D1234372

A GIFT FOR A GHOST

A GIFT FOR A GHOST

A GRAPHIC NOVEL BY
BORJA GONZÁLEZ

Abrams ComicArts • New York

Editor: Charlotte Greenbaum
Designer: Max Temescu
Managing Editor: Mike Richards
Production Manager: Alison Gervais

Library of Congress Control Number: 2019949790

ISBN 978-1-4197-4013-8

Abrams ComicArts books are available at special discounts when purchased
in quantity for premiums and promotions as well as fundraising or educational
use. Special editions can also be created to specification. For details, contact
specialsales@abramsbooks.com or the address below.

ABRAMS The Art of Books
195 Broadway, New York, NY 10007
abramsbooks.com

For Alma

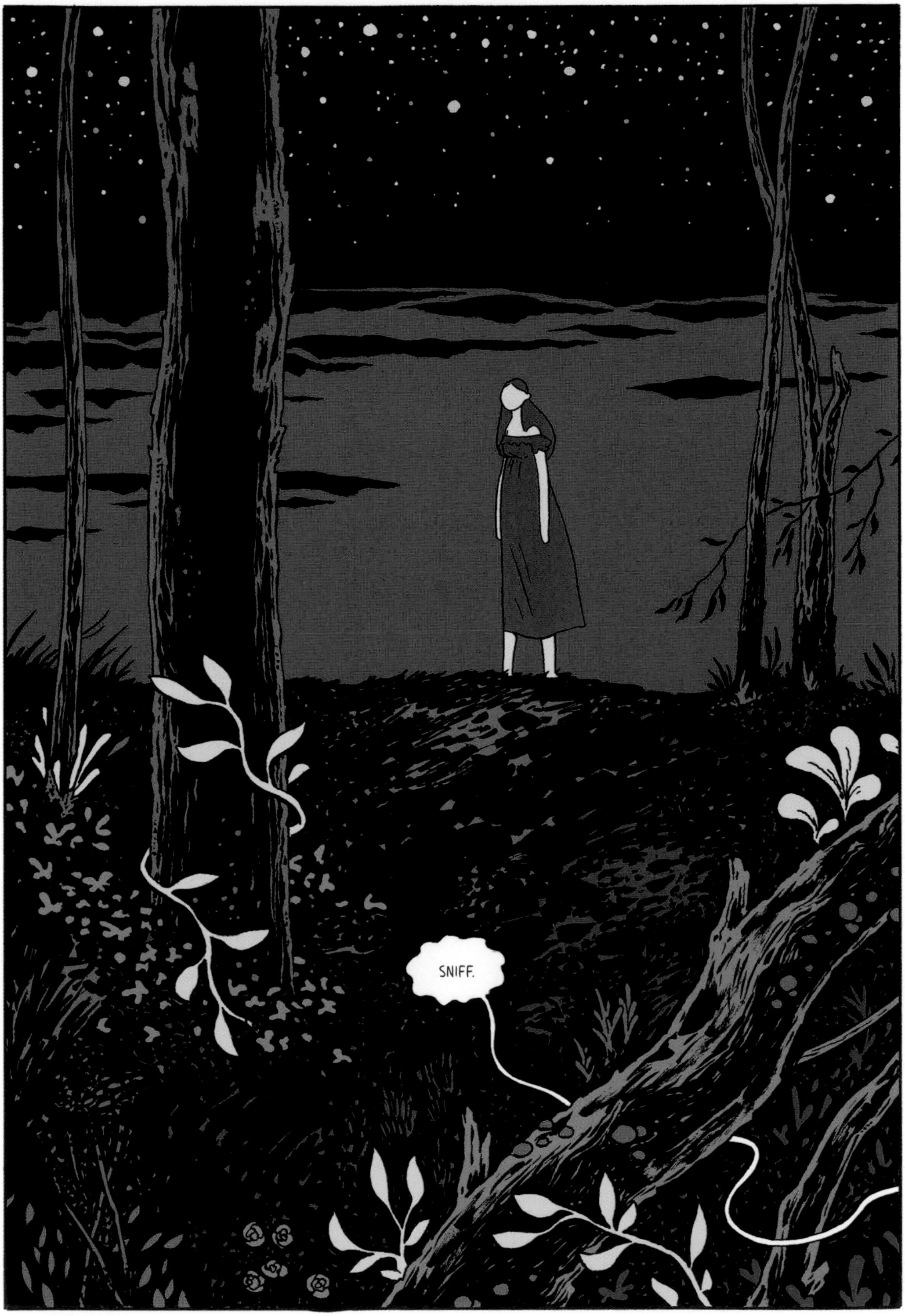
SNIFF.

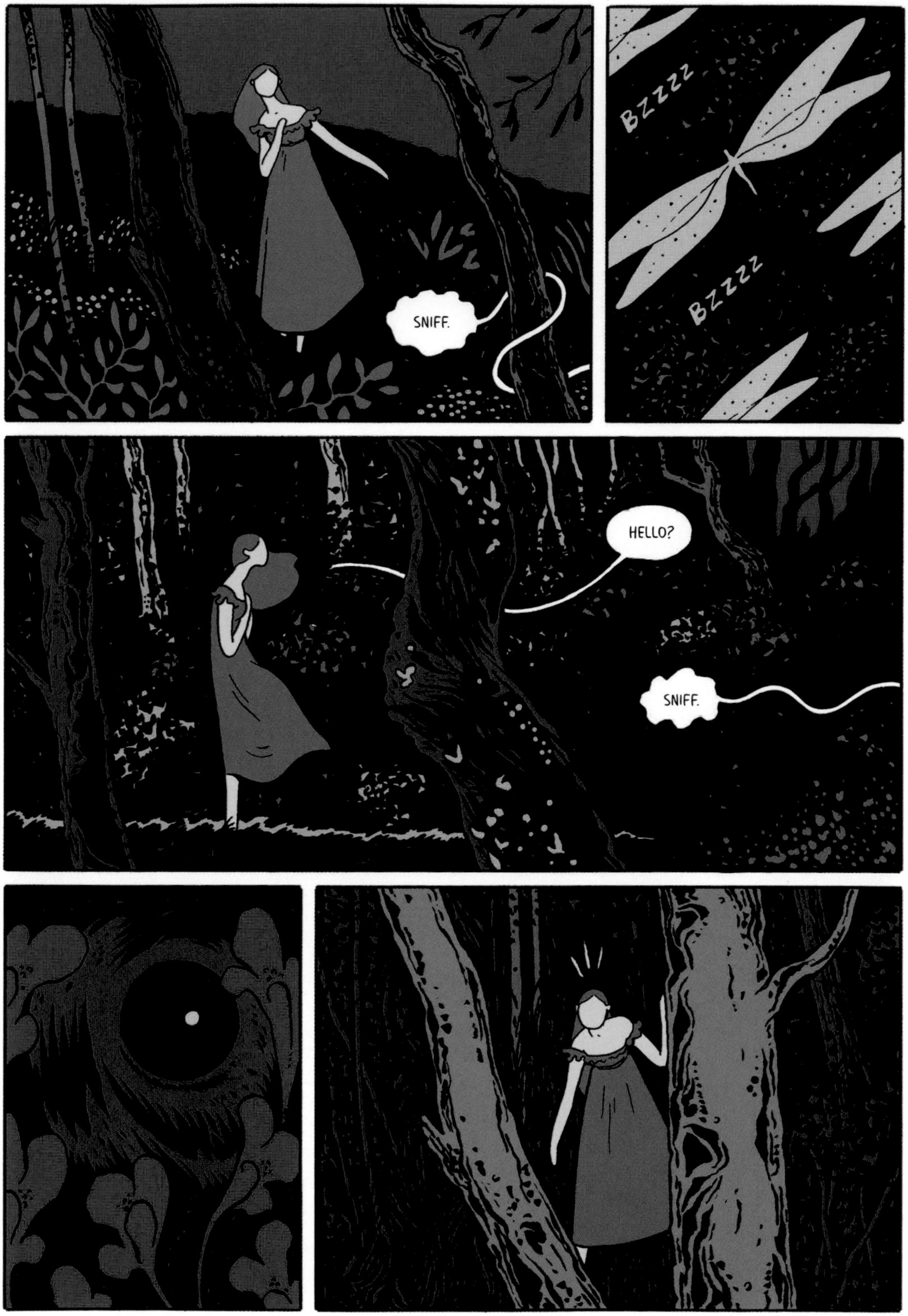
SNIFF.
BZZZZ
BZZZZ
HELLO?
SNIFF.

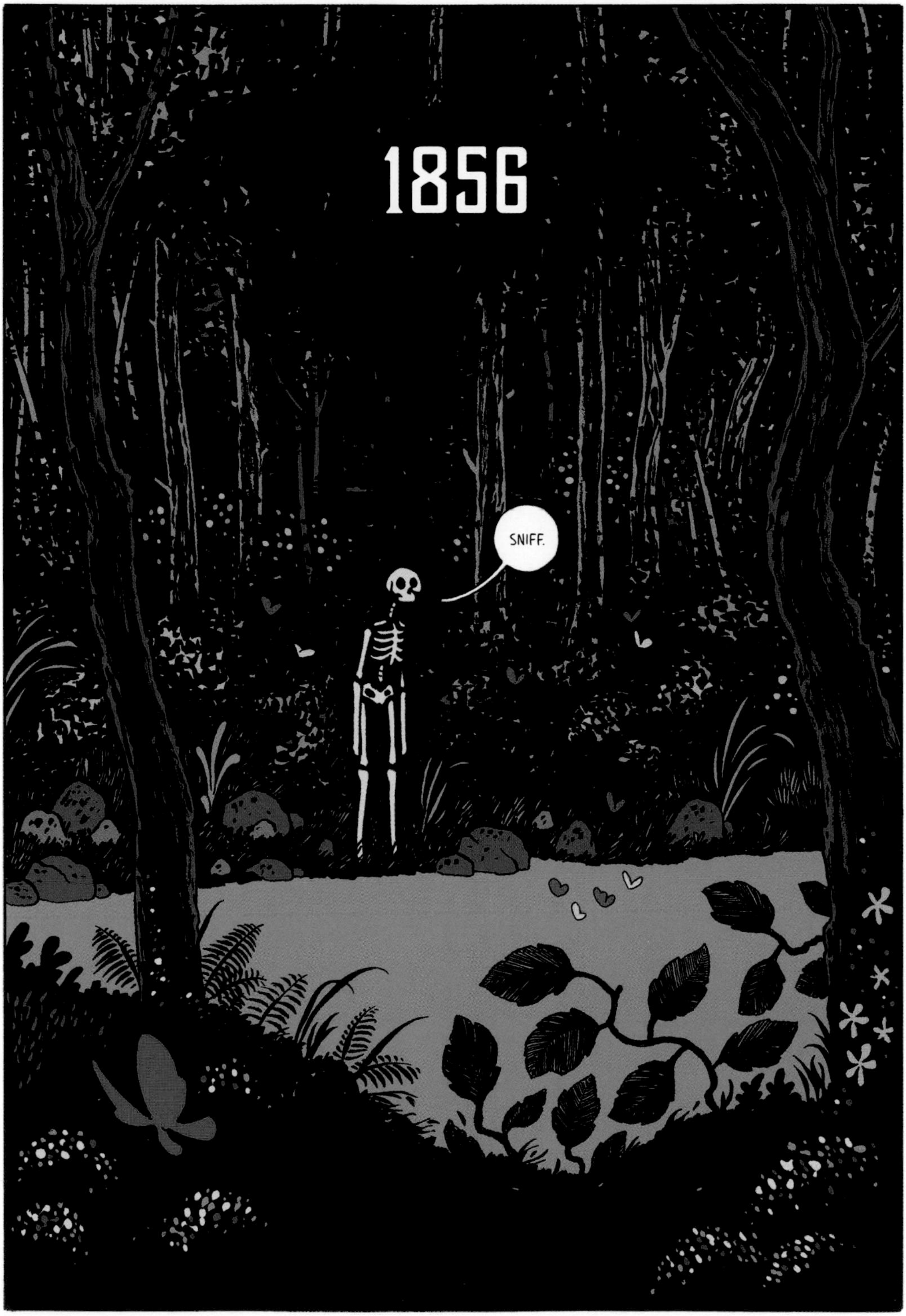
1856
SNIFF.

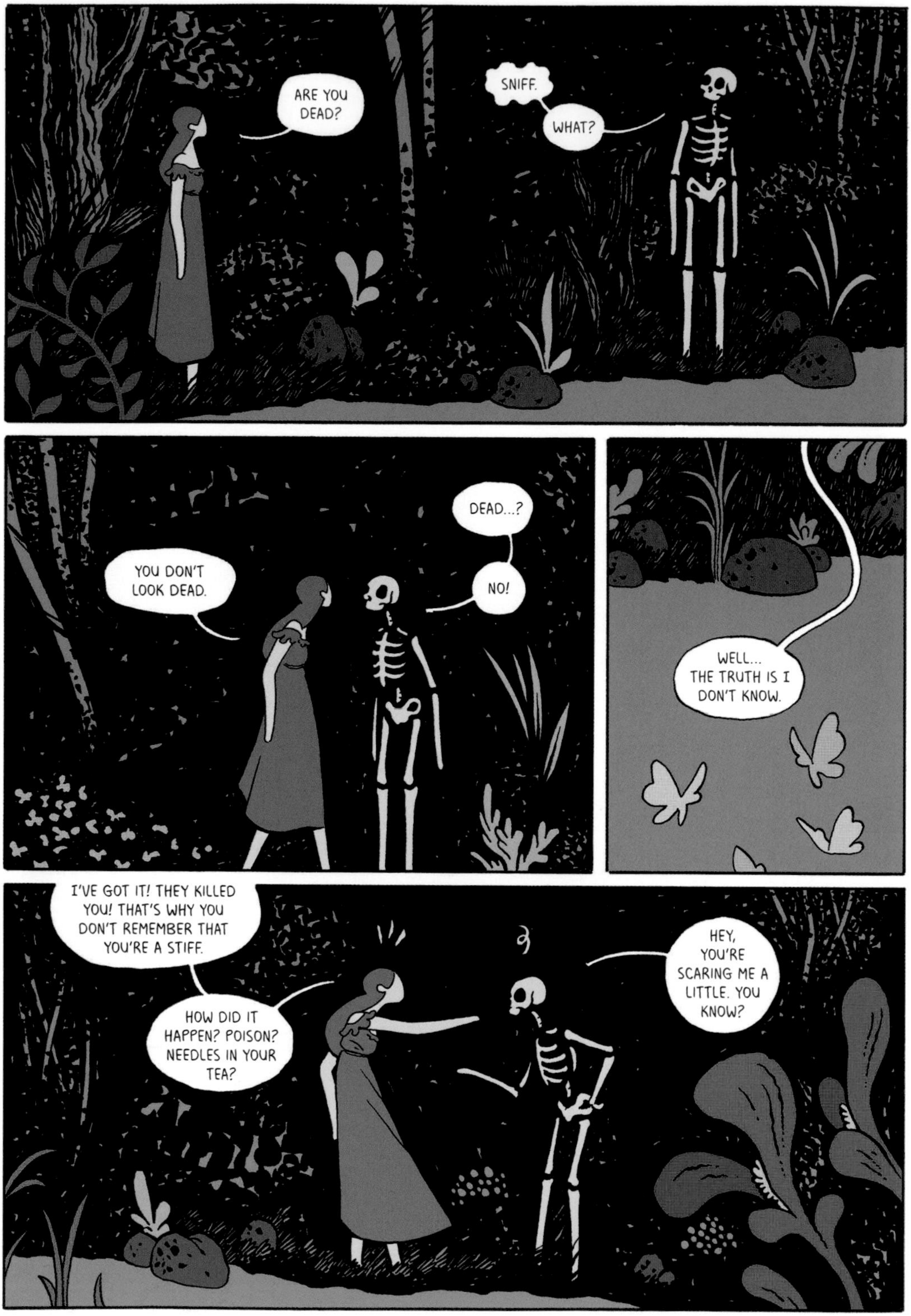
ARE YOU DEAD?
SNIFF.
WHAT?
DEAD...?
NO!
YOU DON'T LOOK DEAD.
WELL... THE TRUTH IS I DON'T KNOW.
I'VE GOT IT! THEY KILLED YOU! THAT'S WHY YOU DON'T REMEMBER THAT YOU'RE A STIFF.
HOW DID IT HAPPEN? POISON? NEEDLES IN YOUR TEA?
HEY, YOU'RE SCARING ME A LITTLE. YOU KNOW?

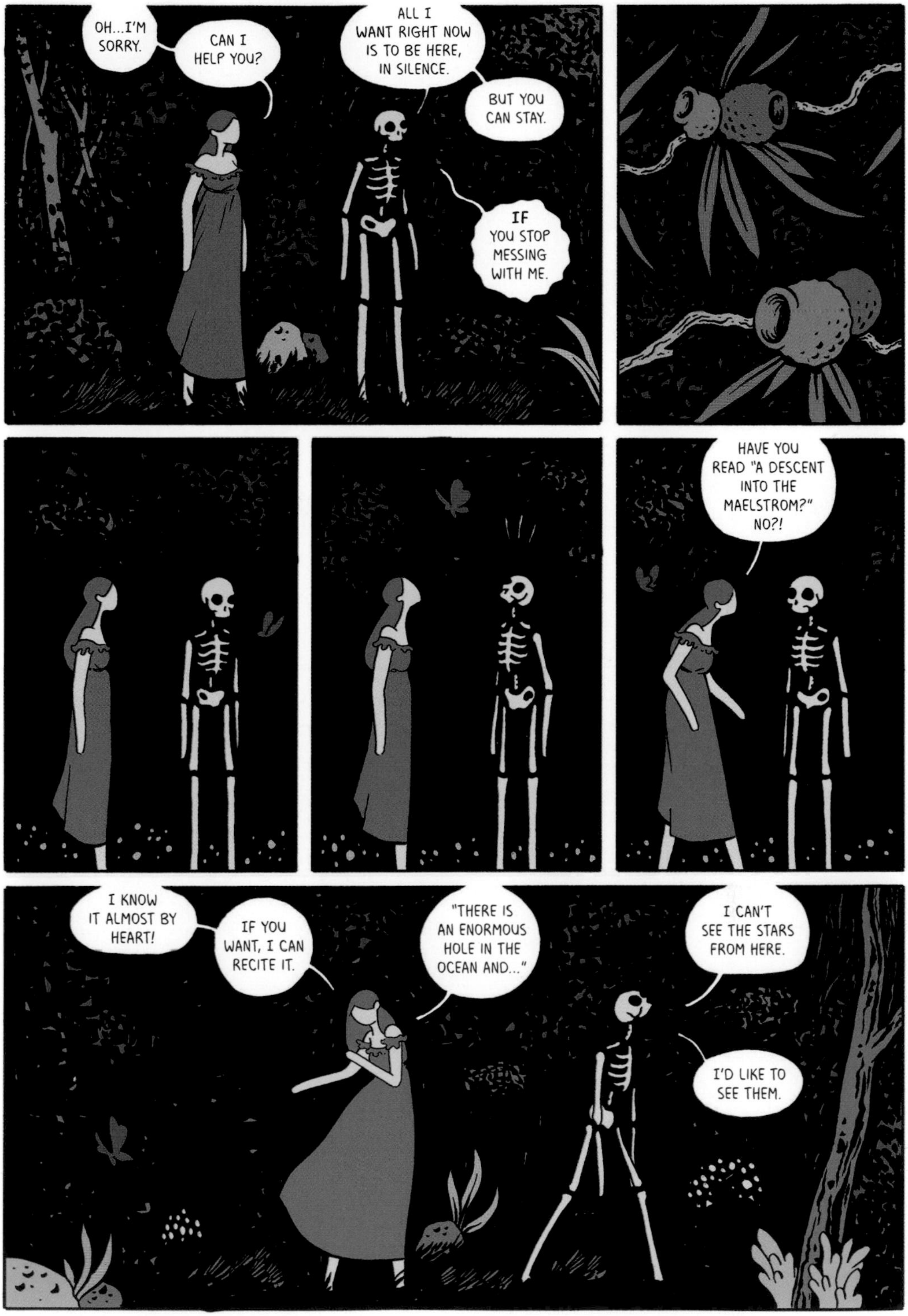
OH...I'M SORRY.
CAN I HELP YOU?
ALL I WANT RIGHT NOW IS TO BE HERE, IN SILENCE.
BUT YOU CAN STAY.
IF YOU STOP MESSING WITH ME.
HAVE YOU READ "A DESCENT INTO THE MAELSTROM?" NO?!
I KNOW IT ALMOST BY HEART!
IF YOU WANT, I CAN RECITE IT.
"THERE IS AN ENORMOUS HOLE IN THE OCEAN AND..."
I CAN'T SEE THE STARS FROM HERE.
I'D LIKE TO SEE THEM.

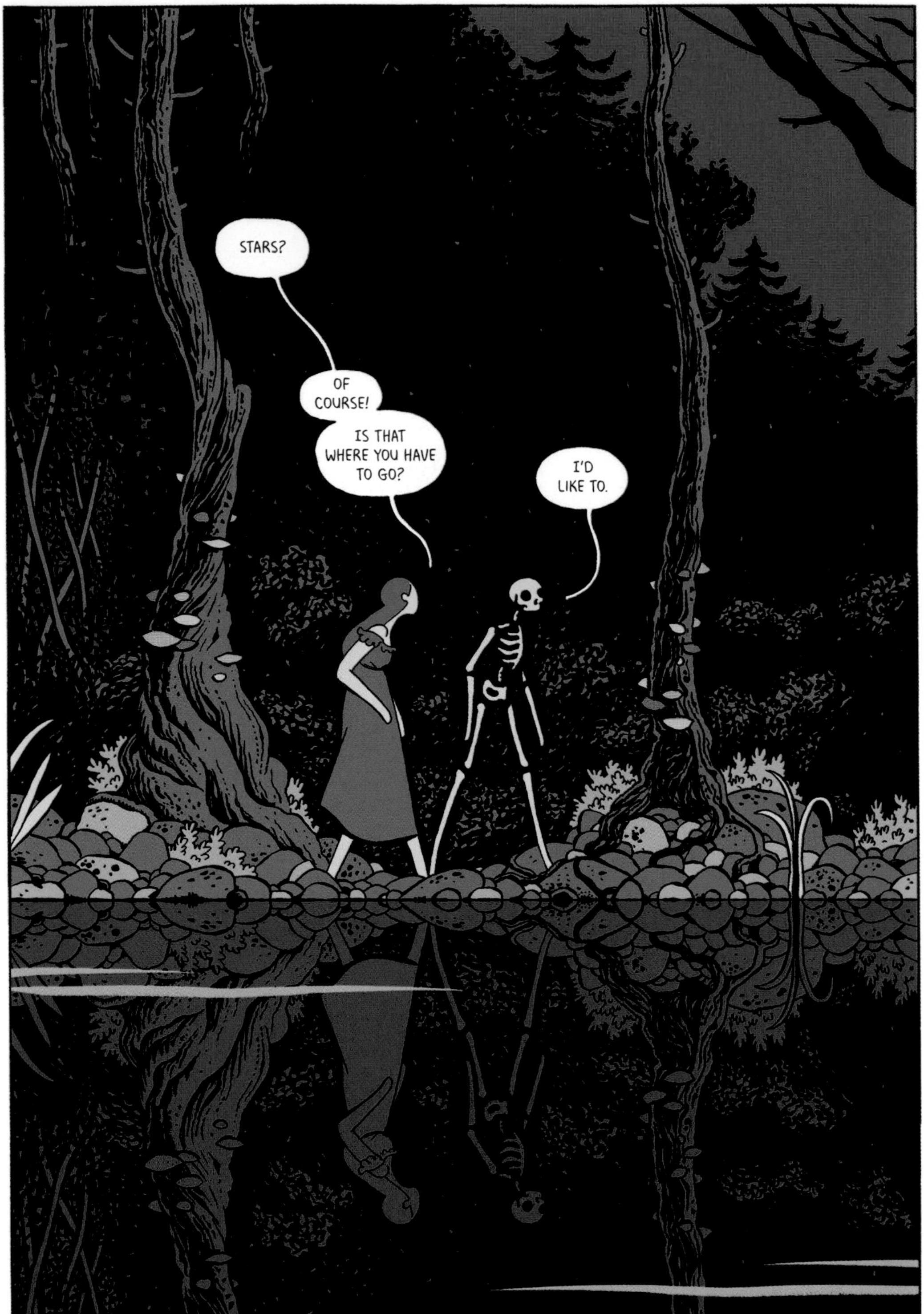
STARS?
OF COURSE!
IS THAT WHERE YOU HAVE TO GO?
I'D LIKE TO.

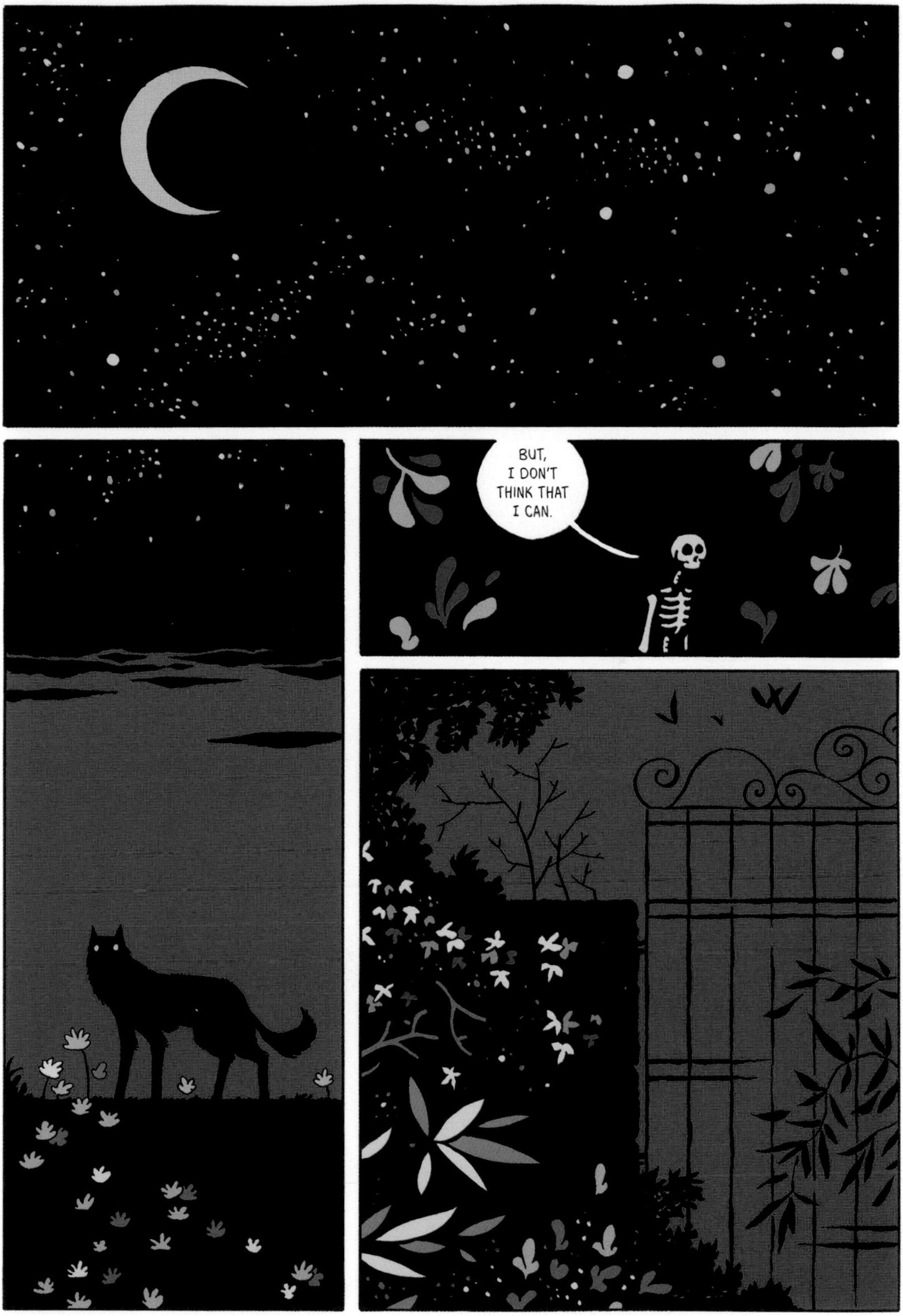
BUT, I DON'T THINK THAT I CAN.

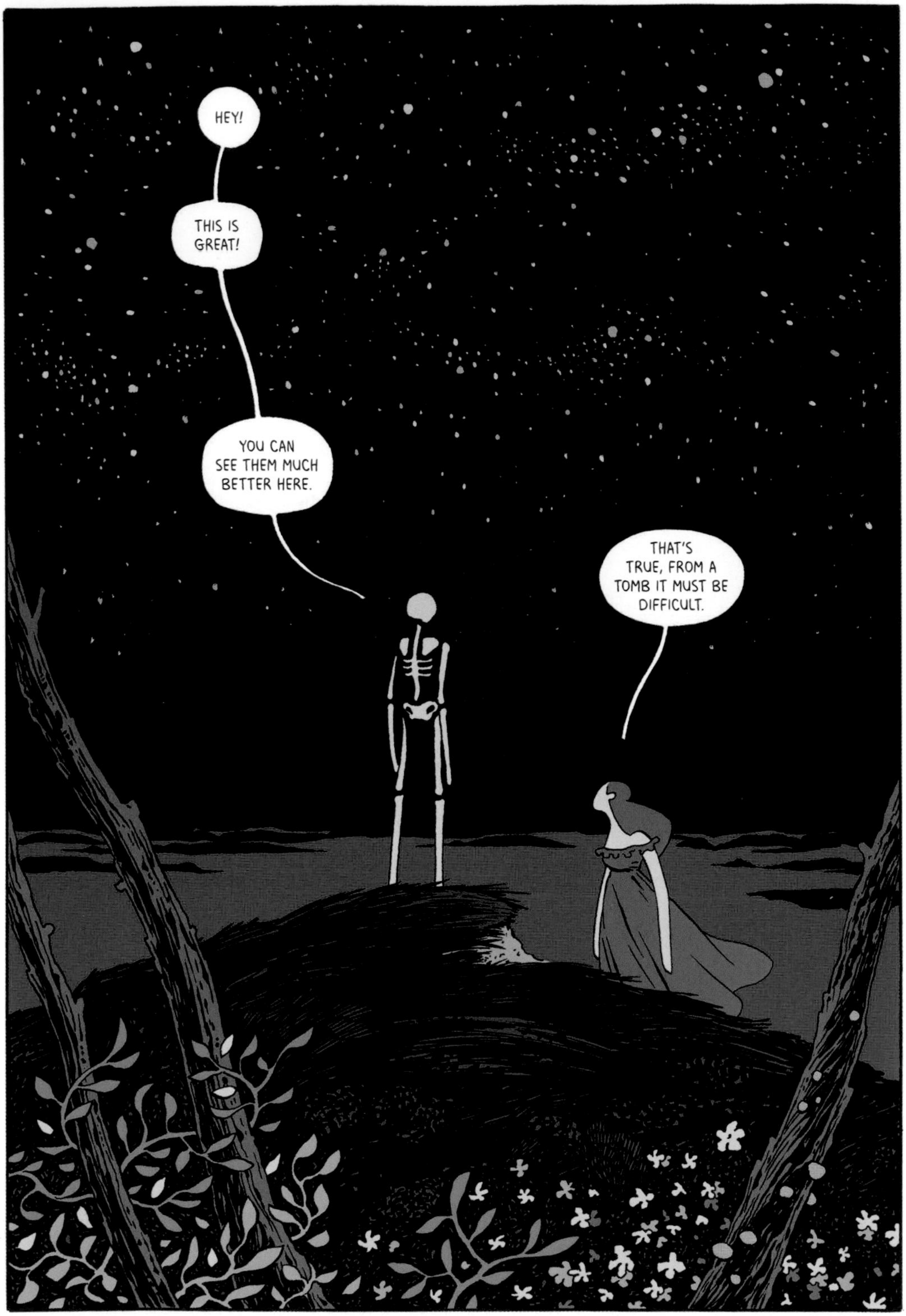
HEY!
THIS IS GREAT!
YOU CAN SEE THEM MUCH BETTER HERE.
THAT'S TRUE, FROM A TOMB IT MUST BE DIFFICULT.

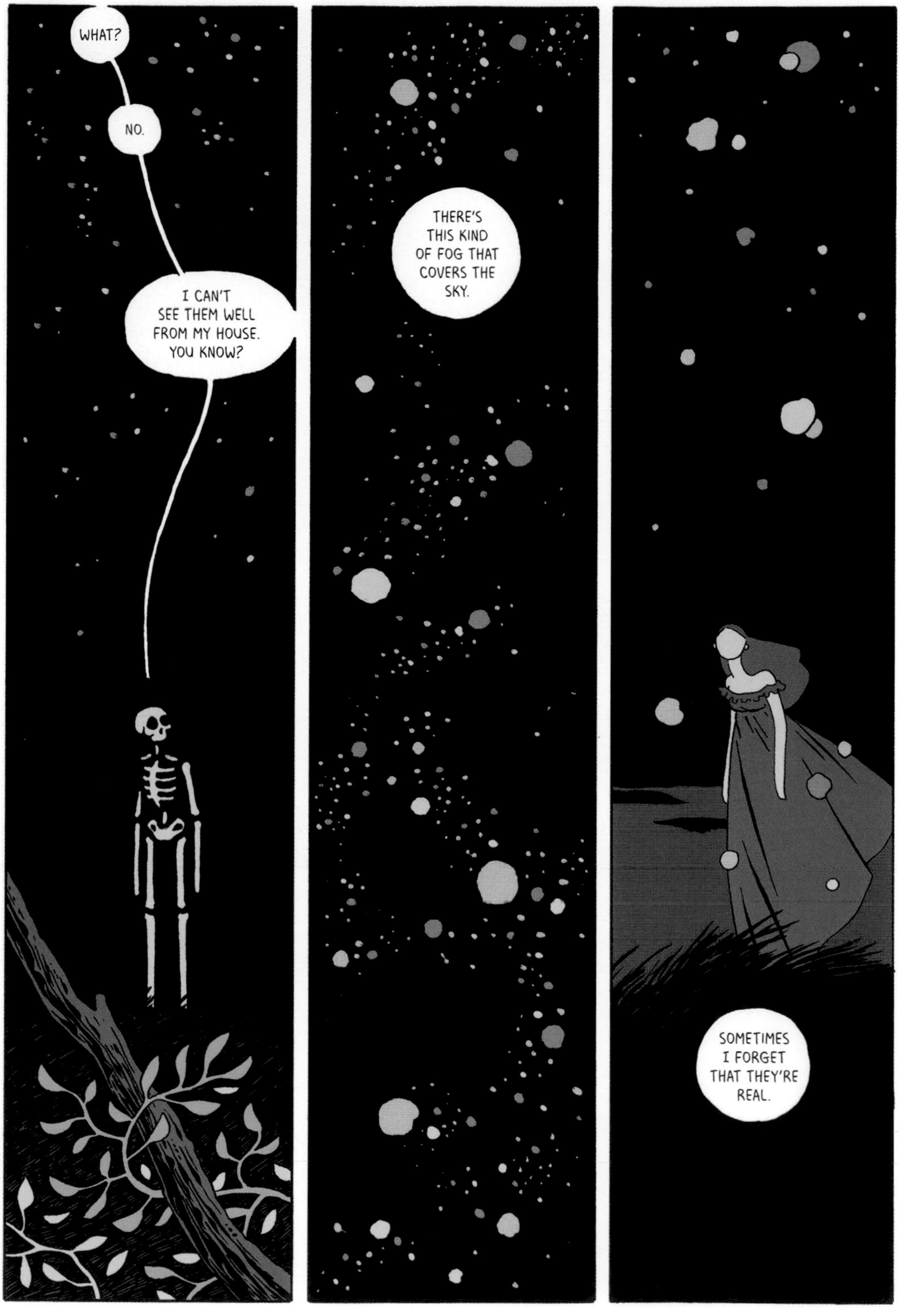
WHAT?
NO.
I CAN'T SEE THEM WELL FROM MY HOUSE. YOU KNOW?
THERE'S THIS KIND OF FOG THAT COVERS THE SKY.
SOMETIMES I FORGET THAT THEY'RE REAL.

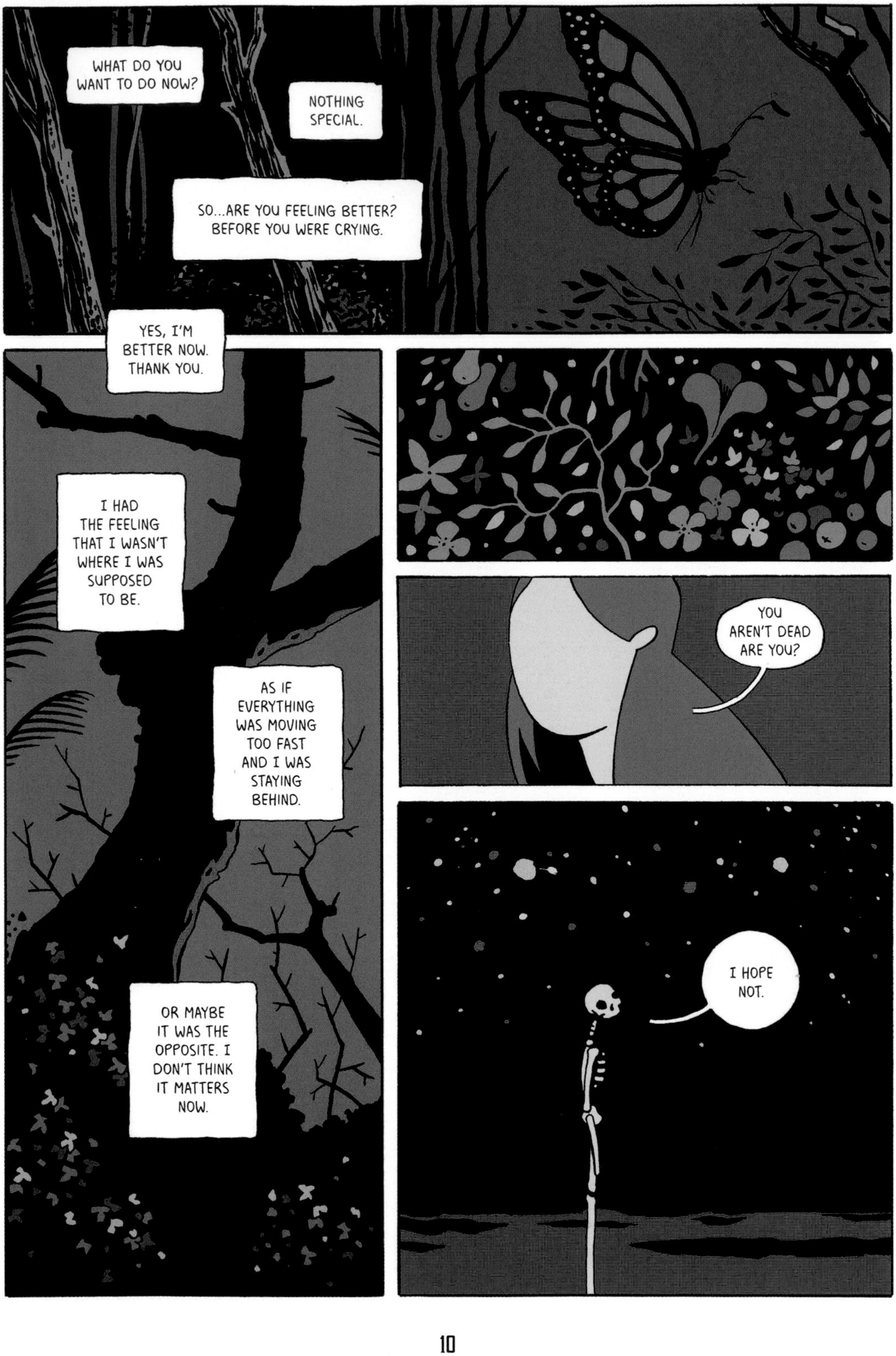
WHAT DO YOU WANT TO DO NOW?
NOTHING SPECIAL.
SO...ARE YOU FEELING BETTER? BEFORE YOU WERE CRYING.
YES, I'M BETTER NOW. THANK YOU.
I HAD THE FEELING THAT I WASN'T WHERE I WAS SUPPOSED TO BE.
AS IF EVERYTHING WAS MOVING TOO FAST AND I WAS STAYING BEHIND.
OR MAYBE IT WAS THE OPPOSITE. I DON'T THINK IT MATTERS NOW.
YOU AREN'T DEAD ARE YOU?
I HOPE NOT.

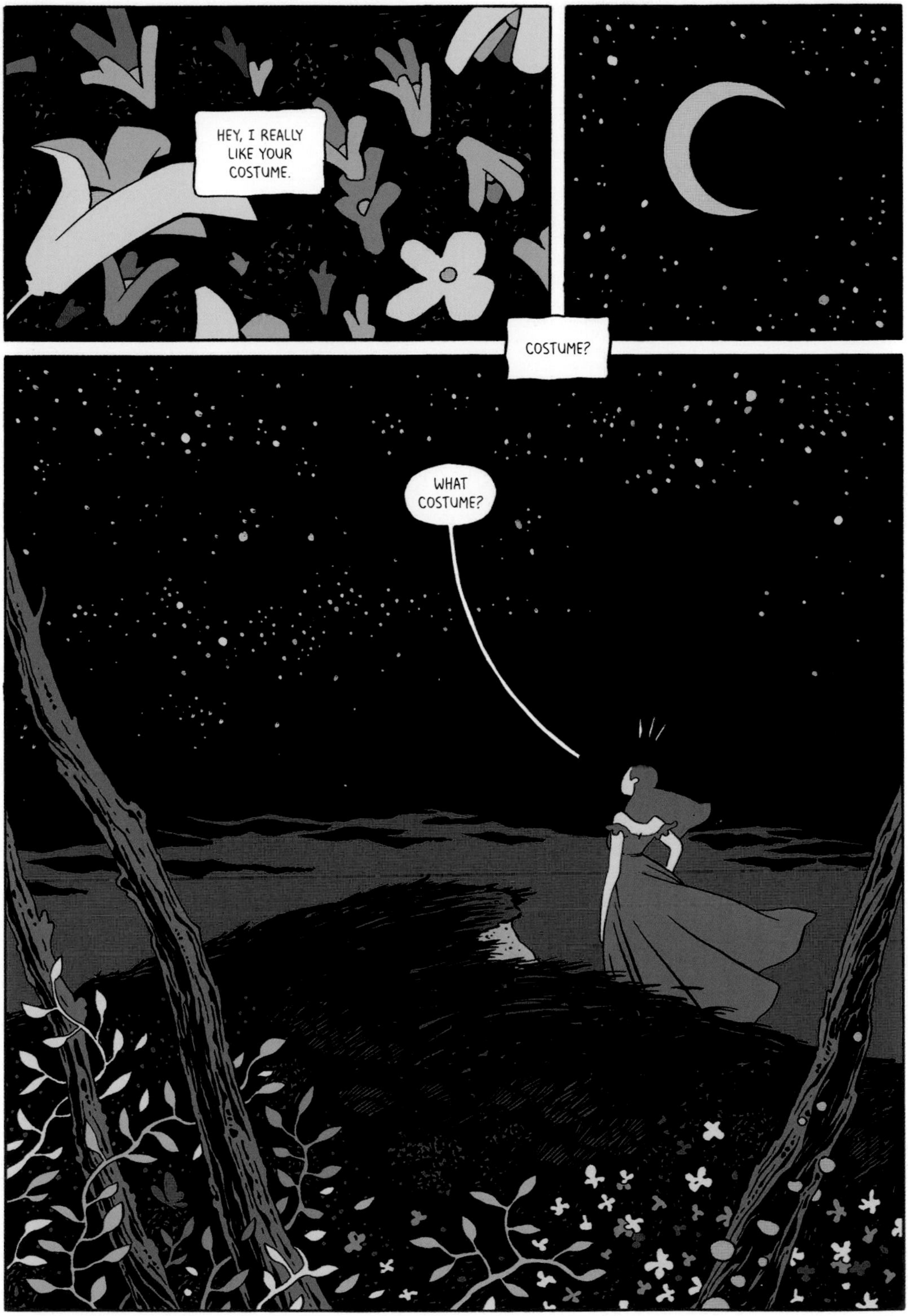
HEY, I REALLY LIKE YOUR COSTUME.
COSTUME?
WHAT COSTUME?

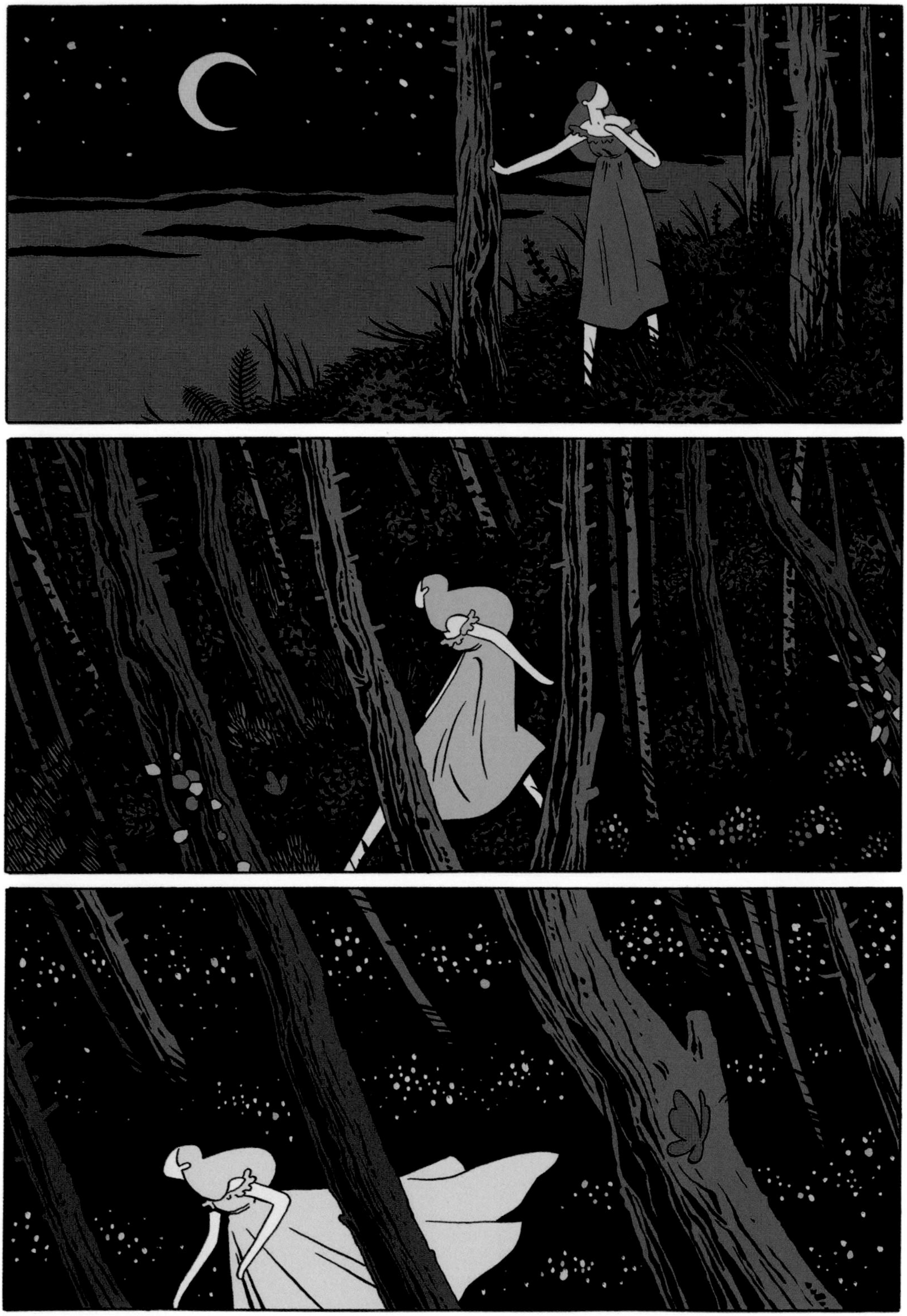

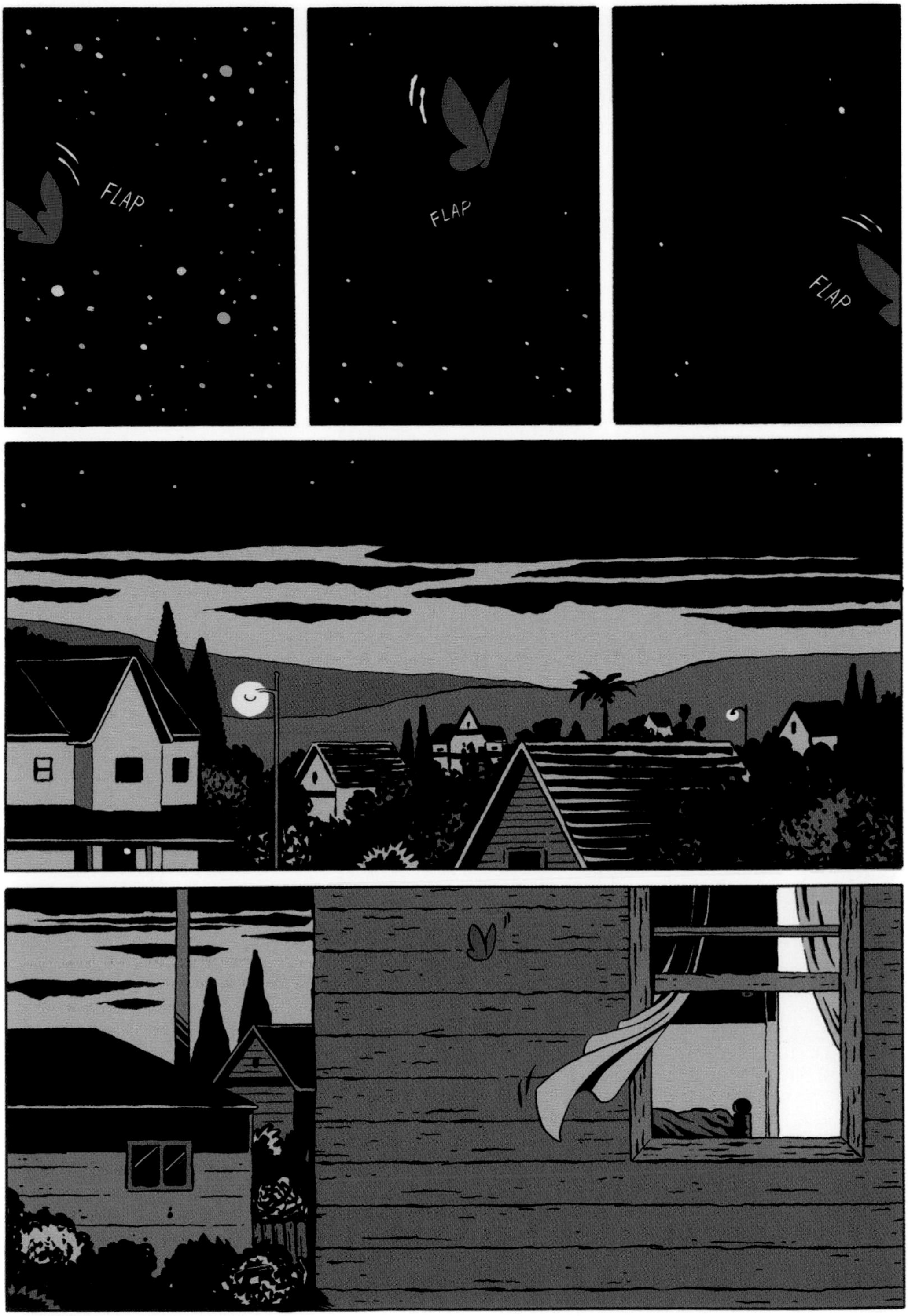
FLAP
FLAP
FLAP

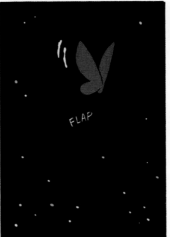

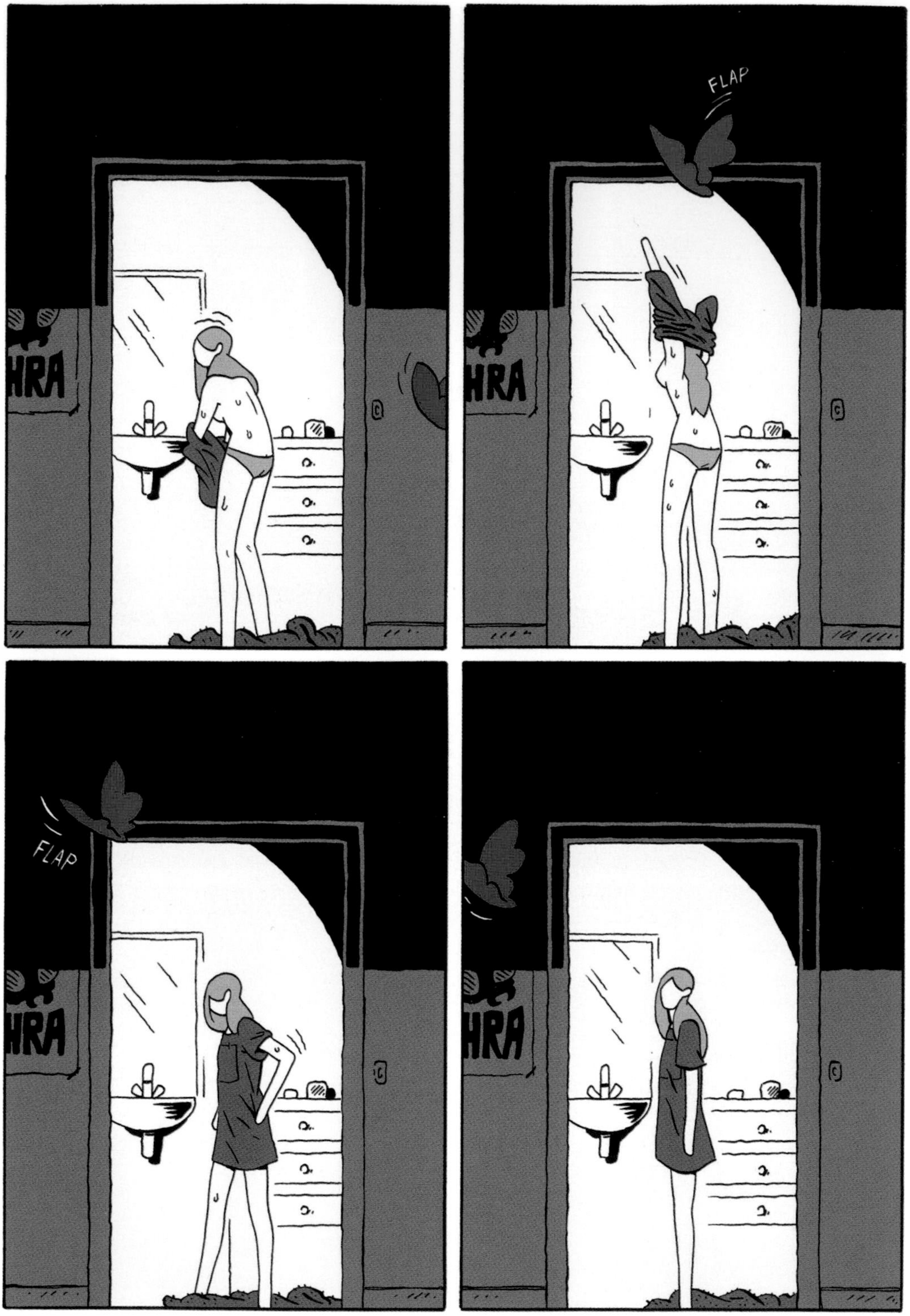
FLAP
FLAP

THE GORGON
HEY.
HI THERE.

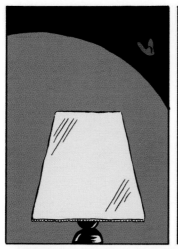

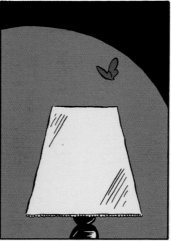

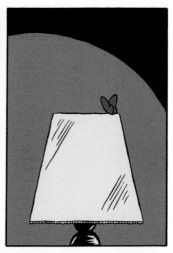

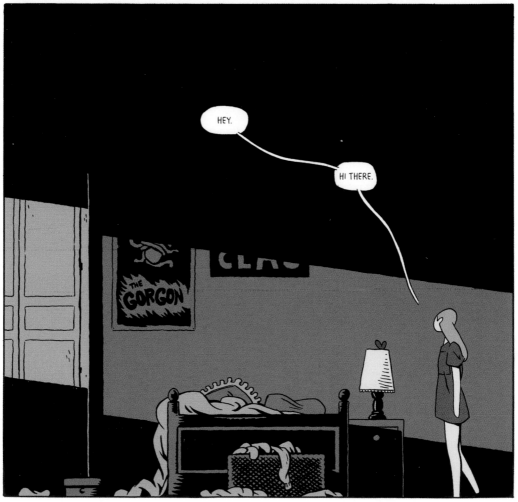

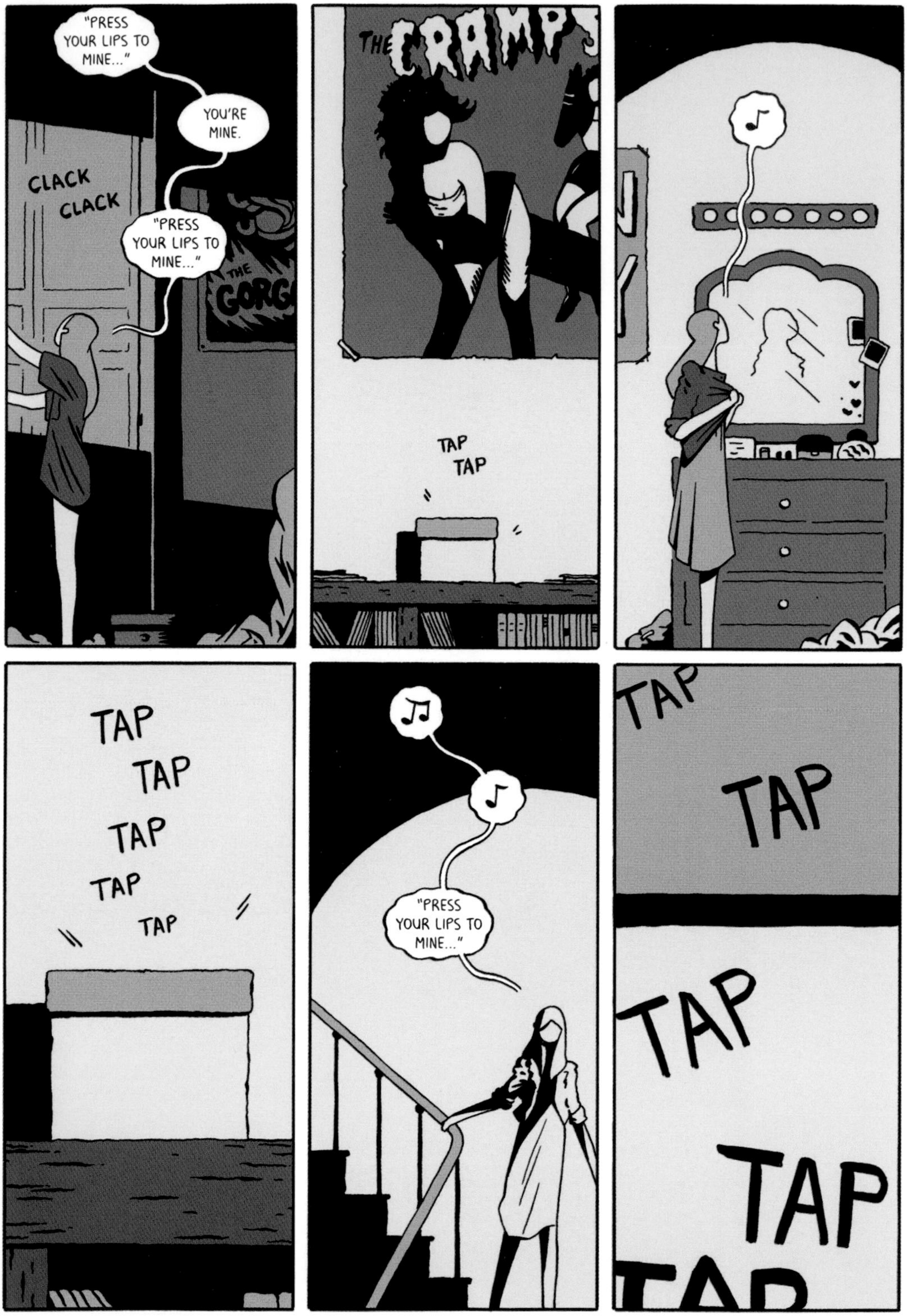
"PRESS YOUR LIPS TO MINE..."
YOU'RE MINE.
CLACK CLACK
"PRESS YOUR LIPS TO MINE..."
TAP TAP
TAP TAP TAP TAP TAP
"PRESS YOUR LIPS TO MINE..."
TAP TAP TAP

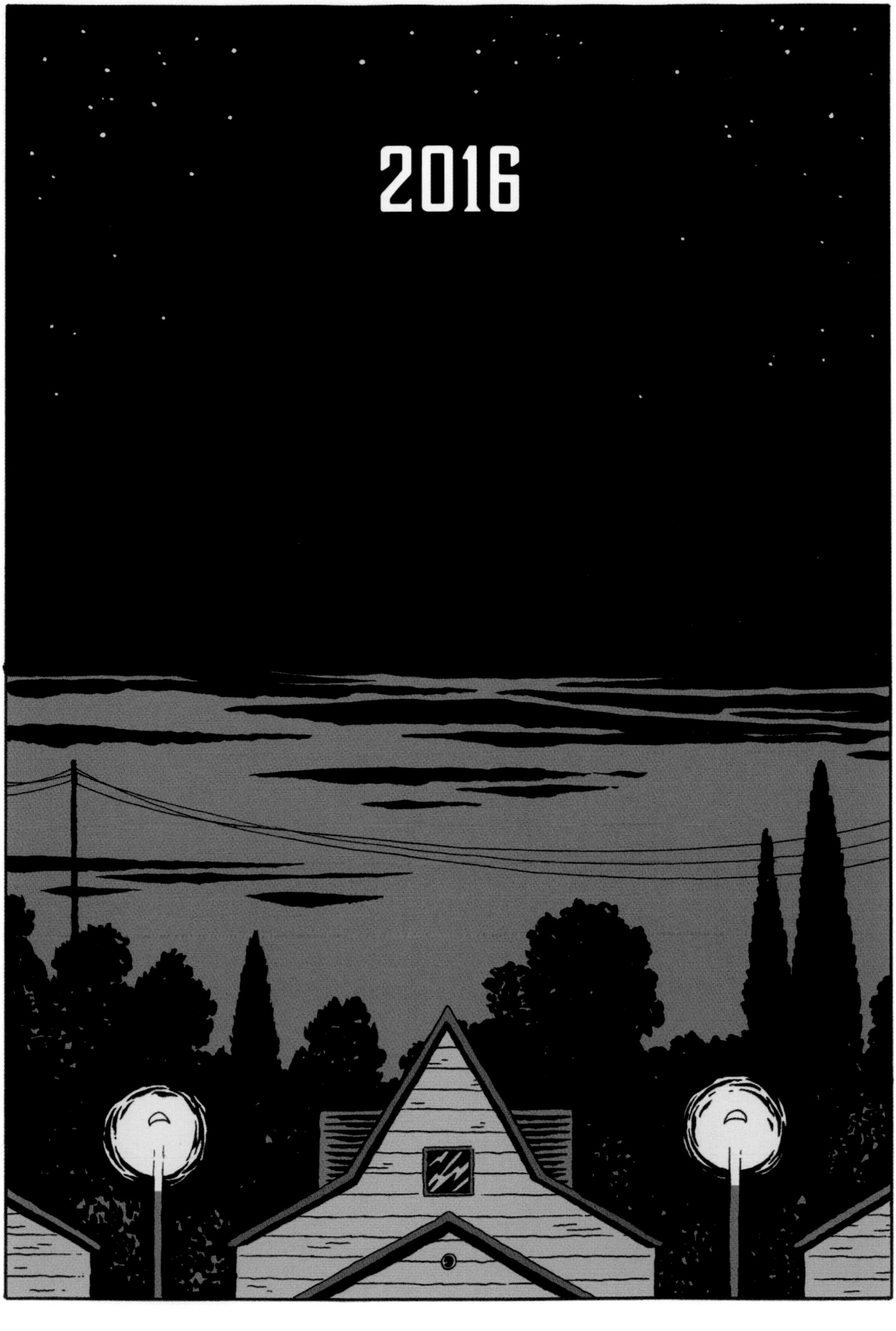
2016

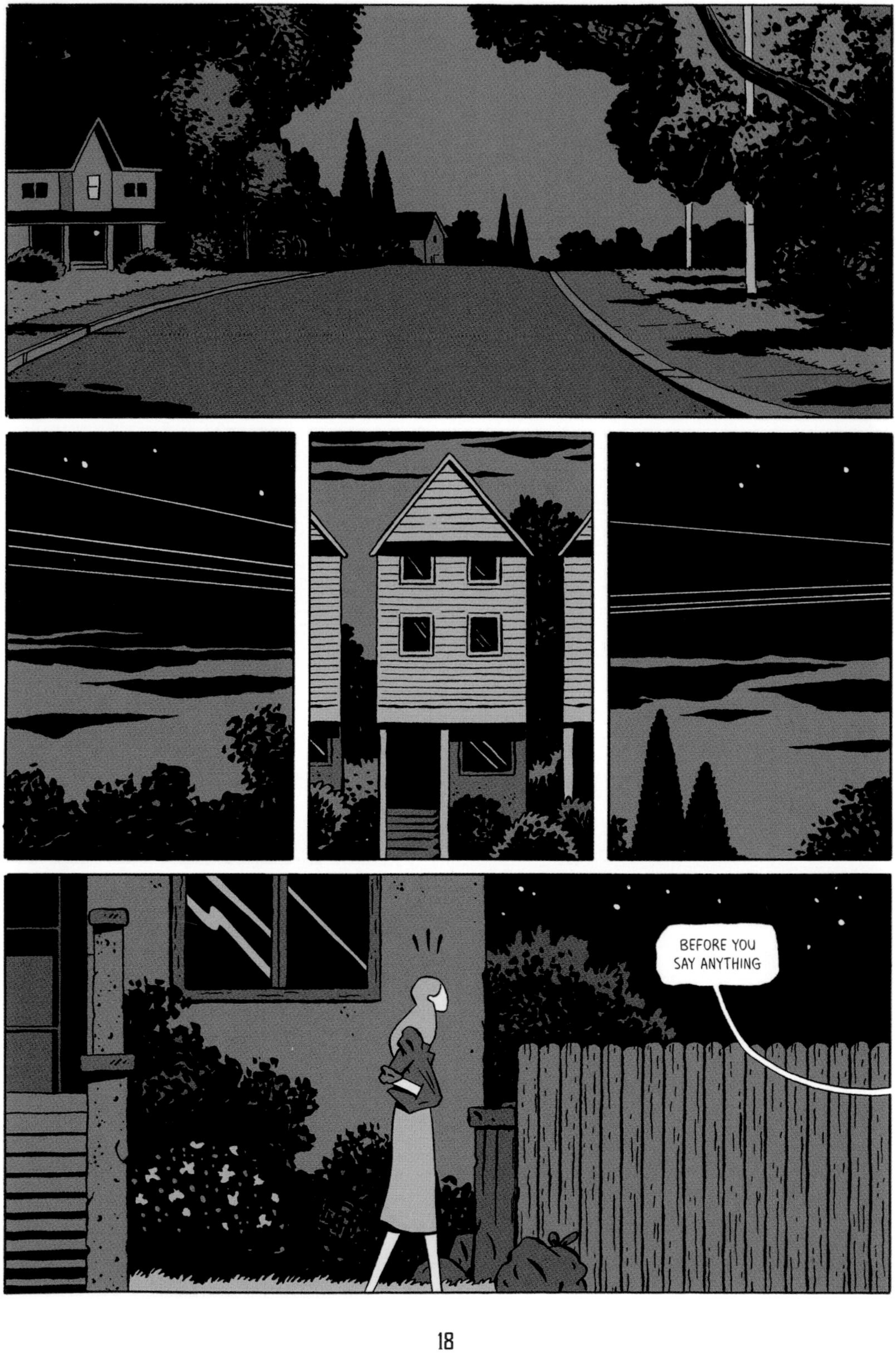
BEFORE YOU SAY ANYTHING

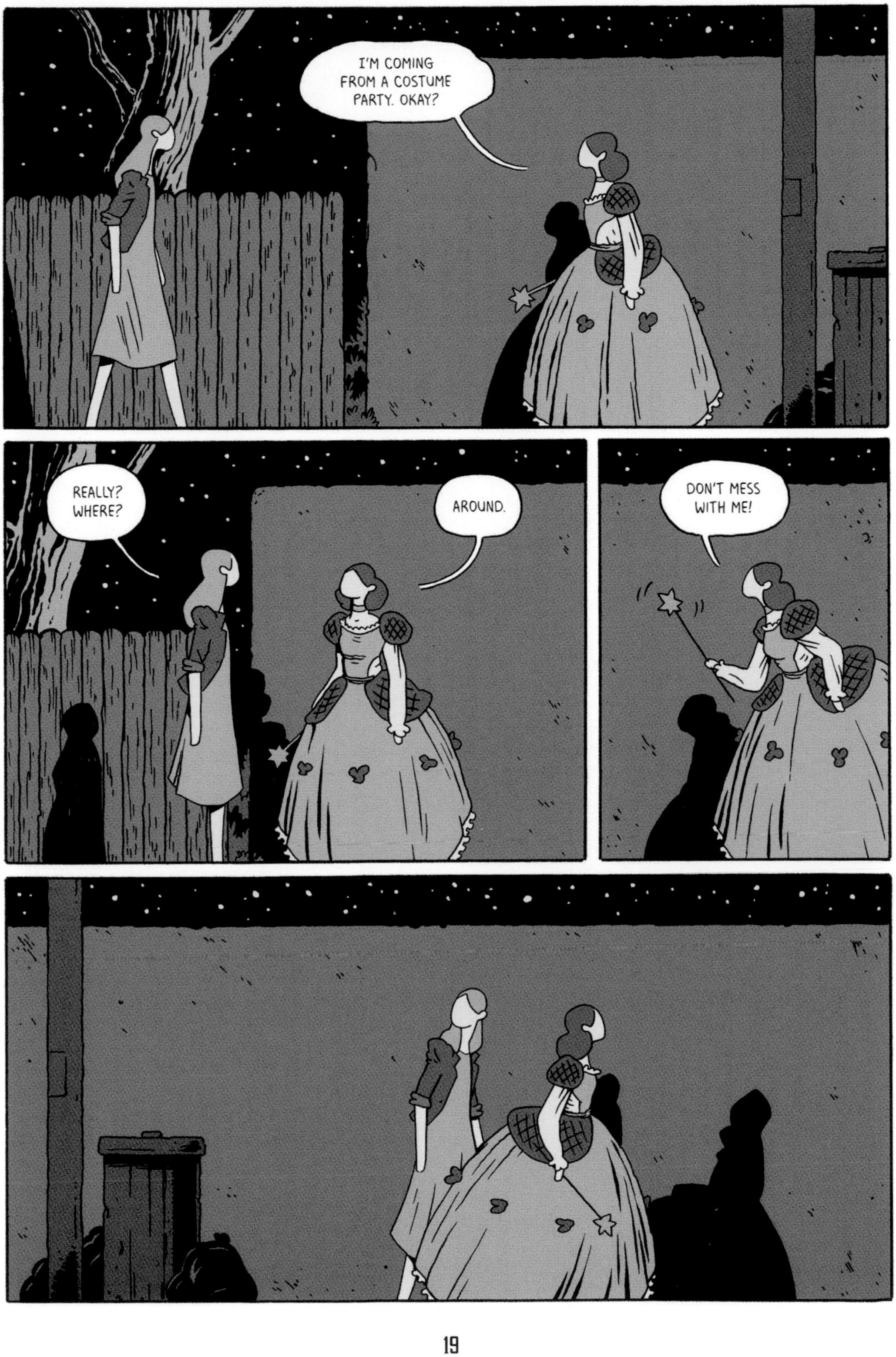
I'M COMING FROM A COSTUME PARTY. OKAY?
REALLY? WHERE?
AROUND.
DON'T MESS WITH ME!

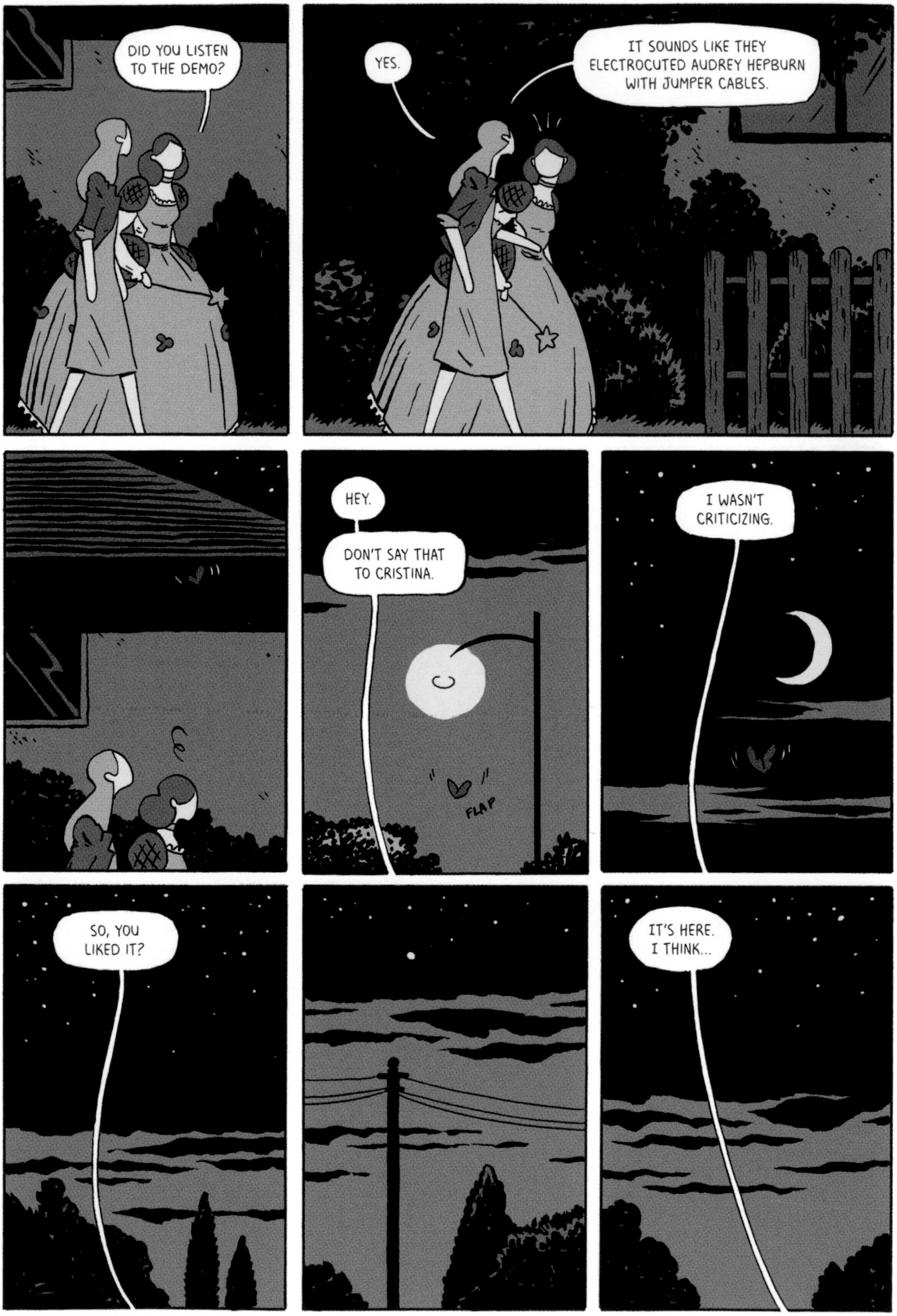
DID YOU LISTEN TO THE DEMO?
YES.
IT SOUNDS LIKE THEY ELECTROCUTED AUDREY HEPBURN WITH JUMPER CABLES.
HEY.
DON'T SAY THAT TO CRISTINA.
FLAP
I WASN'T CRITICIZING.
SO, YOU LIKED IT?
IT'S HERE. I THINK...

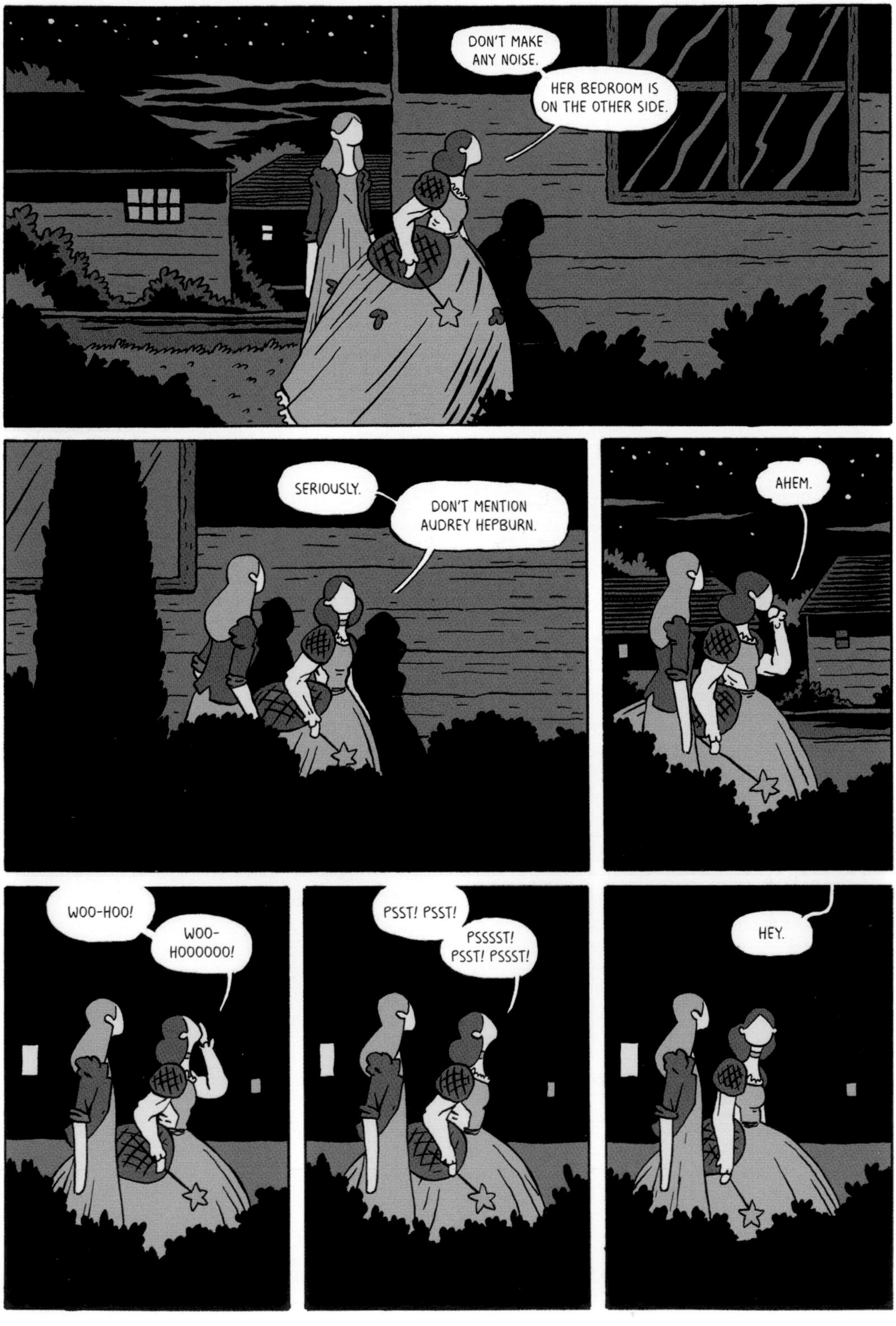
DON'T MAKE ANY NOISE.
HER BEDROOM IS ON THE OTHER SIDE.
SERIOUSLY.
DON'T MENTION AUDREY HEPBURN.
AHEM.
WOO-HOO!
WOO-HOOOOOOO!
PSST! PSST!
PSSSST! PSST! PSSST!
HEY.

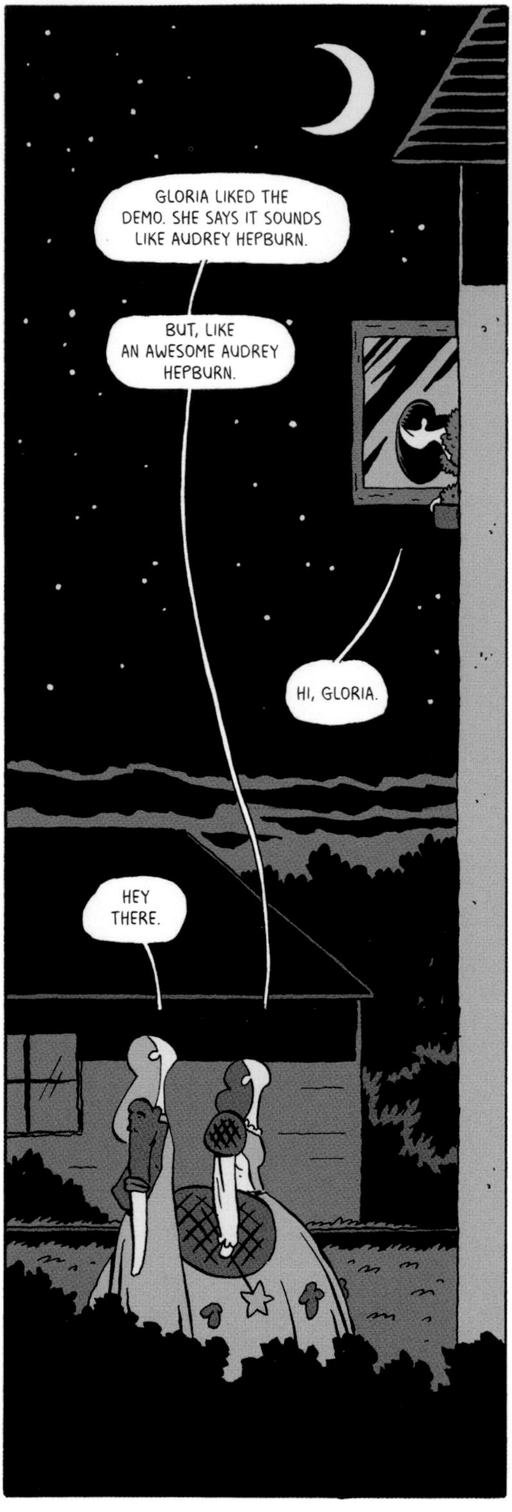
GLORIA LIKED THE DEMO. SHE SAYS IT SOUNDS LIKE AUDREY HEPBURN.
BUT, LIKE AN AWESOME AUDREY HEPBURN.
HI, GLORIA.
HEY THERE.

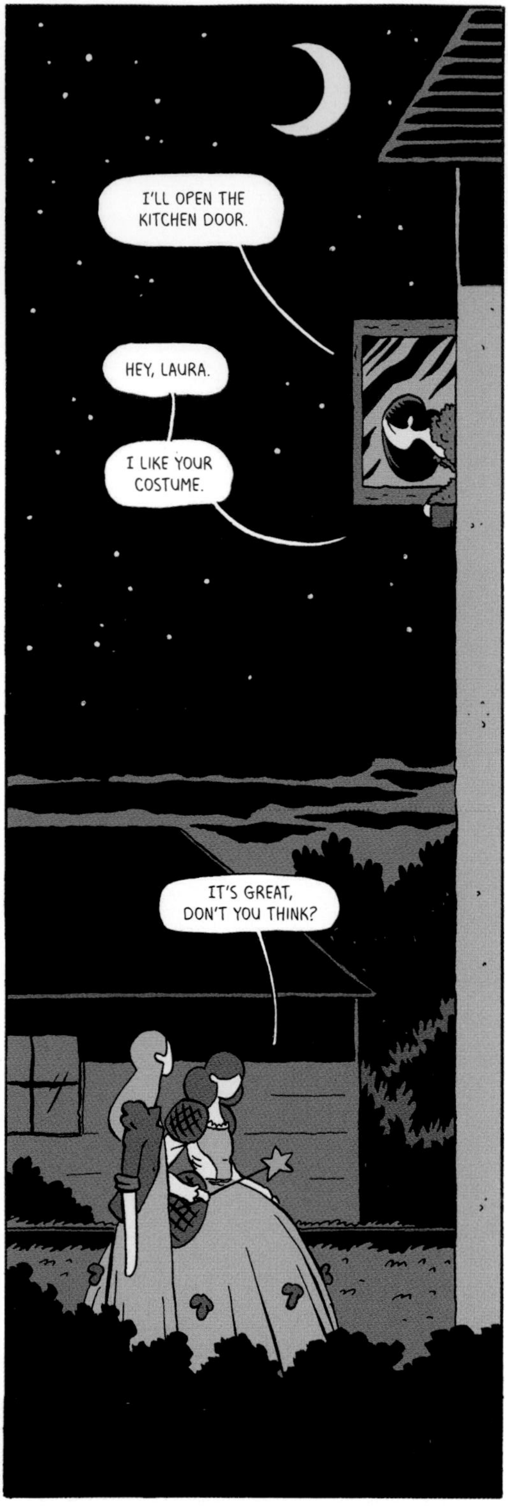
I'LL OPEN THE KITCHEN DOOR.
HEY, LAURA.
I LIKE YOUR COSTUME.
IT'S GREAT, DON'T YOU THINK?

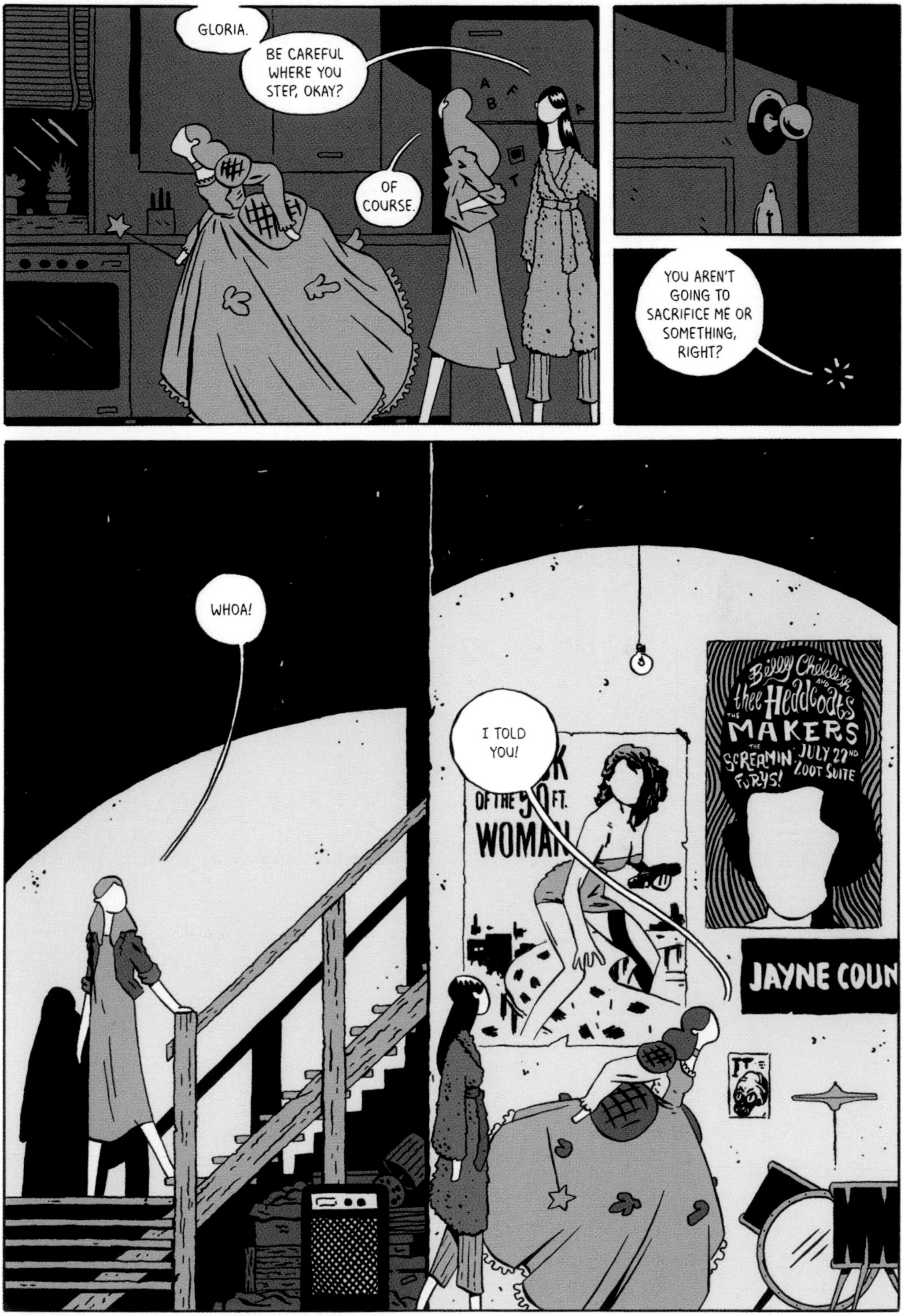
GLORIA.
BE CAREFUL WHERE YOU STEP, OKAY?
OF COURSE.
YOU AREN'T GOING TO SACRIFICE ME OR SOMETHING, RIGHT?
WHOA!
I TOLD YOU!
OF THE 50 FT. WOMAN
Billy Childish and thee Headcoats
THE MAKERS
THE SCREAMIN' FURYS!
JULY 22ND
ZOOT SUITE
JAYNE COUN

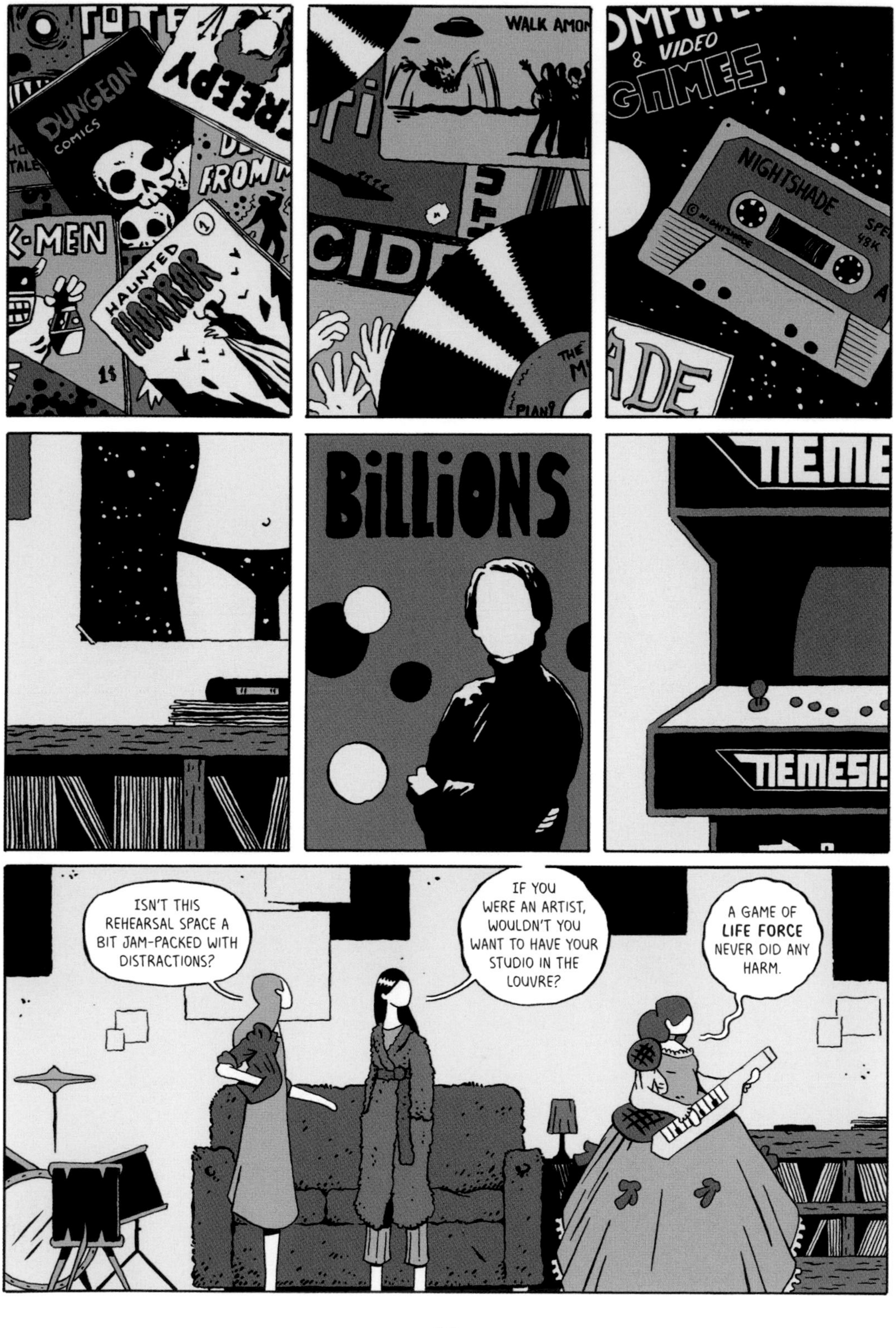
DUNGEON
COMICS
HAUNTED
HORROR
1$
WALK AMON
& VIDEO
GAMES
NIGHTSHADE
48K
BiLLiONS
ISN'T THIS REHEARSAL SPACE A BIT JAM-PACKED WITH DISTRACTIONS?
IF YOU WERE AN ARTIST, WOULDN'T YOU WANT TO HAVE YOUR STUDIO IN THE LOUVRE?
A GAME OF **LIFE FORCE** NEVER DID ANY HARM.

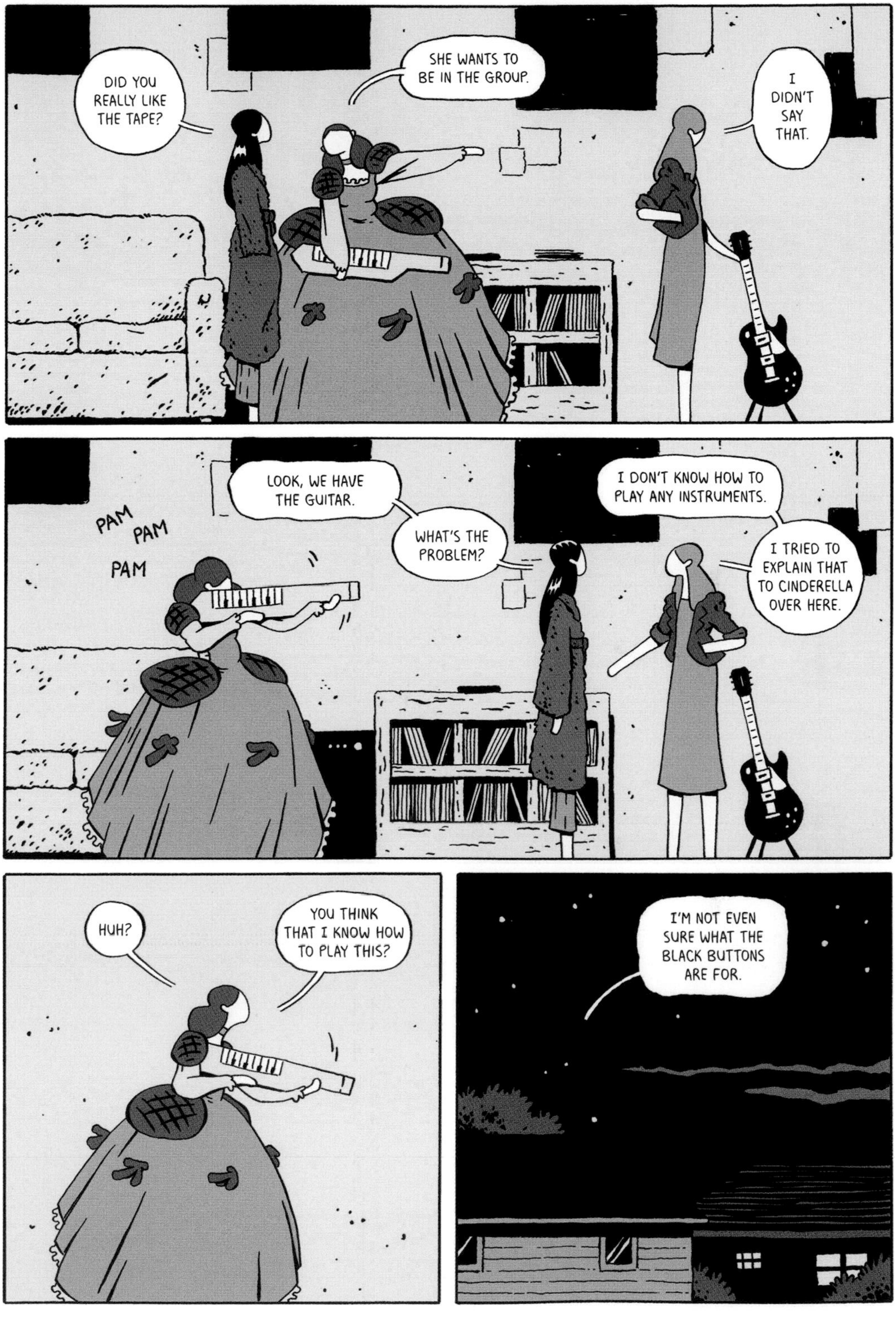
DID YOU REALLY LIKE THE TAPE?
SHE WANTS TO BE IN THE GROUP.
I DIDN'T SAY THAT.
PAM PAM PAM
LOOK, WE HAVE THE GUITAR.
WHAT'S THE PROBLEM?
I DON'T KNOW HOW TO PLAY ANY INSTRUMENTS.
I TRIED TO EXPLAIN THAT TO CINDERELLA OVER HERE.
HUH?
YOU THINK THAT I KNOW HOW TO PLAY THIS?
I'M NOT EVEN SURE WHAT THE BLACK BUTTONS ARE FOR.

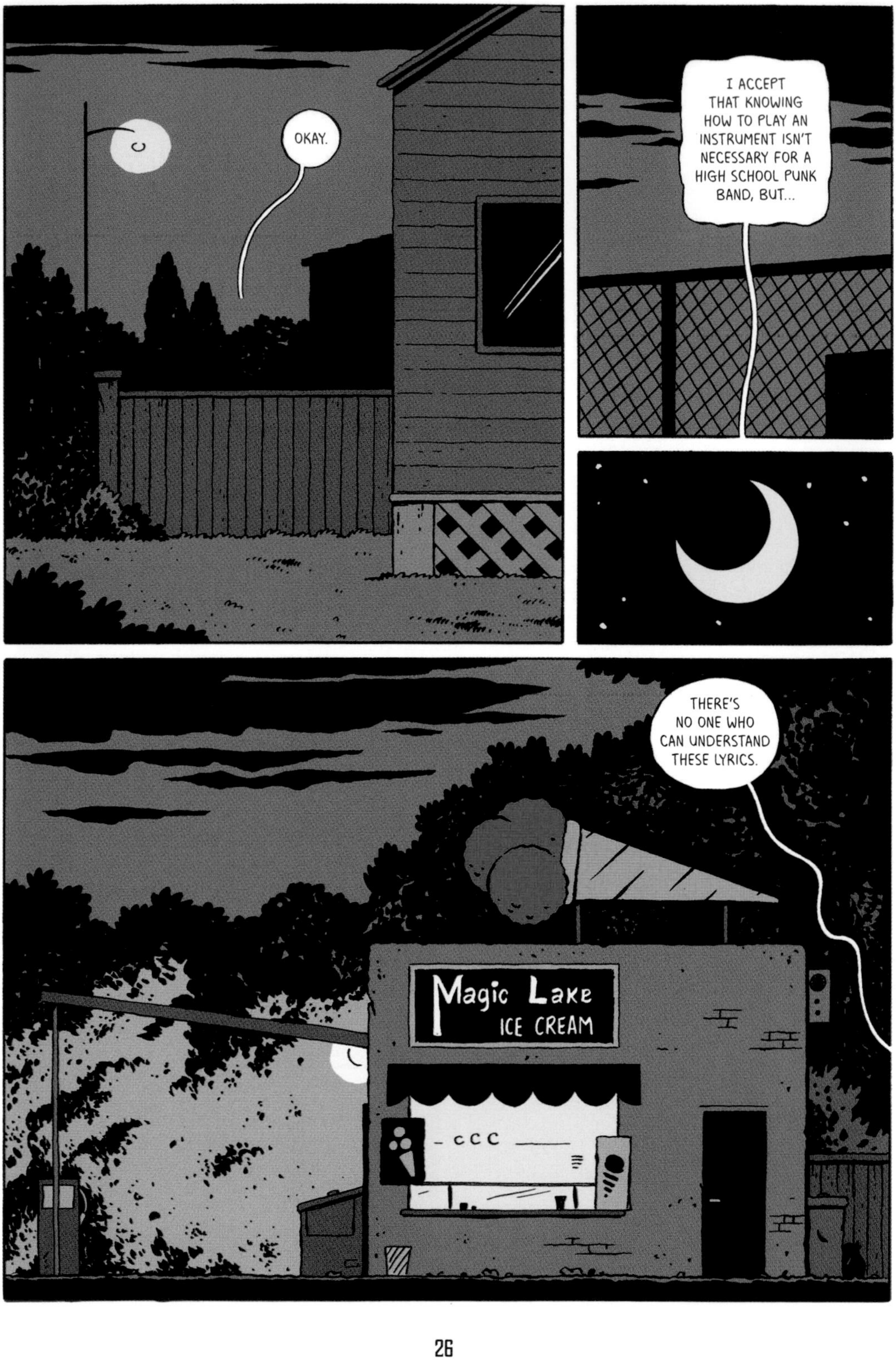
OKAY.
I ACCEPT THAT KNOWING HOW TO PLAY AN INSTRUMENT ISN'T NECESSARY FOR A HIGH SCHOOL PUNK BAND, BUT...
THERE'S NO ONE WHO CAN UNDERSTAND THESE LYRICS.
Magic Lake ICE CREAM

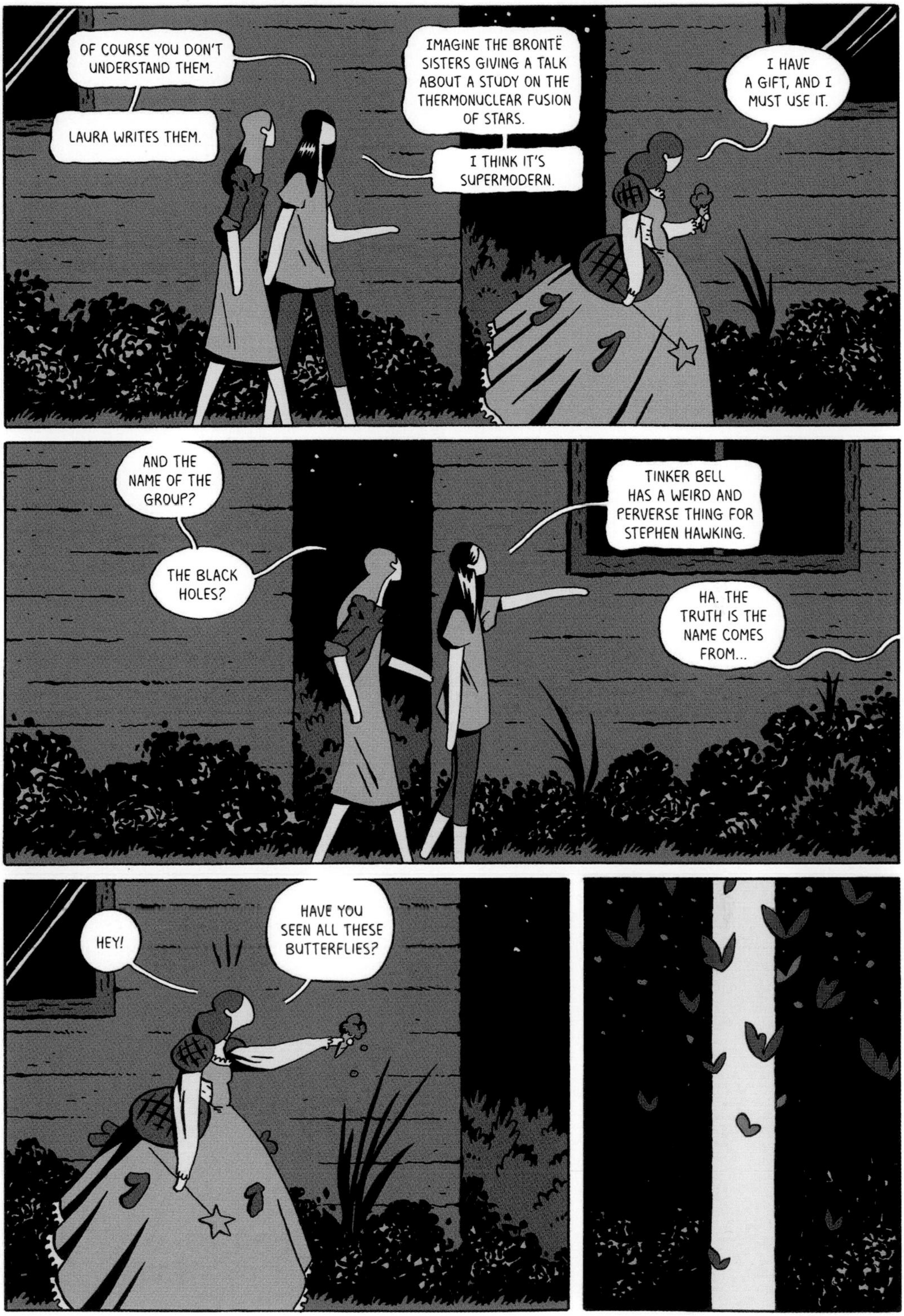
OF COURSE YOU DON'T UNDERSTAND THEM.
LAURA WRITES THEM.
IMAGINE THE BRONTË SISTERS GIVING A TALK ABOUT A STUDY ON THE THERMONUCLEAR FUSION OF STARS.
I THINK IT'S SUPERMODERN.
I HAVE A GIFT, AND I MUST USE IT.
AND THE NAME OF THE GROUP?
THE BLACK HOLES?
TINKER BELL HAS A WEIRD AND PERVERSE THING FOR STEPHEN HAWKING.
HA. THE TRUTH IS THE NAME COMES FROM...
HEY!
HAVE YOU SEEN ALL THESE BUTTERFLIES?

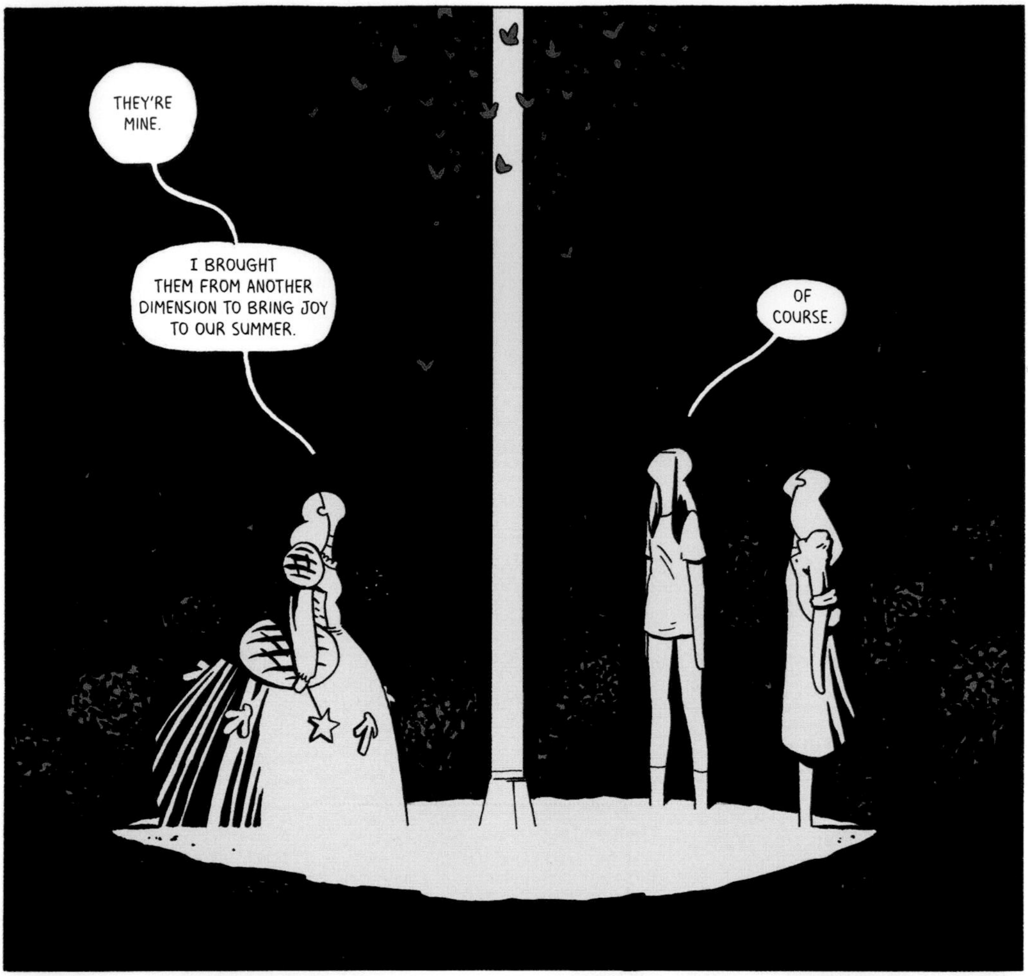
THEY'RE MINE.
I BROUGHT THEM FROM ANOTHER DIMENSION TO BRING JOY TO OUR SUMMER.
OF COURSE.

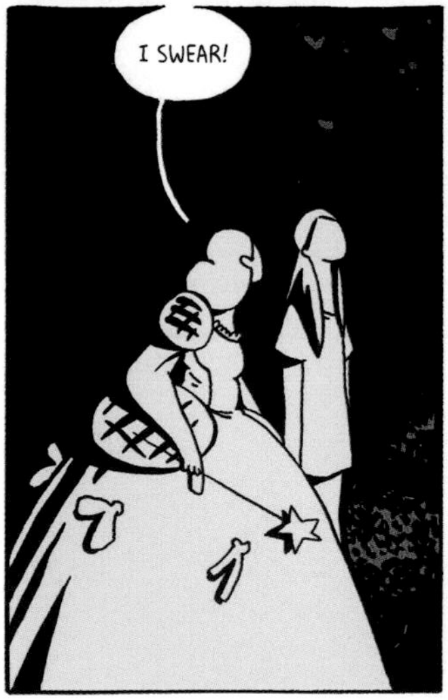
I SWEAR!

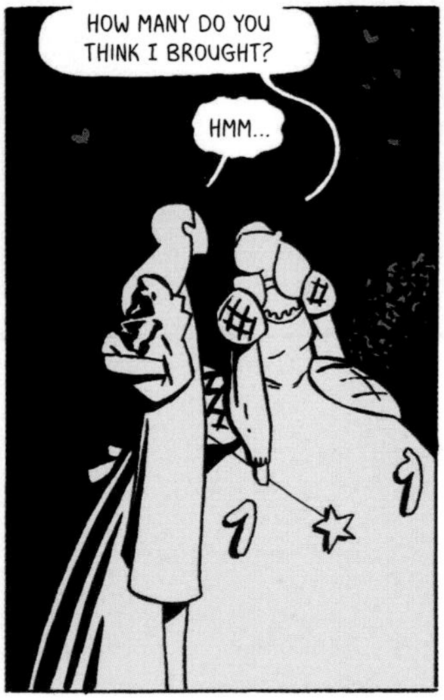
HOW MANY DO YOU THINK I BROUGHT?
HMM...

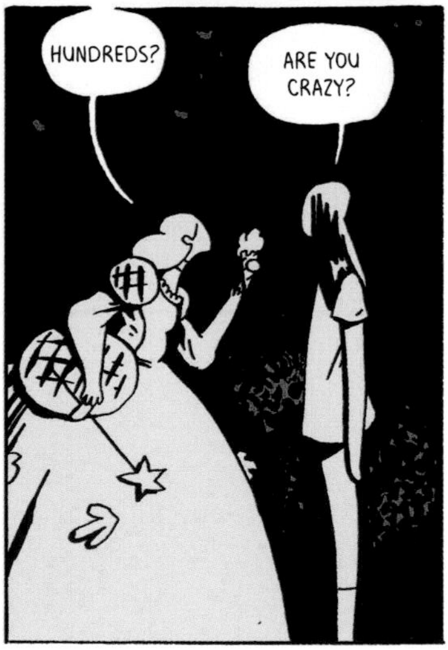
HUNDREDS?
ARE YOU CRAZY?

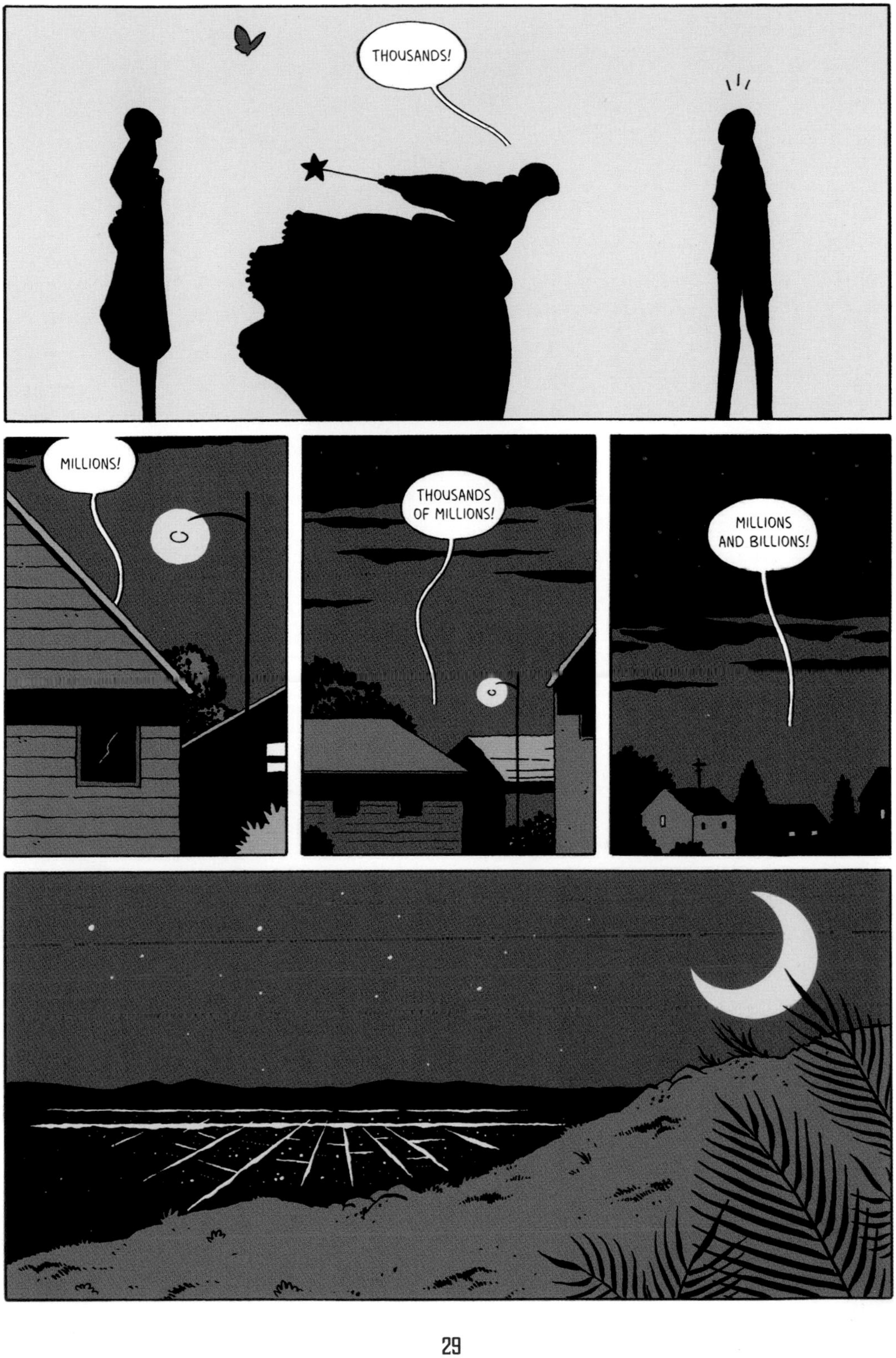
THOUSANDS!
MILLIONS!
THOUSANDS OF MILLIONS!
MILLIONS AND BILLIONS!

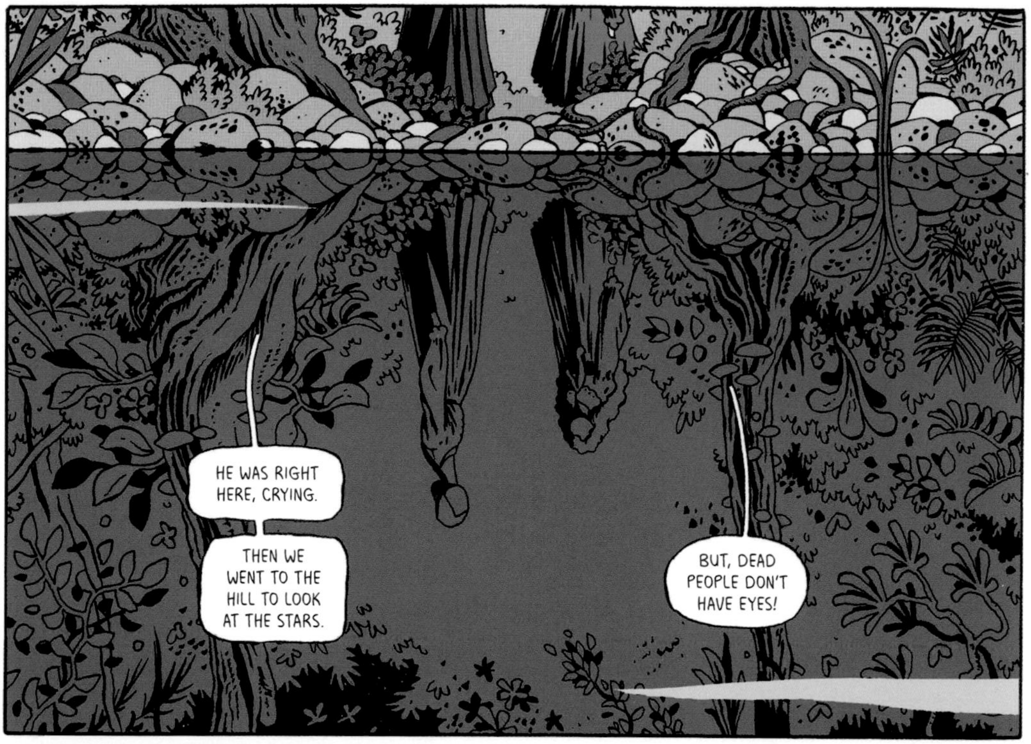
HE WAS RIGHT HERE, CRYING.
THEN WE WENT TO THE HILL TO LOOK AT THE STARS.
BUT, DEAD PEOPLE DON'T HAVE EYES!

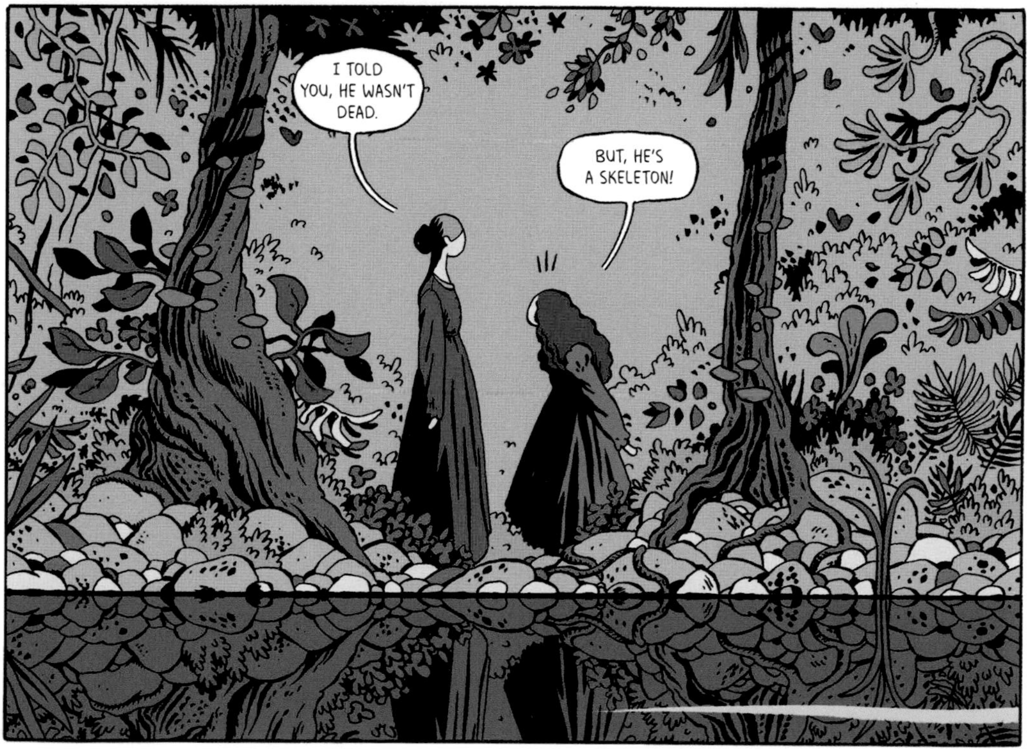
I TOLD YOU, HE WASN'T DEAD.
BUT, HE'S A SKELETON!

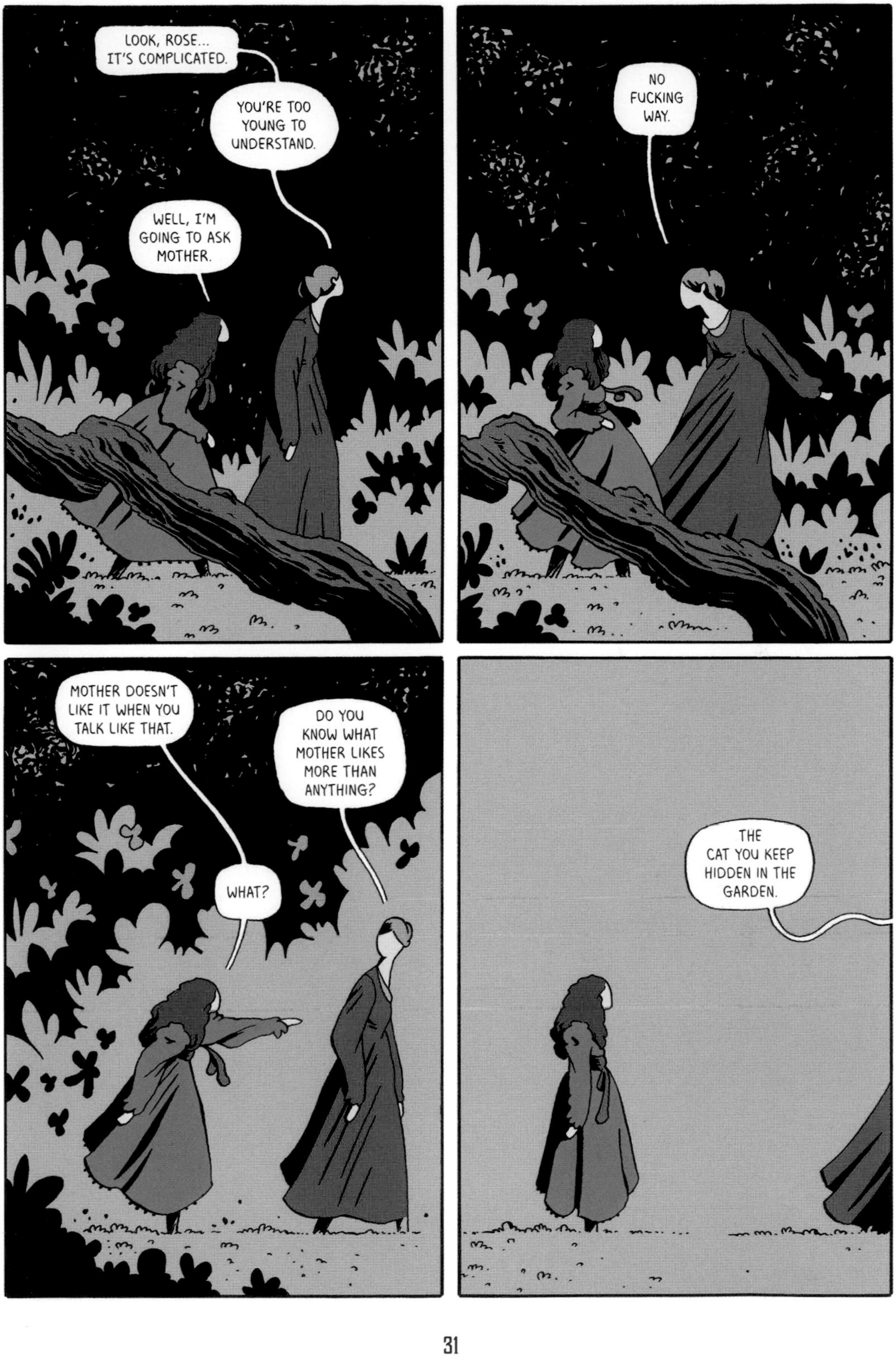
LOOK, ROSE... IT'S COMPLICATED.
YOU'RE TOO YOUNG TO UNDERSTAND.
WELL, I'M GOING TO ASK MOTHER.
NO FUCKING WAY.
MOTHER DOESN'T LIKE IT WHEN YOU TALK LIKE THAT.
DO YOU KNOW WHAT MOTHER LIKES MORE THAN ANYTHING?
WHAT?
THE CAT YOU KEEP HIDDEN IN THE GARDEN.

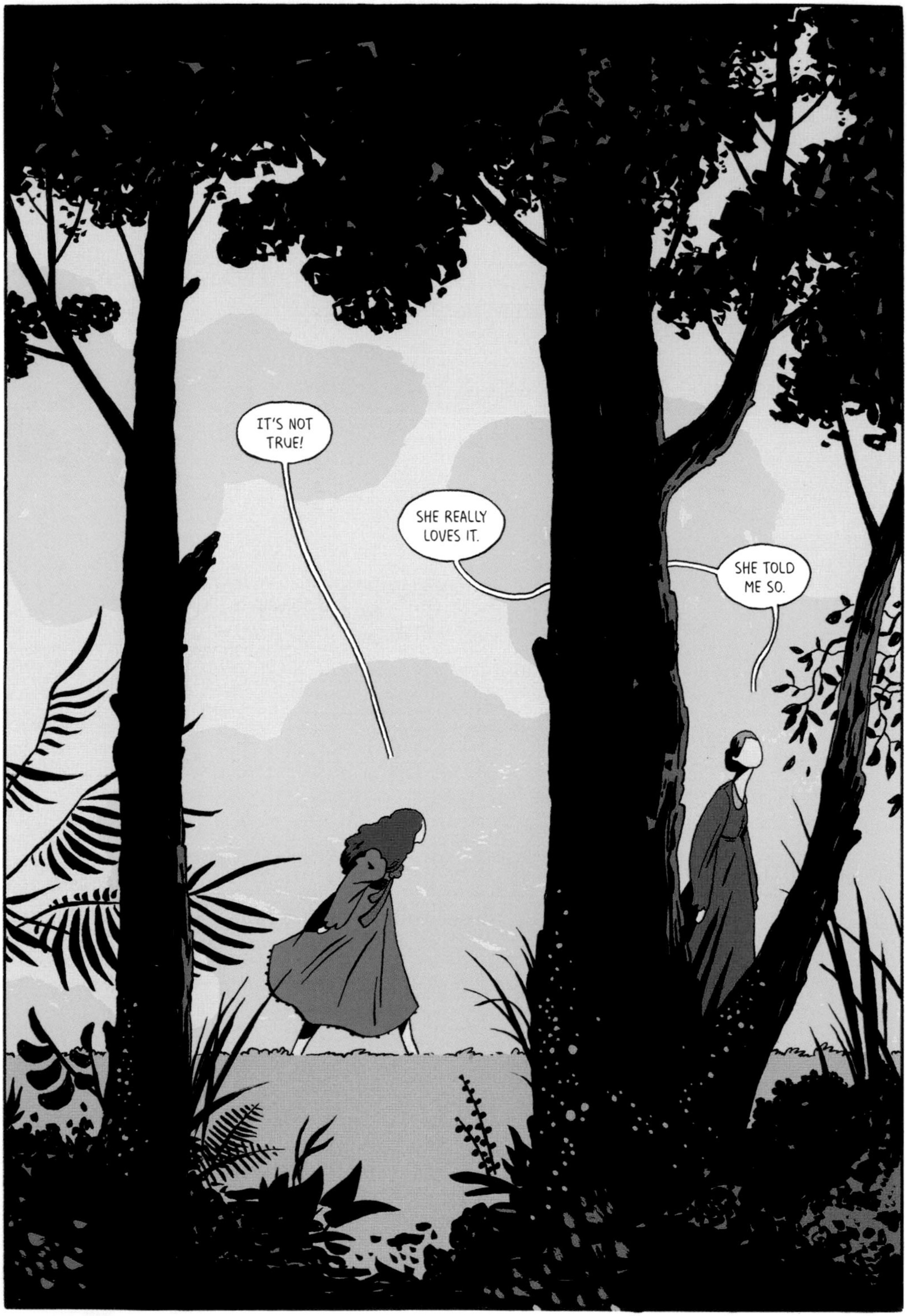
IT'S NOT TRUE!
SHE REALLY LOVES IT.
SHE TOLD ME SO.

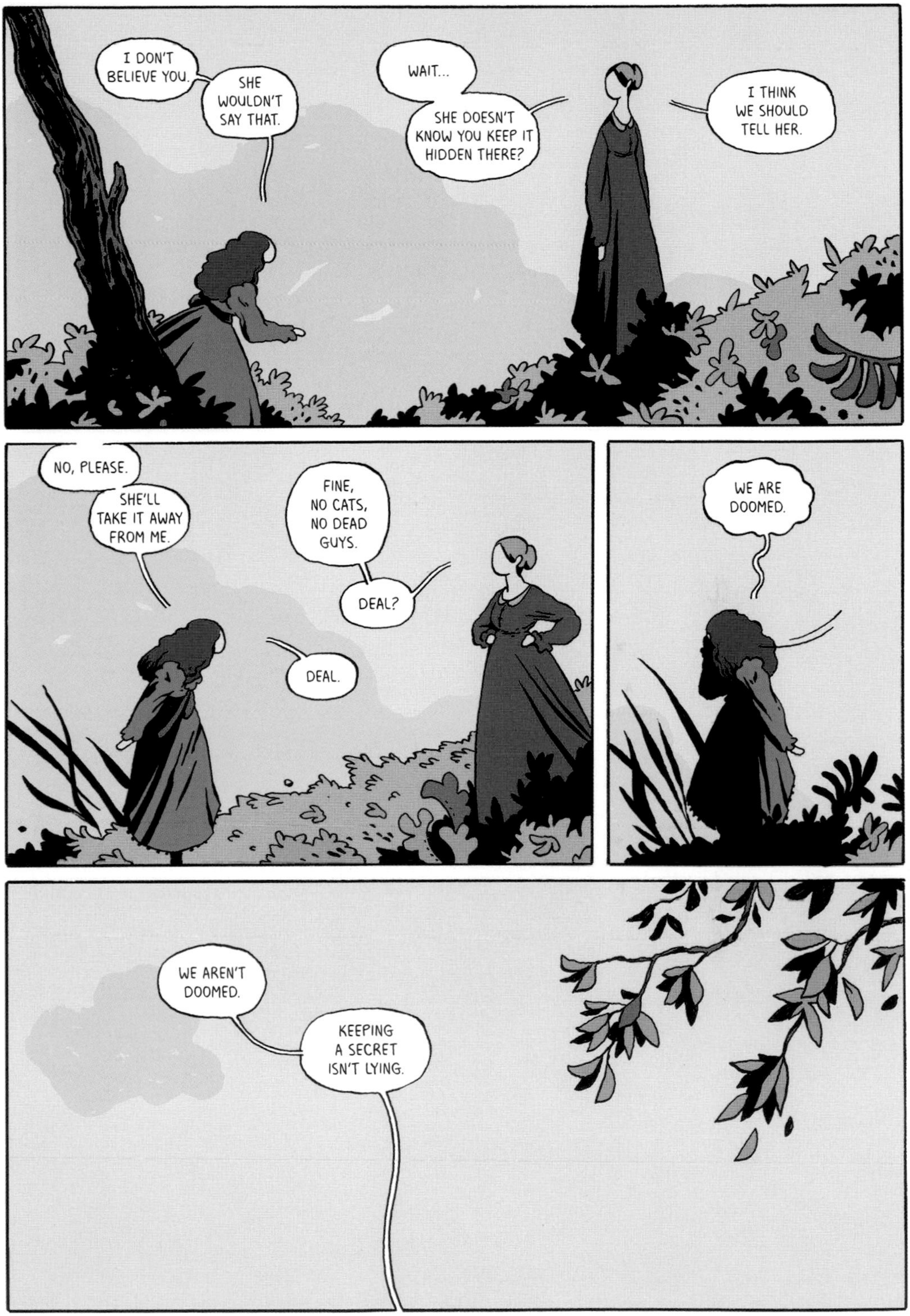
I DON'T BELIEVE YOU.
SHE WOULDN'T SAY THAT.
WAIT...
SHE DOESN'T KNOW YOU KEEP IT HIDDEN THERE?
I THINK WE SHOULD TELL HER.
NO, PLEASE.
SHE'LL TAKE IT AWAY FROM ME.
FINE, NO CATS, NO DEAD GUYS.
DEAL?
DEAL.
WE ARE DOOMED.
WE AREN'T DOOMED.
KEEPING A SECRET ISN'T LYING.

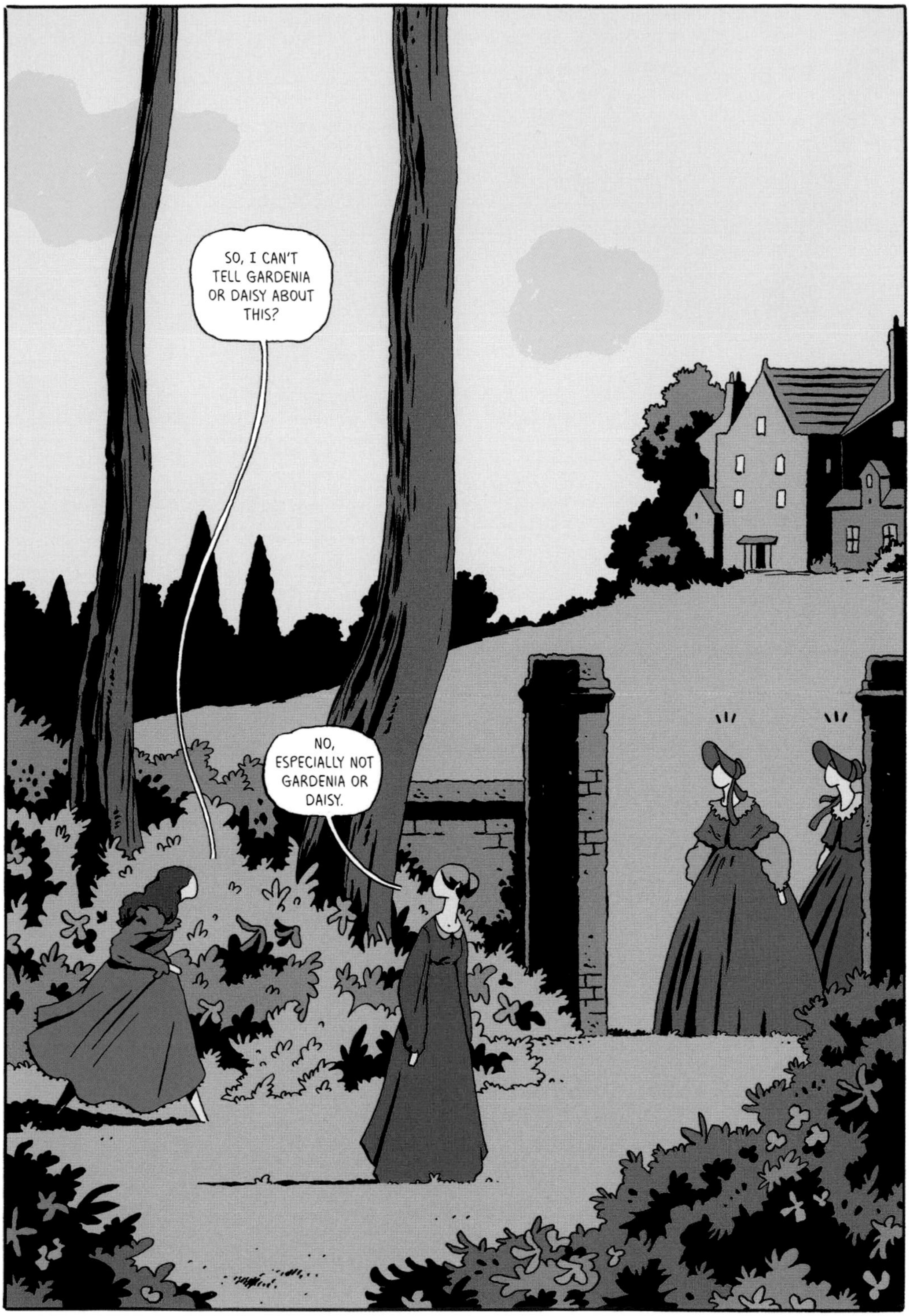
SO, I CAN'T TELL GARDENIA OR DAISY ABOUT THIS?
NO, ESPECIALLY NOT GARDENIA OR DAISY.

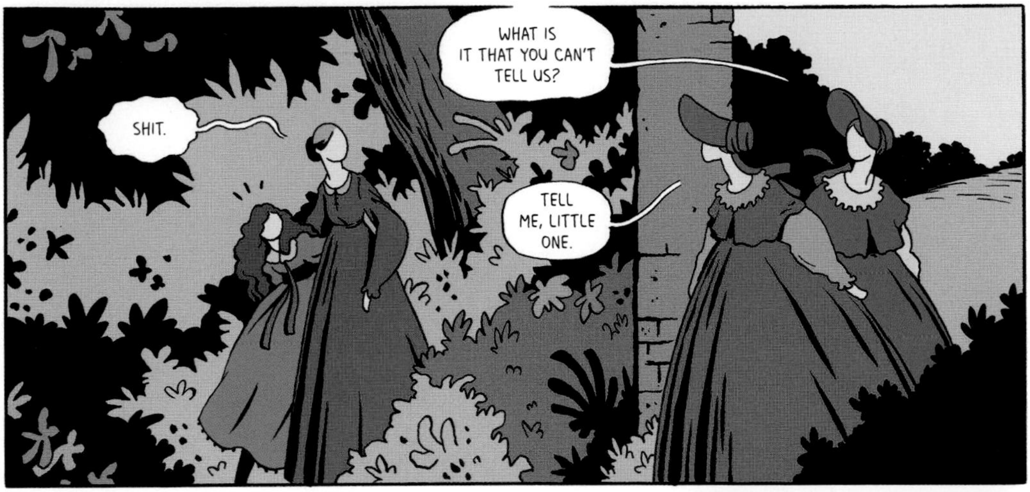
SHIT.
WHAT IS IT THAT YOU CAN'T TELL US?
TELL ME, LITTLE ONE.

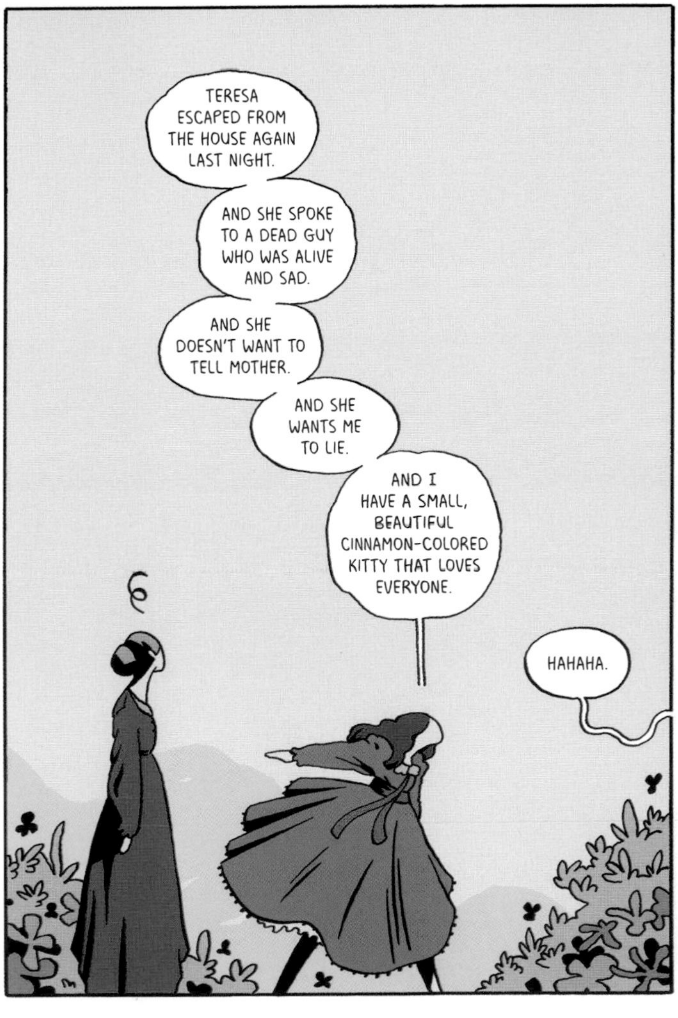
TERESA ESCAPED FROM THE HOUSE AGAIN LAST NIGHT.
AND SHE SPOKE TO A DEAD GUY WHO WAS ALIVE AND SAD.
AND SHE DOESN'T WANT TO TELL MOTHER.
AND SHE WANTS ME TO LIE.
AND I HAVE A SMALL, BEAUTIFUL CINNAMON-COLORED KITTY THAT LOVES EVERYONE.
HAHAHA.

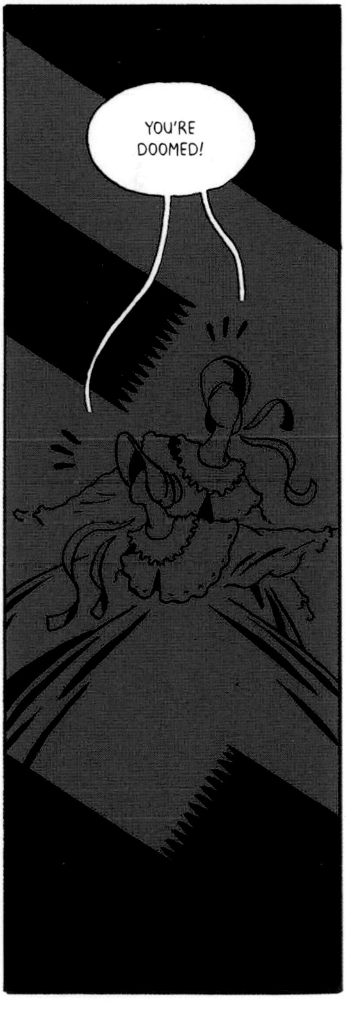
YOU'RE DOOMED!

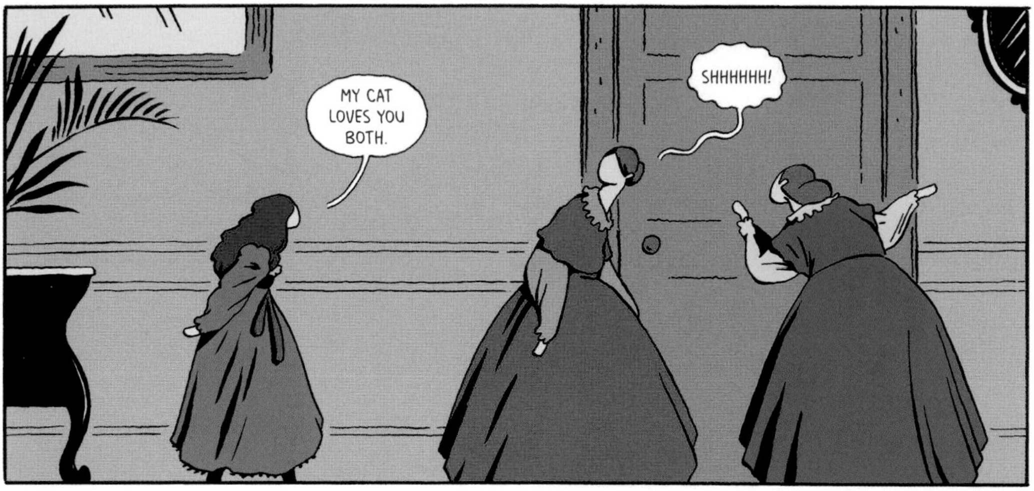
MY CAT LOVES YOU BOTH.
SHHHHHH!

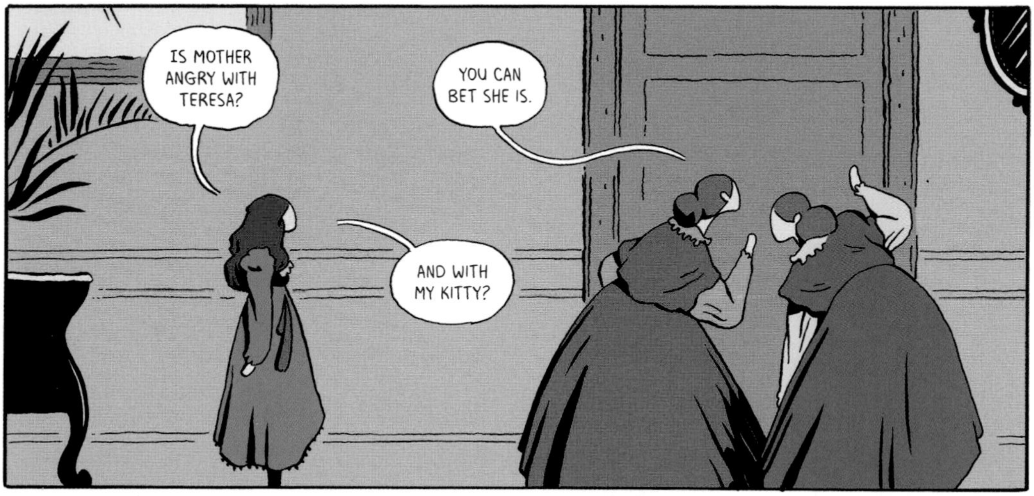
IS MOTHER ANGRY WITH TERESA?
YOU CAN BET SHE IS.
AND WITH MY KITTY?

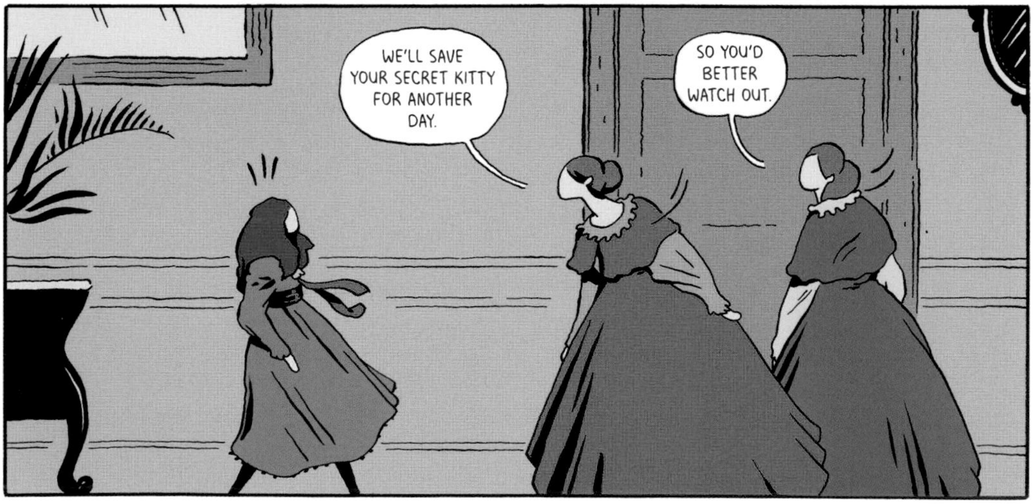
WE'LL SAVE YOUR SECRET KITTY FOR ANOTHER DAY.
SO YOU'D BETTER WATCH OUT.

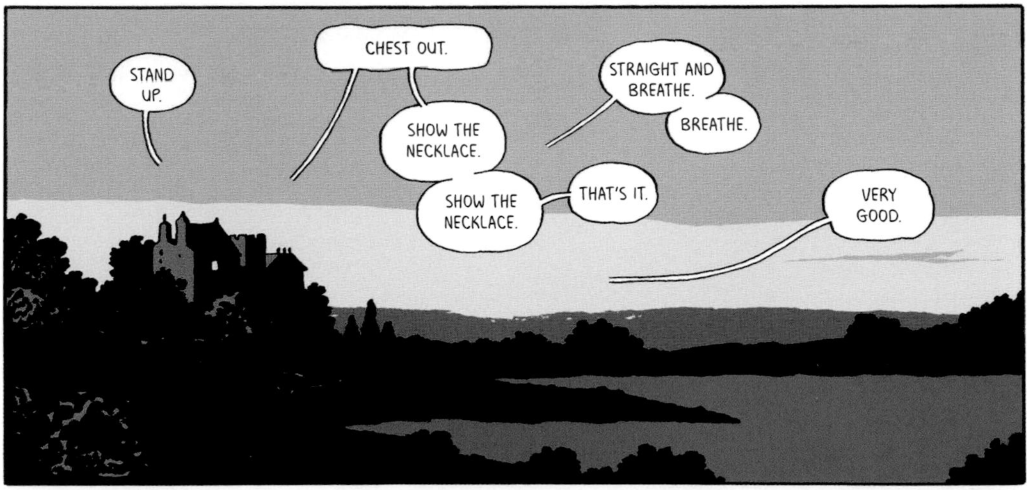
STAND UP.
CHEST OUT.
SHOW THE NECKLACE.
SHOW THE NECKLACE.
STRAIGHT AND BREATHE.
BREATHE.
THAT'S IT.
VERY GOOD.

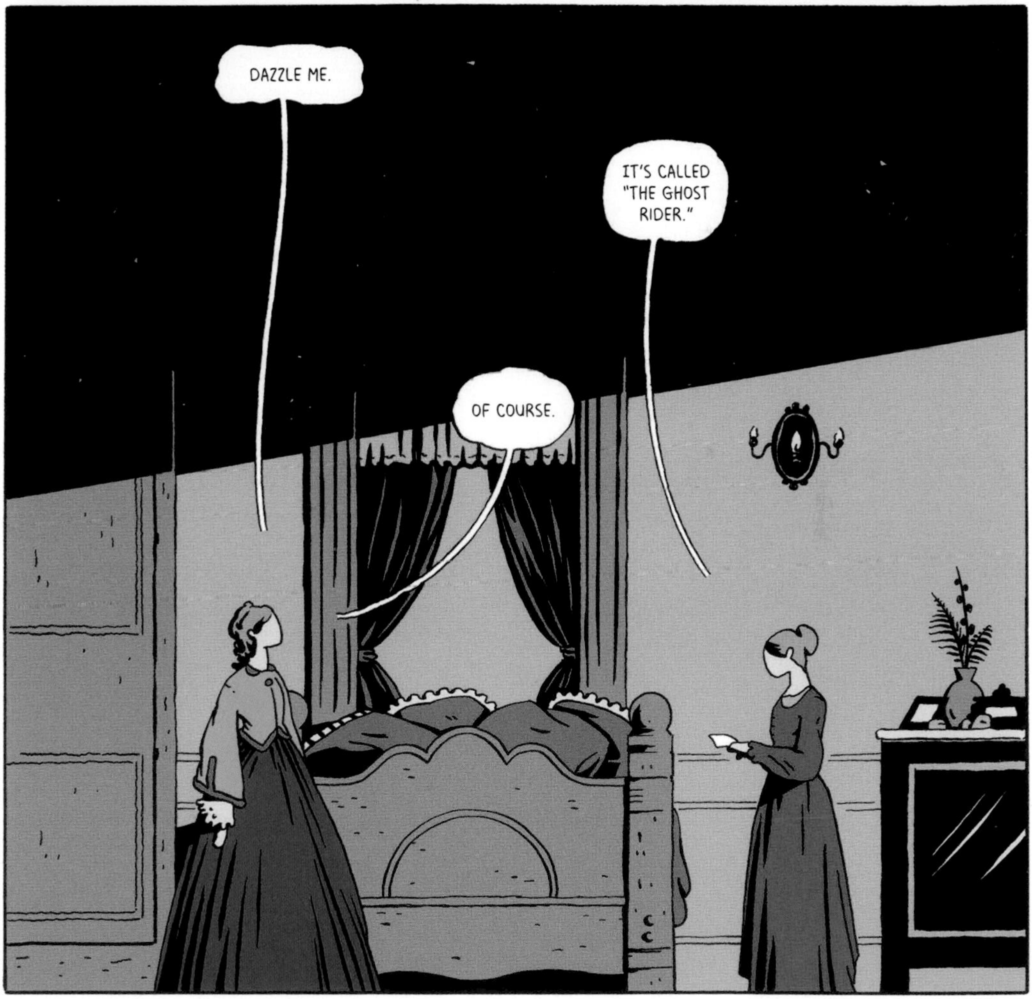
DAZZLE ME.
OF COURSE.
IT'S CALLED "THE GHOST RIDER."

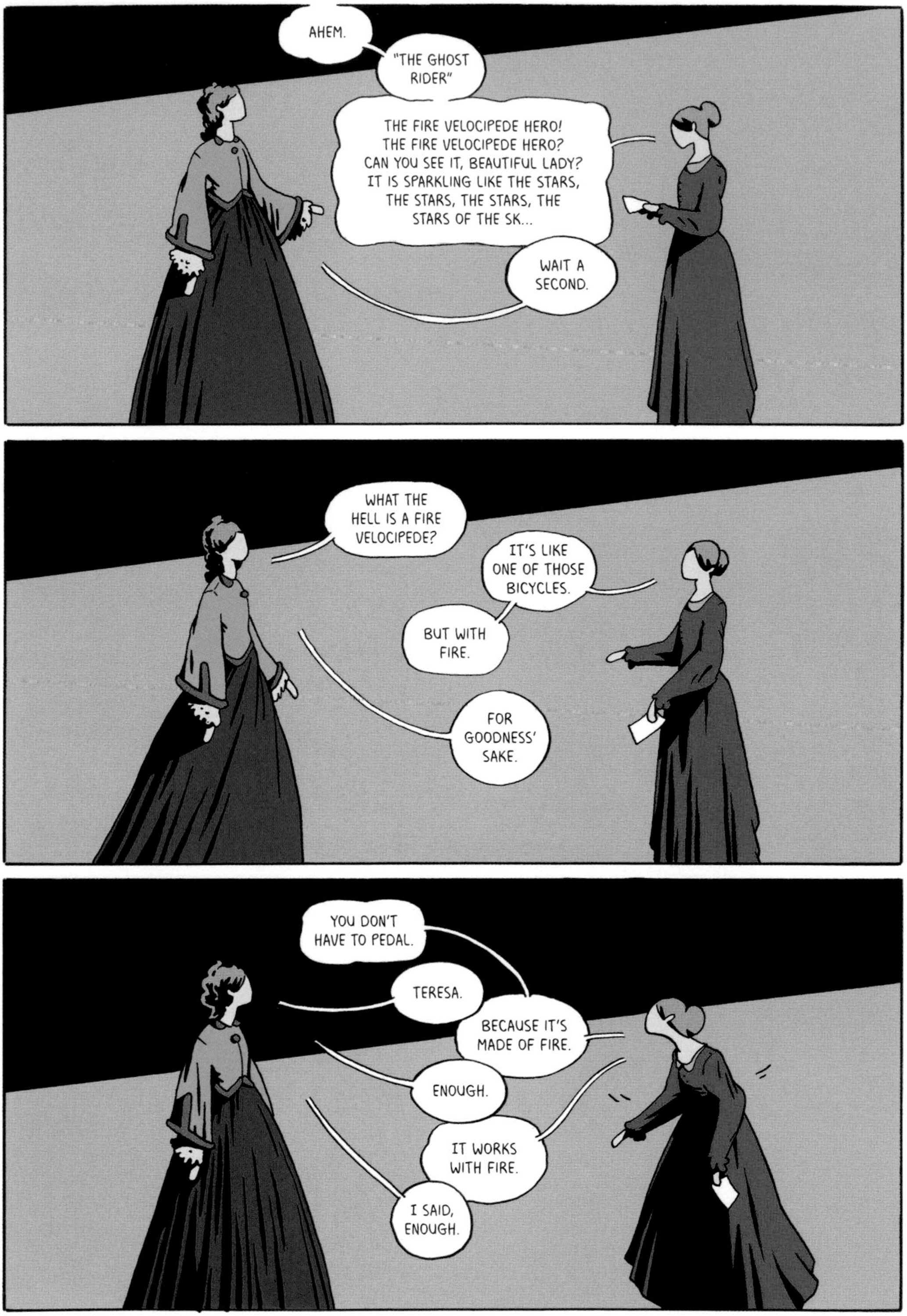
AHEM.
"THE GHOST RIDER"
THE FIRE VELOCIPEDE HERO! THE FIRE VELOCIPEDE HERO? CAN YOU SEE IT, BEAUTIFUL LADY? IT IS SPARKLING LIKE THE STARS, THE STARS, THE STARS, THE STARS OF THE SK...
WAIT A SECOND.
WHAT THE HELL IS A FIRE VELOCIPEDE?
IT'S LIKE ONE OF THOSE BICYCLES.
BUT WITH FIRE.
FOR GOODNESS' SAKE.
YOU DON'T HAVE TO PEDAL.
TERESA.
BECAUSE IT'S MADE OF FIRE.
ENOUGH.
IT WORKS WITH FIRE.
I SAID, ENOUGH.

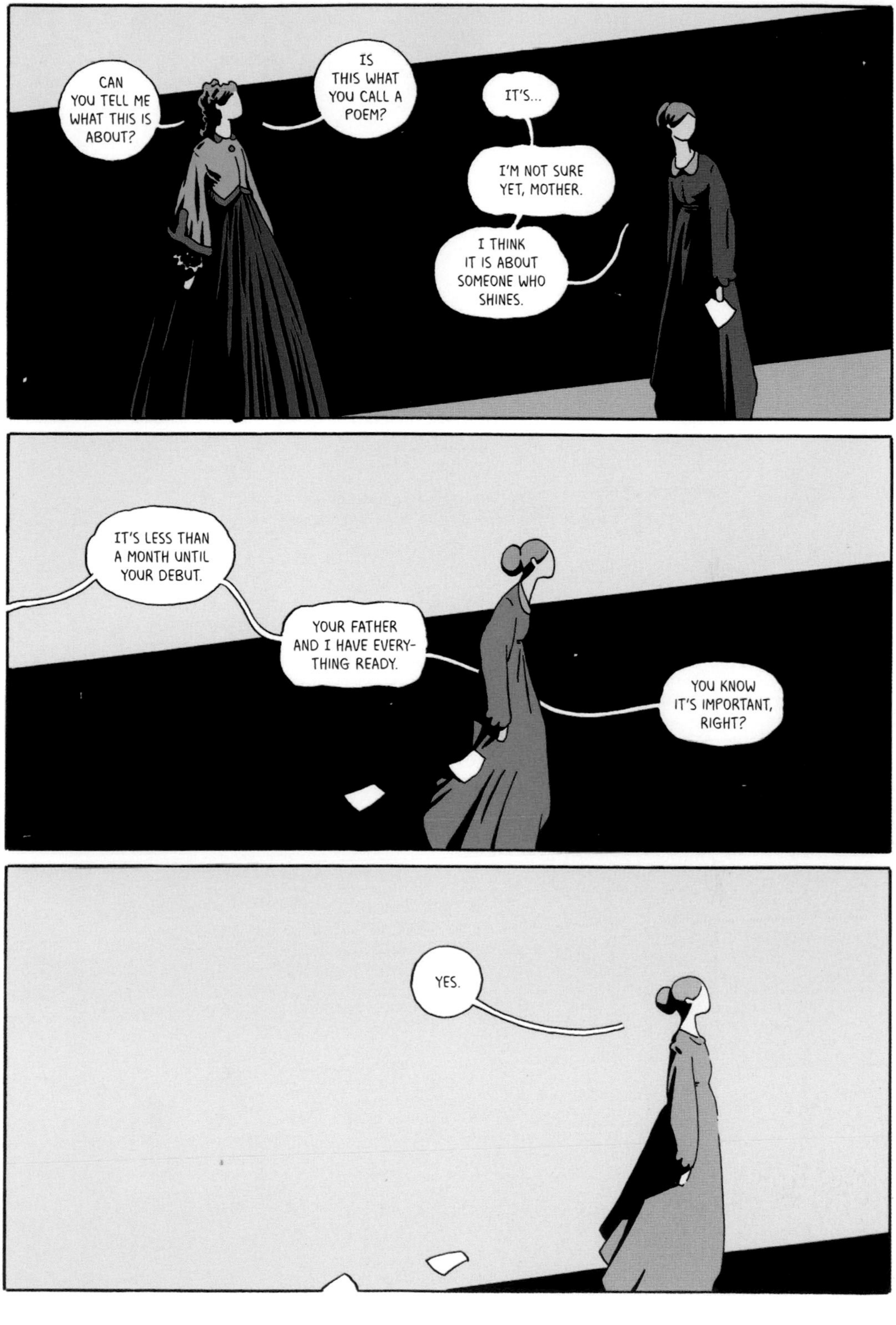
CAN YOU TELL ME WHAT THIS IS ABOUT?
IS THIS WHAT YOU CALL A POEM?
IT'S...
I'M NOT SURE YET, MOTHER.
I THINK IT IS ABOUT SOMEONE WHO SHINES.
IT'S LESS THAN A MONTH UNTIL YOUR DEBUT.
YOUR FATHER AND I HAVE EVERYTHING READY.
YOU KNOW IT'S IMPORTANT, RIGHT?
YES.

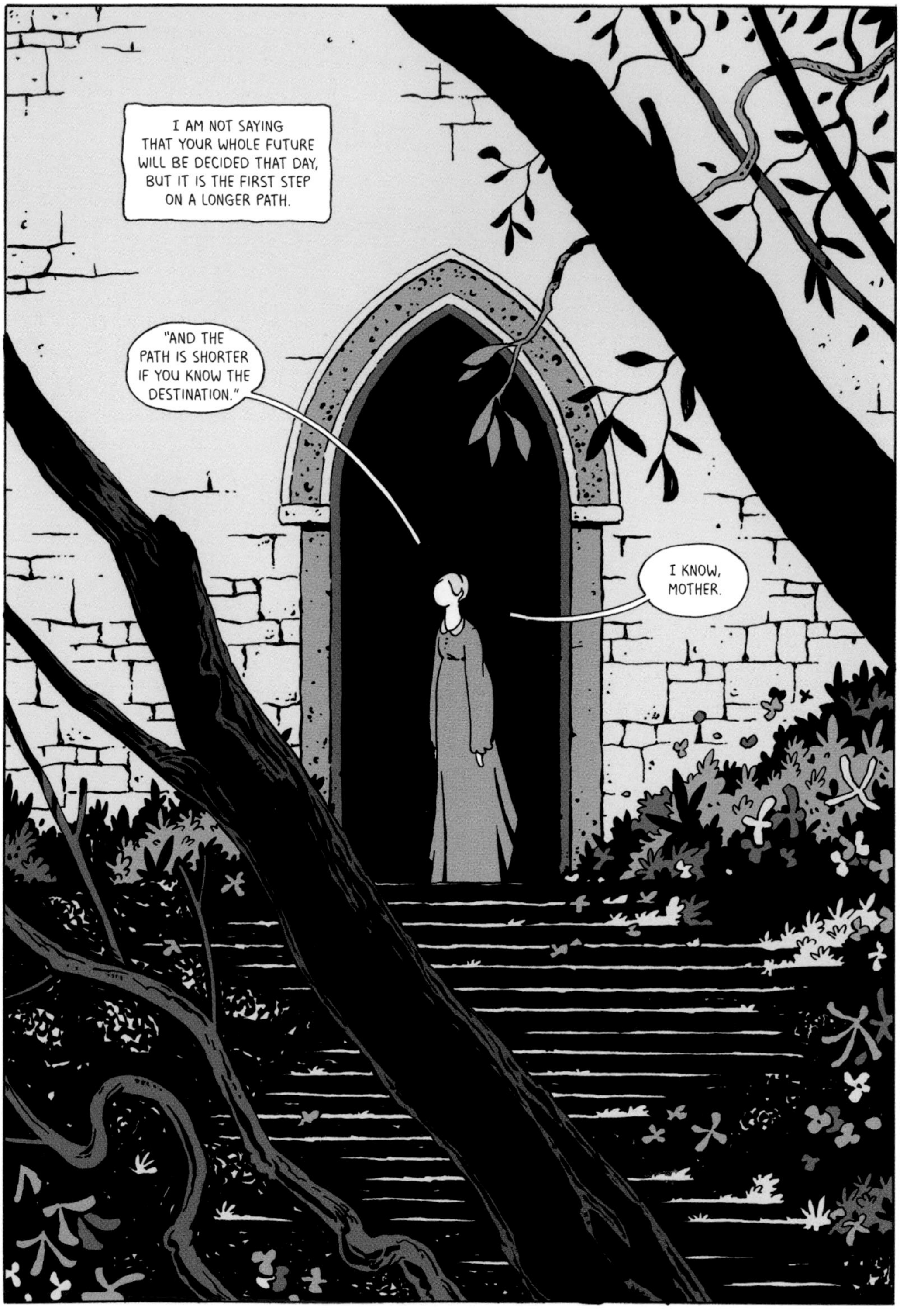
I AM NOT SAYING THAT YOUR WHOLE FUTURE WILL BE DECIDED THAT DAY, BUT IT IS THE FIRST STEP ON A LONGER PATH.
"AND THE PATH IS SHORTER IF YOU KNOW THE DESTINATION."
I KNOW, MOTHER.

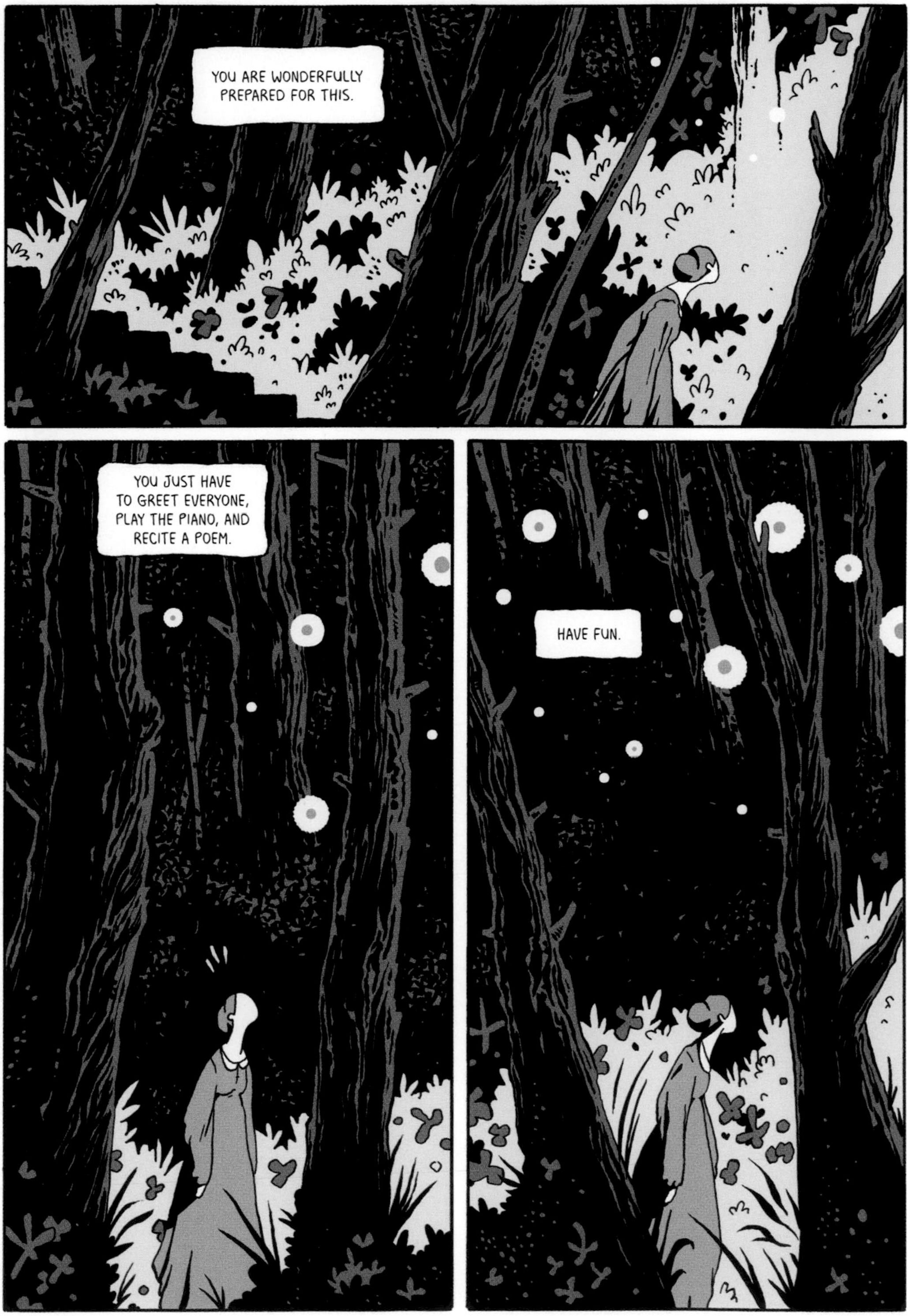
YOU ARE WONDERFULLY PREPARED FOR THIS.
YOU JUST HAVE TO GREET EVERYONE, PLAY THE PIANO, AND RECITE A POEM.
HAVE FUN.

IT ISN'T NECESSARY TO ESCAPE MIDWAY THROUGH THE NIGHT JUST TO HAVE FUN.
I DON'T KNOW WHAT YOU HOPE TO FIND OUT THERE.

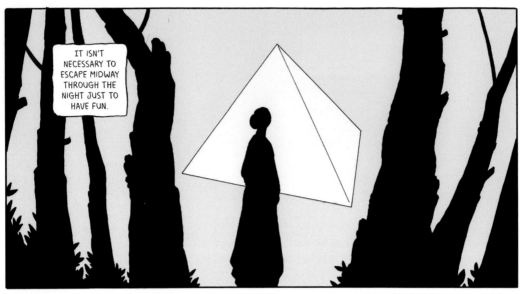

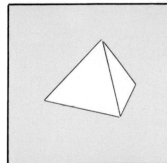

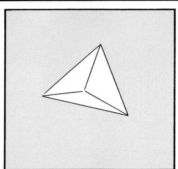

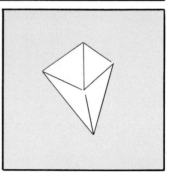

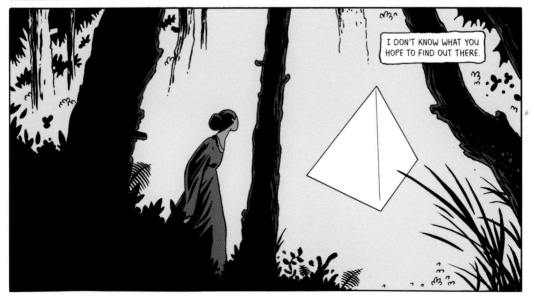

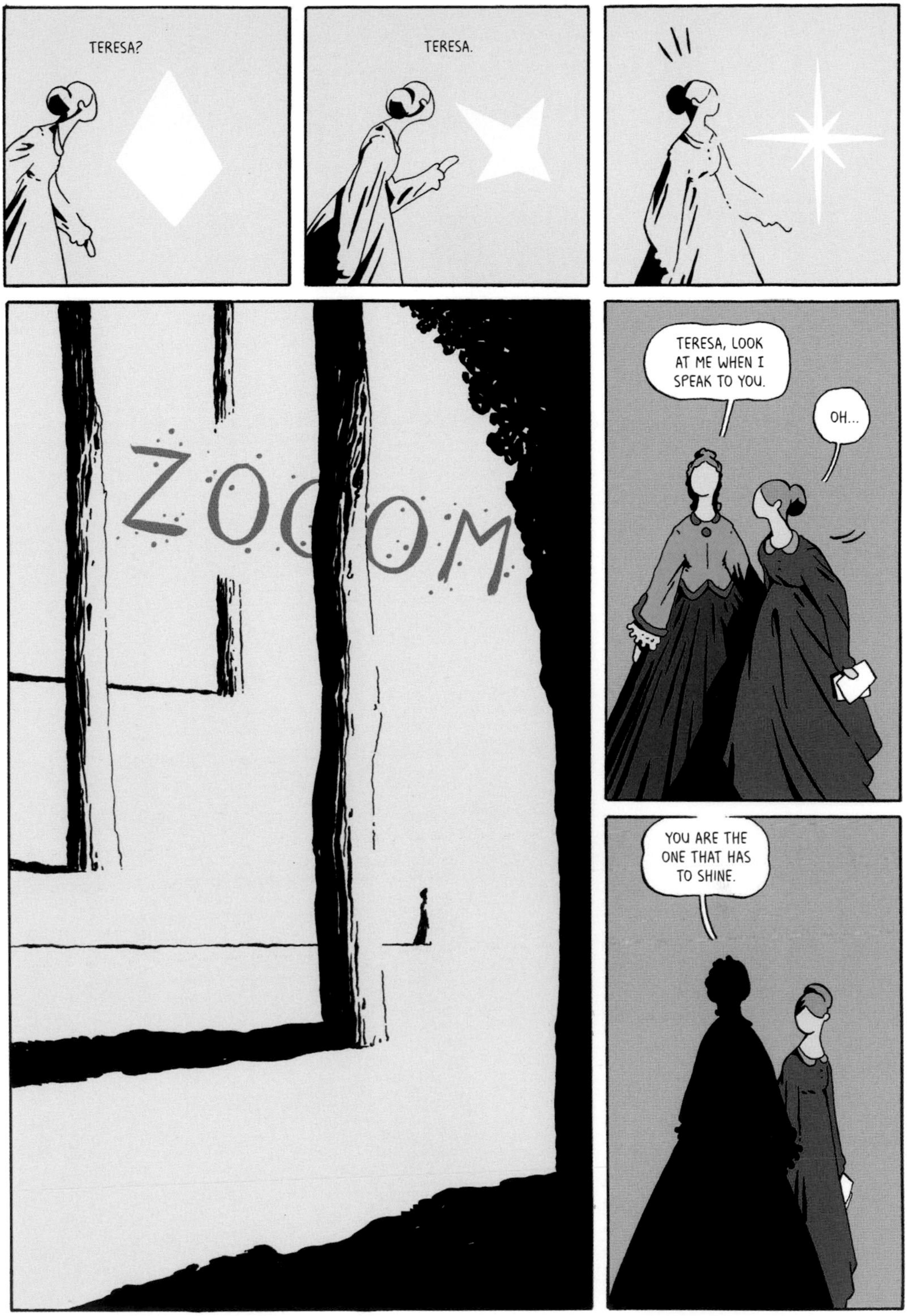
TERESA?
TERESA.
ZOOOM
TERESA, LOOK AT ME WHEN I SPEAK TO YOU.
OH...
YOU ARE THE ONE THAT HAS TO SHINE.

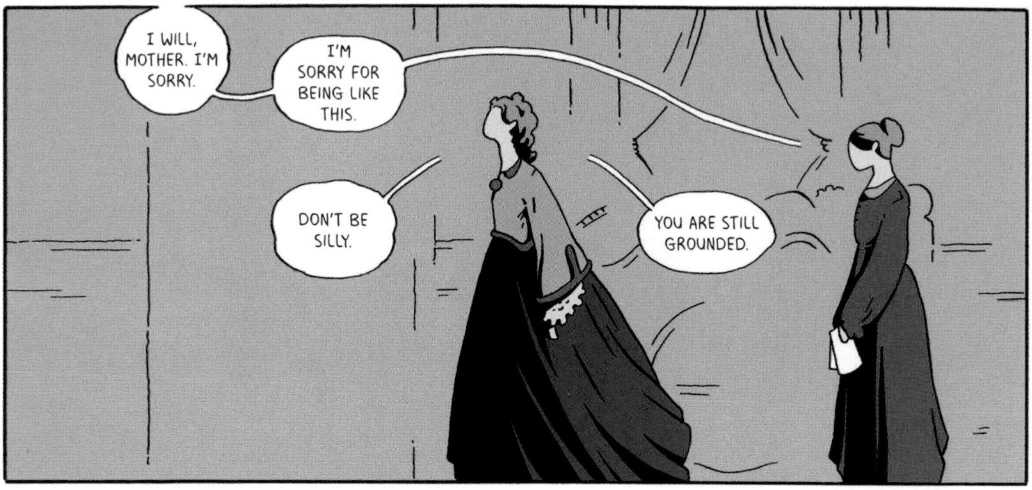
I WILL, MOTHER. I'M SORRY.
I'M SORRY FOR BEING LIKE THIS.
DON'T BE SILLY.
YOU ARE STILL GROUNDED.

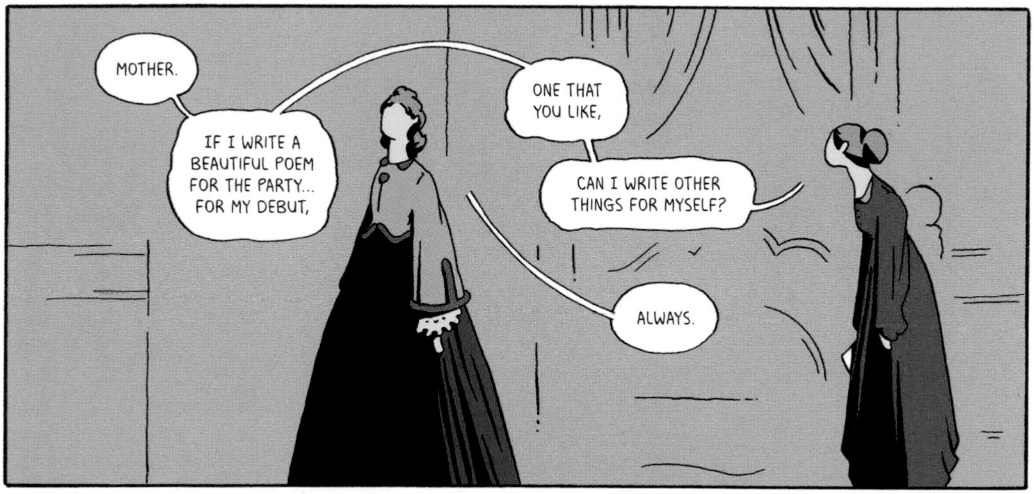
MOTHER.
IF I WRITE A BEAUTIFUL POEM FOR THE PARTY... FOR MY DEBUT,
ONE THAT YOU LIKE,
CAN I WRITE OTHER THINGS FOR MYSELF?
ALWAYS.

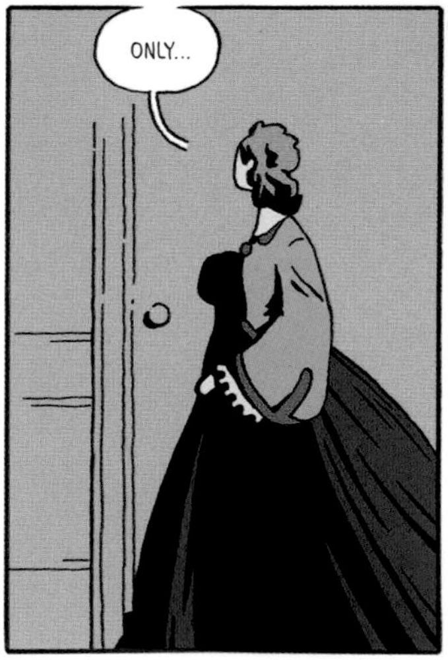
ONLY...

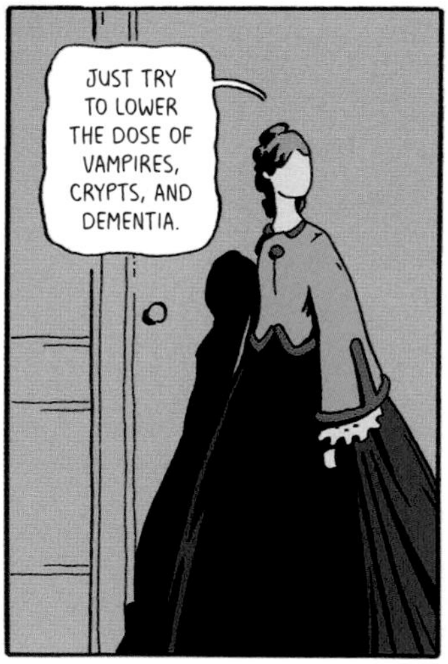
JUST TRY TO LOWER THE DOSE OF VAMPIRES, CRYPTS, AND DEMENTIA.

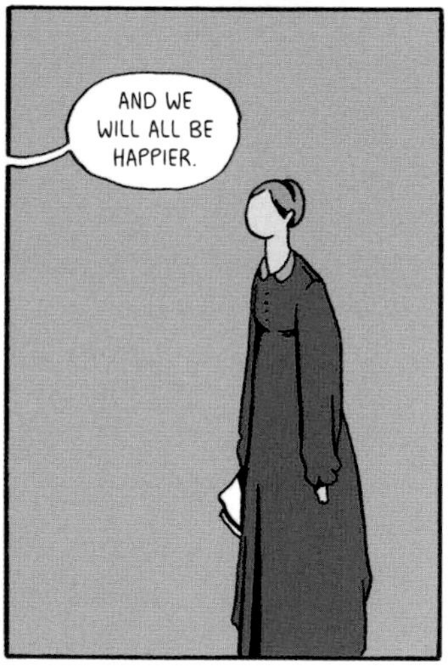
AND WE WILL ALL BE HAPPIER.

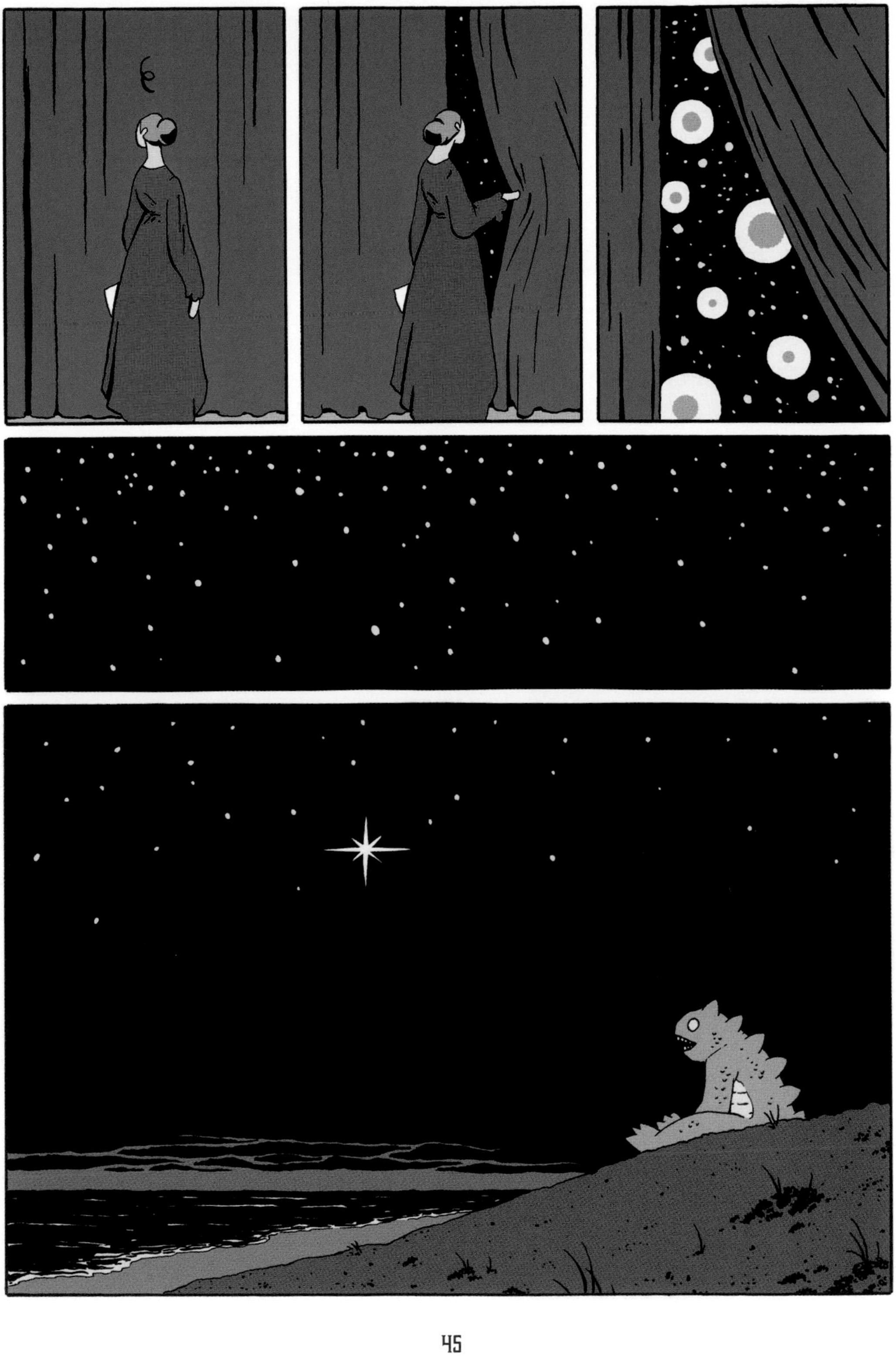

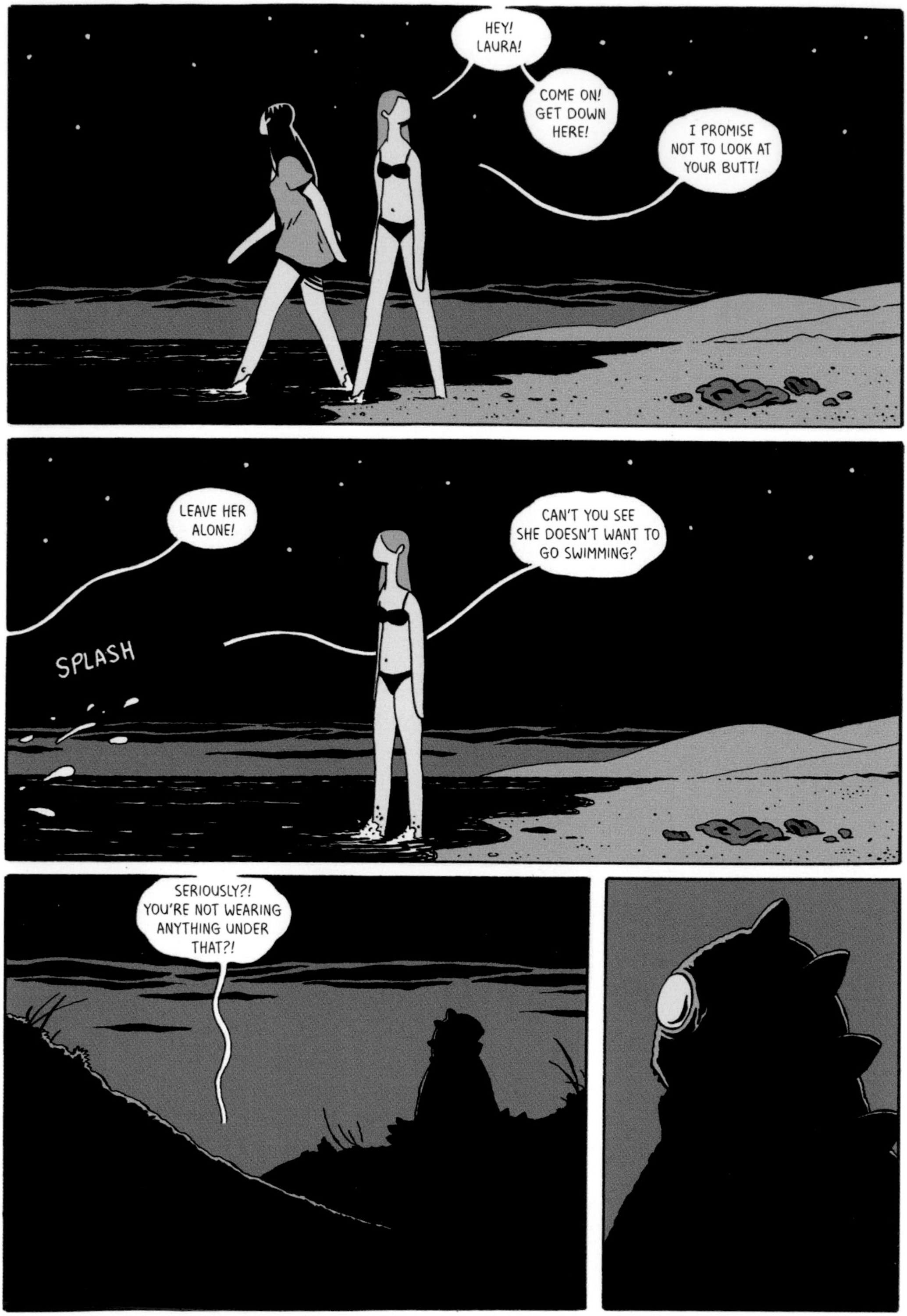
HEY! LAURA!
COME ON! GET DOWN HERE!
I PROMISE NOT TO LOOK AT YOUR BUTT!
LEAVE HER ALONE!
CAN'T YOU SEE SHE DOESN'T WANT TO GO SWIMMING?
SPLASH
SERIOUSLY?! YOU'RE NOT WEARING ANYTHING UNDER THAT?!

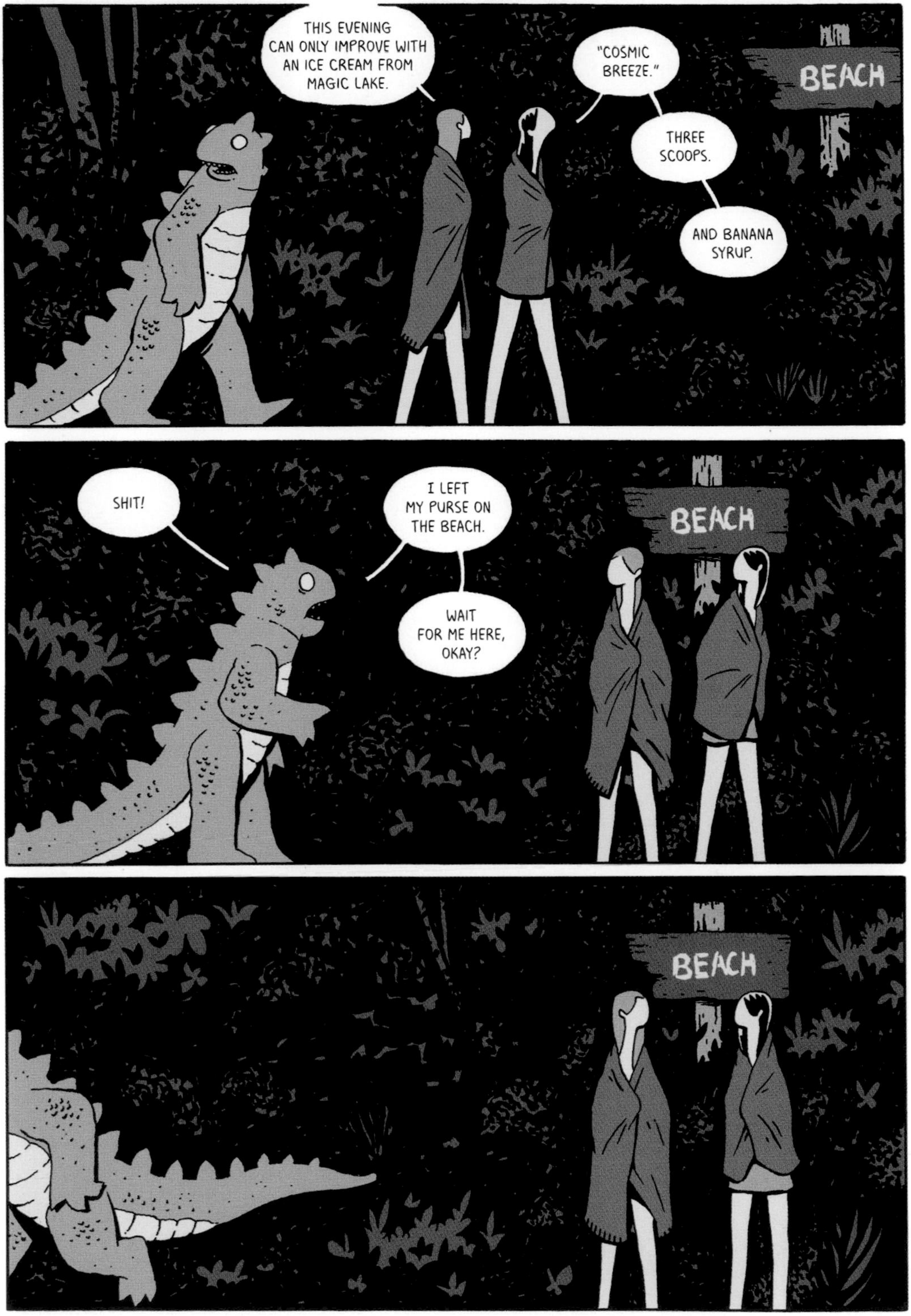
THIS EVENING CAN ONLY IMPROVE WITH AN ICE CREAM FROM MAGIC LAKE.
BEACH
"COSMIC BREEZE."
THREE SCOOPS.
AND BANANA SYRUP.
SHIT!
I LEFT MY PURSE ON THE BEACH.
BEACH
WAIT FOR ME HERE, OKAY?
BEACH

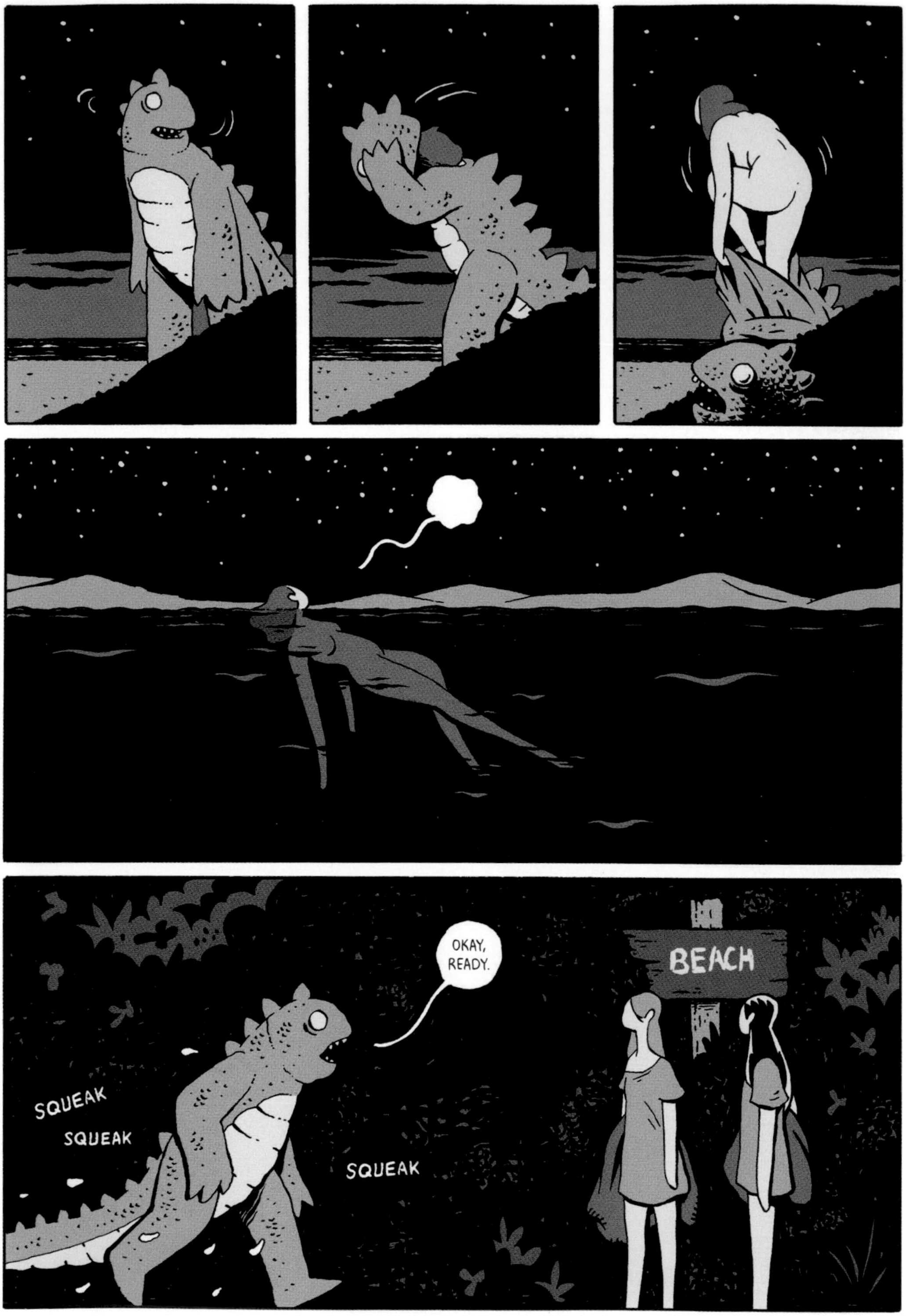
SQUEAK
SQUEAK
SQUEAK
OKAY, READY.
BEACH

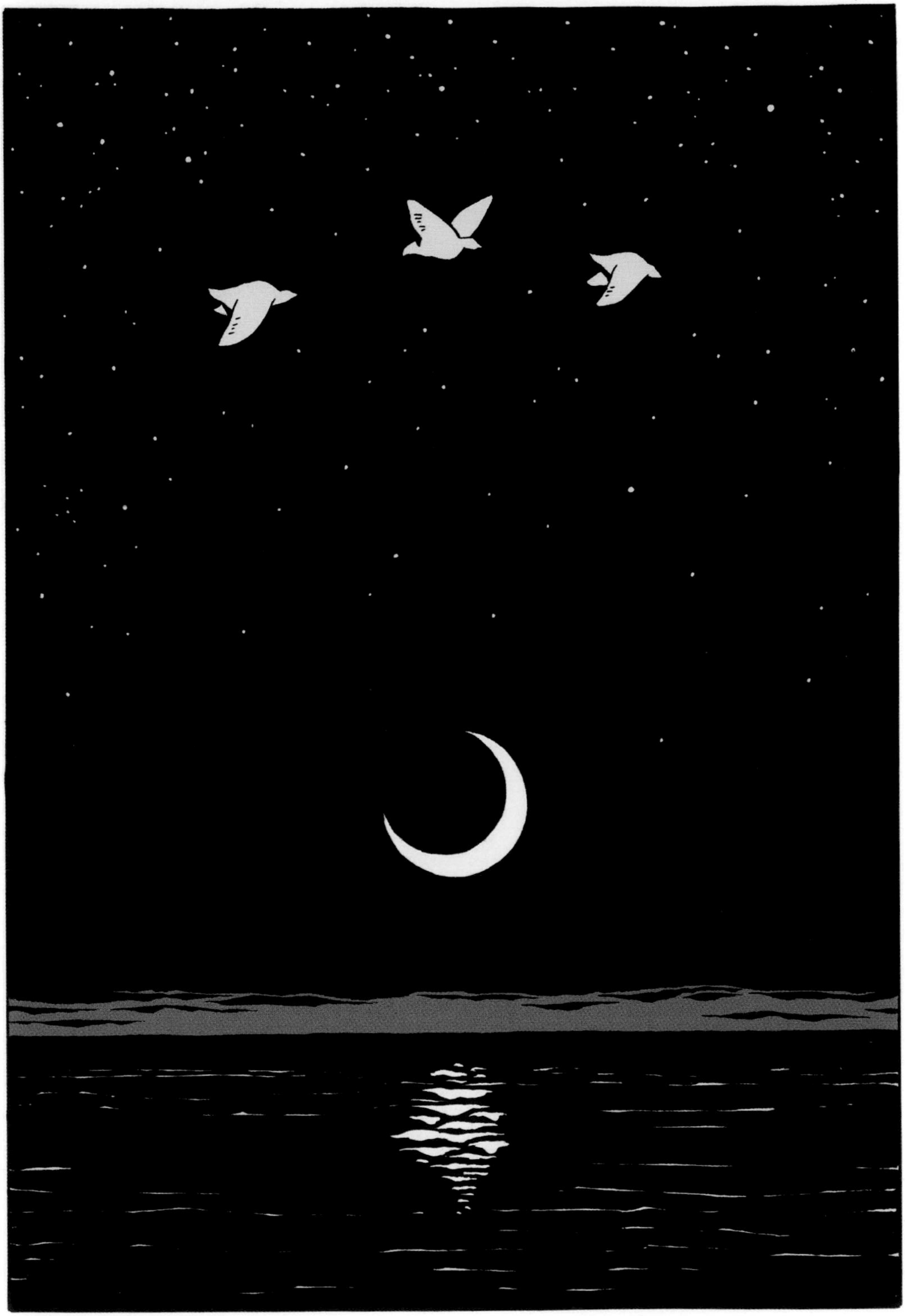

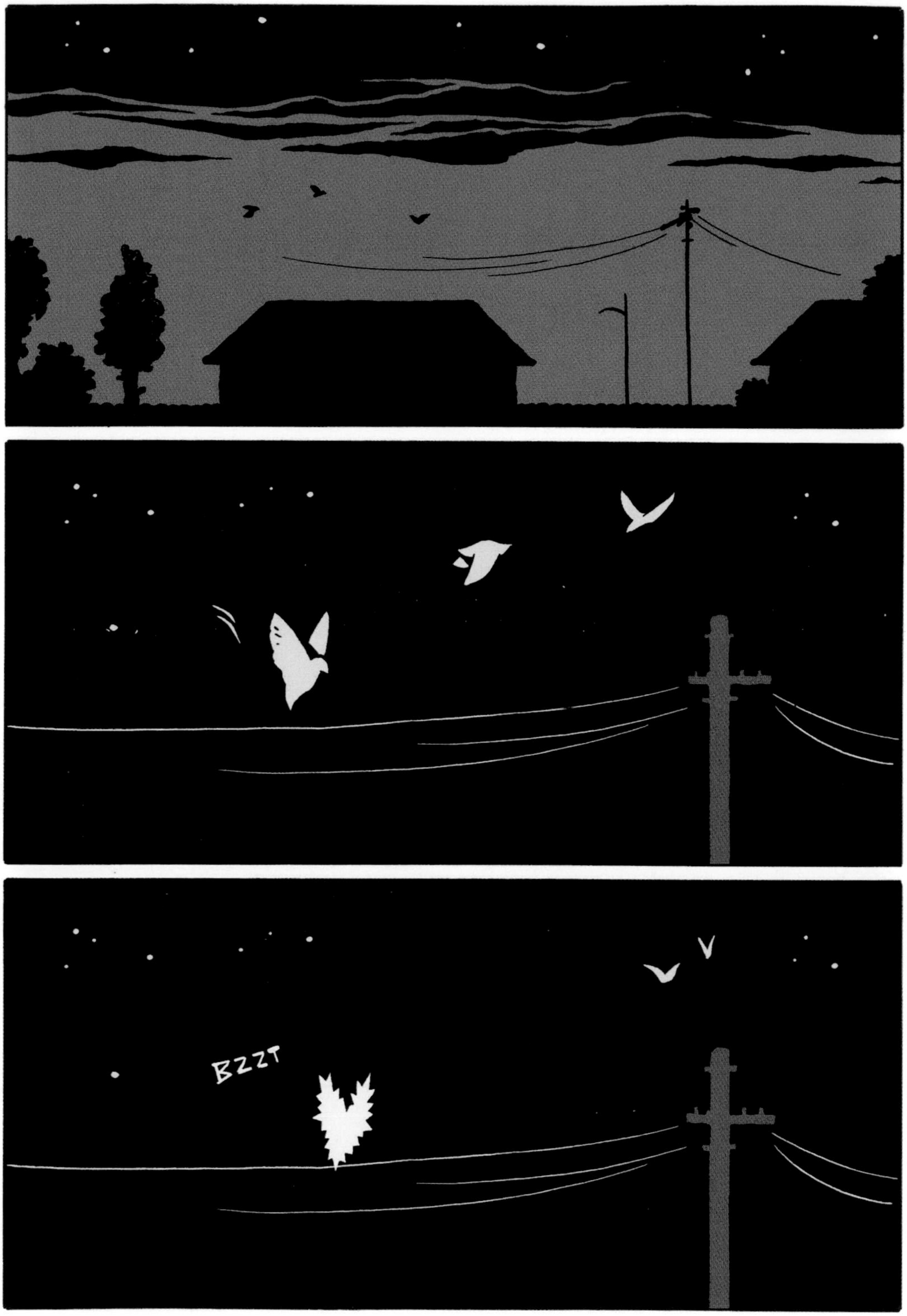
BZZT

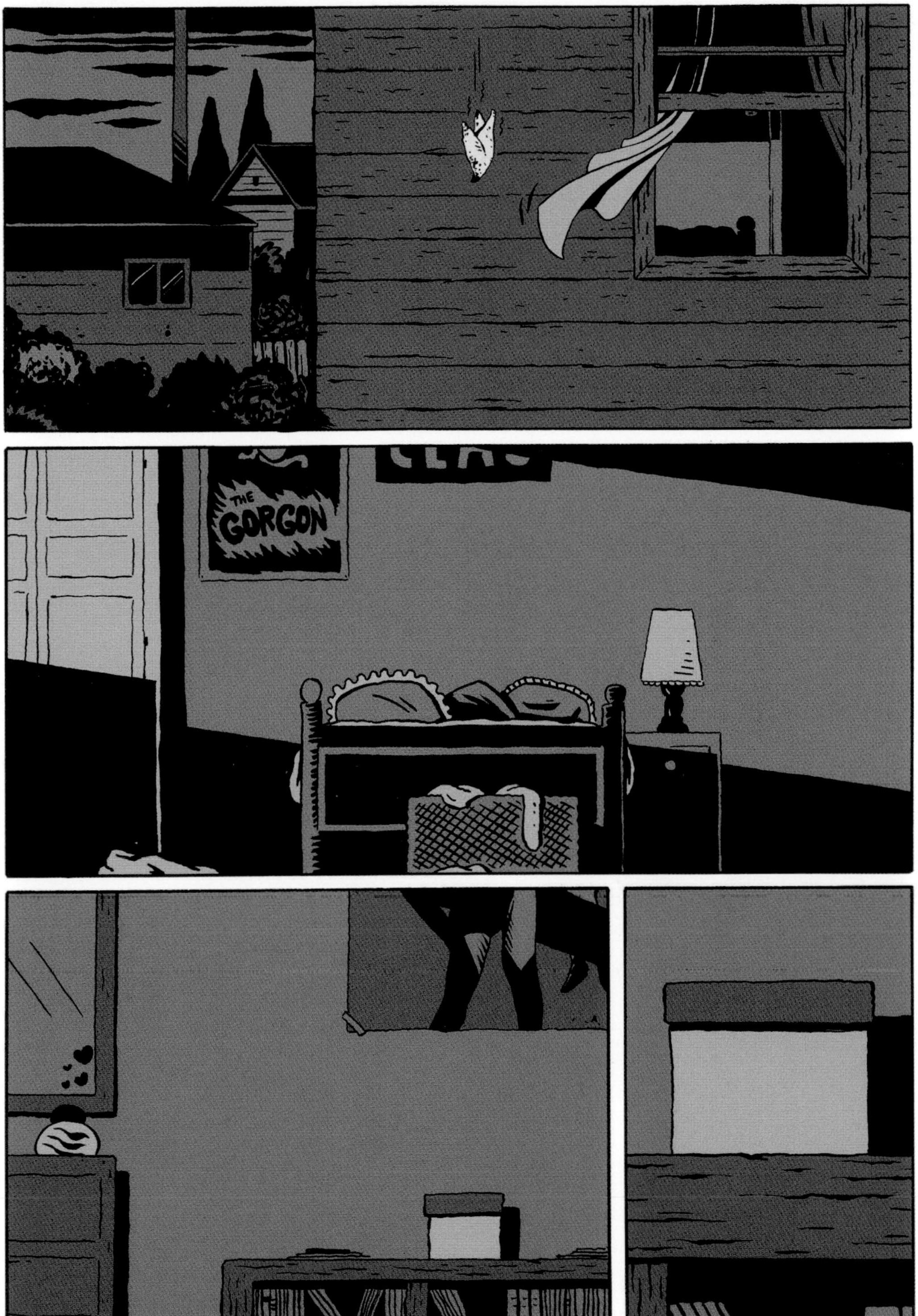
THE GORGON

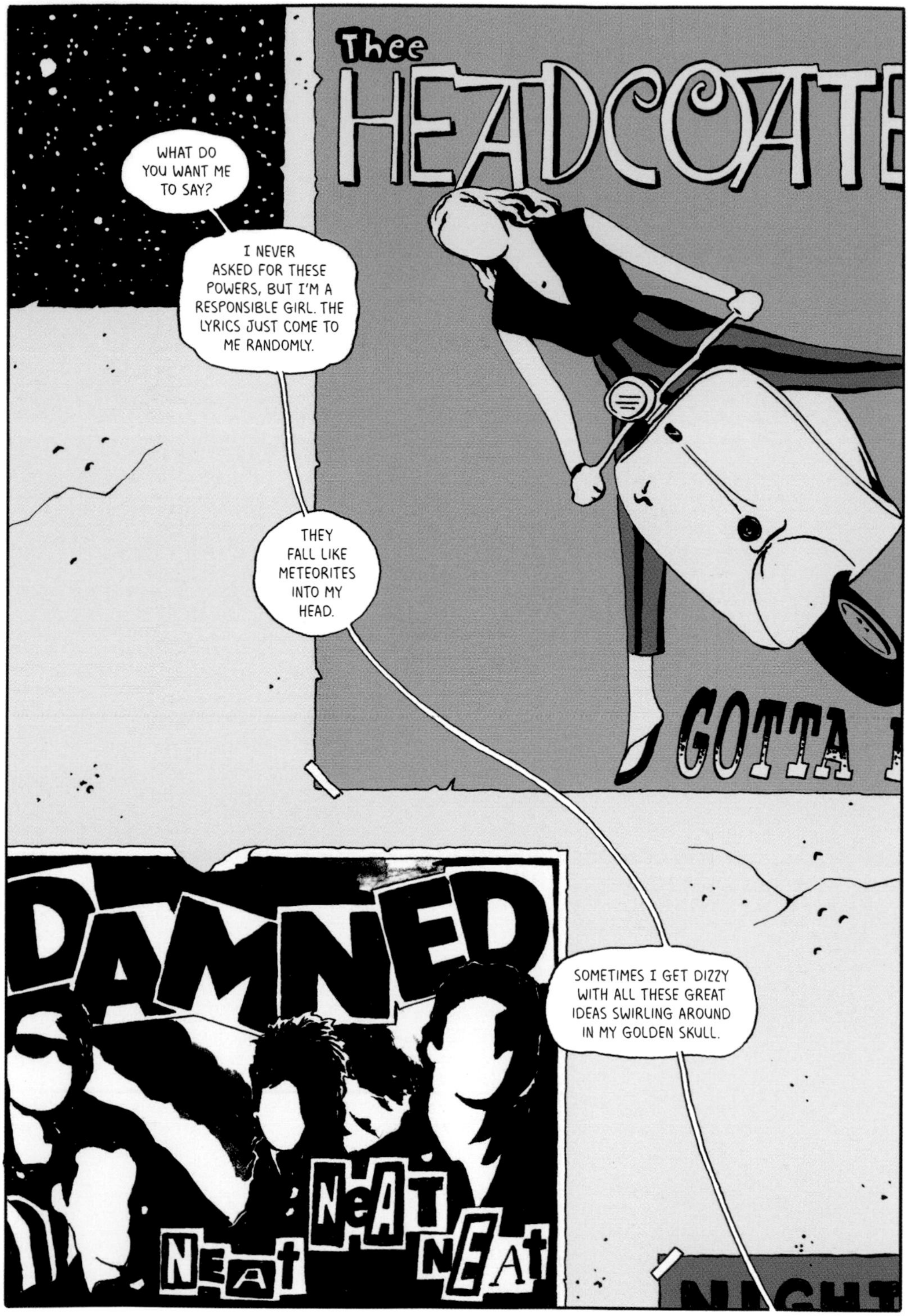
Thee HEADCOATE
GOTTA
WHAT DO YOU WANT ME TO SAY?
I NEVER ASKED FOR THESE POWERS, BUT I'M A RESPONSIBLE GIRL. THE LYRICS JUST COME TO ME RANDOMLY.
THEY FALL LIKE METEORITES INTO MY HEAD.
DAMNED
SOMETIMES I GET DIZZY WITH ALL THESE GREAT IDEAS SWIRLING AROUND IN MY GOLDEN SKULL.
NEAT NEAT NEAT
NIGHT

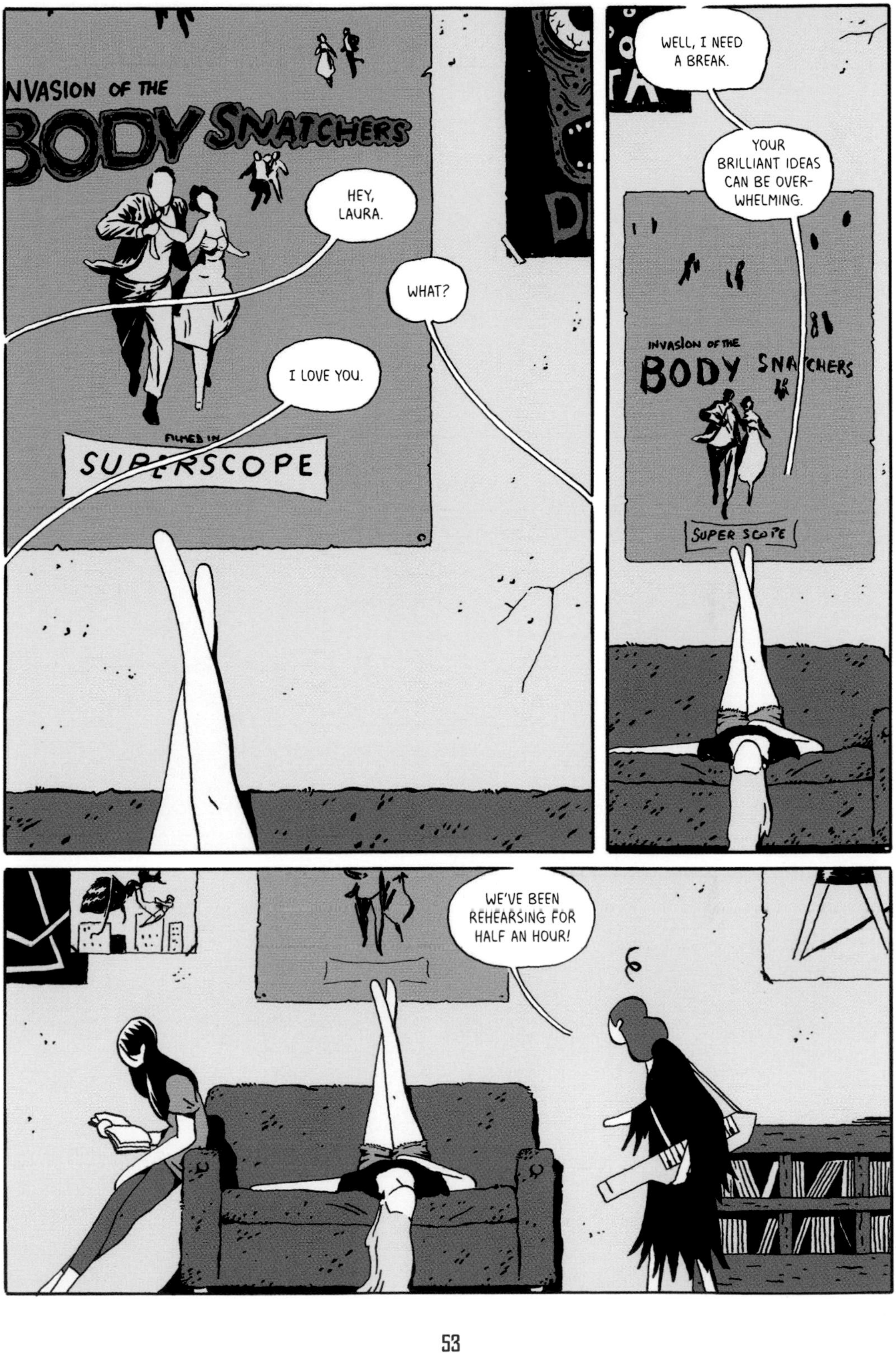
INVASION OF THE BODY SNATCHERS
FILMED IN SUPERSCOPE
HEY, LAURA.
WHAT?
I LOVE YOU.
WELL, I NEED A BREAK.
YOUR BRILLIANT IDEAS CAN BE OVER-WHELMING.
INVASION OF THE BODY SNATCHERS
SUPER SCOPE
WE'VE BEEN REHEARSING FOR HALF AN HOUR!

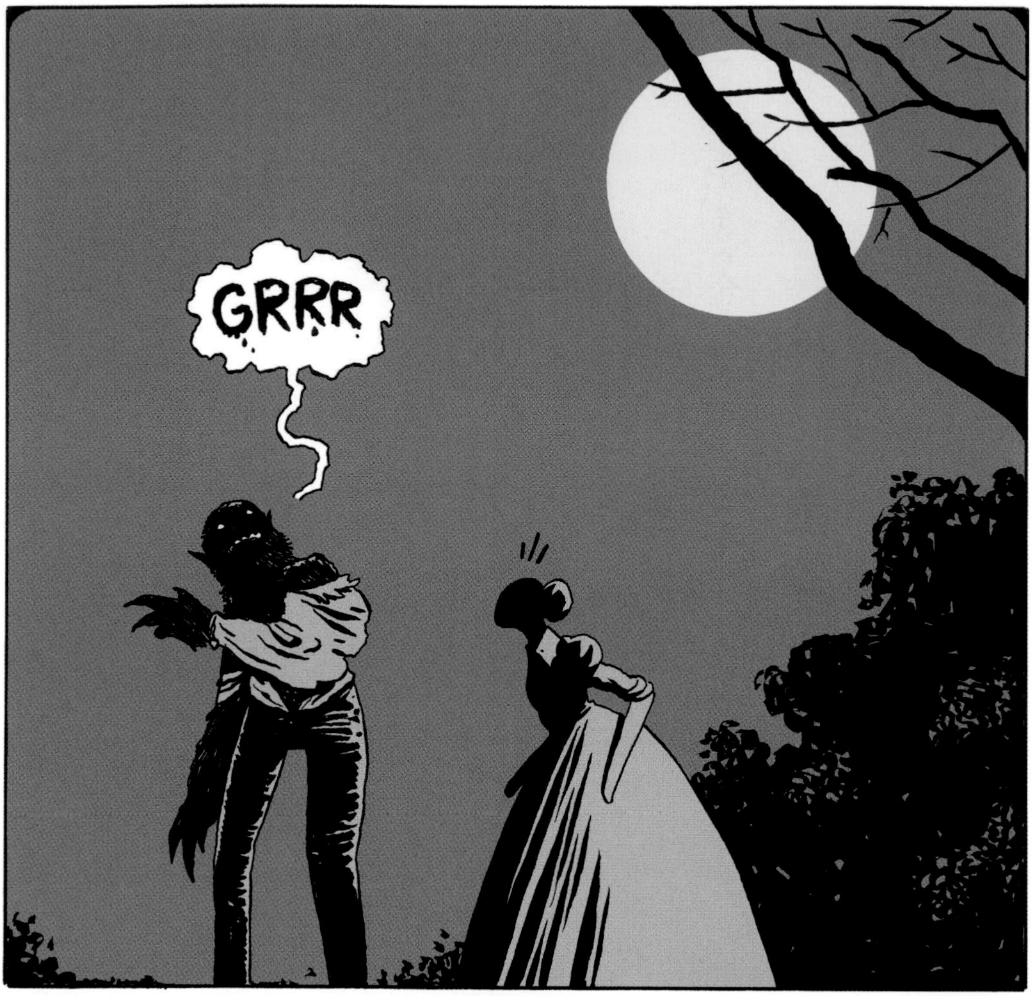
GRRR

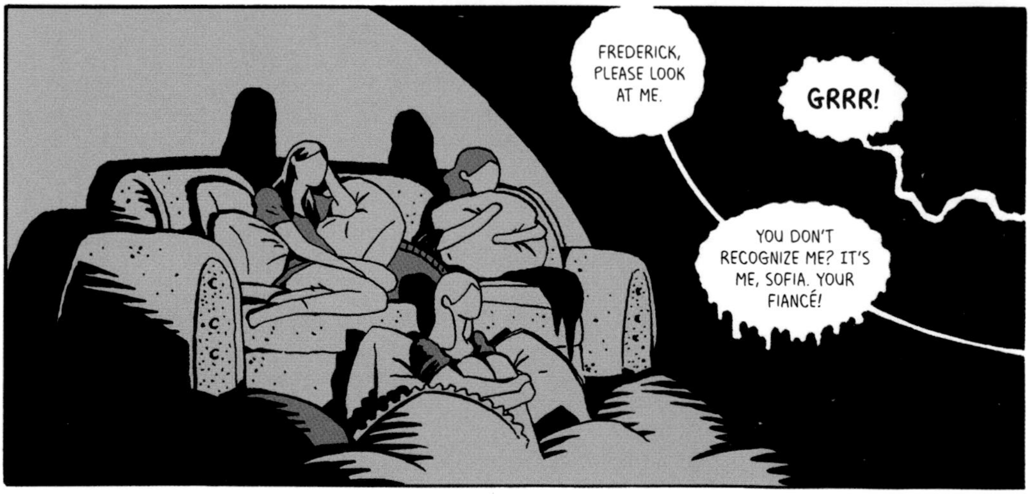
FREDERICK, PLEASE LOOK AT ME.
GRRR!
YOU DON'T RECOGNIZE ME? IT'S ME, SOFIA. YOUR FIANCÉ!

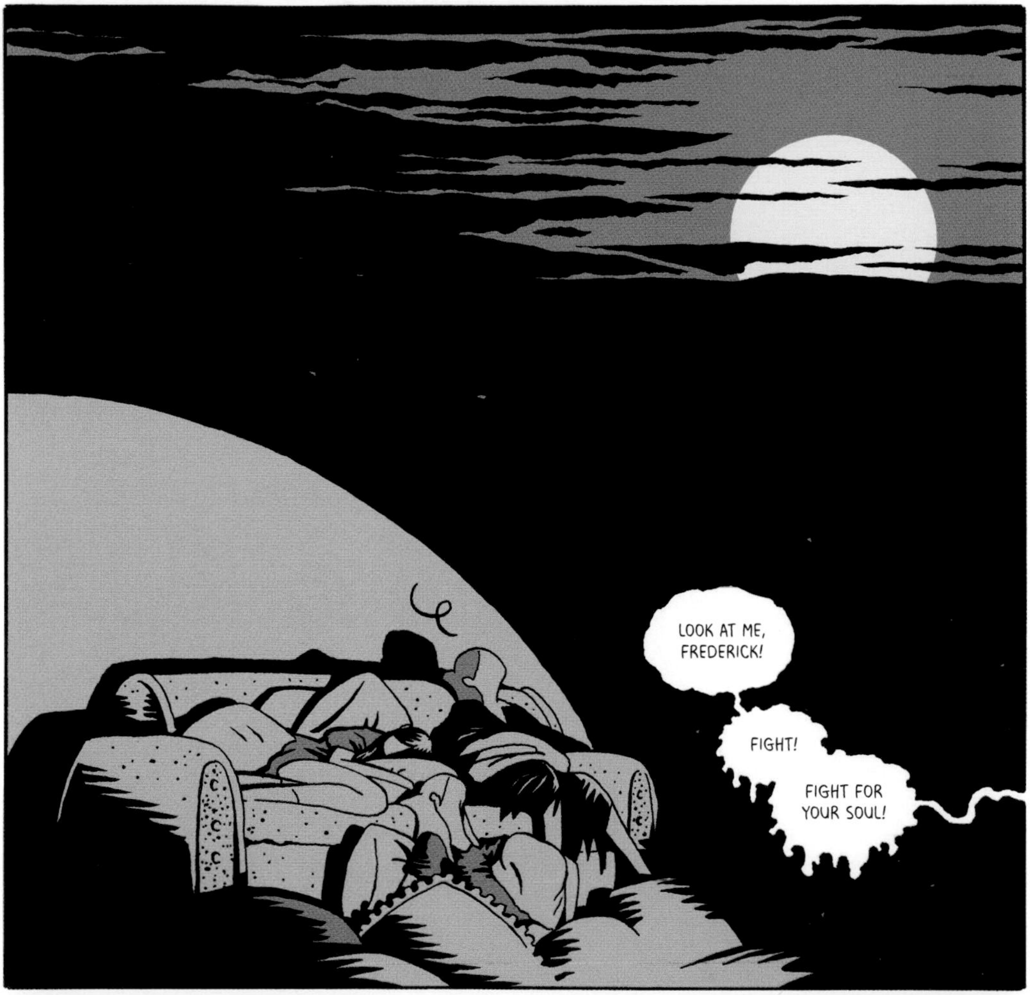
LOOK AT ME, FREDERICK!
FIGHT!
FIGHT FOR YOUR SOUL!

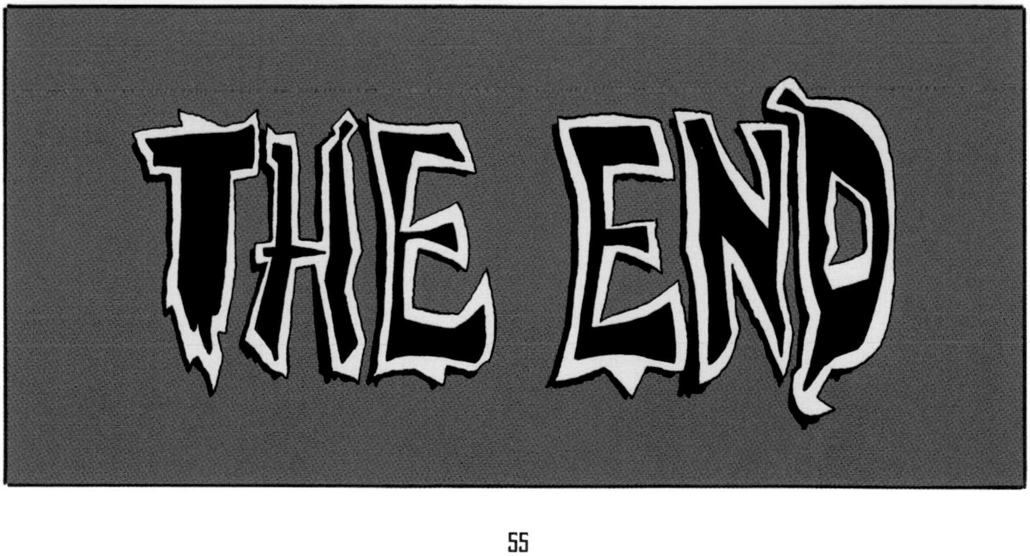
THE END

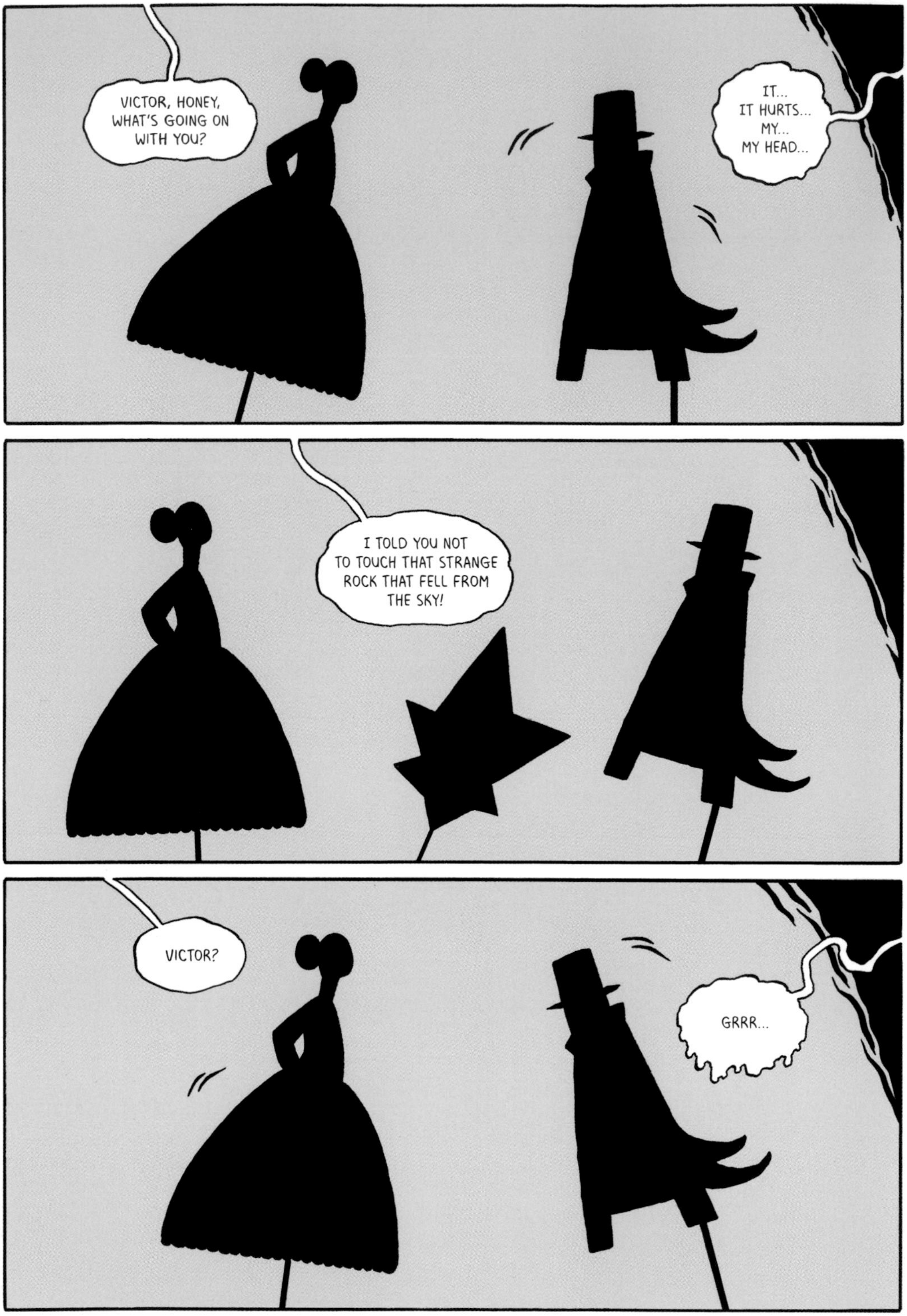
VICTOR, HONEY, WHAT'S GOING ON WITH YOU?
IT... IT HURTS... MY... MY HEAD...
I TOLD YOU NOT TO TOUCH THAT STRANGE ROCK THAT FELL FROM THE SKY!
VICTOR?
GRRR...

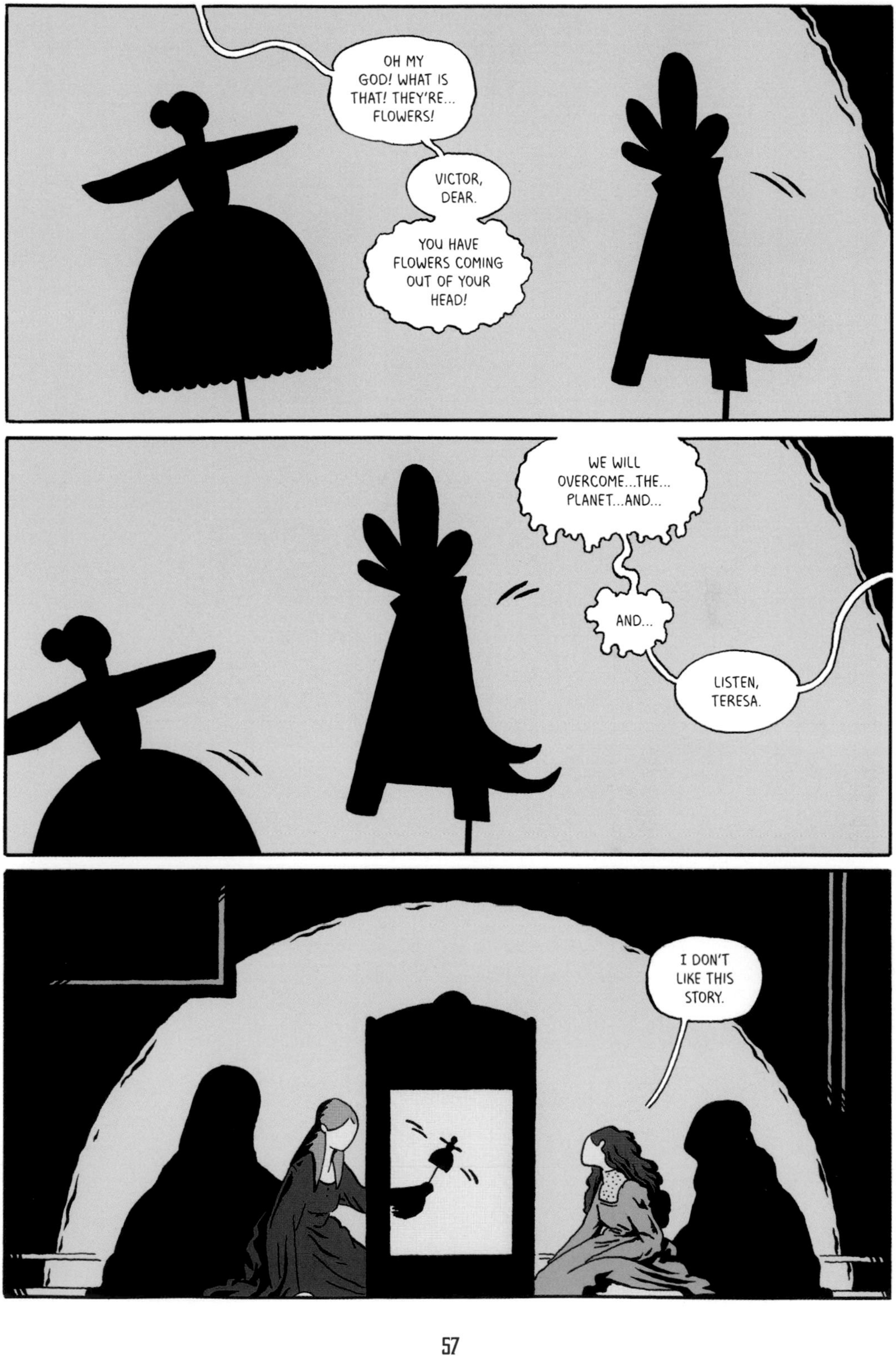
OH MY GOD! WHAT IS THAT! THEY'RE... FLOWERS!
VICTOR, DEAR.
YOU HAVE FLOWERS COMING OUT OF YOUR HEAD!
WE WILL OVERCOME...THE... PLANET...AND...
AND...
LISTEN, TERESA.
I DON'T LIKE THIS STORY.

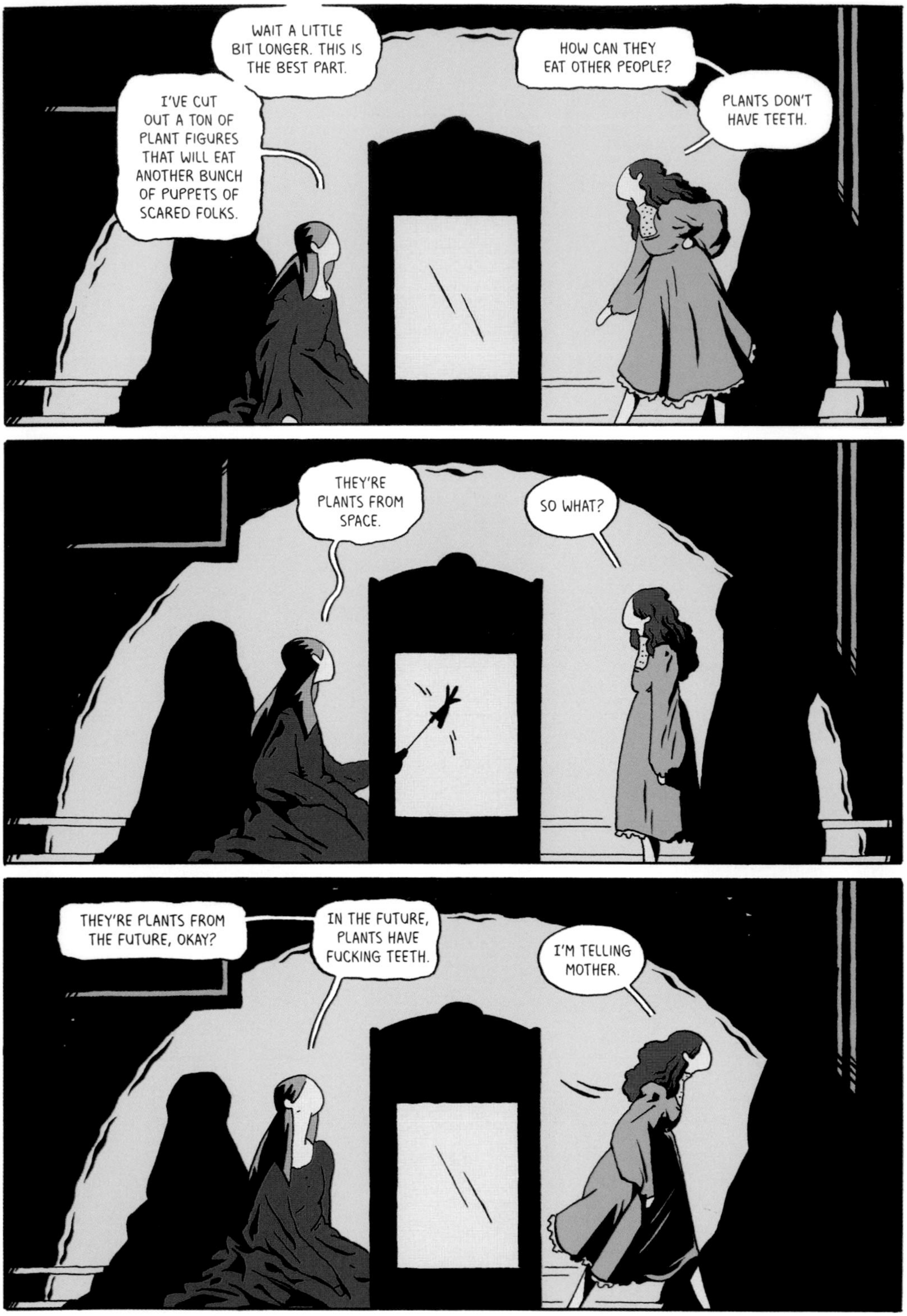

I'VE CUT OUT A TON OF PLANT FIGURES THAT WILL EAT ANOTHER BUNCH OF PUPPETS OF SCARED FOLKS.
WAIT A LITTLE BIT LONGER. THIS IS THE BEST PART.
HOW CAN THEY EAT OTHER PEOPLE?
PLANTS DON'T HAVE TEETH.
THEY'RE PLANTS FROM SPACE.
SO WHAT?
THEY'RE PLANTS FROM THE FUTURE, OKAY?
IN THE FUTURE, PLANTS HAVE FUCKING TEETH.
I'M TELLING MOTHER.

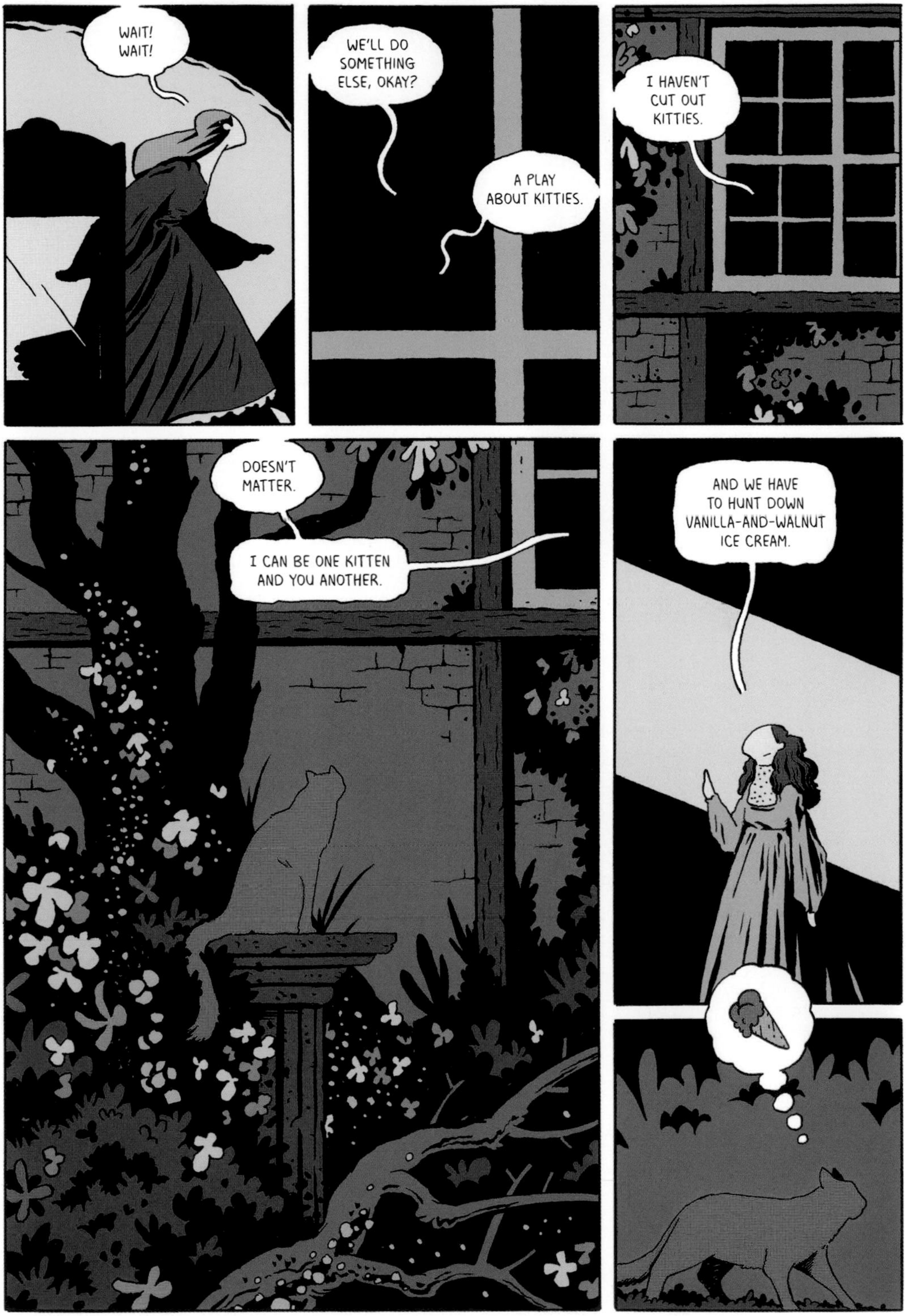
WAIT! WAIT!
WE'LL DO SOMETHING ELSE, OKAY?
A PLAY ABOUT KITTIES.
I HAVEN'T CUT OUT KITTIES.
DOESN'T MATTER.
I CAN BE ONE KITTEN AND YOU ANOTHER.
AND WE HAVE TO HUNT DOWN VANILLA-AND-WALNUT ICE CREAM.

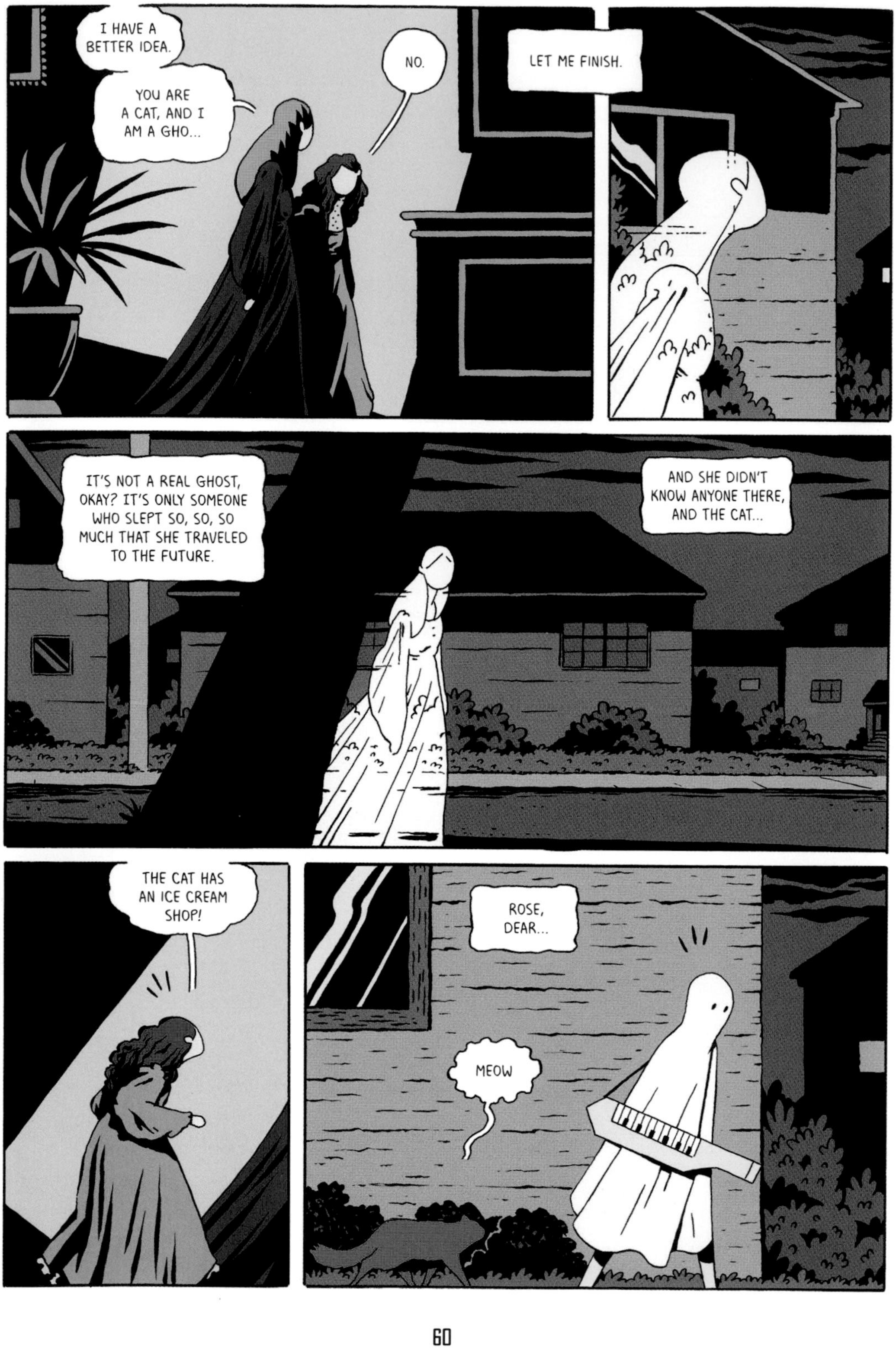
I HAVE A BETTER IDEA.
YOU ARE A CAT, AND I AM A GHO...
NO.
LET ME FINISH.
IT'S NOT A REAL GHOST, OKAY? IT'S ONLY SOMEONE WHO SLEPT SO, SO, SO MUCH THAT SHE TRAVELED TO THE FUTURE.
AND SHE DIDN'T KNOW ANYONE THERE, AND THE CAT...
THE CAT HAS AN ICE CREAM SHOP!
ROSE, DEAR...
MEOW

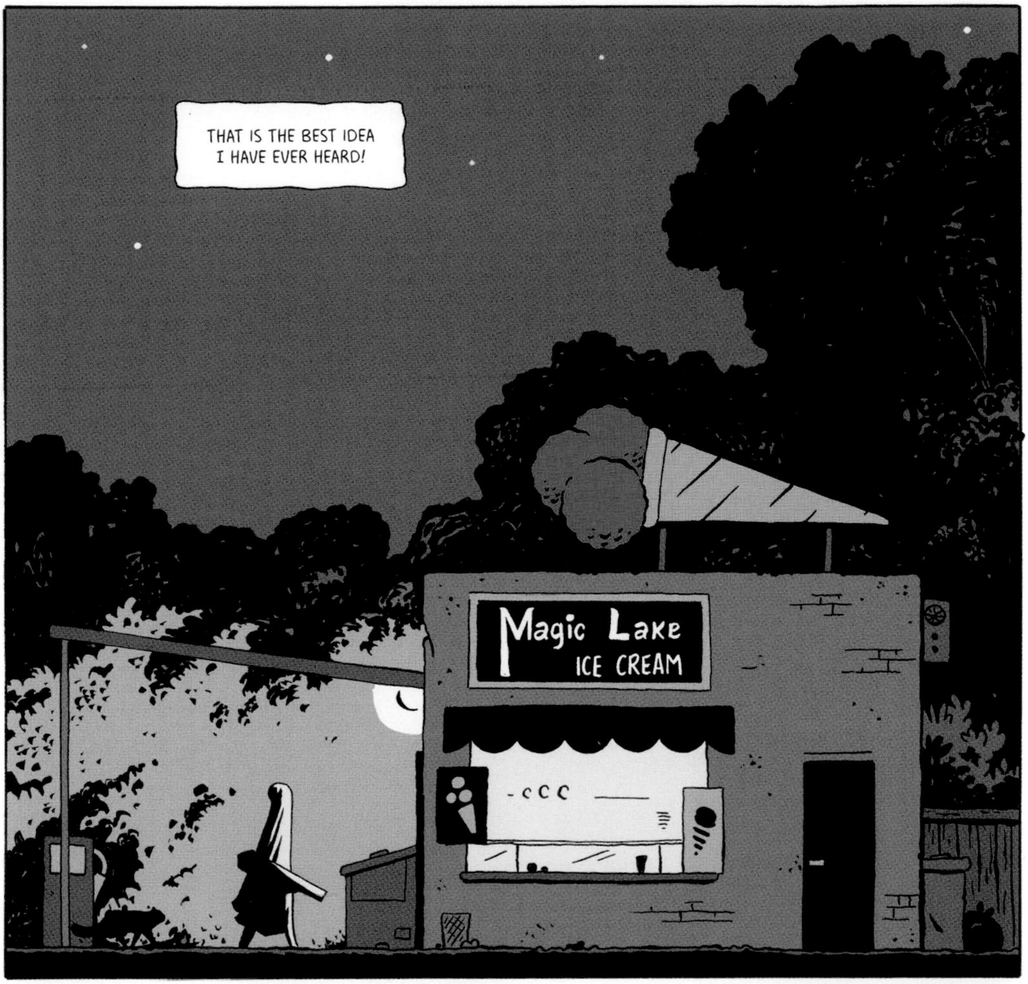
THAT IS THE BEST IDEA I HAVE EVER HEARD!
Magic Lake ICE CREAM

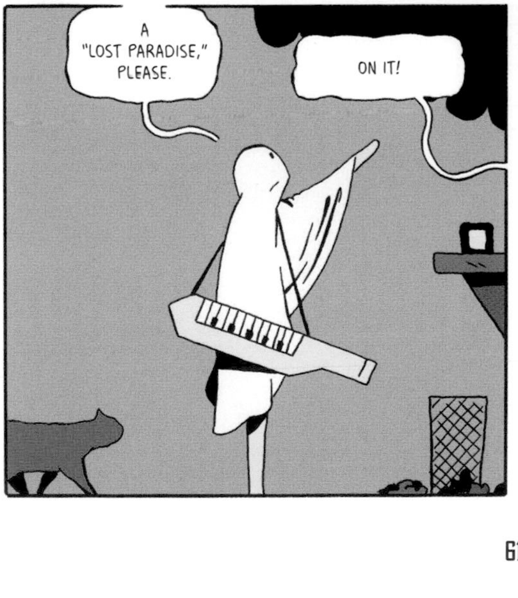
A "LOST PARADISE," PLEASE.
ON IT!

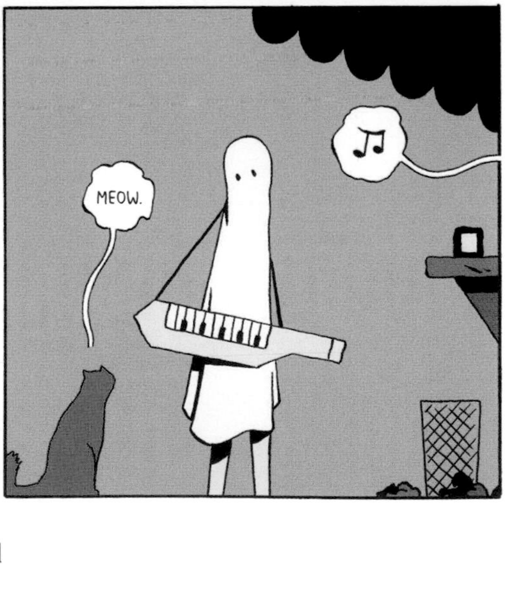
MEOW.
♫

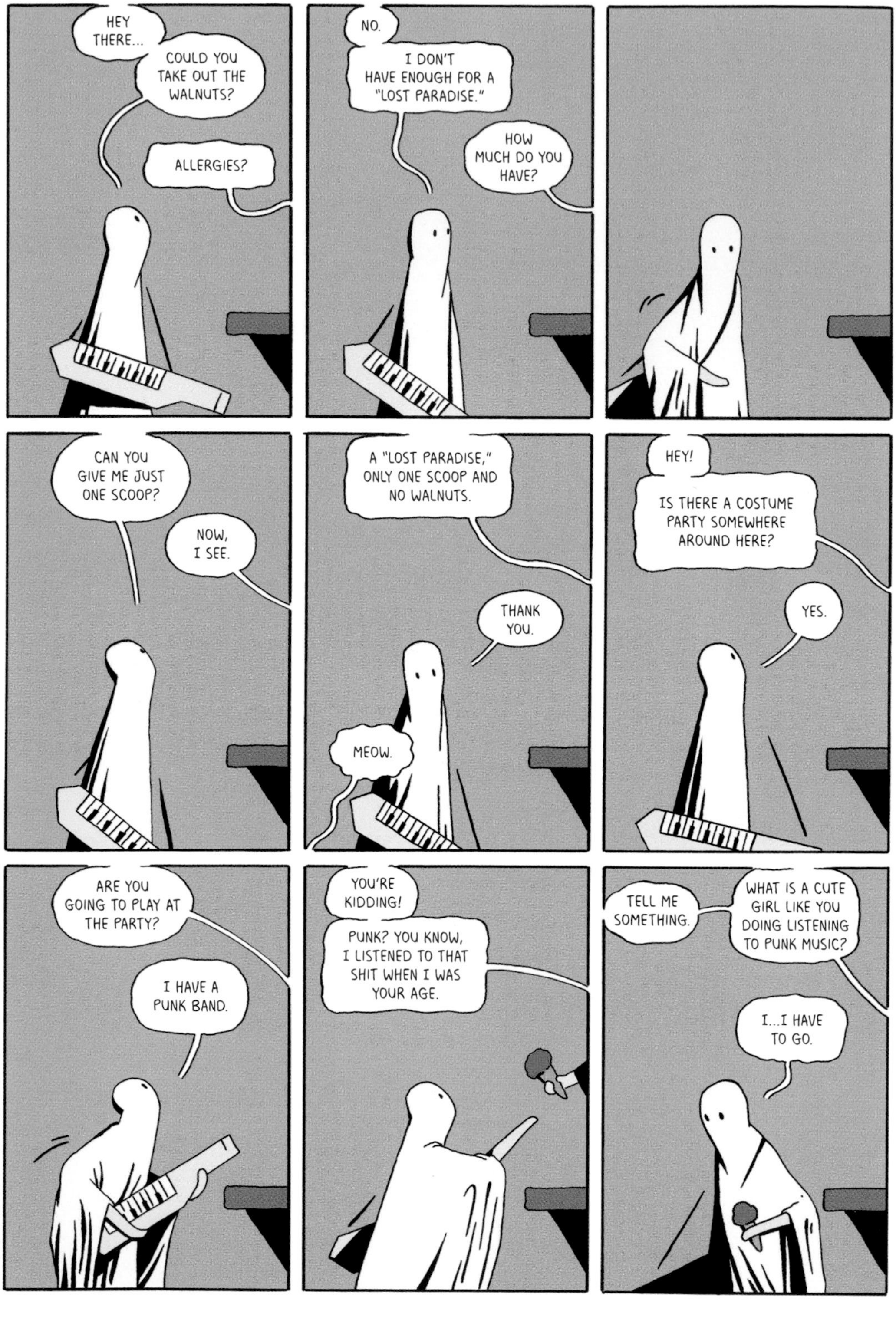
HEY THERE...
COULD YOU TAKE OUT THE WALNUTS?
ALLERGIES?
NO.
I DON'T HAVE ENOUGH FOR A "LOST PARADISE."
HOW MUCH DO YOU HAVE?
CAN YOU GIVE ME JUST ONE SCOOP?
NOW, I SEE.
A "LOST PARADISE," ONLY ONE SCOOP AND NO WALNUTS.
THANK YOU.
MEOW.
HEY!
IS THERE A COSTUME PARTY SOMEWHERE AROUND HERE?
YES.
ARE YOU GOING TO PLAY AT THE PARTY?
I HAVE A PUNK BAND.
YOU'RE KIDDING!
PUNK? YOU KNOW, I LISTENED TO THAT SHIT WHEN I WAS YOUR AGE.
TELL ME SOMETHING.
WHAT IS A CUTE GIRL LIKE YOU DOING LISTENING TO PUNK MUSIC?
I...I HAVE TO GO.

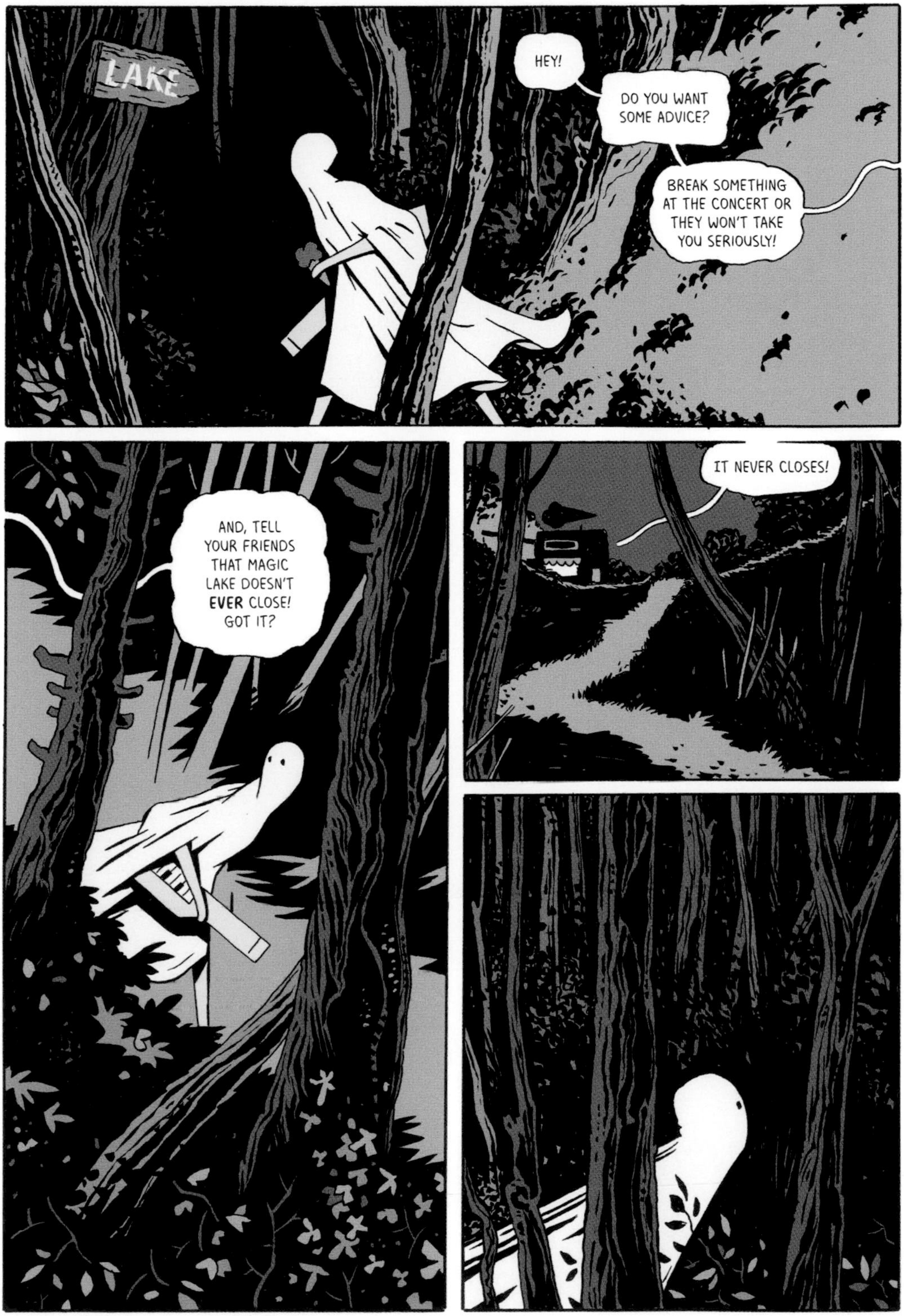
LAKE
HEY!
DO YOU WANT SOME ADVICE?
BREAK SOMETHING AT THE CONCERT OR THEY WON'T TAKE YOU SERIOUSLY!
AND, TELL YOUR FRIENDS THAT MAGIC LAKE DOESN'T **EVER** CLOSE! GOT IT?
IT NEVER CLOSES!

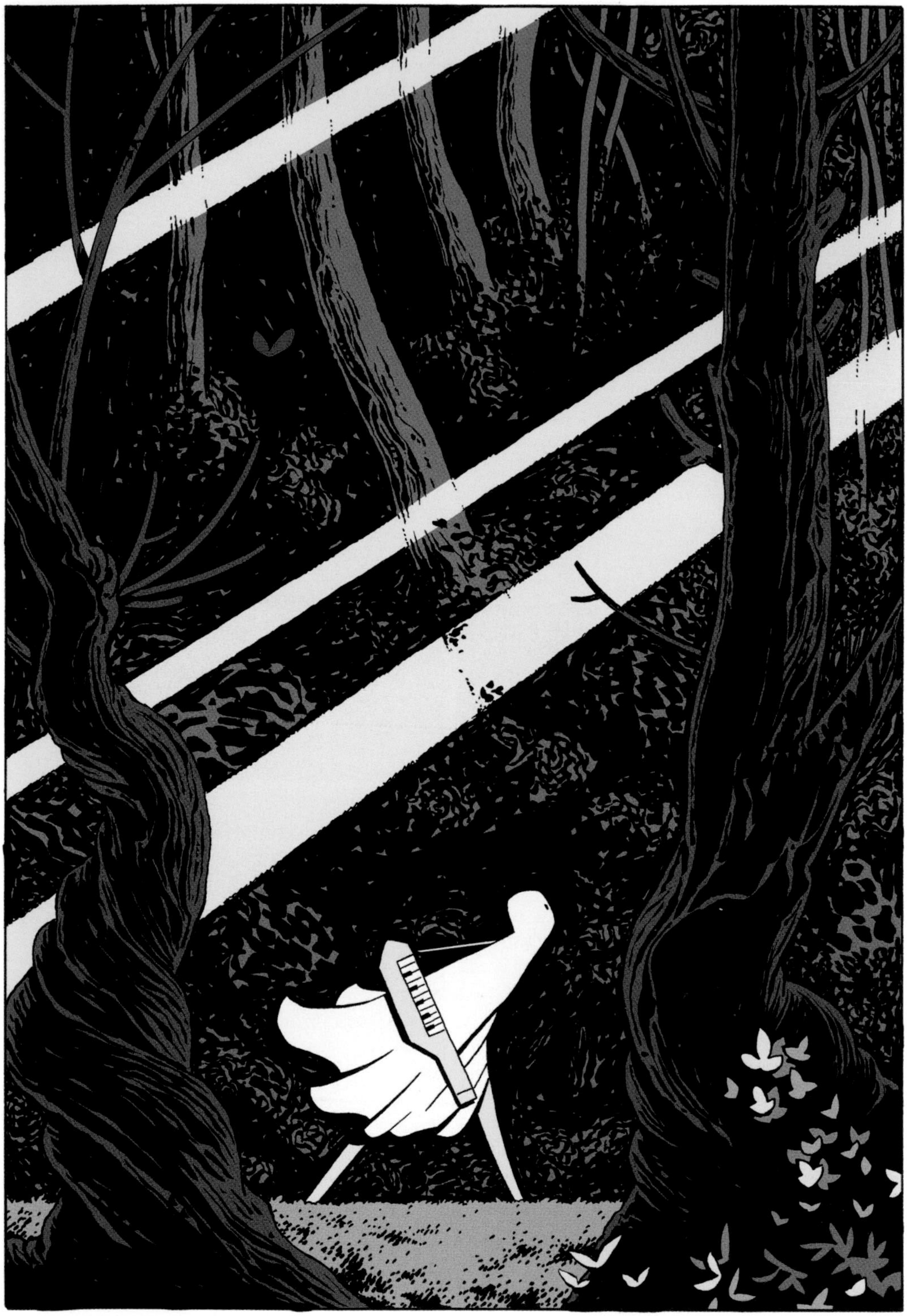

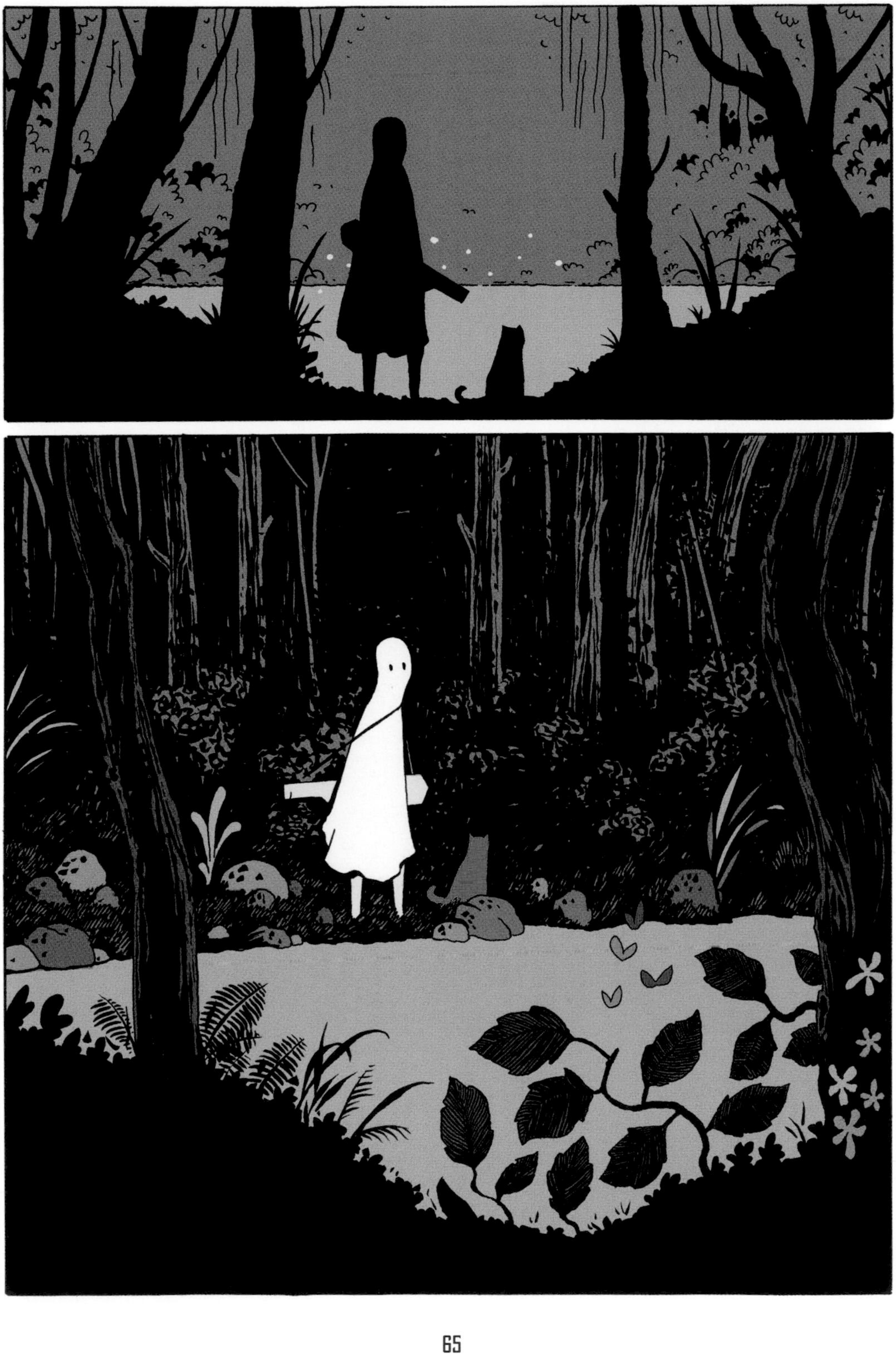

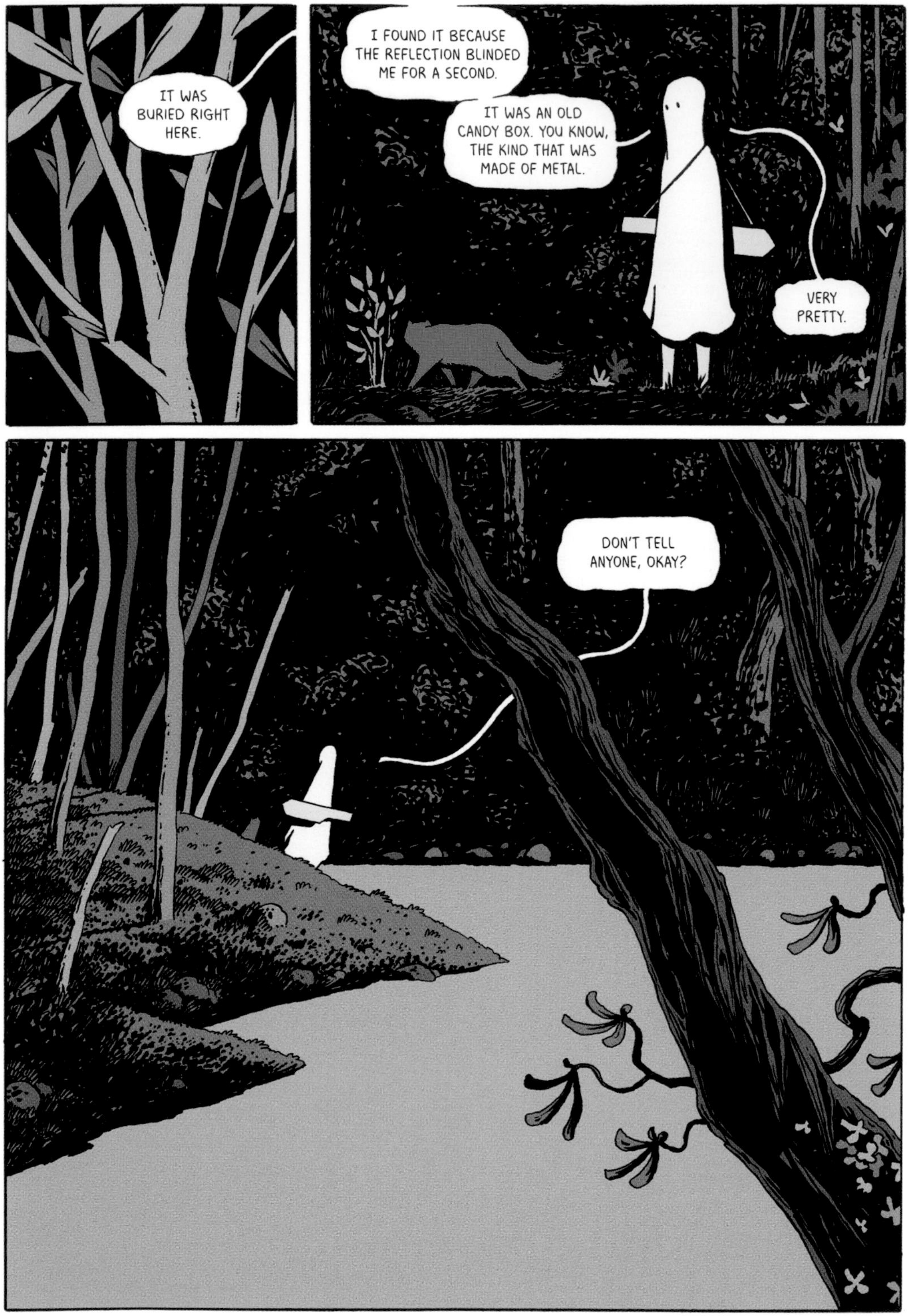
IT WAS BURIED RIGHT HERE.
I FOUND IT BECAUSE THE REFLECTION BLINDED ME FOR A SECOND.
IT WAS AN OLD CANDY BOX. YOU KNOW, THE KIND THAT WAS MADE OF METAL.
VERY PRETTY.
DON'T TELL ANYONE, OKAY?

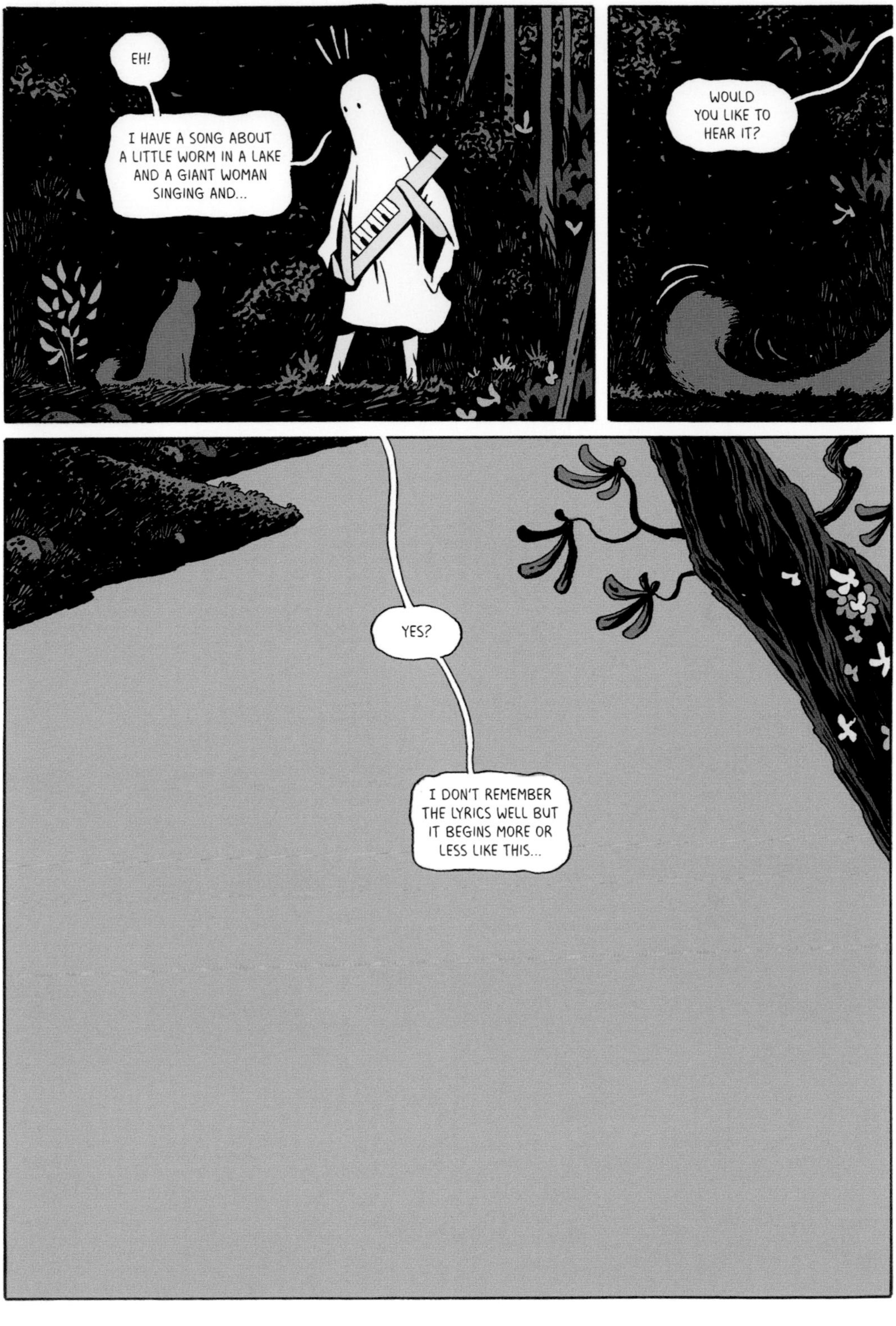
EH!
I HAVE A SONG ABOUT A LITTLE WORM IN A LAKE AND A GIANT WOMAN SINGING AND...
WOULD YOU LIKE TO HEAR IT?
YES?
I DON'T REMEMBER THE LYRICS WELL BUT IT BEGINS MORE OR LESS LIKE THIS...

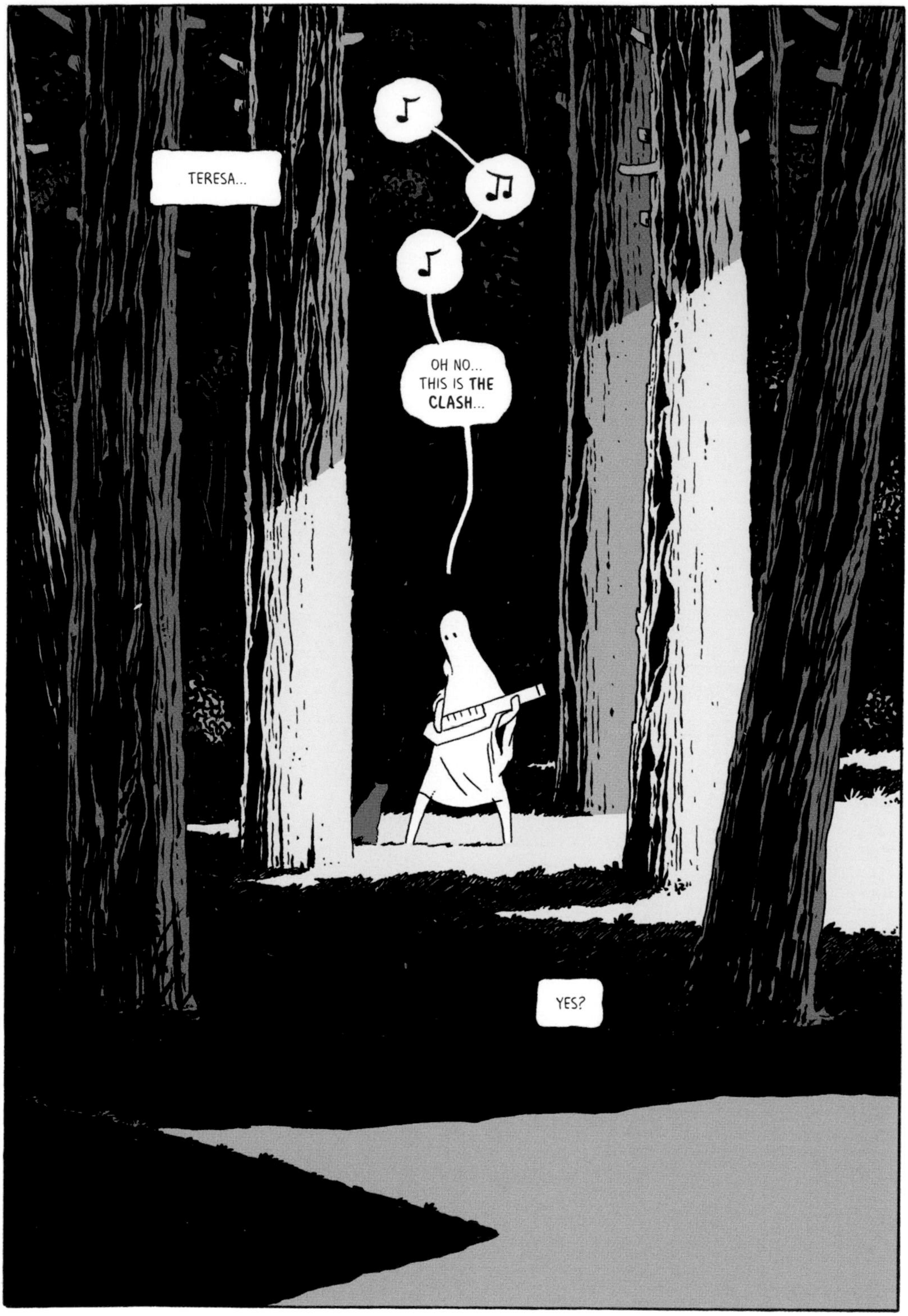
TERESA...
OH NO... THIS IS THE CLASH...
YES?

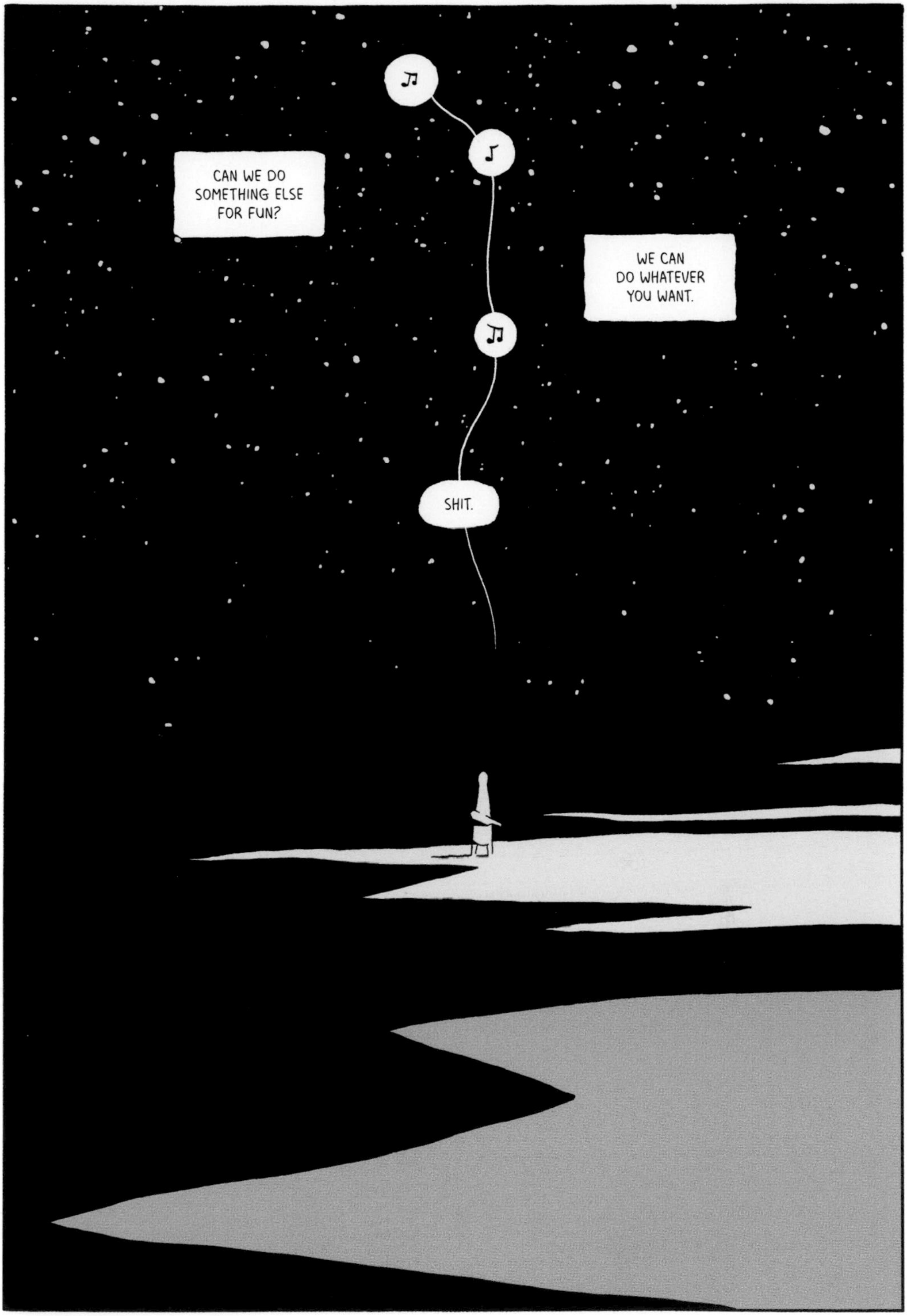
CAN WE DO SOMETHING ELSE FOR FUN?
WE CAN DO WHATEVER YOU WANT.
SHIT.

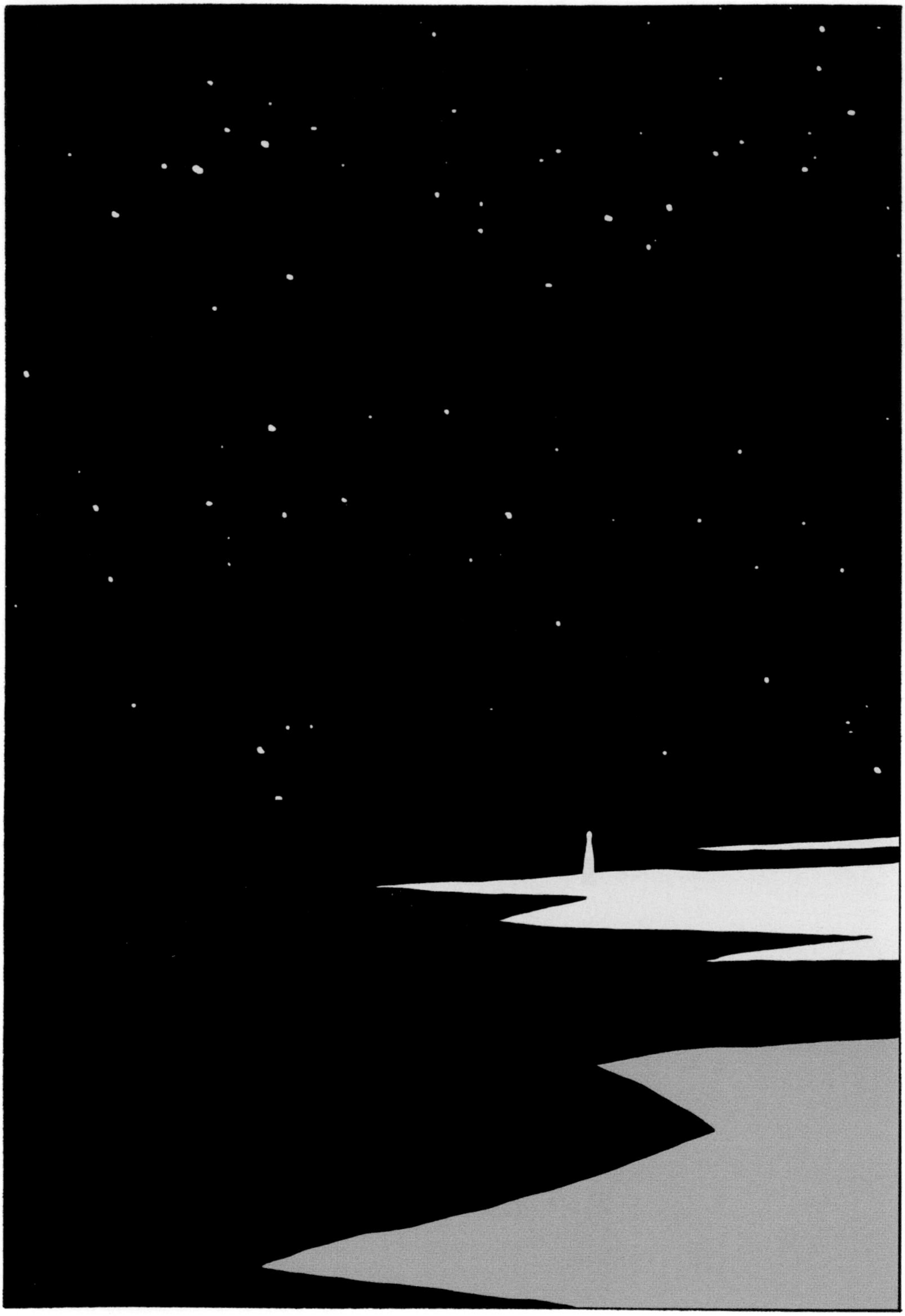

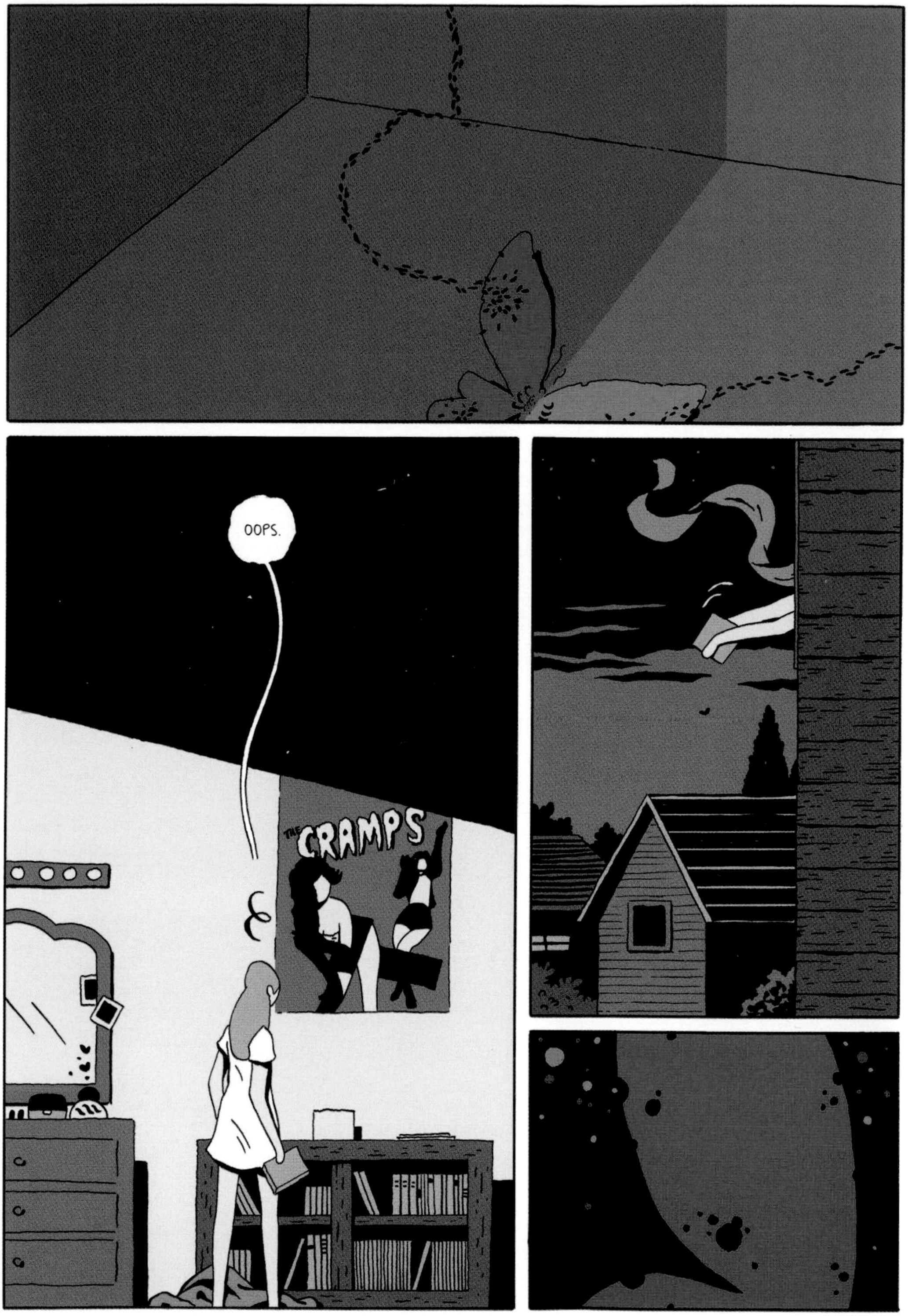
OOPS.
THE CRAMPS

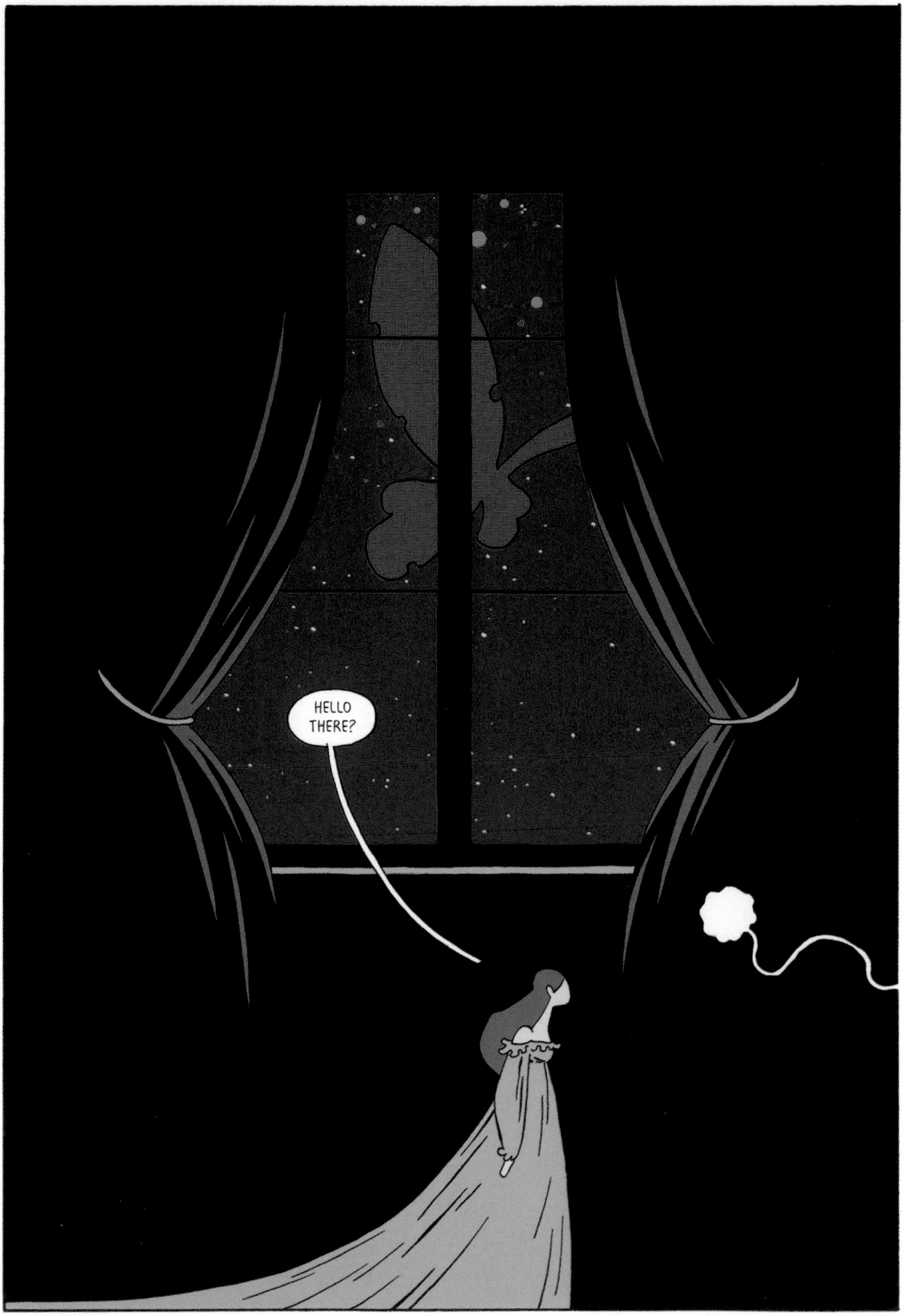
HELLO THERE?

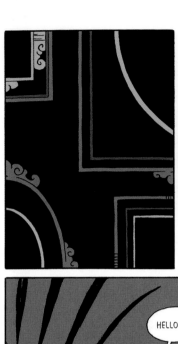

HELLO?!?!

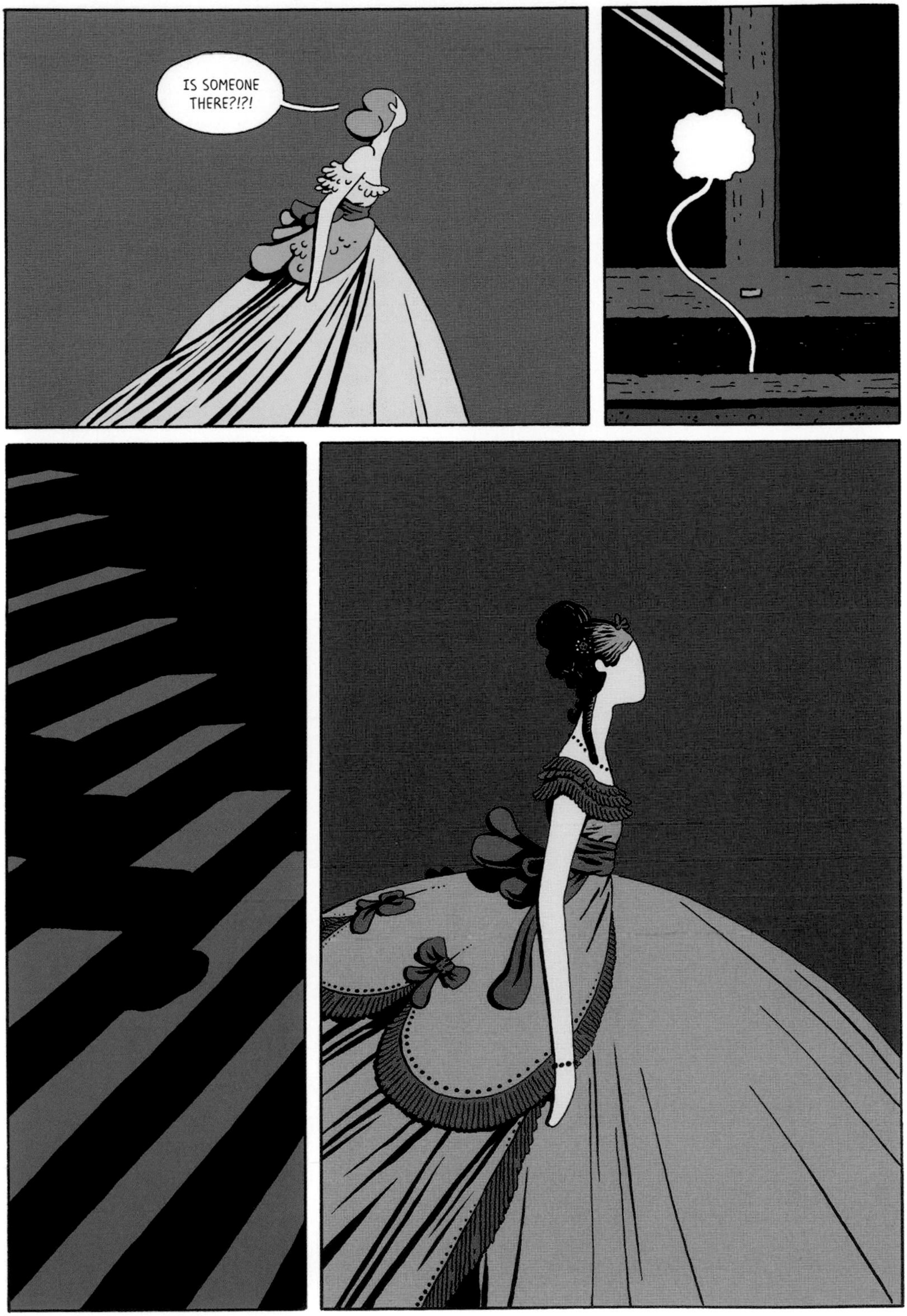
IS SOMEONE
THERE?!?!

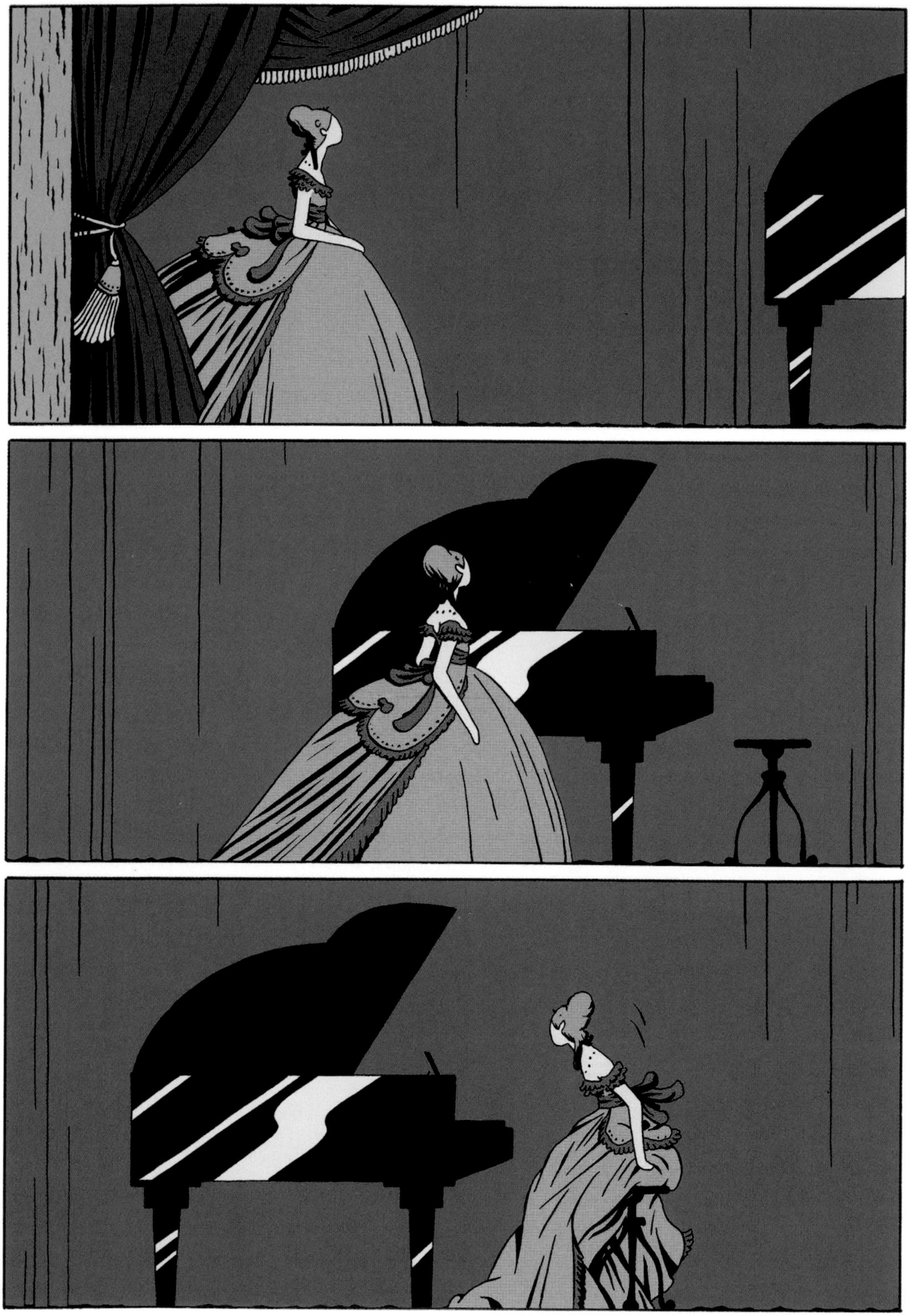

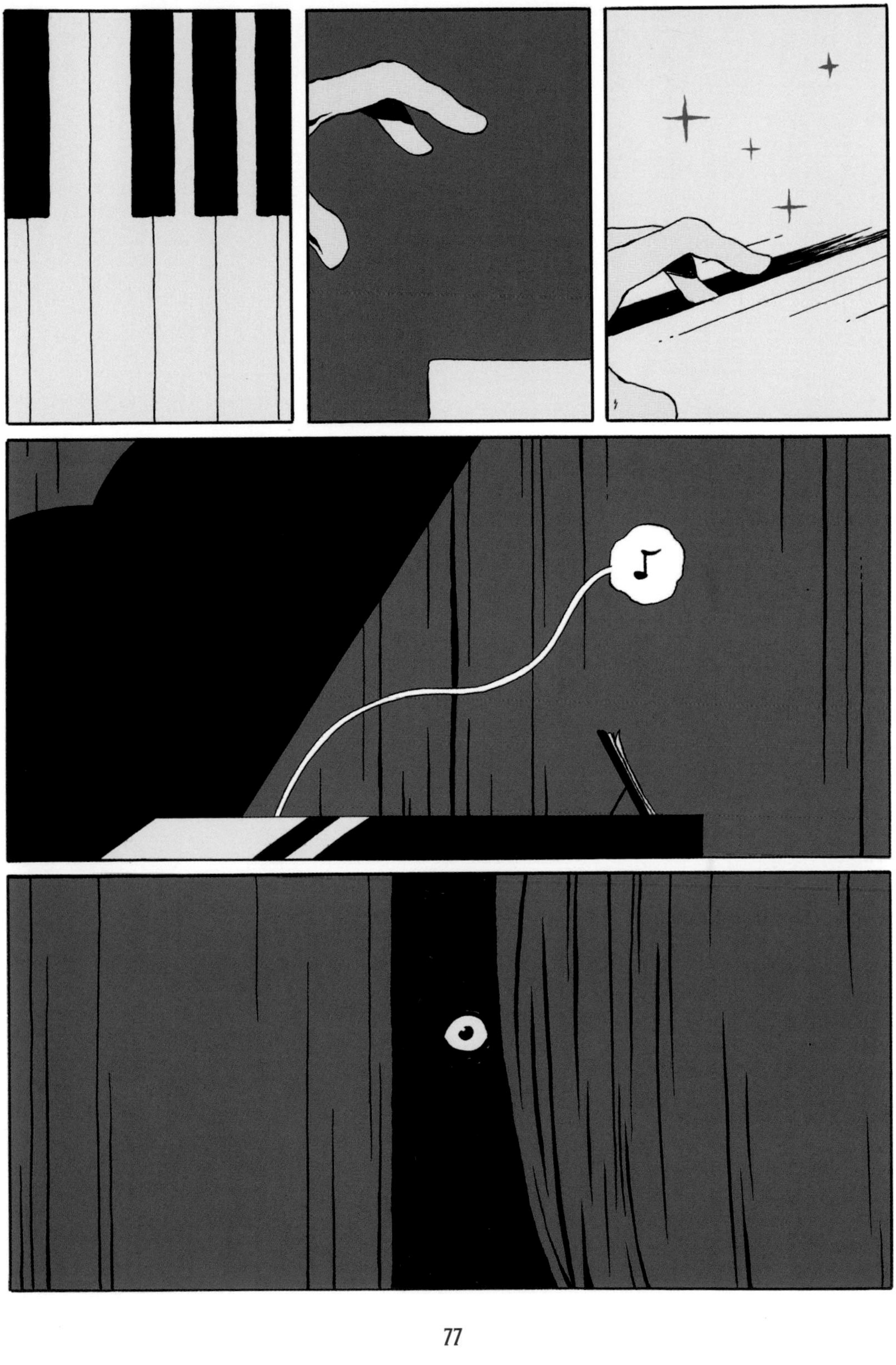

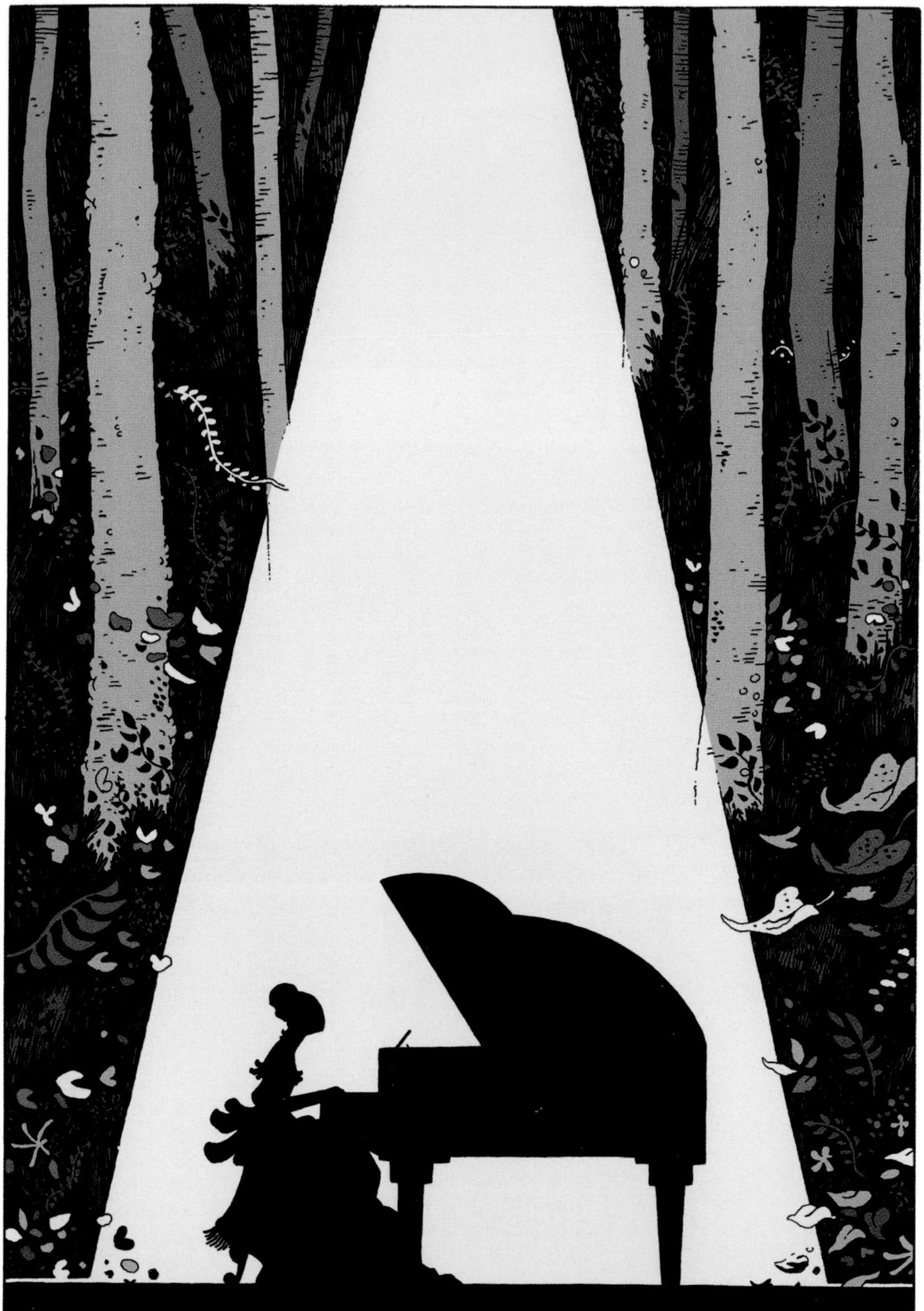

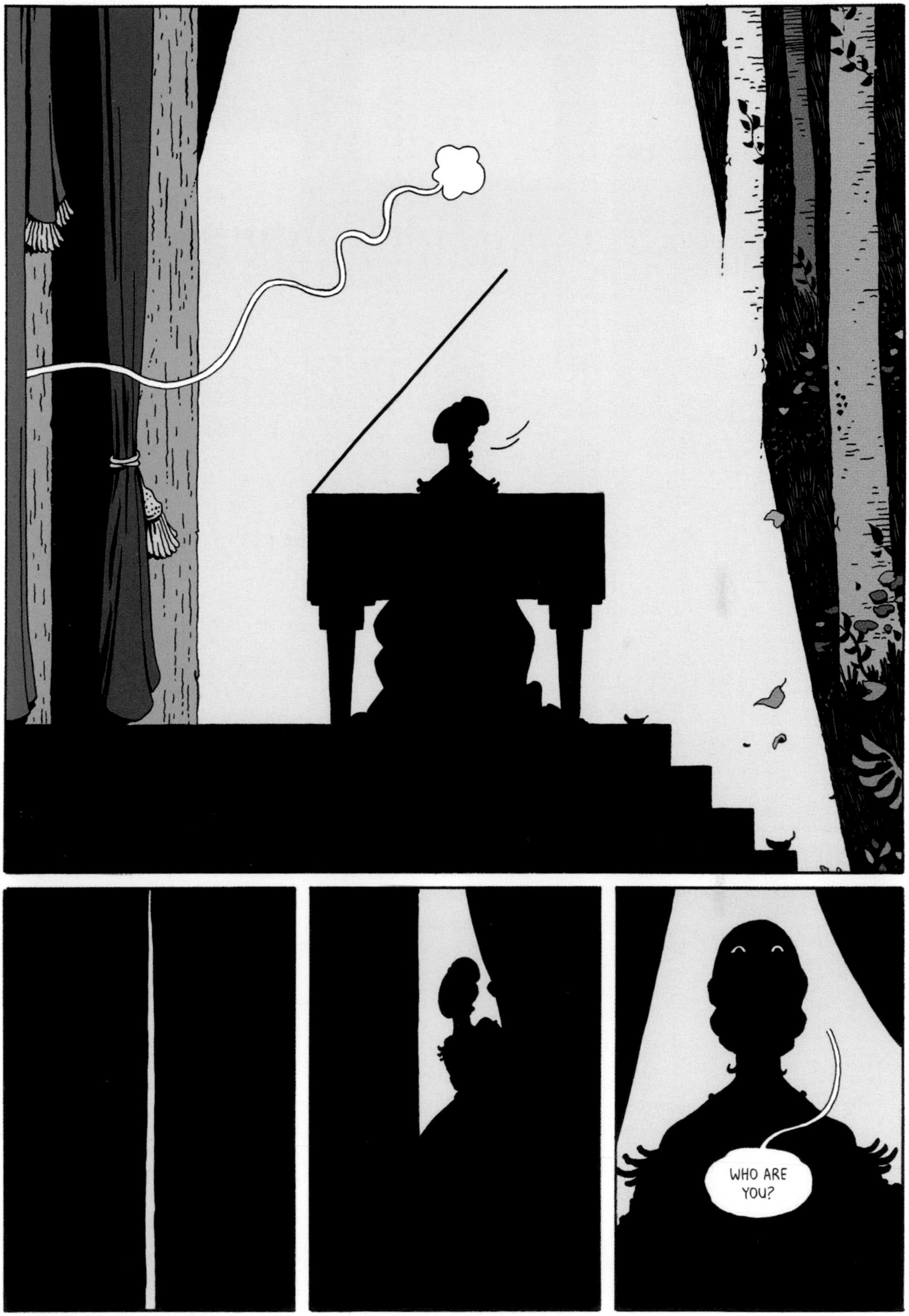
WHO ARE YOU?

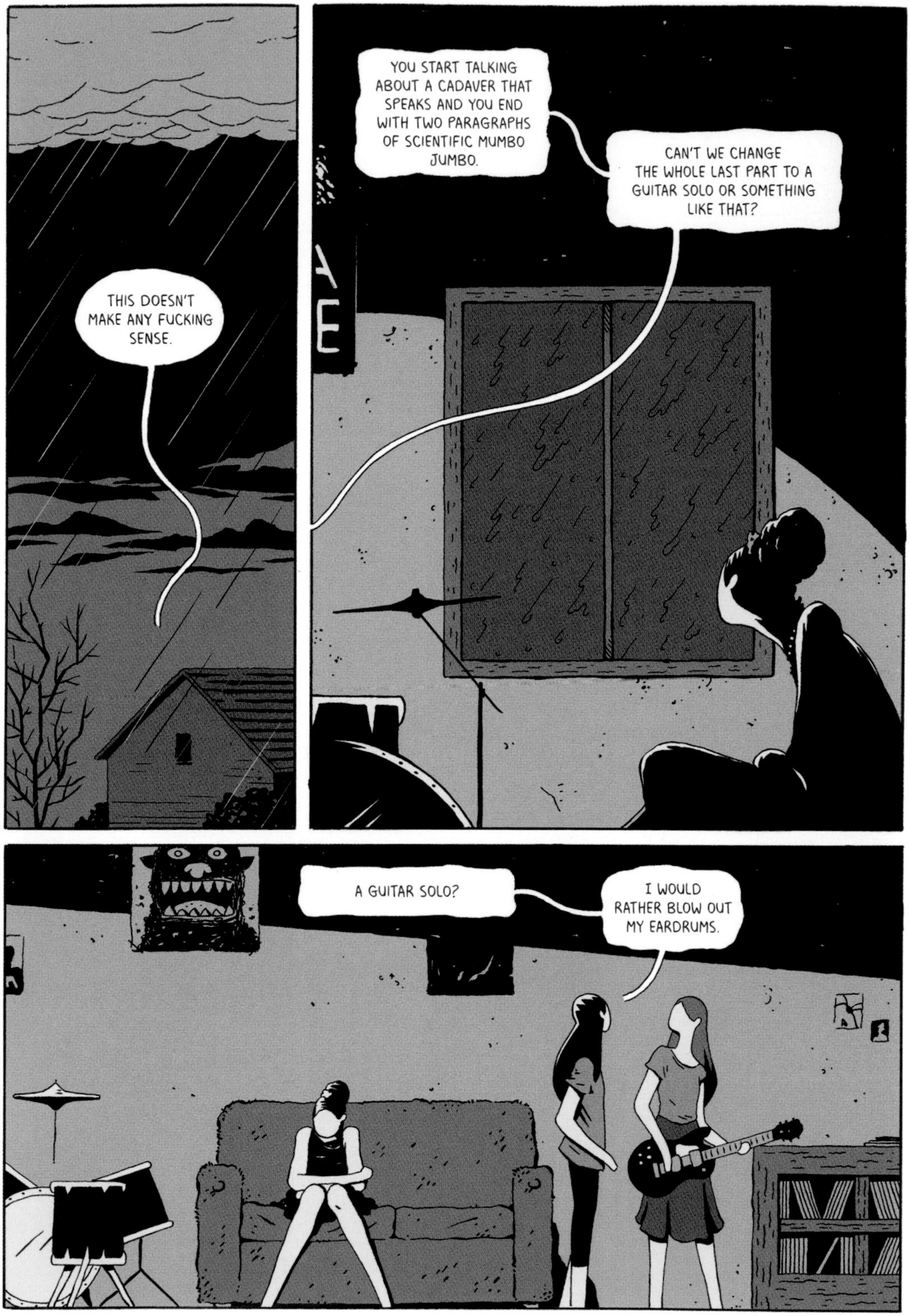
THIS DOESN'T MAKE ANY FUCKING SENSE.
YOU START TALKING ABOUT A CADAVER THAT SPEAKS AND YOU END WITH TWO PARAGRAPHS OF SCIENTIFIC MUMBO JUMBO.
CAN'T WE CHANGE THE WHOLE LAST PART TO A GUITAR SOLO OR SOMETHING LIKE THAT?
A GUITAR SOLO?
I WOULD RATHER BLOW OUT MY EARDRUMS.

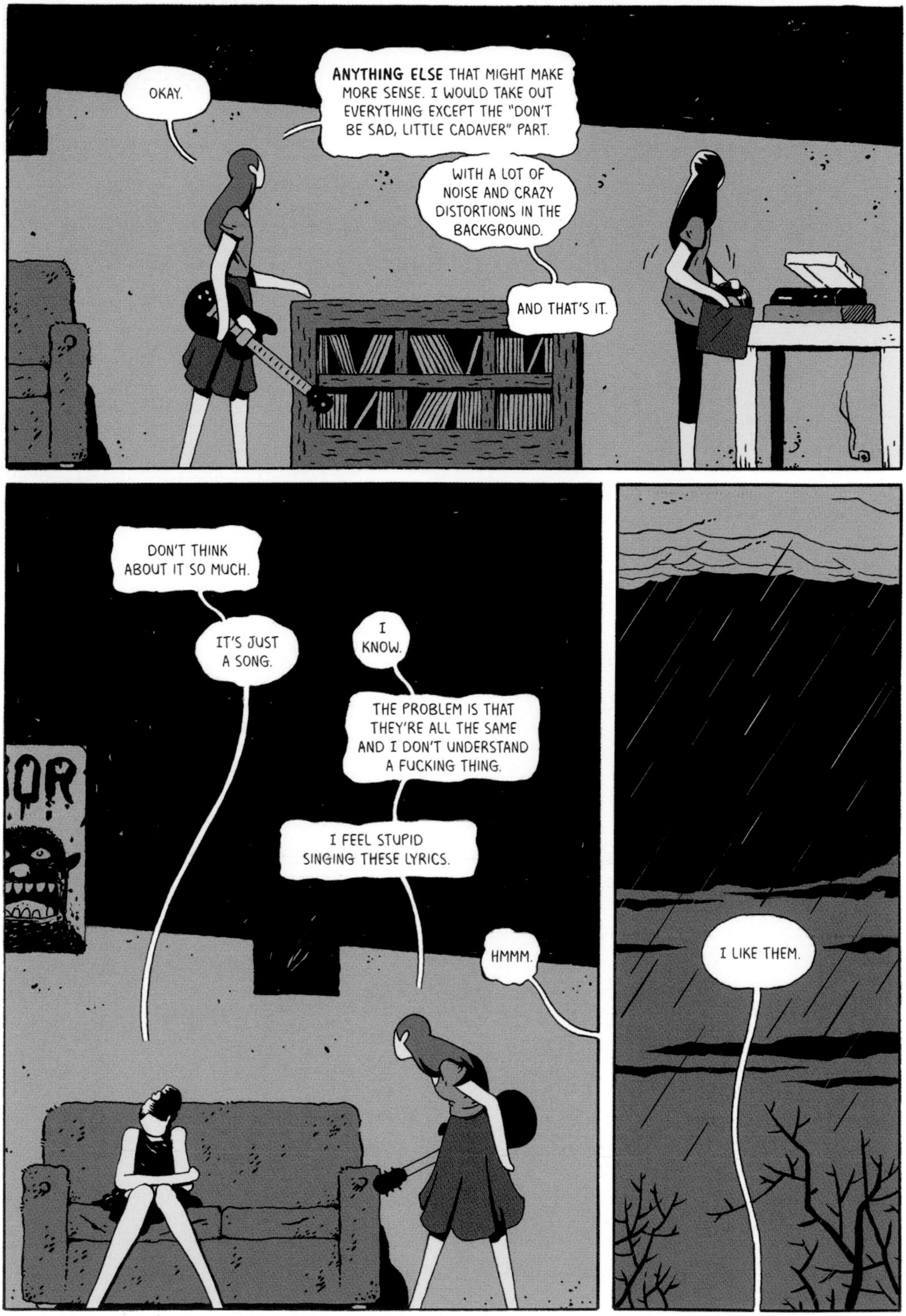
OKAY.
ANYTHING ELSE THAT MIGHT MAKE MORE SENSE. I WOULD TAKE OUT EVERYTHING EXCEPT THE "DON'T BE SAD, LITTLE CADAVER" PART.
WITH A LOT OF NOISE AND CRAZY DISTORTIONS IN THE BACKGROUND.
AND THAT'S IT.
DON'T THINK ABOUT IT SO MUCH.
IT'S JUST A SONG.
I KNOW.
THE PROBLEM IS THAT THEY'RE ALL THE SAME AND I DON'T UNDERSTAND A FUCKING THING.
I FEEL STUPID SINGING THESE LYRICS.
HMMM.
I LIKE THEM.

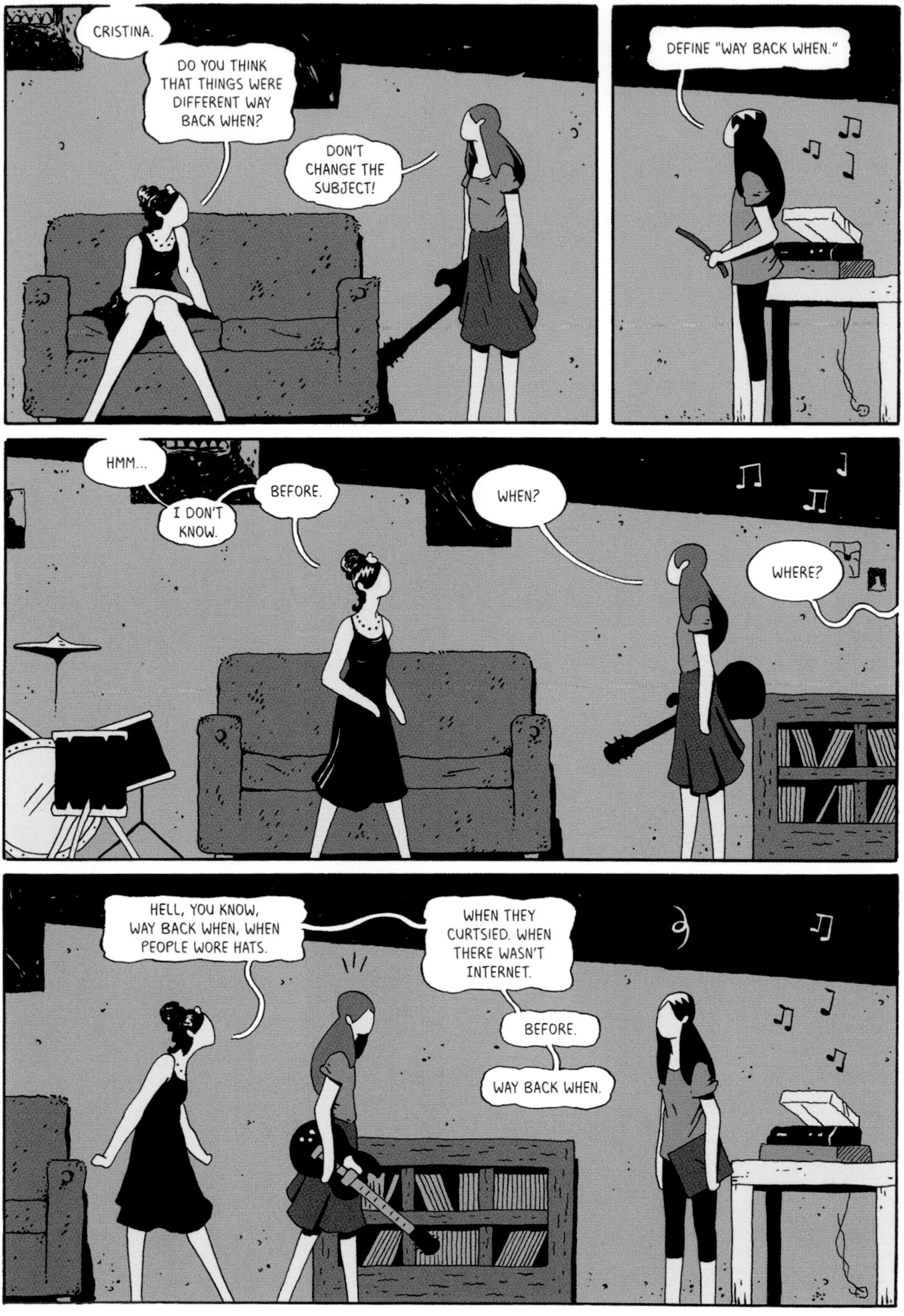
CRISTINA.
DO YOU THINK THAT THINGS WERE DIFFERENT WAY BACK WHEN?
DON'T CHANGE THE SUBJECT!
DEFINE "WAY BACK WHEN."
HMM...
I DON'T KNOW.
BEFORE.
WHEN?
WHERE?
HELL, YOU KNOW, WAY BACK WHEN, WHEN PEOPLE WORE HATS.
WHEN THEY CURTSIED. WHEN THERE WASN'T INTERNET.
BEFORE.
WAY BACK WHEN.

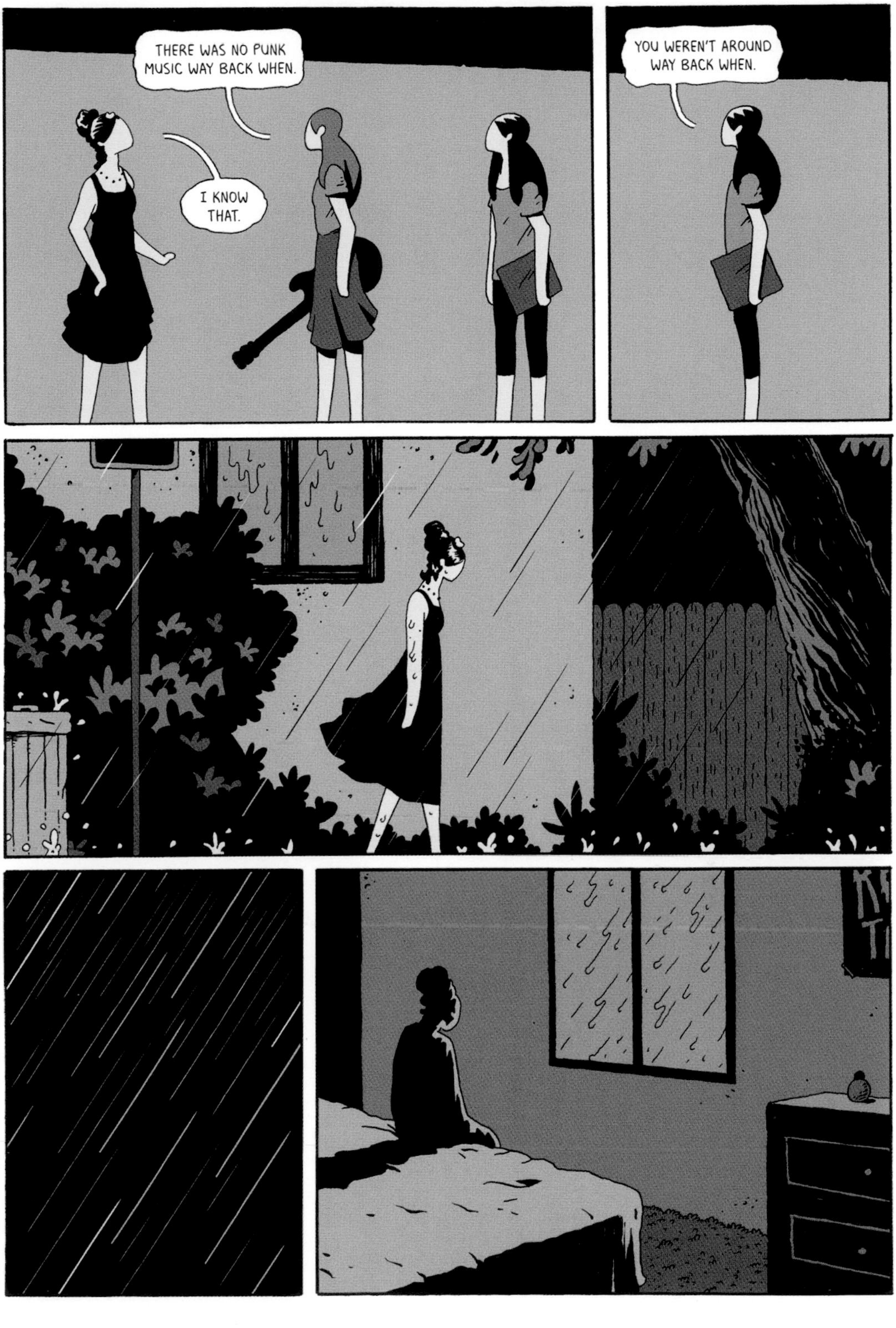
THERE WAS NO PUNK MUSIC WAY BACK WHEN.
I KNOW THAT.
YOU WEREN'T AROUND WAY BACK WHEN.

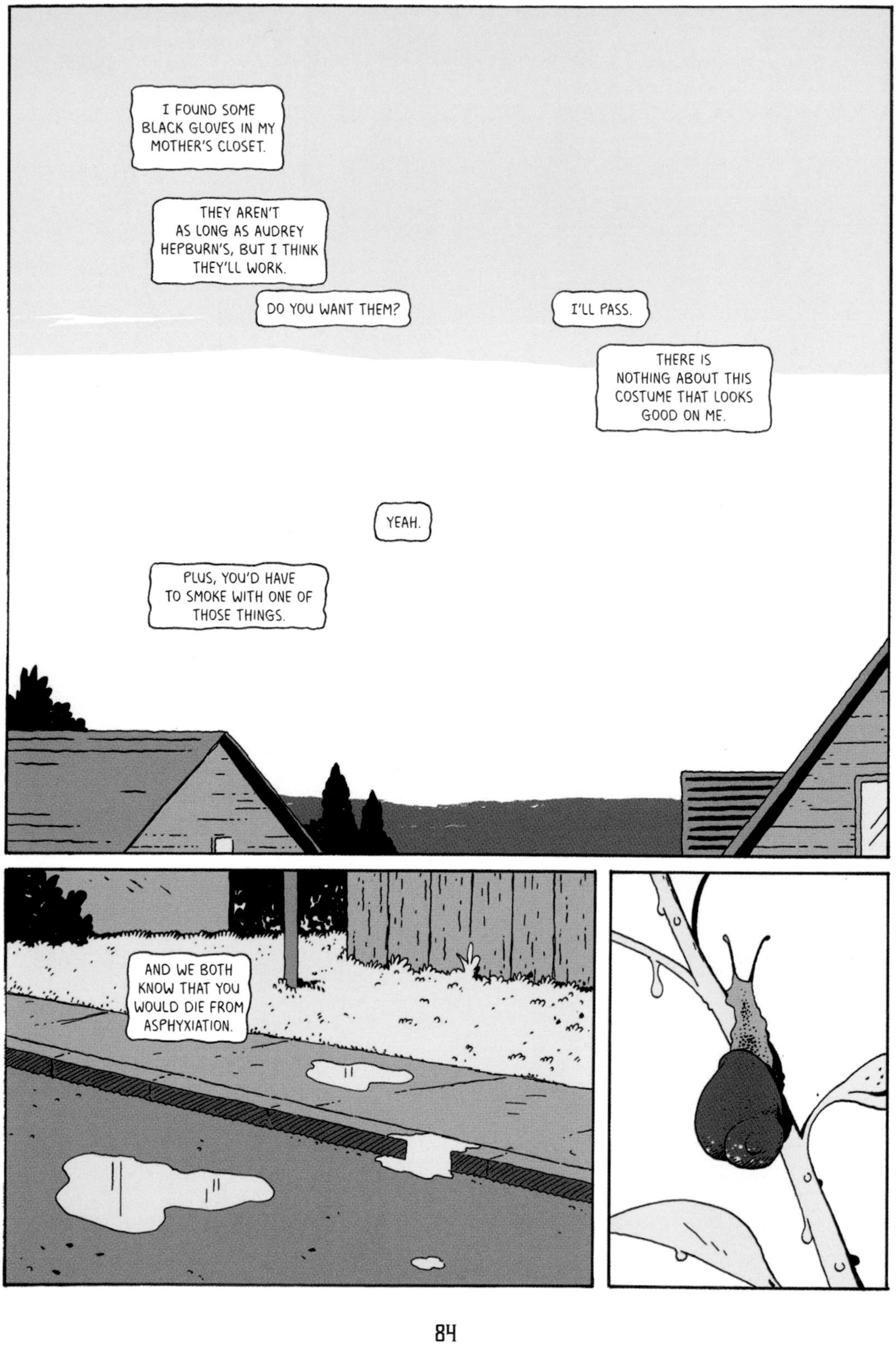
I FOUND SOME BLACK GLOVES IN MY MOTHER'S CLOSET.
THEY AREN'T AS LONG AS AUDREY HEPBURN'S, BUT I THINK THEY'LL WORK.
DO YOU WANT THEM?
I'LL PASS.
THERE IS NOTHING ABOUT THIS COSTUME THAT LOOKS GOOD ON ME.
YEAH.
PLUS, YOU'D HAVE TO SMOKE WITH ONE OF THOSE THINGS.
AND WE BOTH KNOW THAT YOU WOULD DIE FROM ASPHYXIATION.

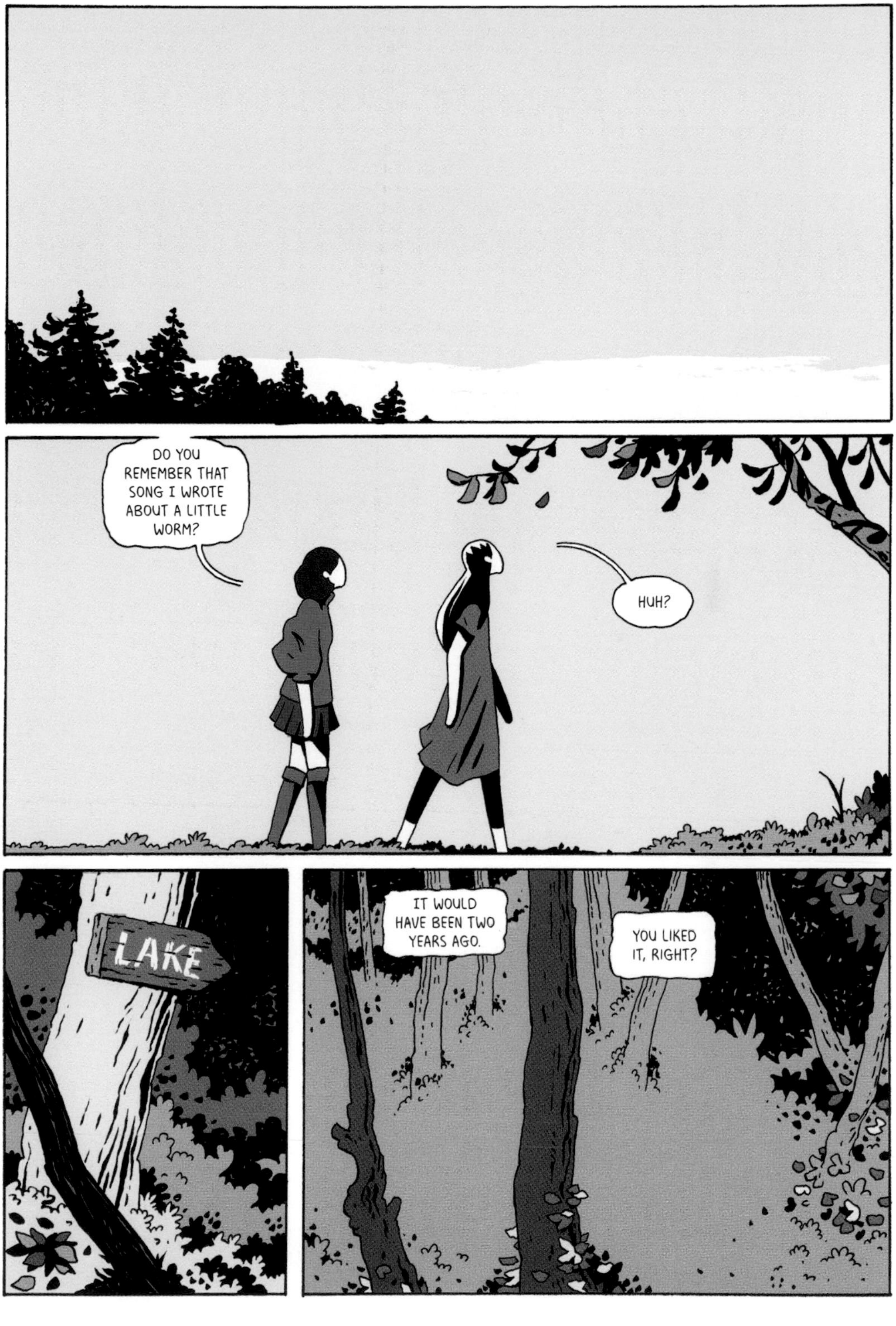
DO YOU REMEMBER THAT SONG I WROTE ABOUT A LITTLE WORM?
HUH?
LAKE
IT WOULD HAVE BEEN TWO YEARS AGO.
YOU LIKED IT, RIGHT?

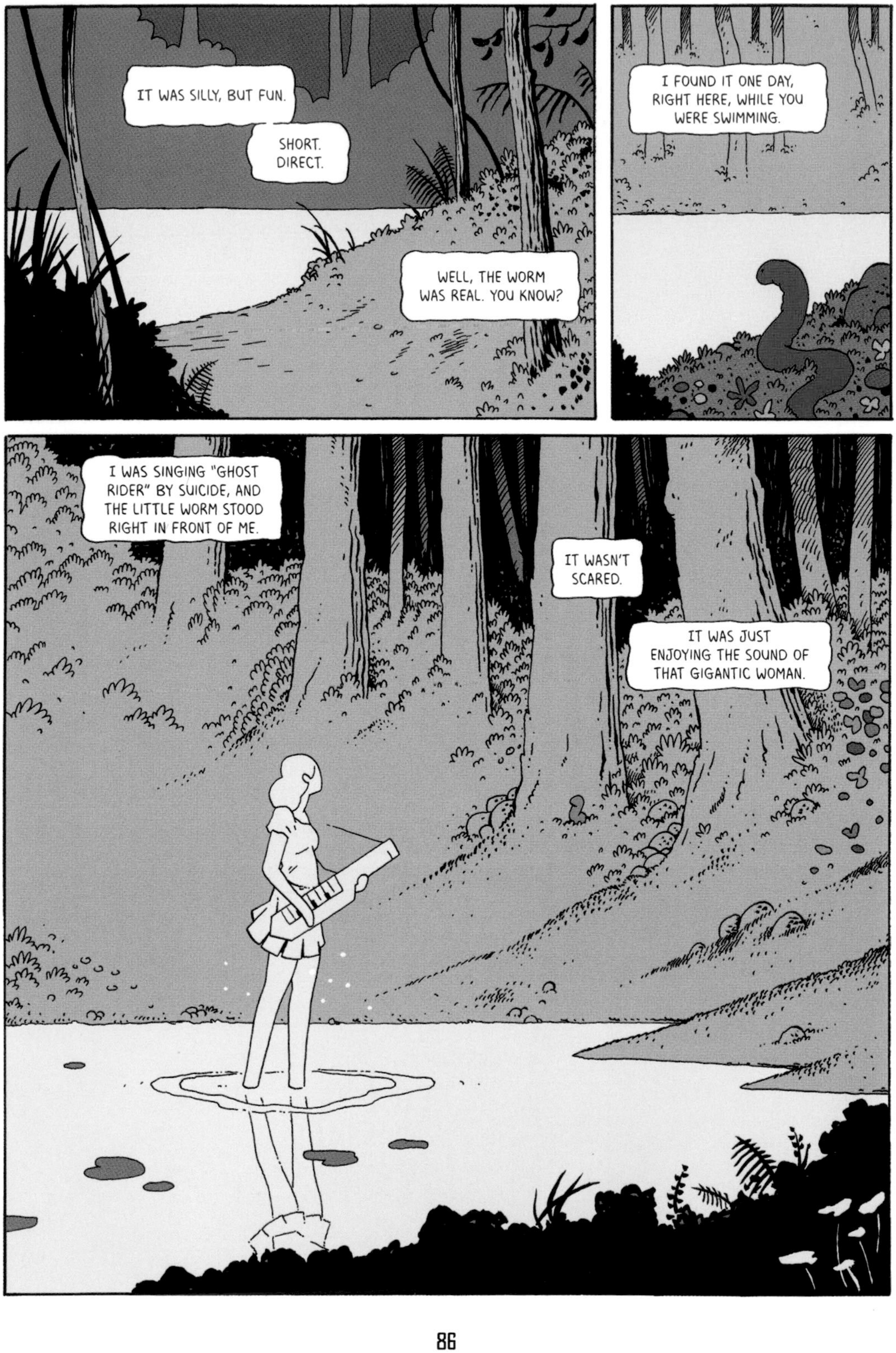
IT WAS SILLY, BUT FUN.
SHORT. DIRECT.
WELL, THE WORM WAS REAL. YOU KNOW?
I FOUND IT ONE DAY, RIGHT HERE, WHILE YOU WERE SWIMMING.
I WAS SINGING "GHOST RIDER" BY SUICIDE, AND THE LITTLE WORM STOOD RIGHT IN FRONT OF ME.
IT WASN'T SCARED.
IT WAS JUST ENJOYING THE SOUND OF THAT GIGANTIC WOMAN.

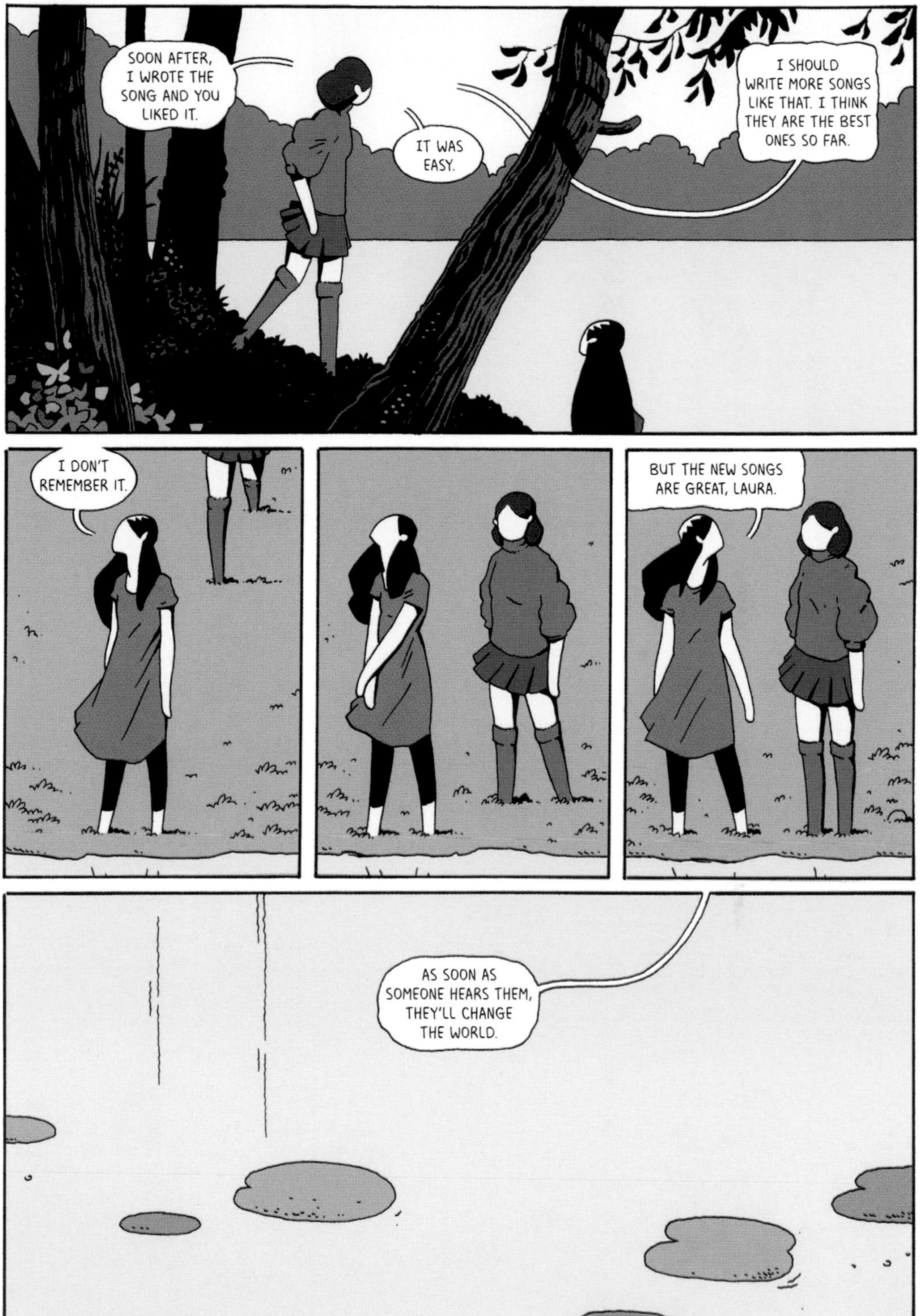
SOON AFTER, I WROTE THE SONG AND YOU LIKED IT.
IT WAS EASY.
I SHOULD WRITE MORE SONGS LIKE THAT. I THINK THEY ARE THE BEST ONES SO FAR.
I DON'T REMEMBER IT.
BUT THE NEW SONGS ARE GREAT, LAURA.
AS SOON AS SOMEONE HEARS THEM, THEY'LL CHANGE THE WORLD.

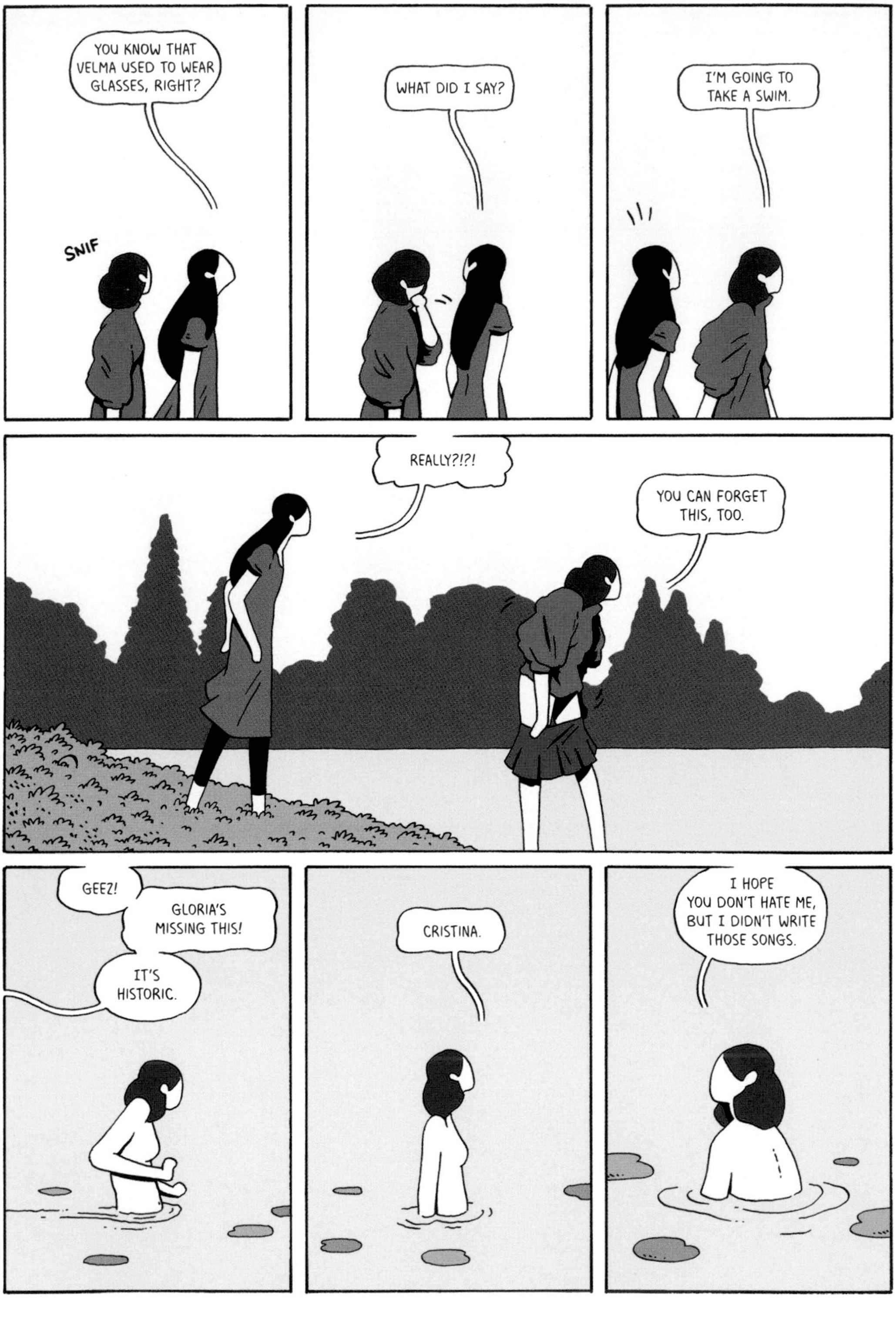
YOU KNOW THAT VELMA USED TO WEAR GLASSES, RIGHT?
SNIF
WHAT DID I SAY?
I'M GOING TO TAKE A SWIM.
REALLY?!?!
YOU CAN FORGET THIS, TOO.
GEEZ!
GLORIA'S MISSING THIS!
IT'S HISTORIC.
CRISTINA.
I HOPE YOU DON'T HATE ME, BUT I DIDN'T WRITE THOSE SONGS.

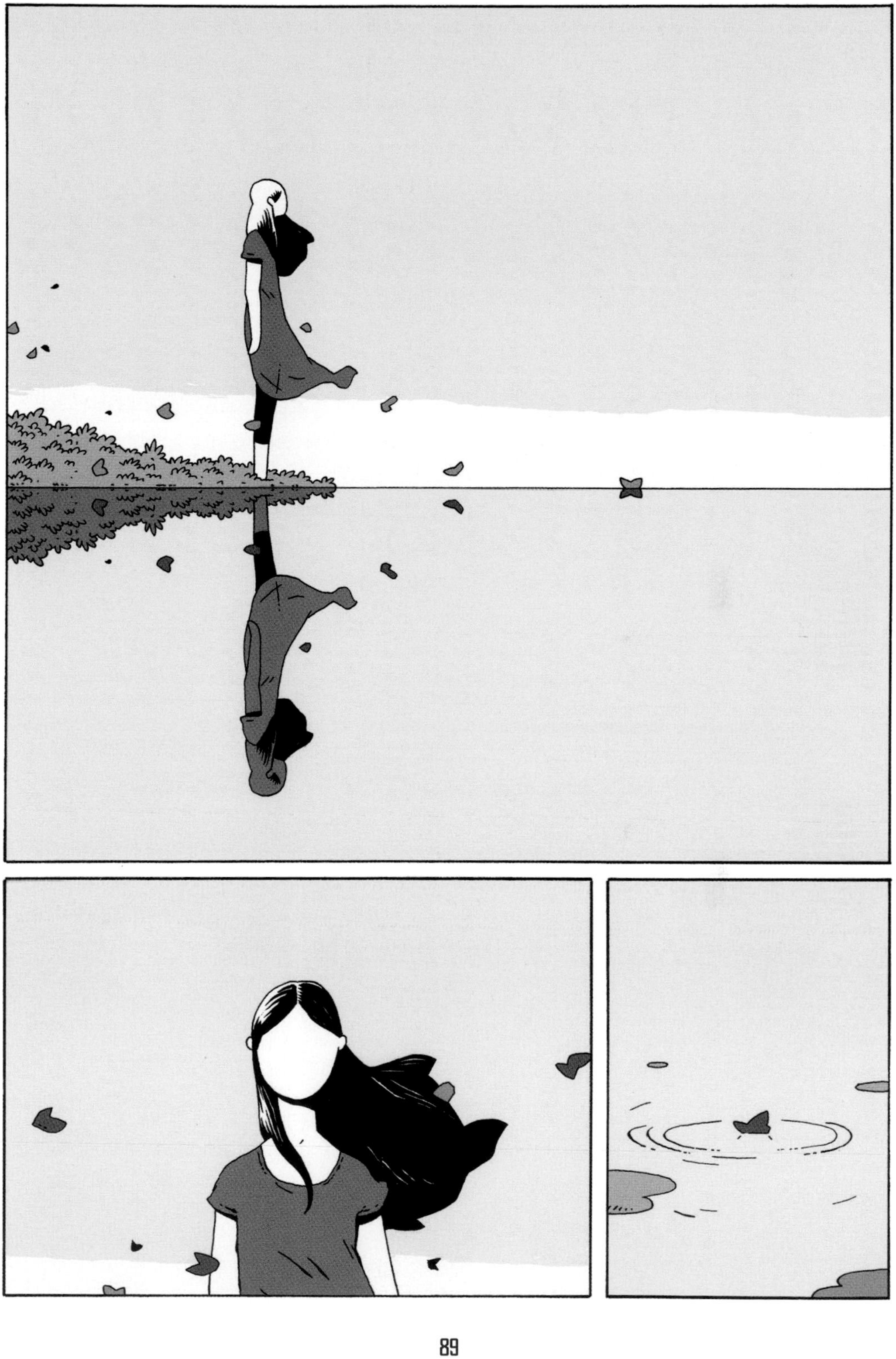

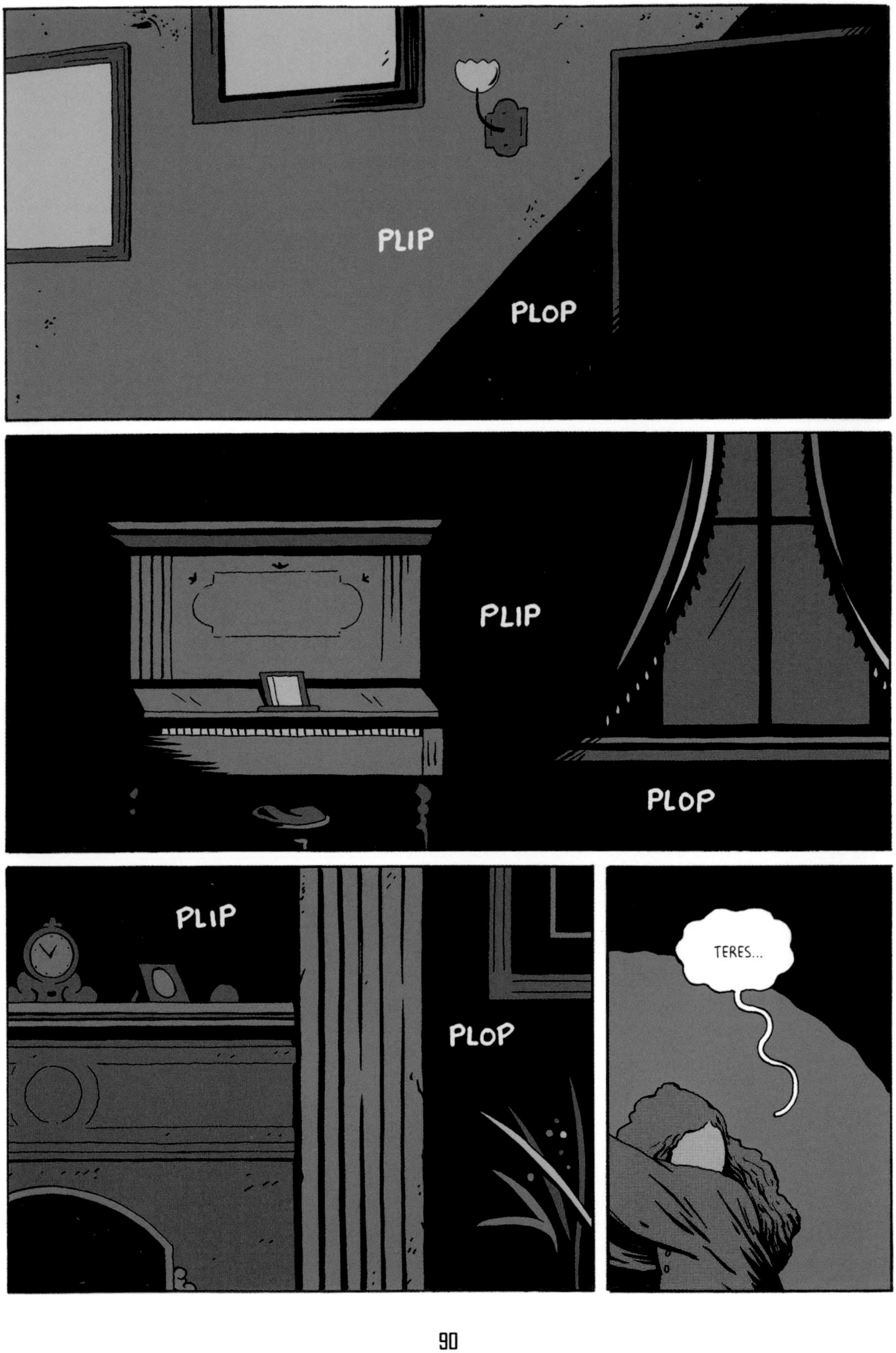
PLIP
PLOP
PLIP
PLOP
PLIP
PLOP
TERES...

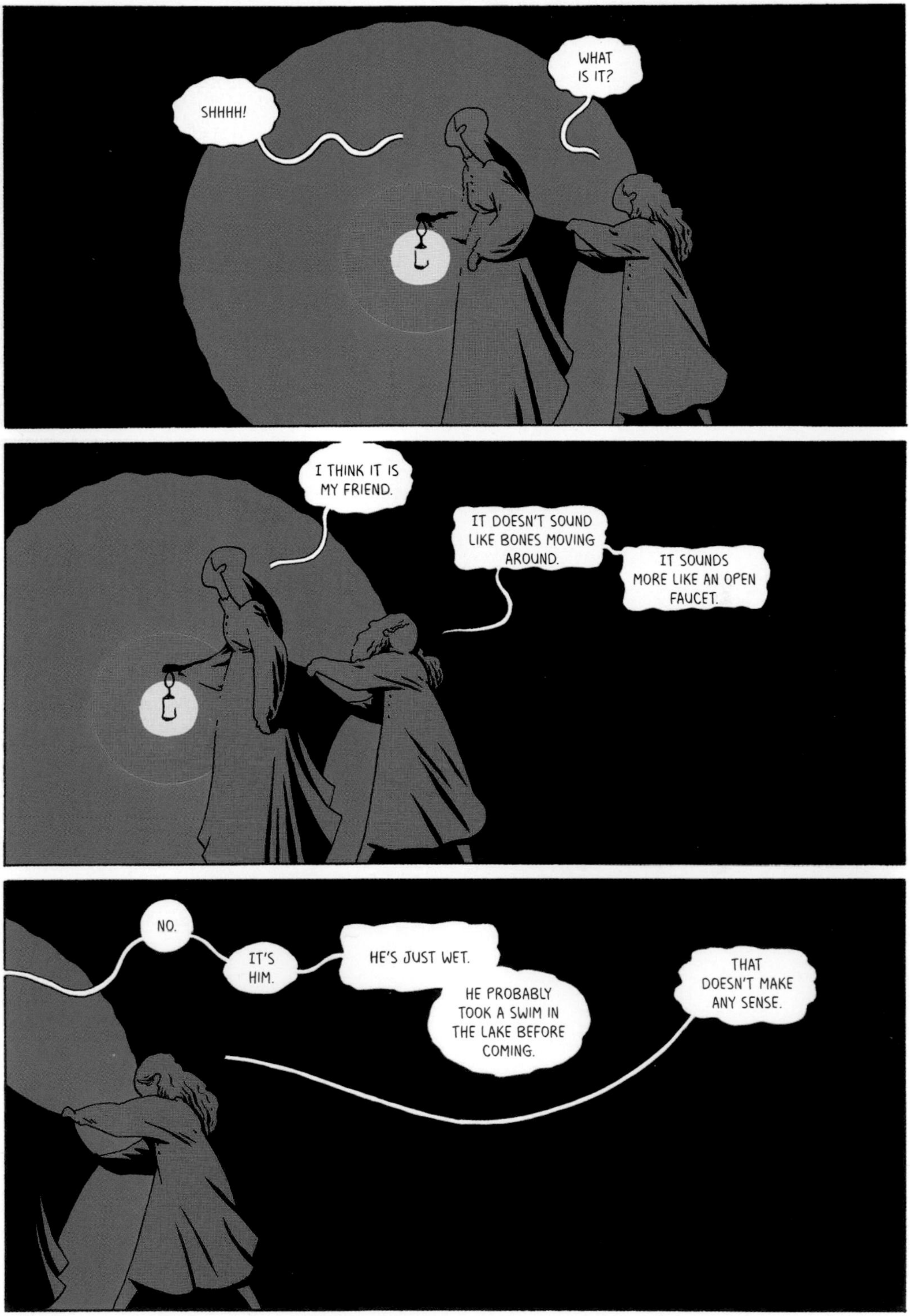
SHHHH!
WHAT IS IT?
I THINK IT IS MY FRIEND.
IT DOESN'T SOUND LIKE BONES MOVING AROUND.
IT SOUNDS MORE LIKE AN OPEN FAUCET.
NO.
IT'S HIM.
HE'S JUST WET.
HE PROBABLY TOOK A SWIM IN THE LAKE BEFORE COMING.
THAT DOESN'T MAKE ANY SENSE.

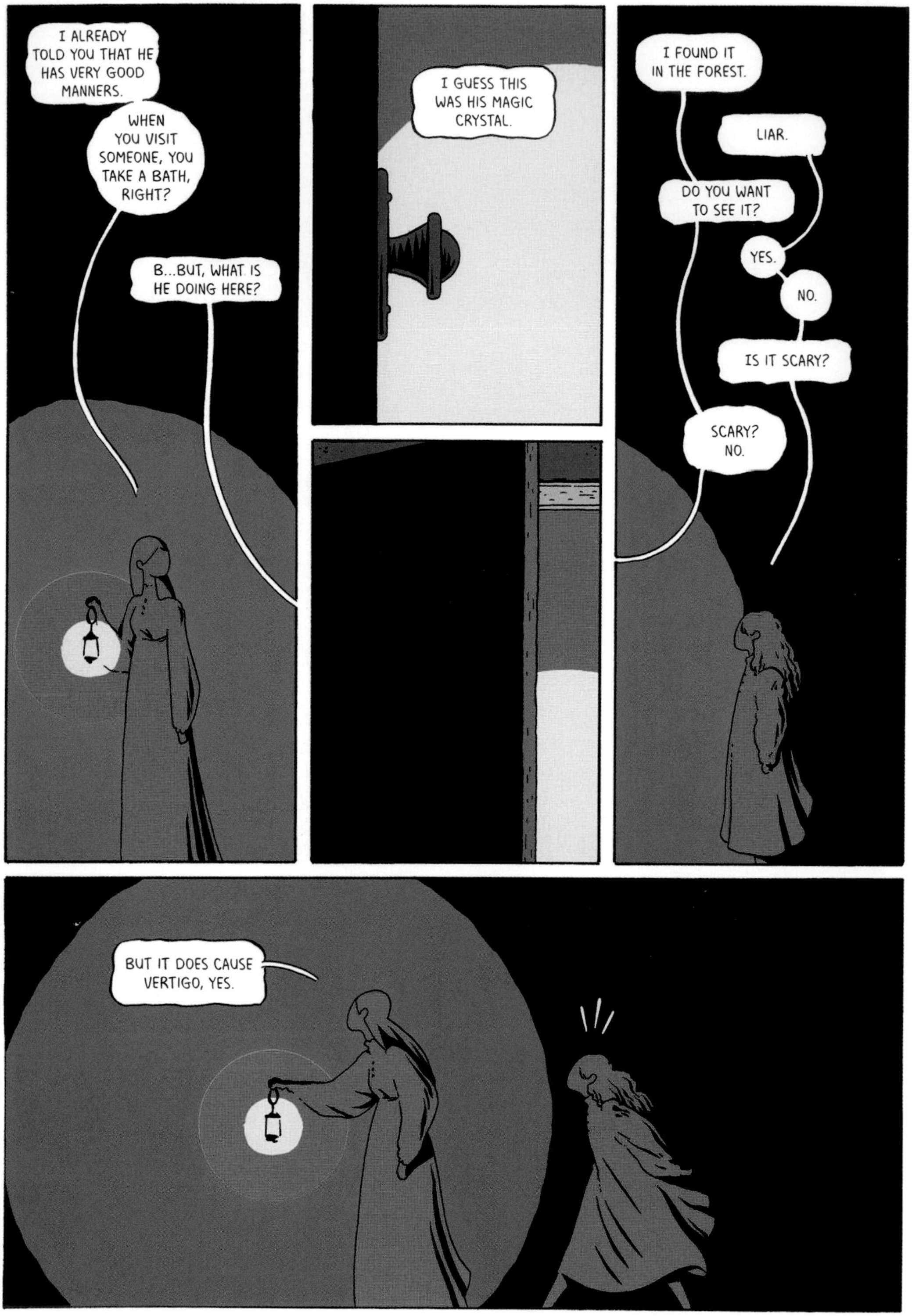
I ALREADY TOLD YOU THAT HE HAS VERY GOOD MANNERS.
WHEN YOU VISIT SOMEONE, YOU TAKE A BATH, RIGHT?
B...BUT, WHAT IS HE DOING HERE?
I GUESS THIS WAS HIS MAGIC CRYSTAL.
I FOUND IT IN THE FOREST.
LIAR.
DO YOU WANT TO SEE IT?
YES.
NO.
IS IT SCARY?
SCARY? NO.
BUT IT DOES CAUSE VERTIGO, YES.

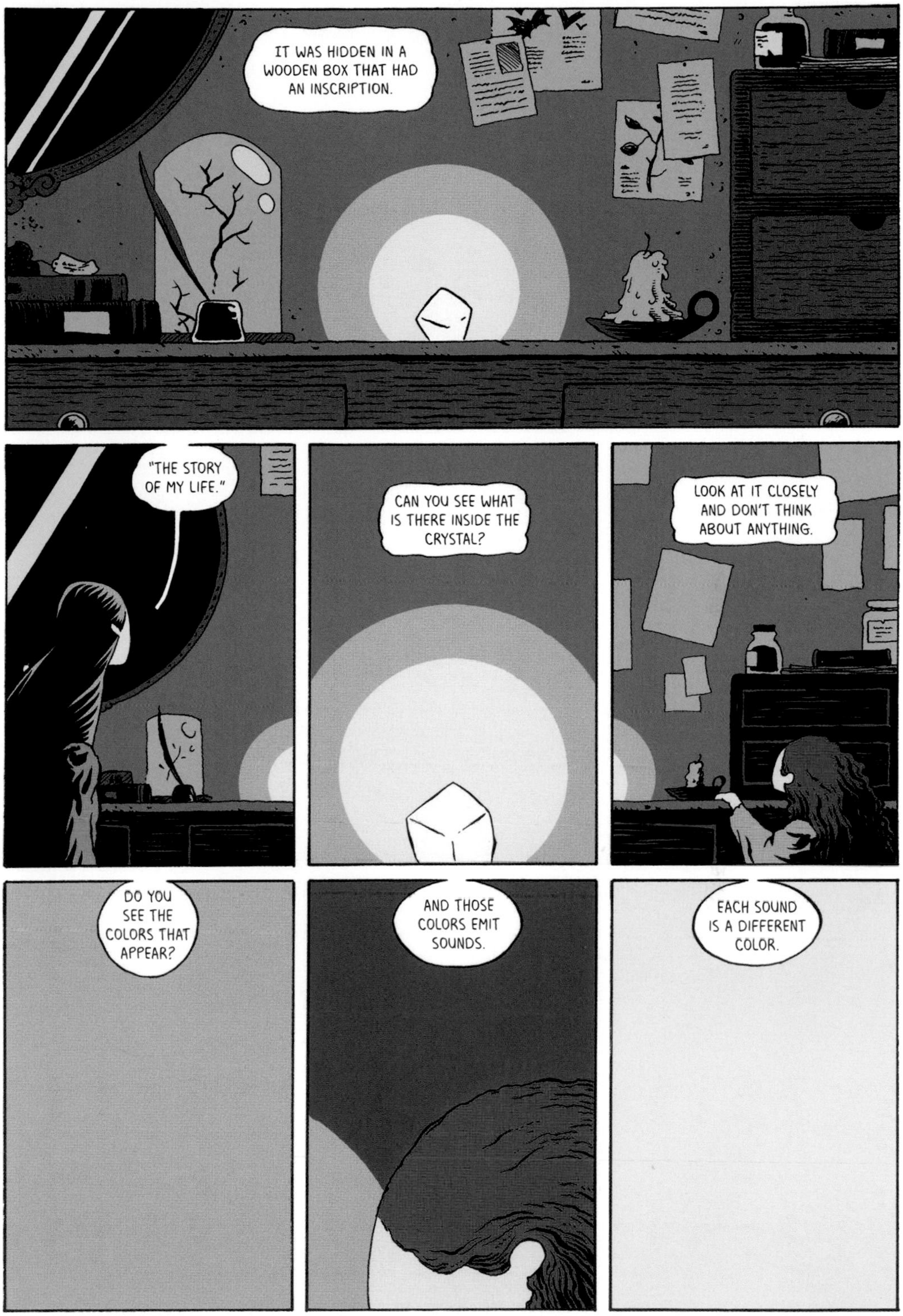
IT WAS HIDDEN IN A WOODEN BOX THAT HAD AN INSCRIPTION.
"THE STORY OF MY LIFE."
CAN YOU SEE WHAT IS THERE INSIDE THE CRYSTAL?
LOOK AT IT CLOSELY AND DON'T THINK ABOUT ANYTHING.
DO YOU SEE THE COLORS THAT APPEAR?
AND THOSE COLORS EMIT SOUNDS.
EACH SOUND IS A DIFFERENT COLOR.

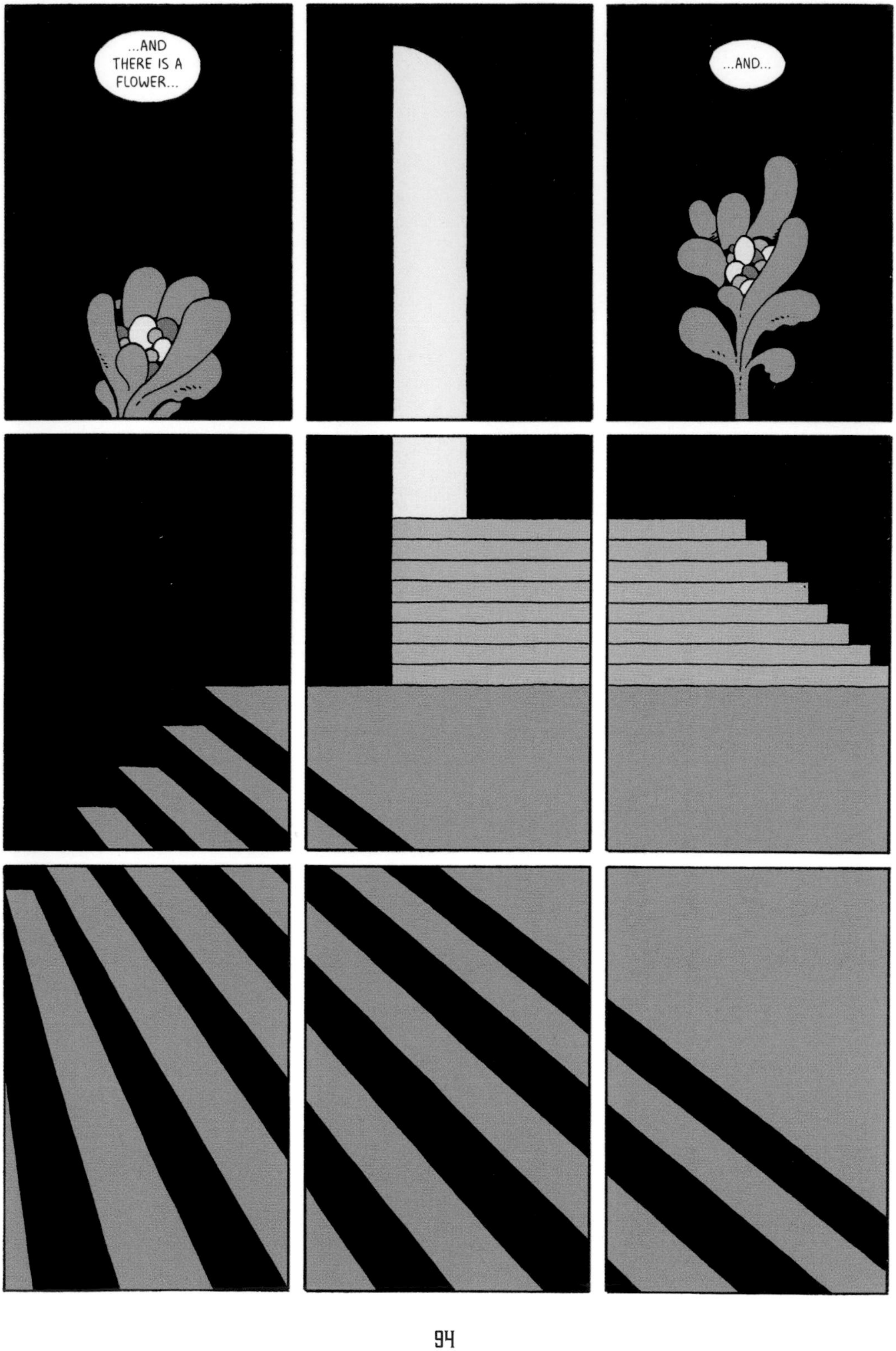
...AND THERE IS A FLOWER...
...AND...

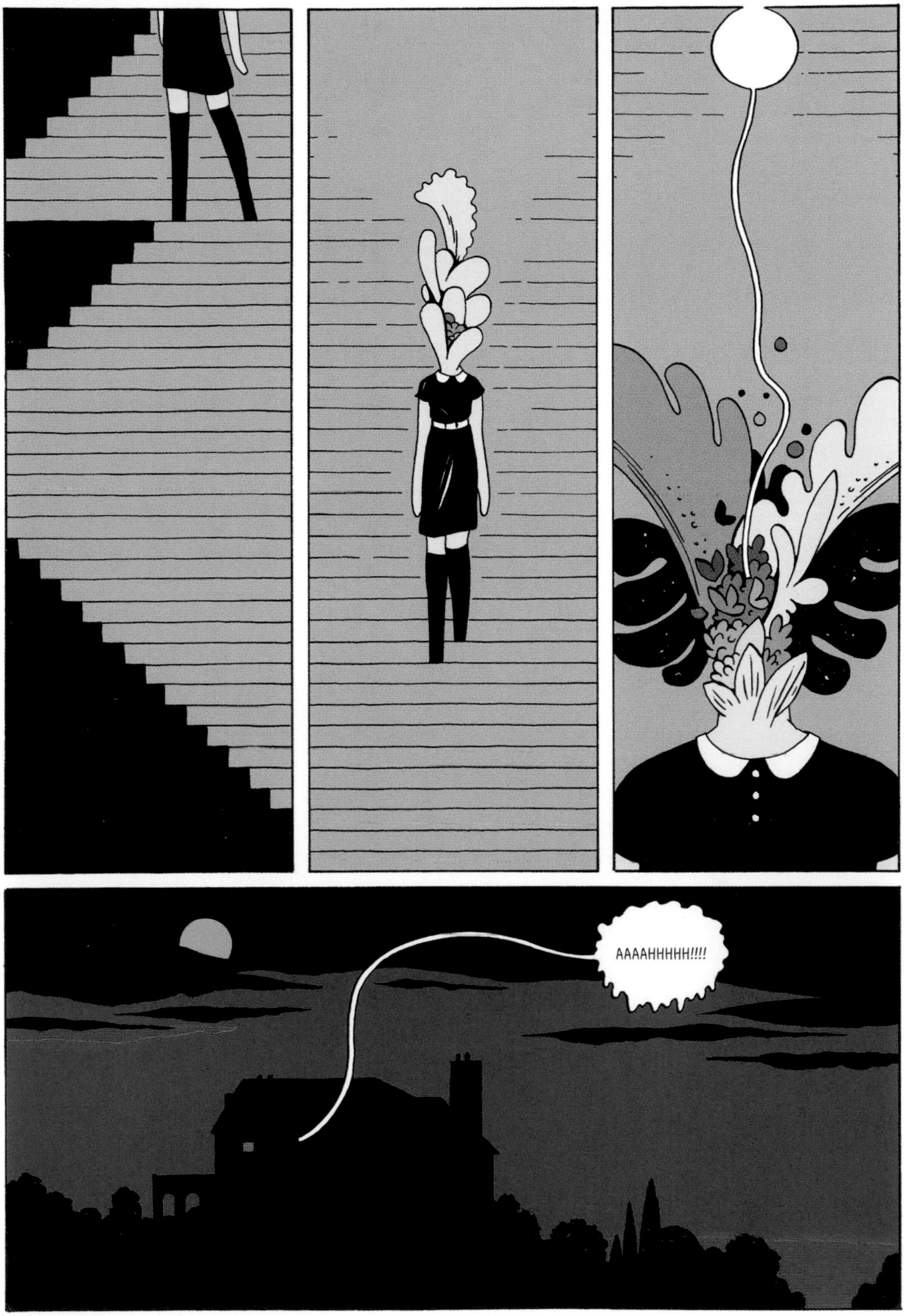
AAAAHHHHH!!!!

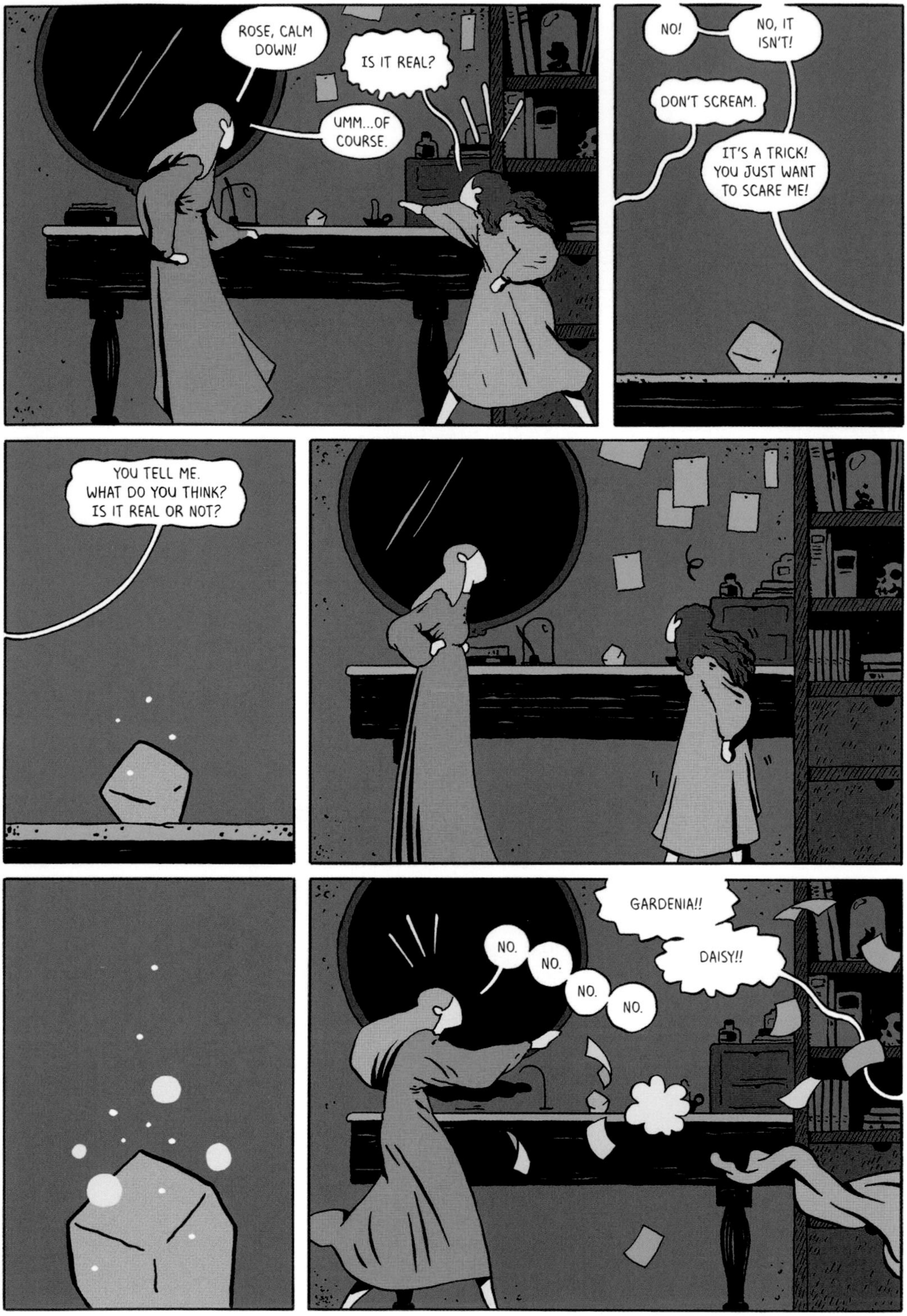
ROSE, CALM DOWN!
IS IT REAL?
UMM...OF COURSE.
NO!
NO, IT ISN'T!
DON'T SCREAM.
IT'S A TRICK! YOU JUST WANT TO SCARE ME!
YOU TELL ME. WHAT DO YOU THINK? IS IT REAL OR NOT?
NO.
NO.
NO.
NO.
GARDENIA!!
DAISY!!

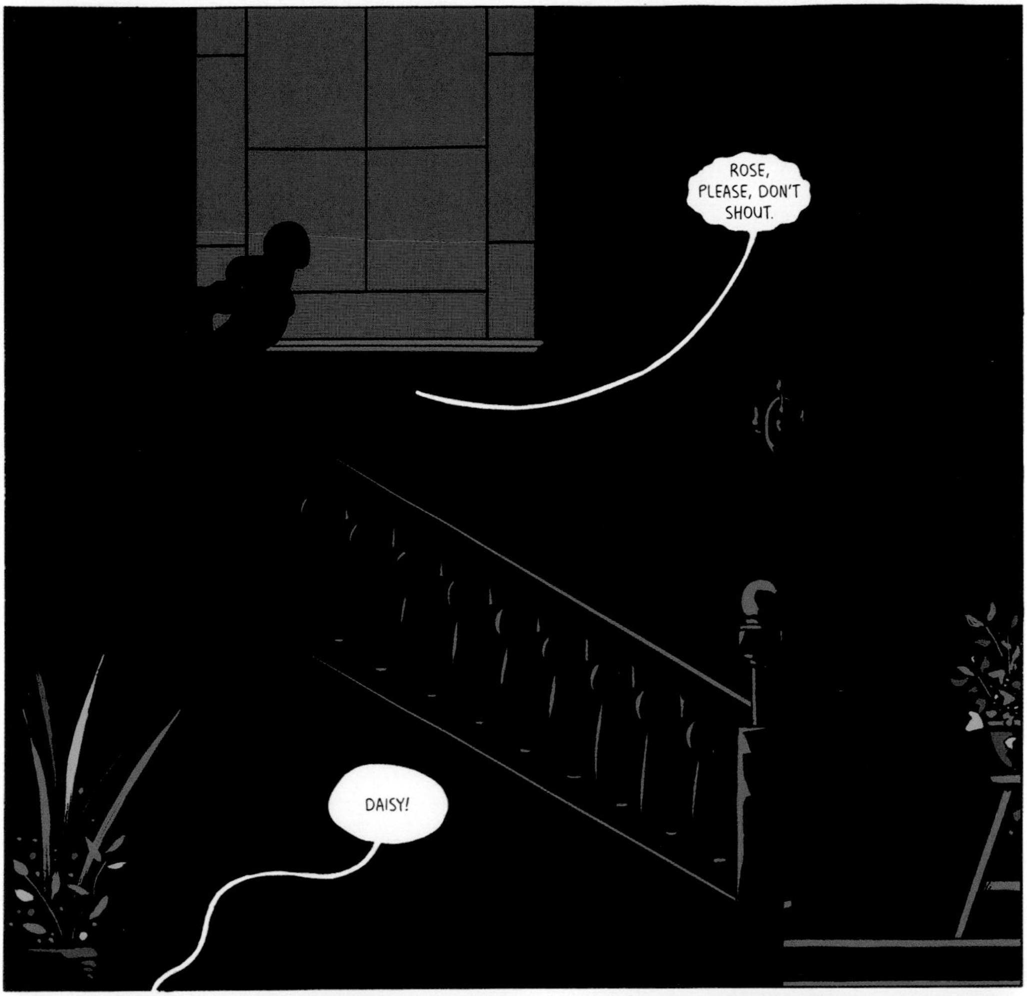
ROSE, PLEASE, DON'T SHOUT.
DAISY!

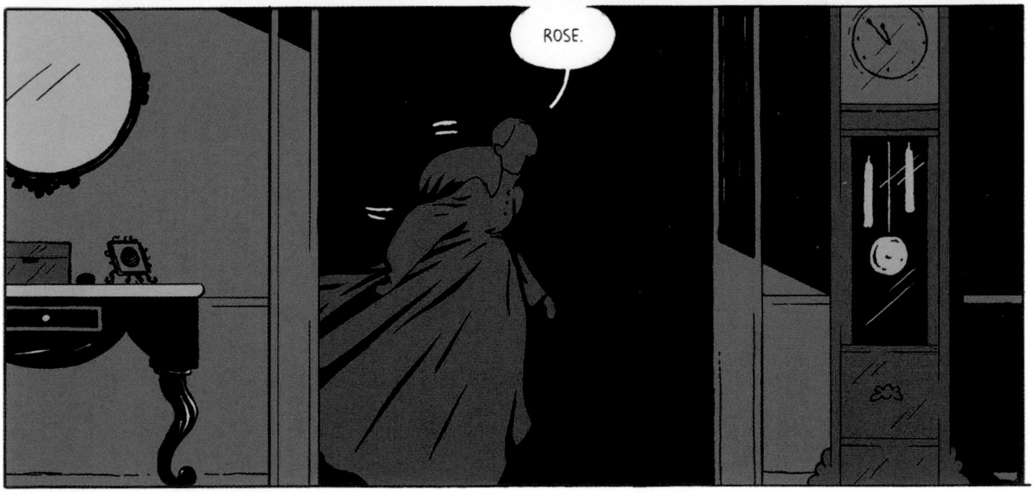
ROSE.

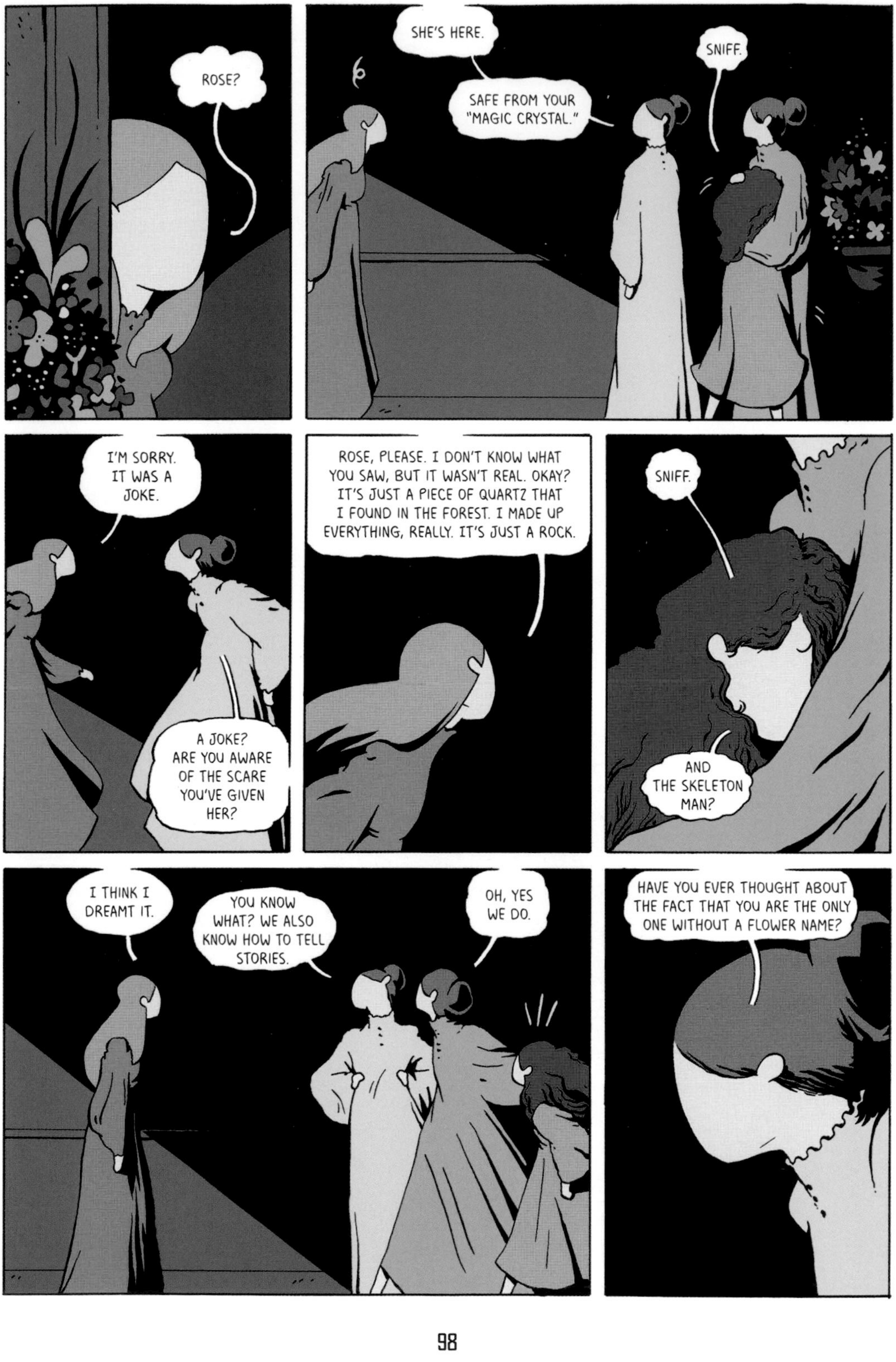
ROSE?
SHE'S HERE.
SAFE FROM YOUR "MAGIC CRYSTAL."
SNIFF.
I'M SORRY. IT WAS A JOKE.
A JOKE? ARE YOU AWARE OF THE SCARE YOU'VE GIVEN HER?
ROSE, PLEASE. I DON'T KNOW WHAT YOU SAW, BUT IT WASN'T REAL. OKAY? IT'S JUST A PIECE OF QUARTZ THAT I FOUND IN THE FOREST. I MADE UP EVERYTHING, REALLY. IT'S JUST A ROCK.
SNIFF.
AND THE SKELETON MAN?
I THINK I DREAMT IT.
YOU KNOW WHAT? WE ALSO KNOW HOW TO TELL STORIES.
OH, YES WE DO.
HAVE YOU EVER THOUGHT ABOUT THE FACT THAT YOU ARE THE ONLY ONE WITHOUT A FLOWER NAME?

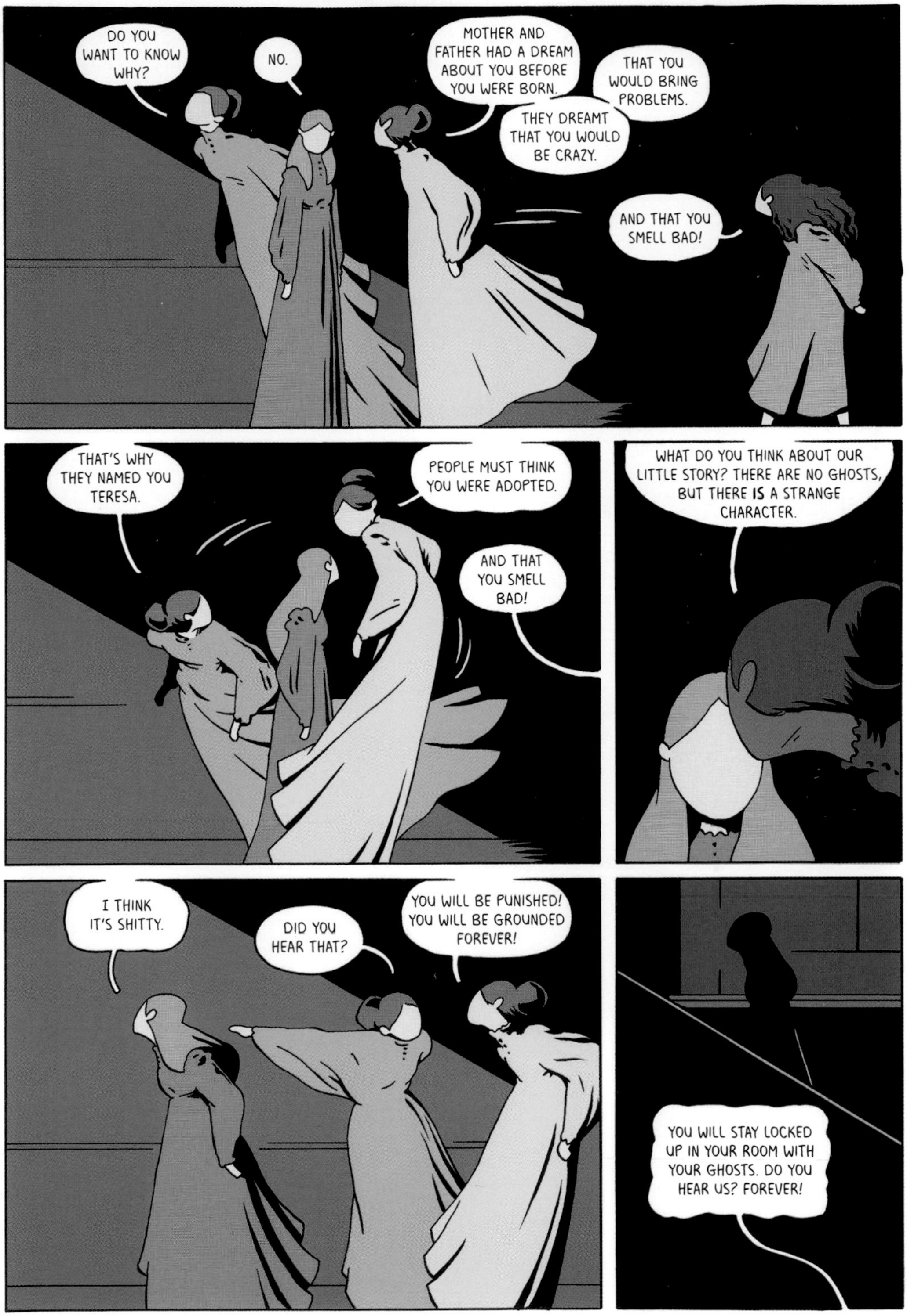
DO YOU WANT TO KNOW WHY?
NO.
MOTHER AND FATHER HAD A DREAM ABOUT YOU BEFORE YOU WERE BORN.
THAT YOU WOULD BRING PROBLEMS.
THEY DREAMT THAT YOU WOULD BE CRAZY.
AND THAT YOU SMELL BAD!
THAT'S WHY THEY NAMED YOU TERESA.
PEOPLE MUST THINK YOU WERE ADOPTED.
AND THAT YOU SMELL BAD!
WHAT DO YOU THINK ABOUT OUR LITTLE STORY? THERE ARE NO GHOSTS, BUT THERE IS A STRANGE CHARACTER.
I THINK IT'S SHITTY.
DID YOU HEAR THAT?
YOU WILL BE PUNISHED! YOU WILL BE GROUNDED FOREVER!
YOU WILL STAY LOCKED UP IN YOUR ROOM WITH YOUR GHOSTS. DO YOU HEAR US? FOREVER!

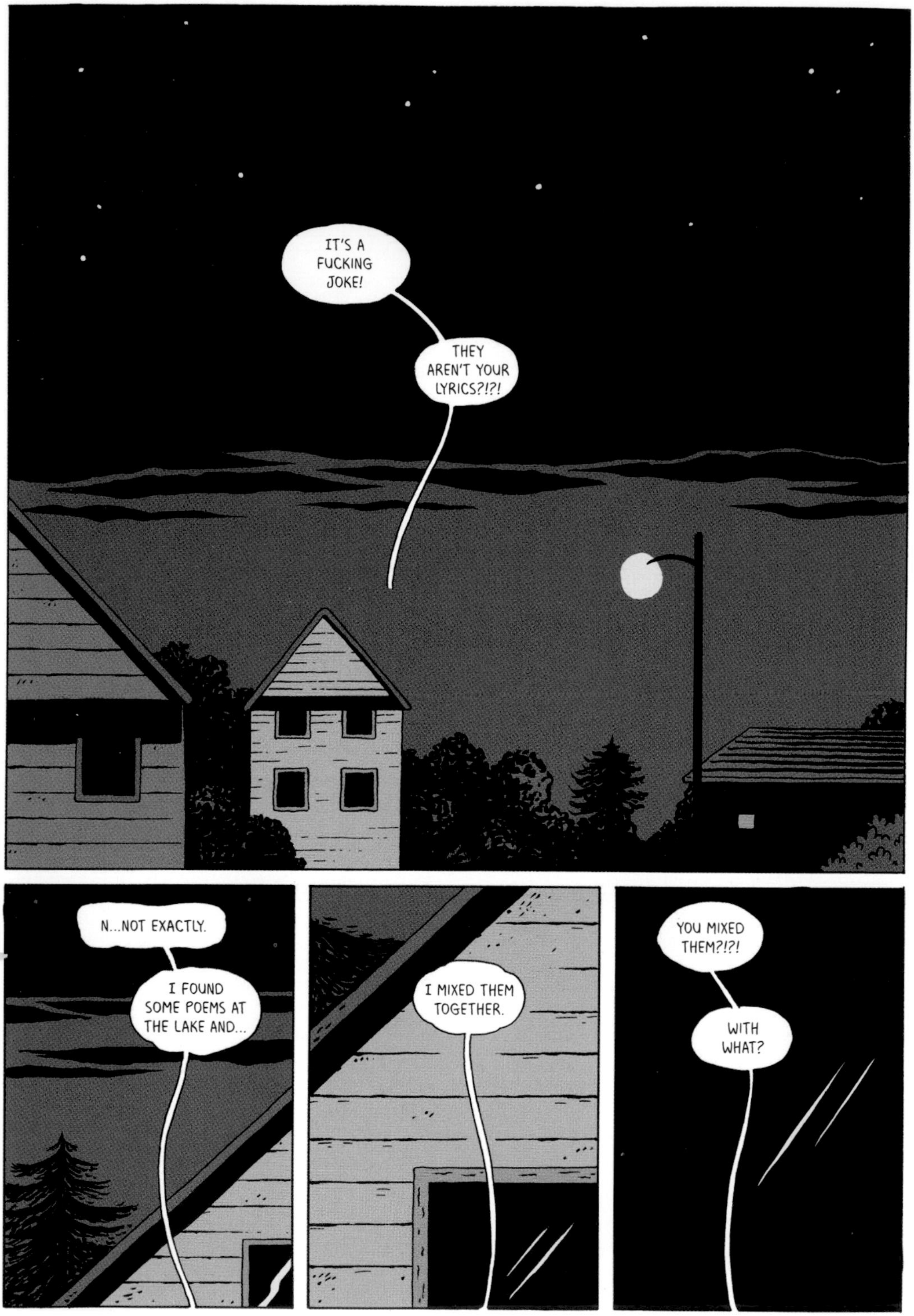
IT'S A FUCKING JOKE!
THEY AREN'T YOUR LYRICS?!?!
N...NOT EXACTLY.
I FOUND SOME POEMS AT THE LAKE AND...
I MIXED THEM TOGETHER.
YOU MIXED THEM?!?!
WITH WHAT?

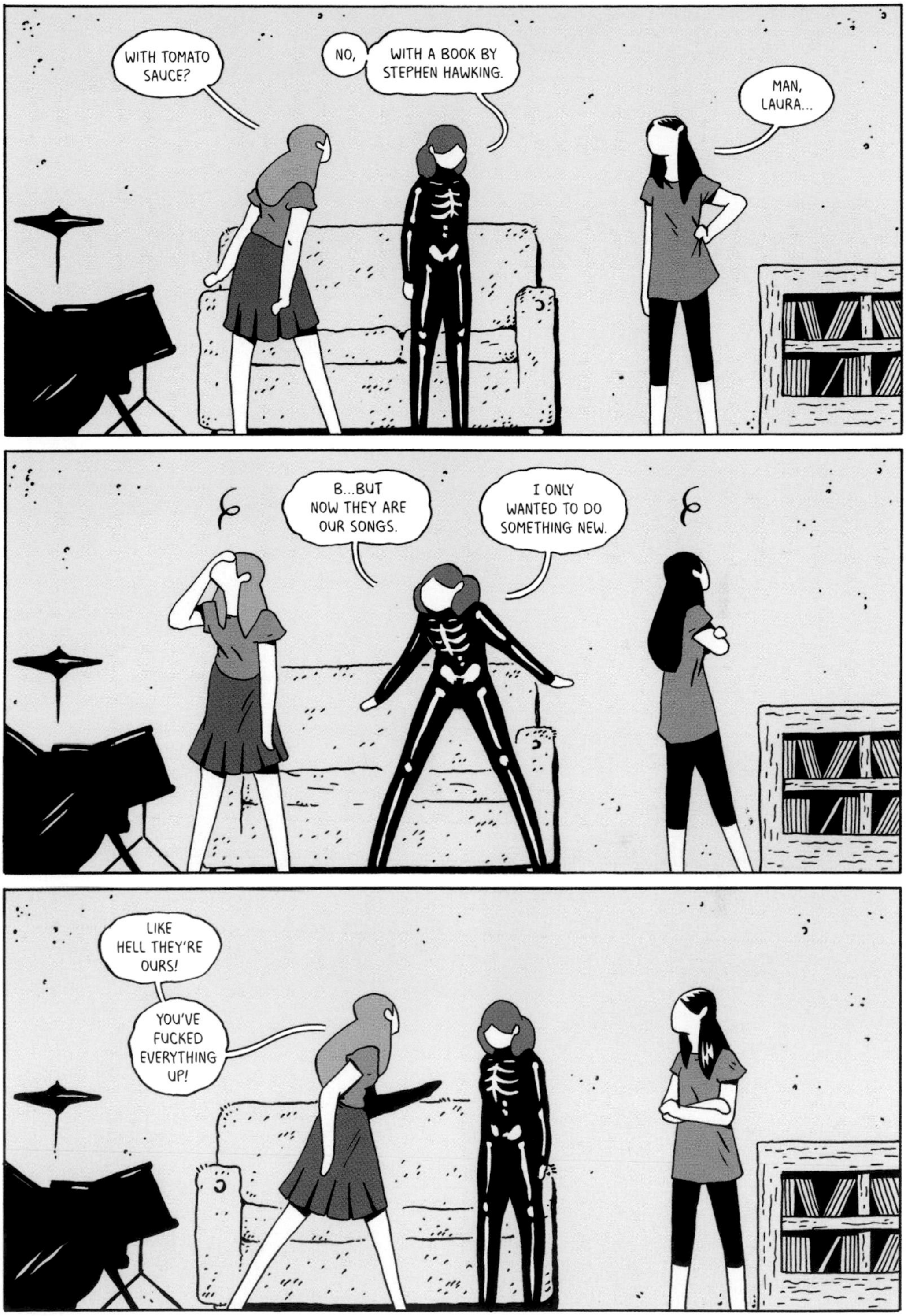
WITH TOMATO SAUCE?
NO,
WITH A BOOK BY STEPHEN HAWKING.
MAN, LAURA...
B...BUT NOW THEY ARE OUR SONGS.
I ONLY WANTED TO DO SOMETHING NEW.
LIKE HELL THEY'RE OURS!
YOU'VE FUCKED EVERYTHING UP!

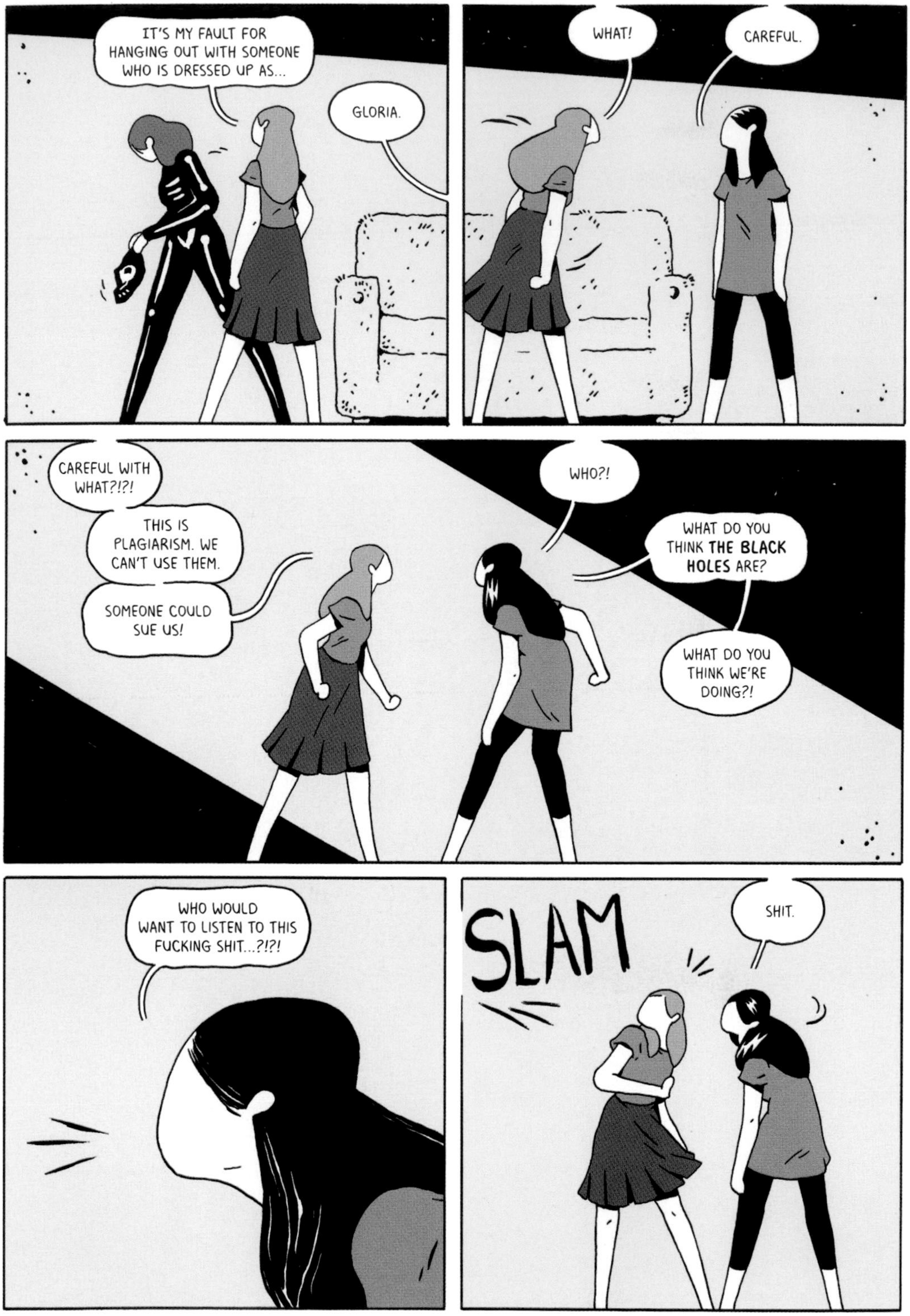
IT'S MY FAULT FOR HANGING OUT WITH SOMEONE WHO IS DRESSED UP AS...
GLORIA.
WHAT!
CAREFUL.
CAREFUL WITH WHAT?!?!
THIS IS PLAGIARISM. WE CAN'T USE THEM.
SOMEONE COULD SUE US!
WHO?!
WHAT DO YOU THINK **THE BLACK HOLES** ARE?
WHAT DO YOU THINK WE'RE DOING?!
WHO WOULD WANT TO LISTEN TO THIS FUCKING SHIT...?!?!
SLAM
SHIT.

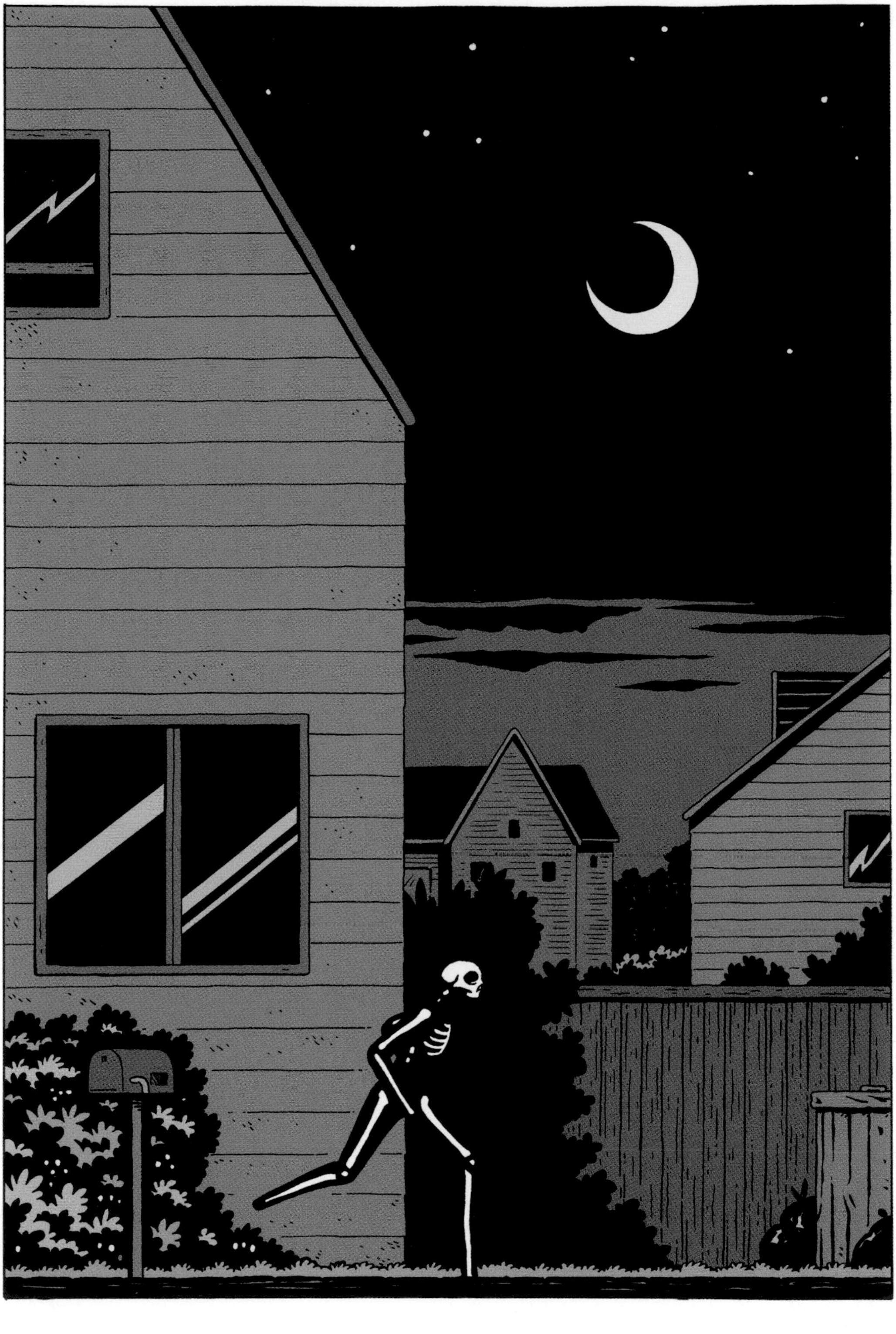

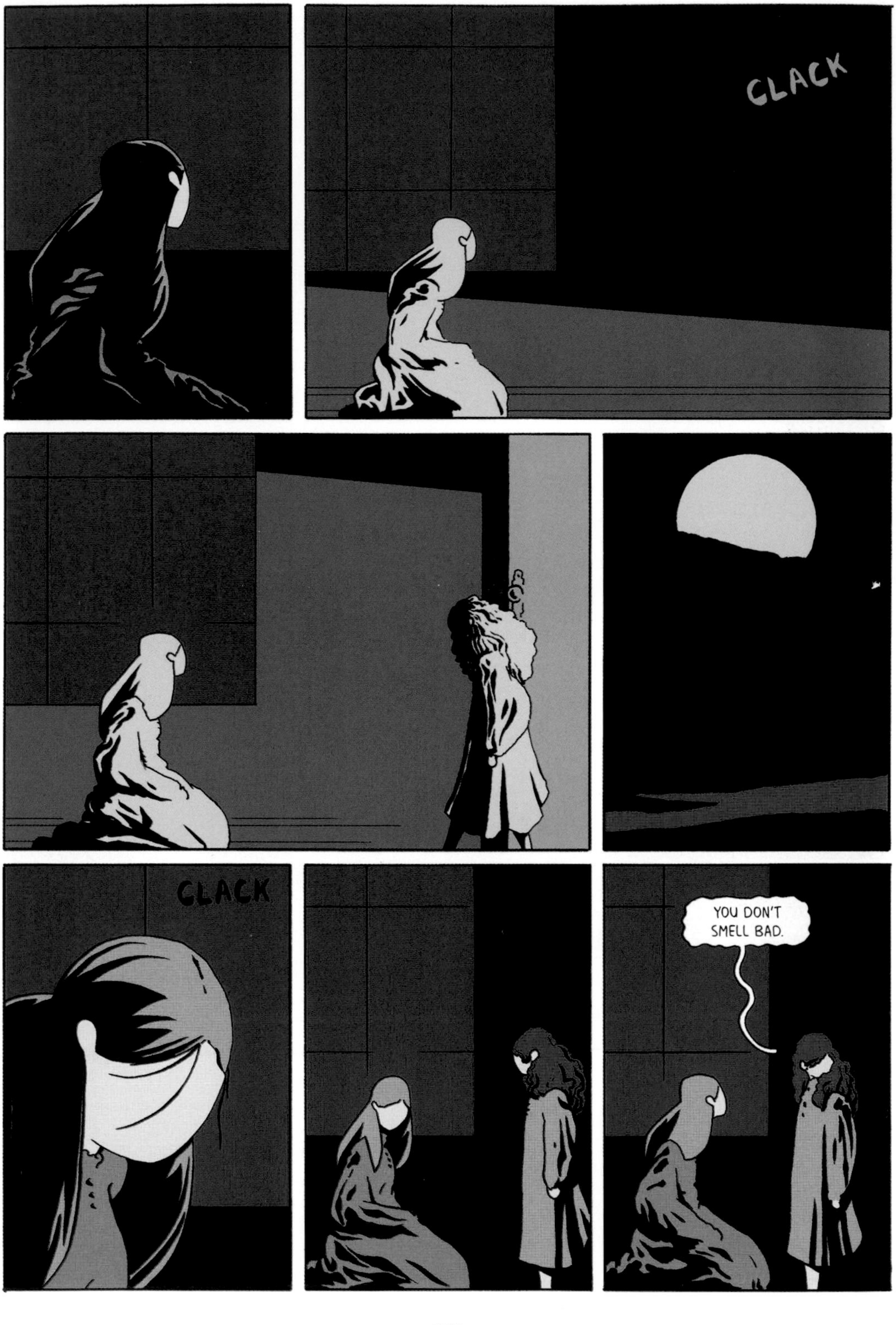
CLACK
CLACK
YOU DON'T SMELL BAD.

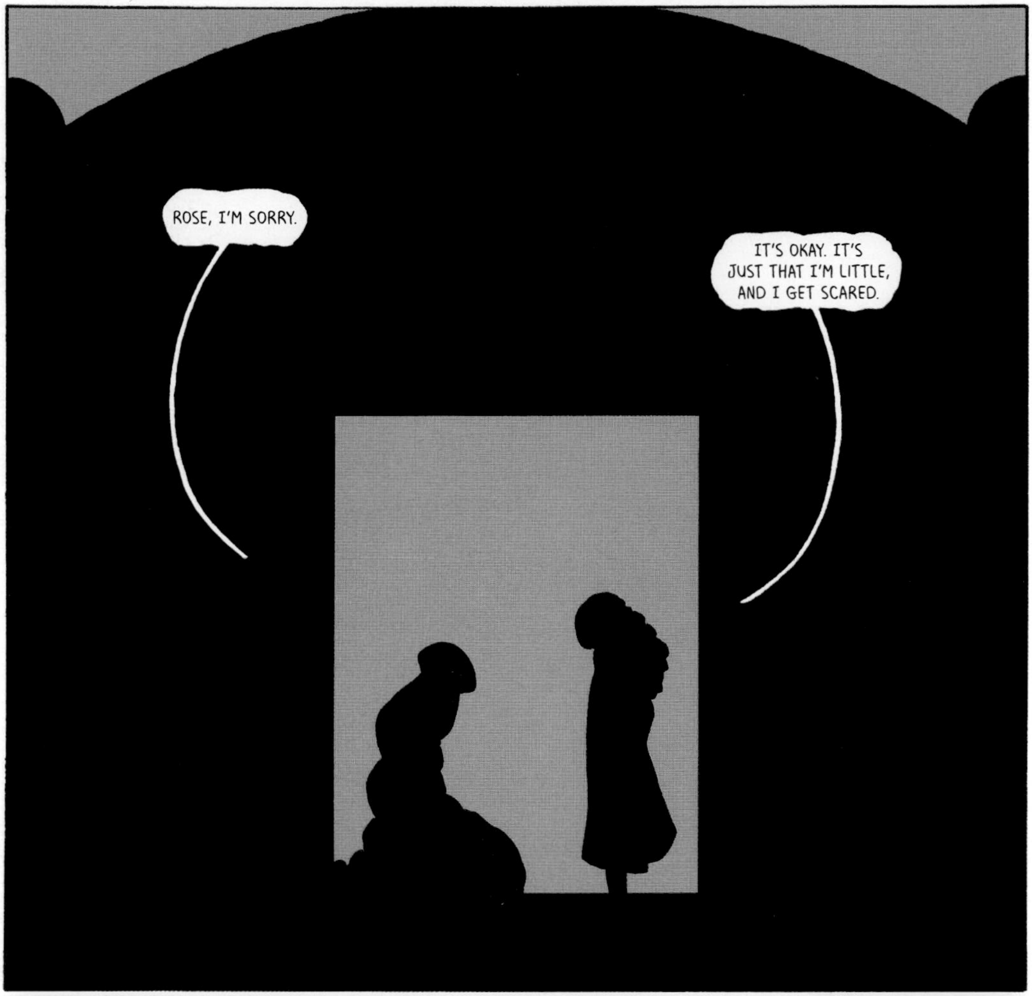
ROSE, I'M SORRY.
IT'S OKAY. IT'S JUST THAT I'M LITTLE, AND I GET SCARED.

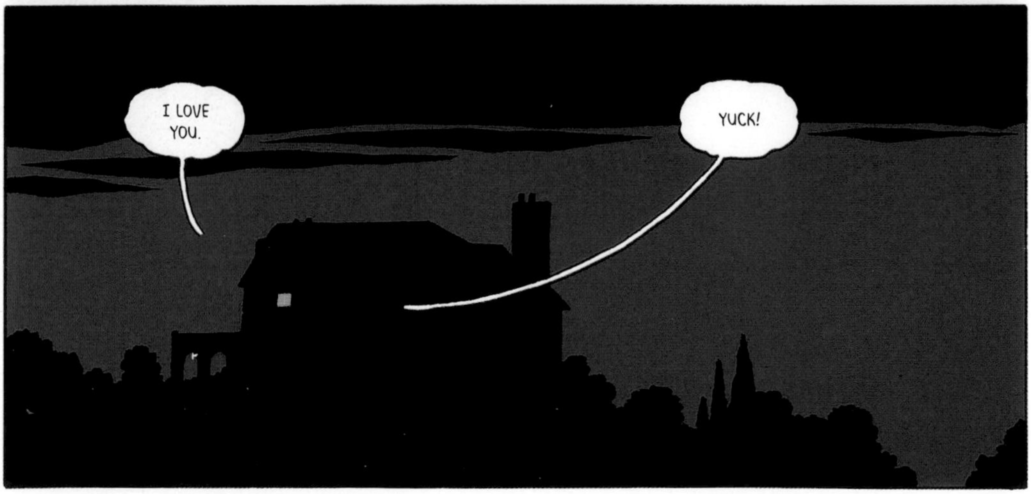
I LOVE YOU.
YUCK!

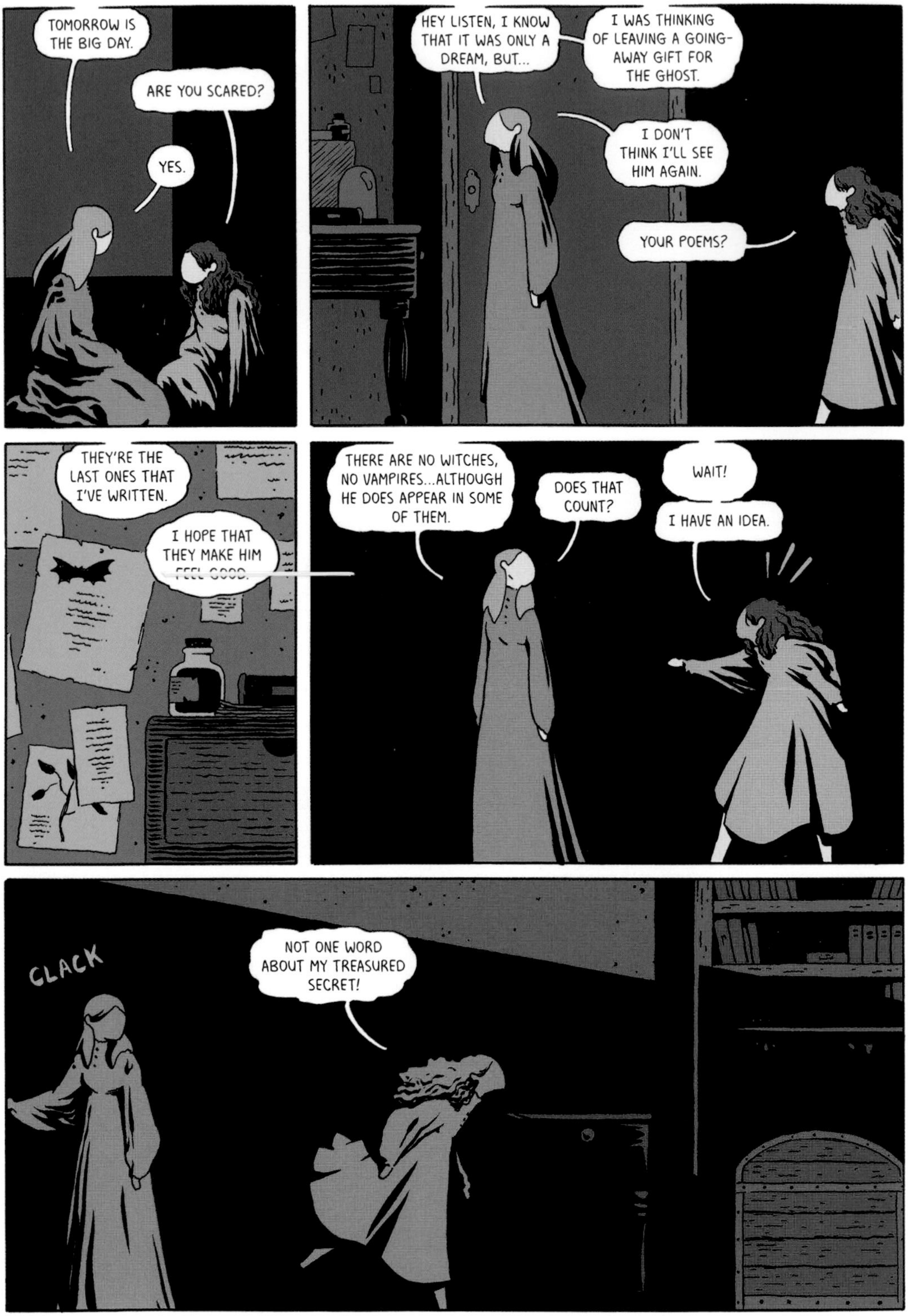
TOMORROW IS THE BIG DAY.
ARE YOU SCARED?
YES.
HEY LISTEN, I KNOW THAT IT WAS ONLY A DREAM, BUT...
I WAS THINKING OF LEAVING A GOING-AWAY GIFT FOR THE GHOST.
I DON'T THINK I'LL SEE HIM AGAIN.
YOUR POEMS?
THEY'RE THE LAST ONES THAT I'VE WRITTEN.
I HOPE THAT THEY MAKE HIM FEEL GOOD.
THERE ARE NO WITCHES, NO VAMPIRES...ALTHOUGH HE DOES APPEAR IN SOME OF THEM.
DOES THAT COUNT?
WAIT!
I HAVE AN IDEA.
CLACK
NOT ONE WORD ABOUT MY TREASURED SECRET!

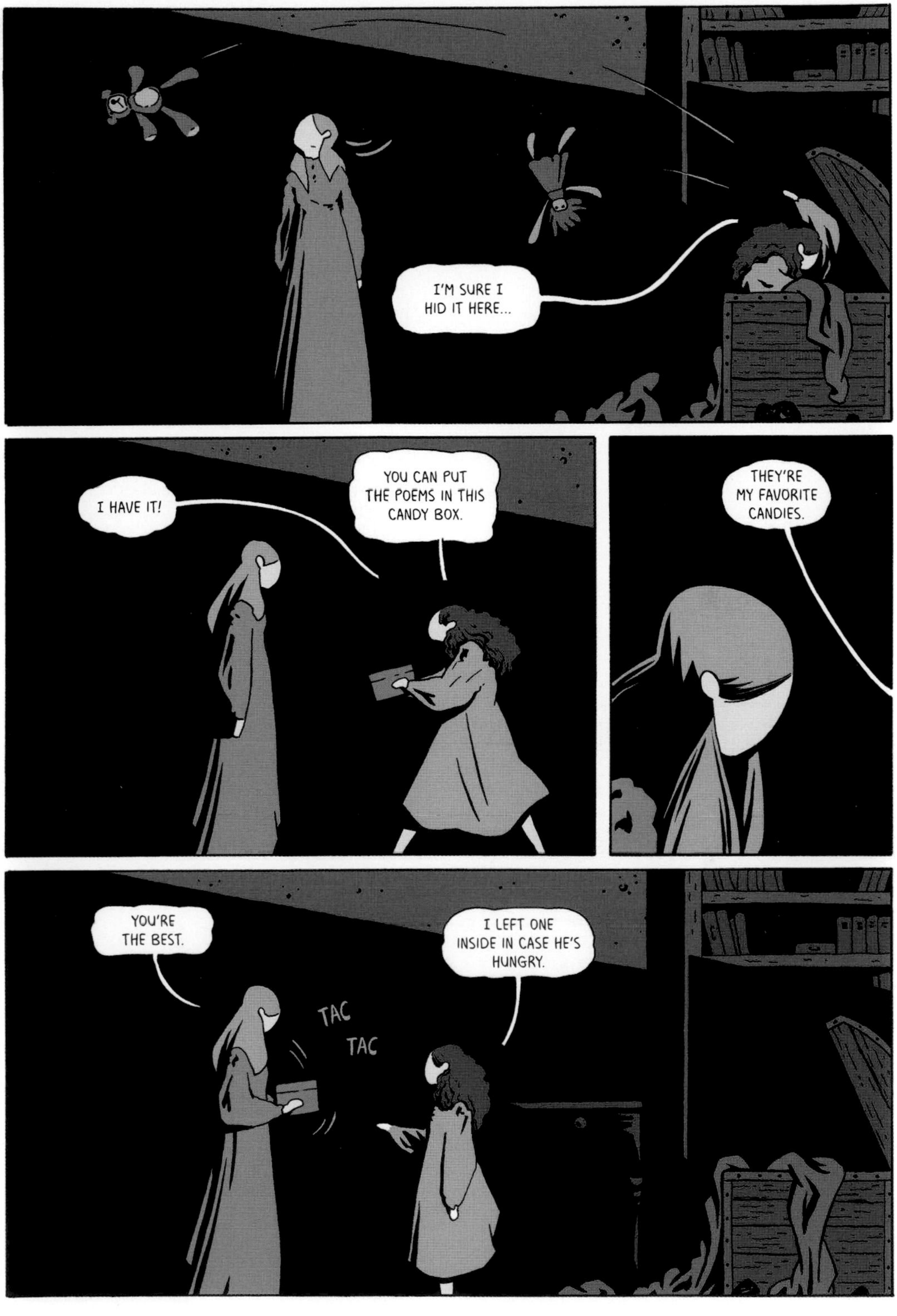
I'M SURE I HID IT HERE...
I HAVE IT!
YOU CAN PUT THE POEMS IN THIS CANDY BOX.
THEY'RE MY FAVORITE CANDIES.
YOU'RE THE BEST.
TAC
TAC
I LEFT ONE INSIDE IN CASE HE'S HUNGRY.

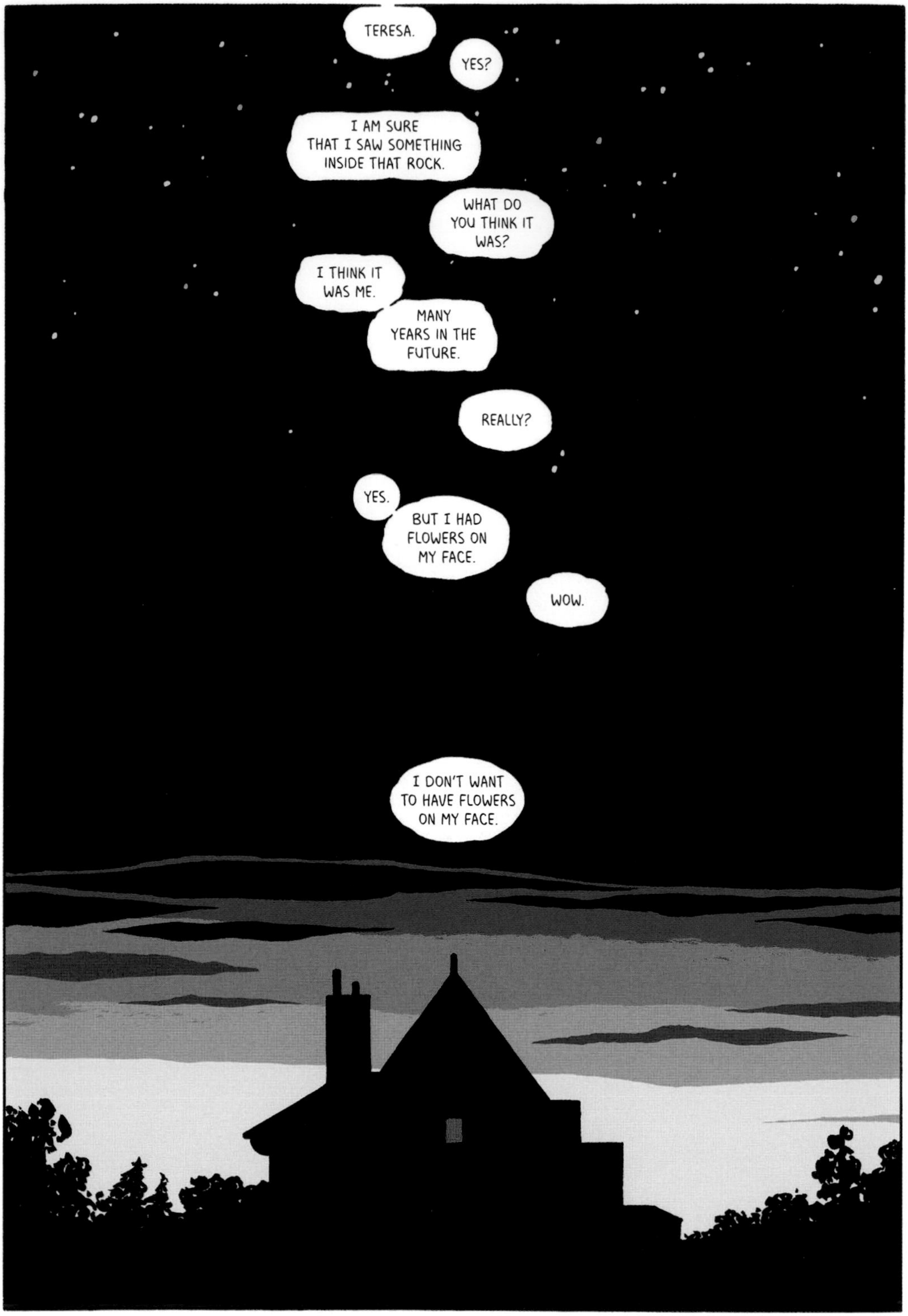
TERESA.
YES?
I AM SURE THAT I SAW SOMETHING INSIDE THAT ROCK.
WHAT DO YOU THINK IT WAS?
I THINK IT WAS ME.
MANY YEARS IN THE FUTURE.
REALLY?
YES.
BUT I HAD FLOWERS ON MY FACE.
WOW.
I DON'T WANT TO HAVE FLOWERS ON MY FACE.

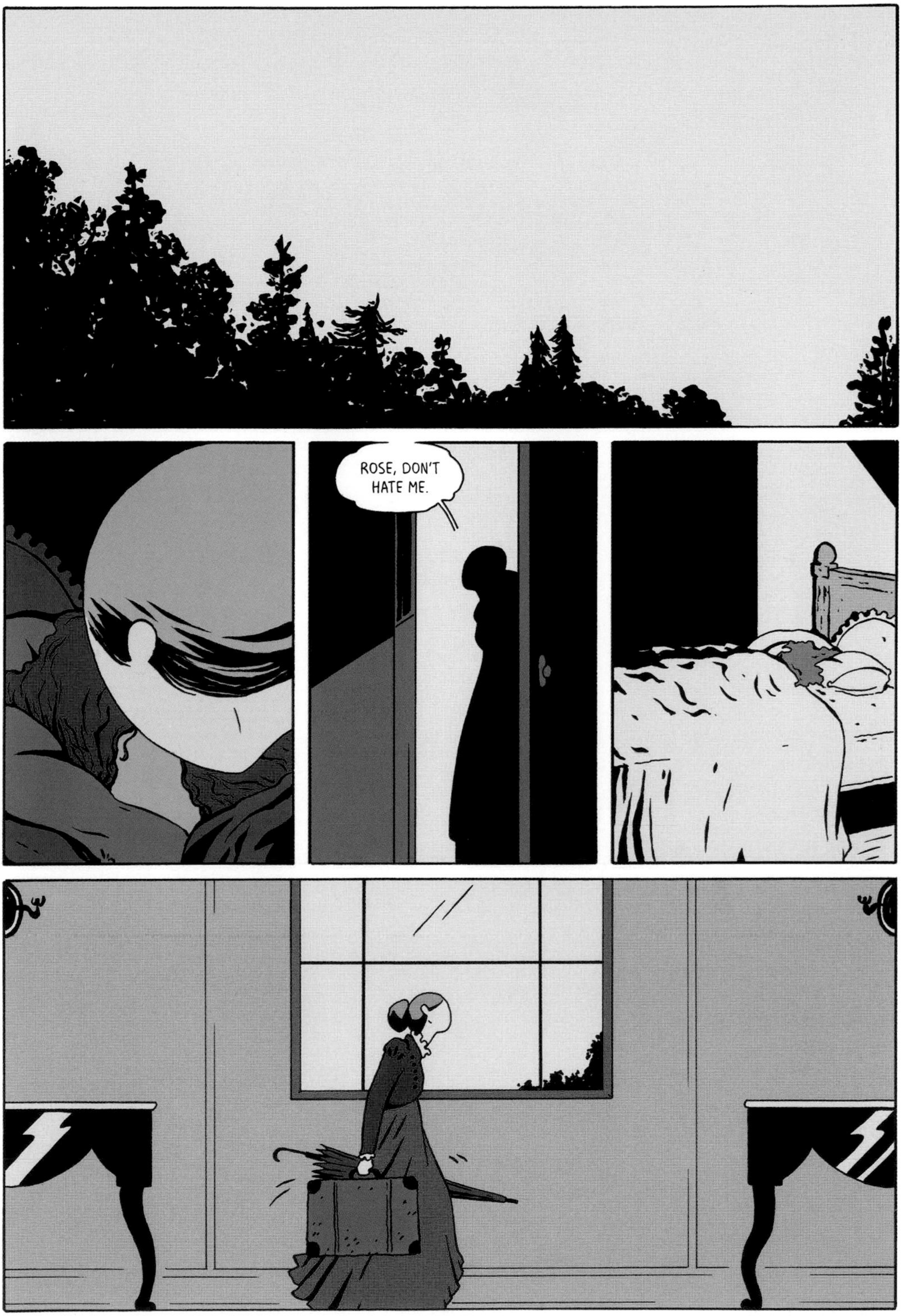
ROSE, DON'T HATE ME.

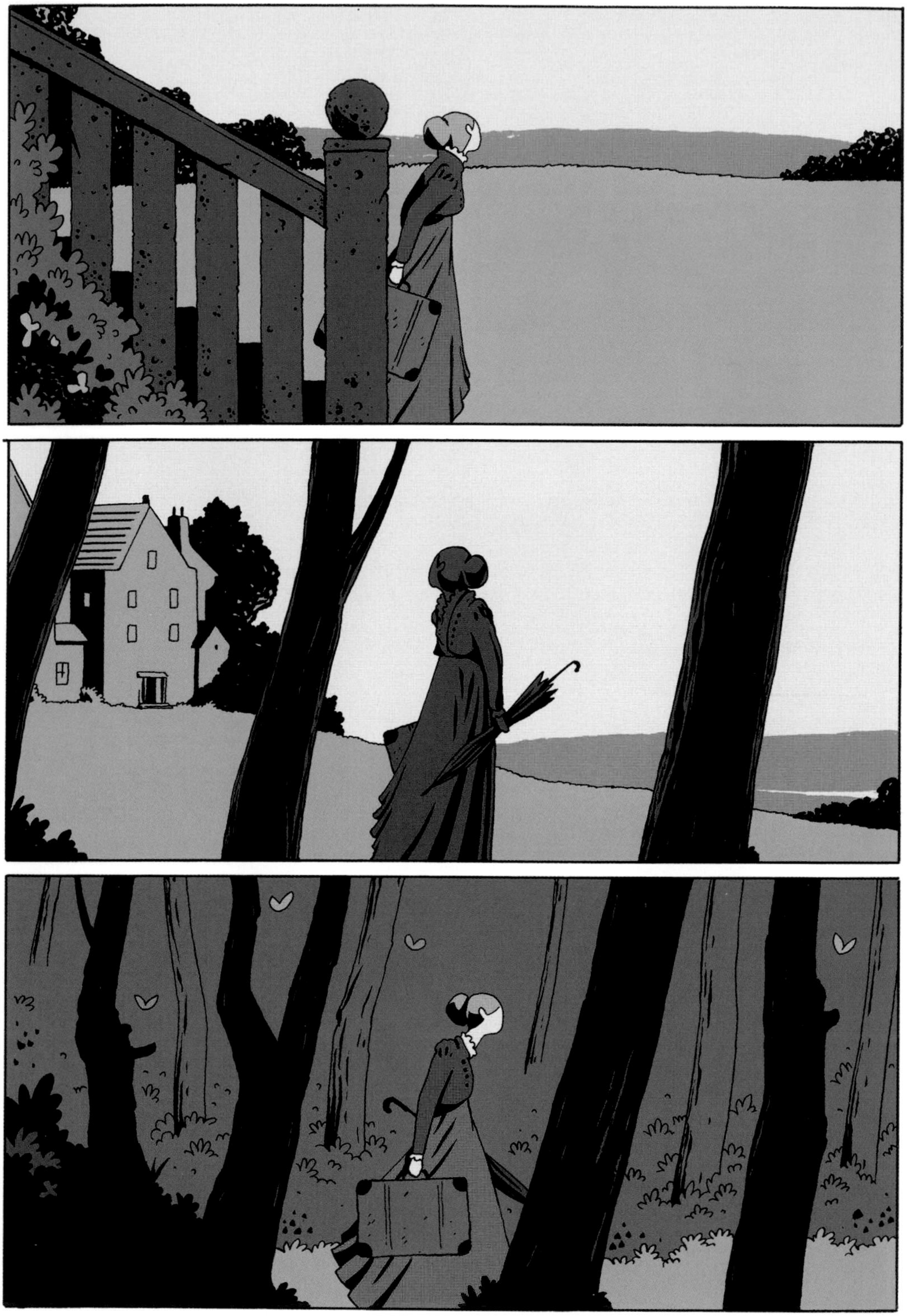

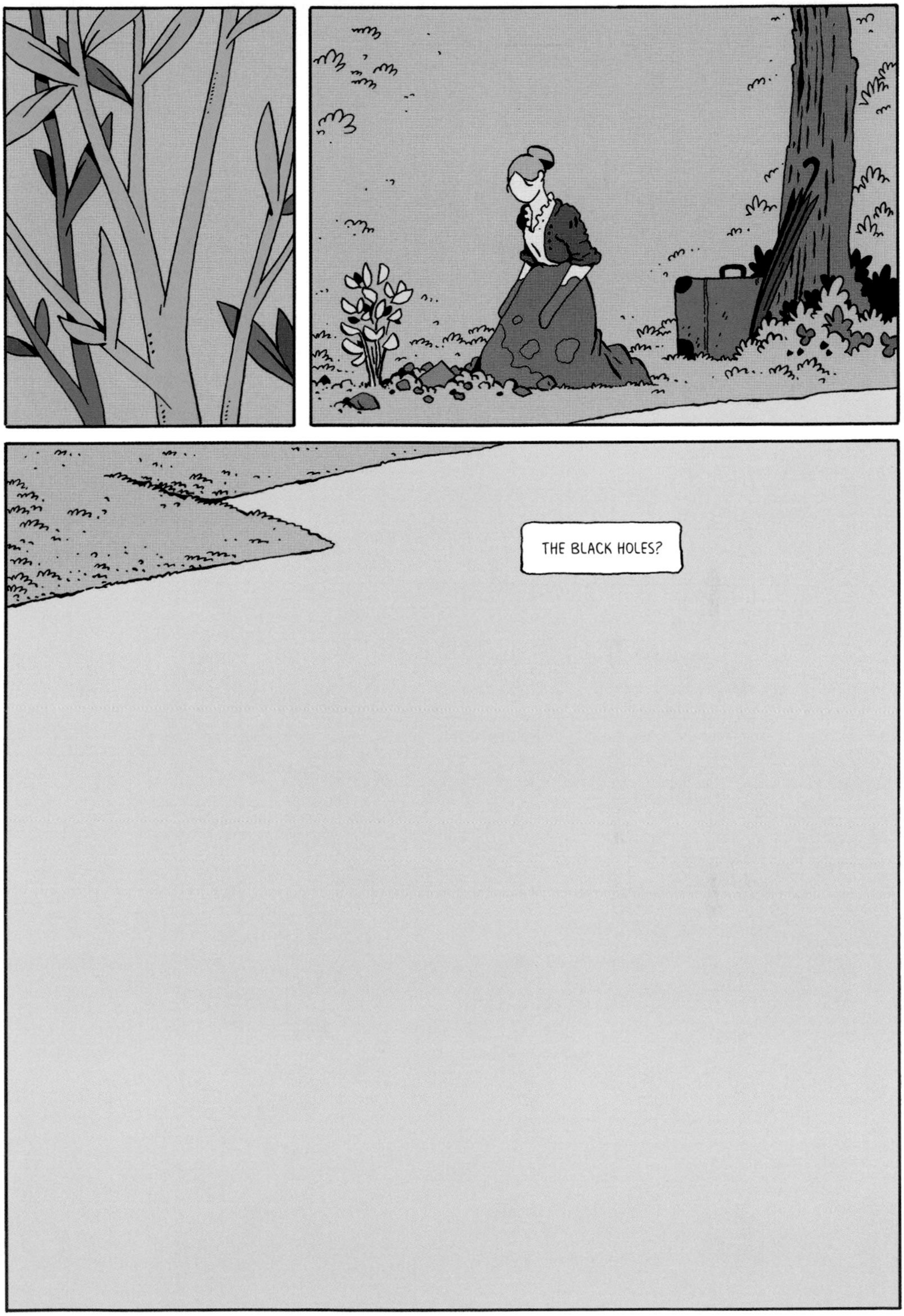
THE BLACK HOLES?

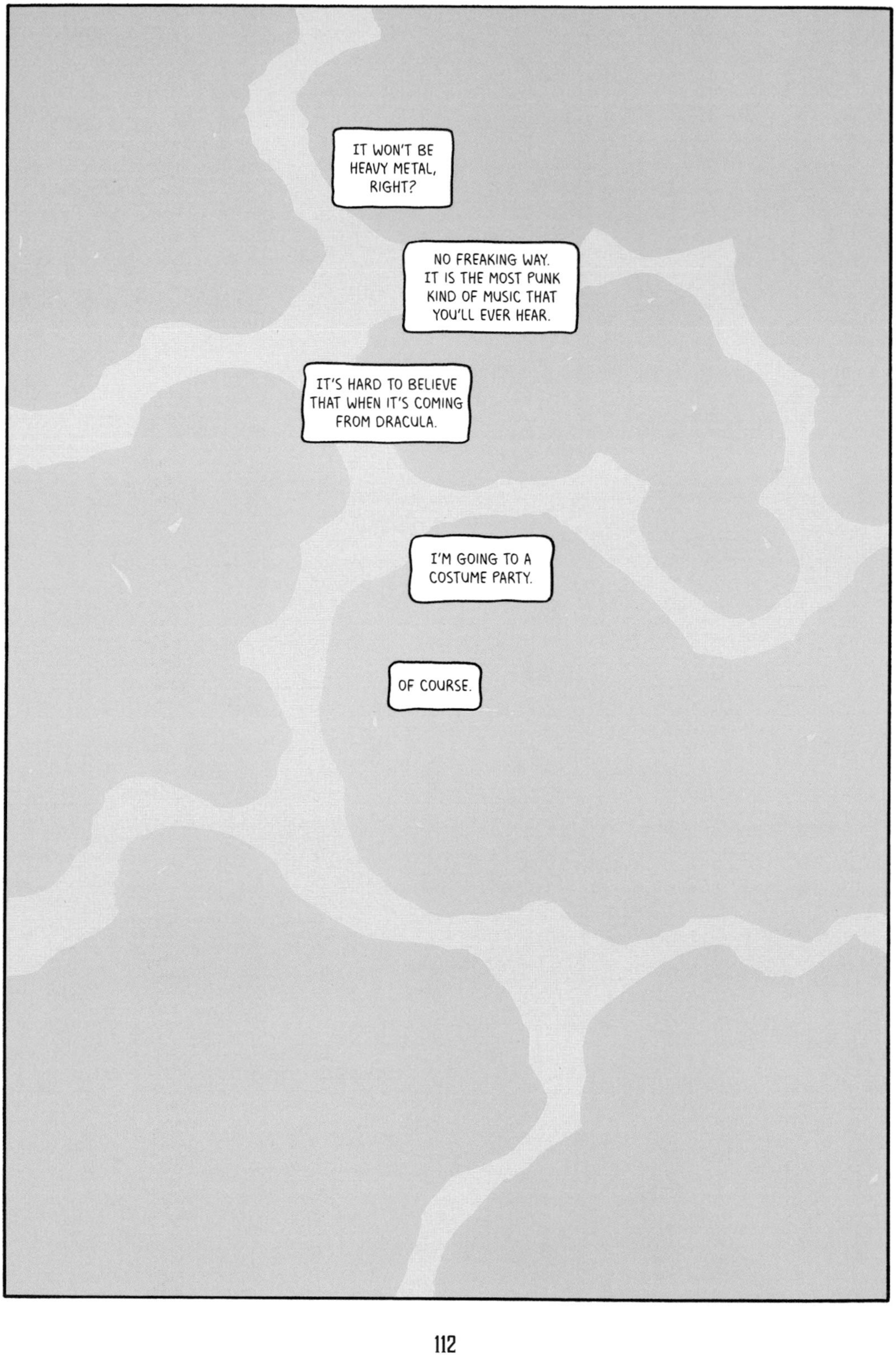
IT WON'T BE HEAVY METAL, RIGHT?
NO FREAKING WAY. IT IS THE MOST PUNK KIND OF MUSIC THAT YOU'LL EVER HEAR.
IT'S HARD TO BELIEVE THAT WHEN IT'S COMING FROM DRACULA.
I'M GOING TO A COSTUME PARTY.
OF COURSE.

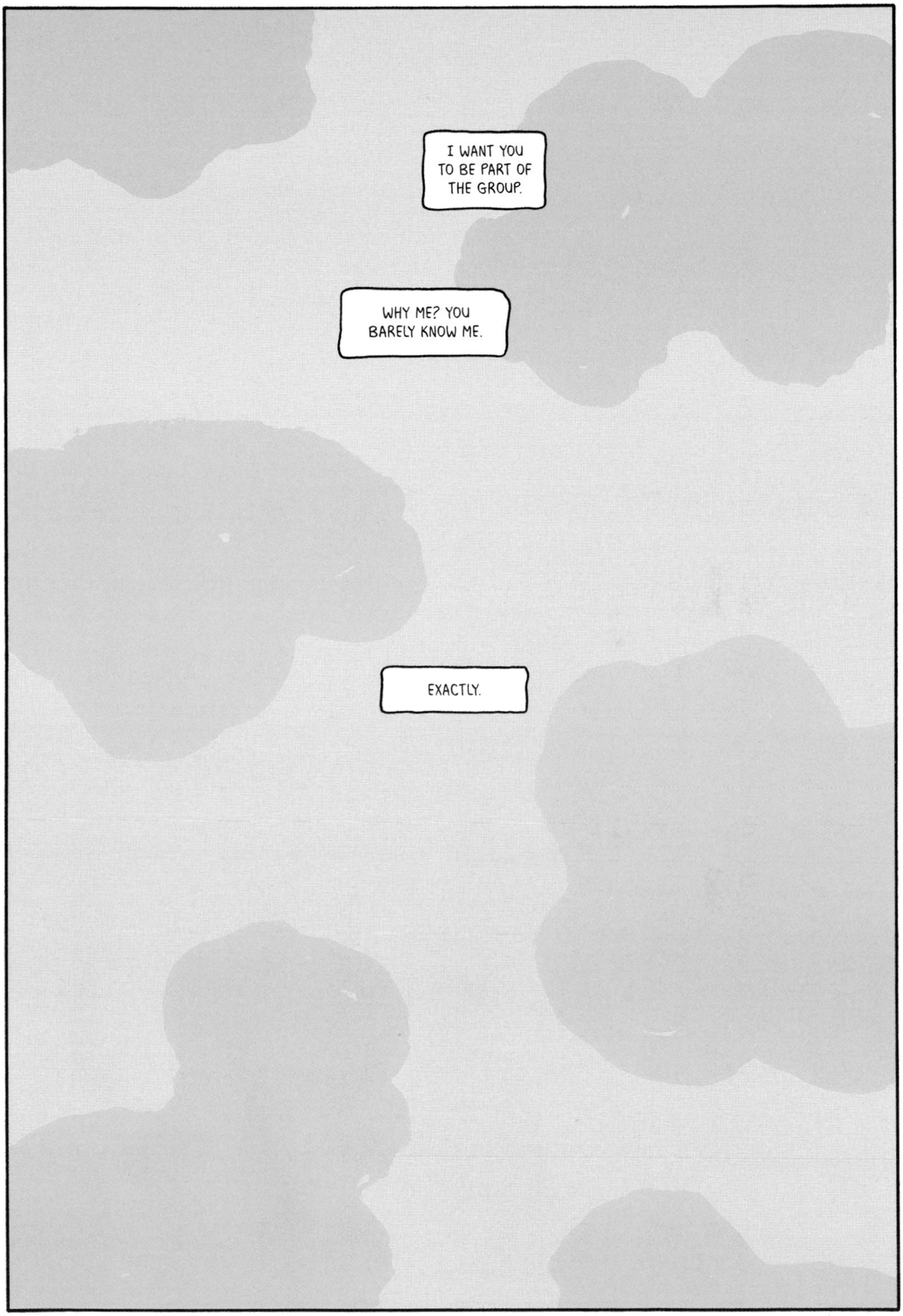
I WANT YOU TO BE PART OF THE GROUP.
WHY ME? YOU BARELY KNOW ME.
EXACTLY.

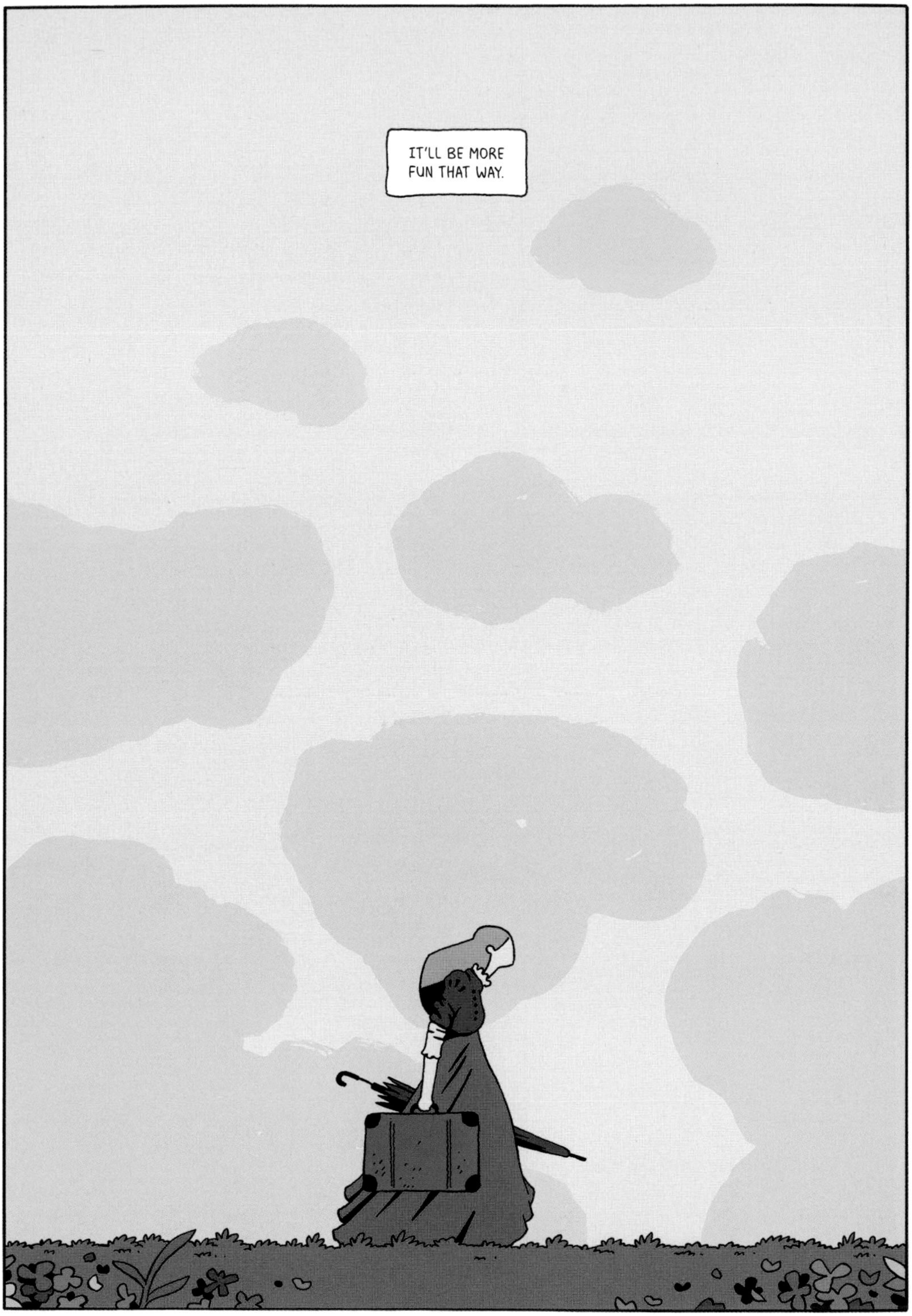
IT'LL BE MORE FUN THAT WAY.

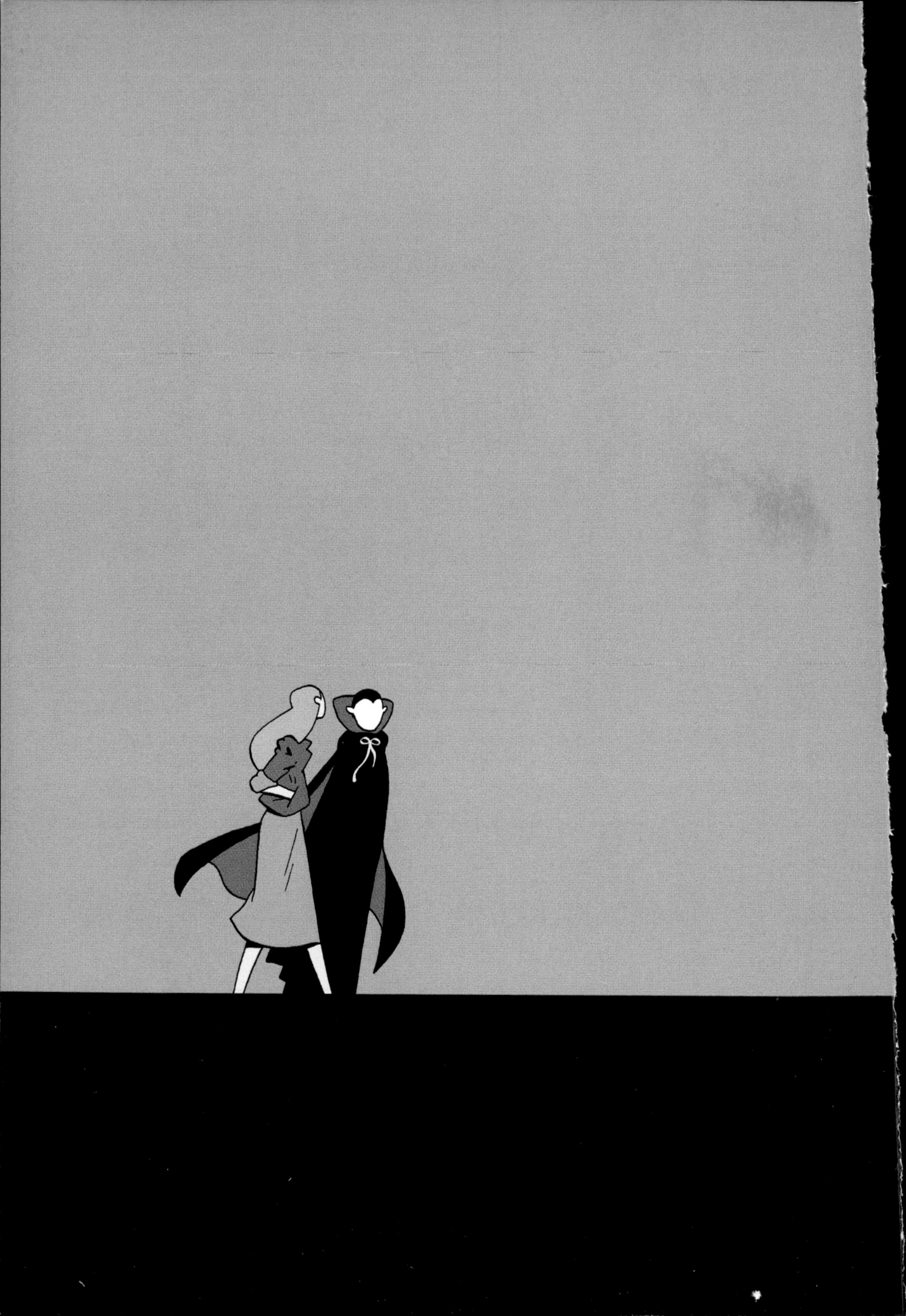